for CATHY

THANKS FOR YOUR SUPPORT
& BEST WISHES

Frank Prete

NIGHTSHADE

by

FRANK PRETE

Inquiries should be directed to:

The Weidner Publishing Group
490 Cornwall Avenue
Cheshire CT 06410
Phone: 1-800-783-9654
Fax: (203) 271-1813

This book is dedicated to:

Donna, Janine and David

*"May you never be touched
by the arrogant powers of indifference.
You are my heart and soul."*

*Eh per la cara mia mama e cara papa
ti voligo bene assi, assi.*

Acknowledgements:

Thanks to Suzanne Wescott, her insights and assistance were of great value.

Mike Andreozzi

Thanks to Gary Null, the staff of WBAI (Pacifica Radio), F.A.I.R.
"May your voices never be silenced."

And,
Especially Christopher Smith, I am extremely grateful for his help and guidance.
"Thanks Chris!"

"....I don't trust secrecy."

Gloria Tennley

ONE

October, 1970

The dark Virginia sky was giving way to a beautiful sunrise as Emmet Prescott drove his official car to the Dolly Madison gate leading into the headquarters of the CIA. A stern looking guard with closely cropped hair and rigid movements emerged from the glass-enclosed guard booth and approached the car. He checked Prescott's name on a clip board then threw a quick, suspicious glance into the car. The guard stepped away and with an awkward attempt at friendliness motioned for Prescott to proceed.

As Prescott drove through the gate he could see a horizontal streak of muted pastel red separating the dark earth from the fading night sky. He drew personal homage from the emerging dawn, equating his work with a new dawn of a different order.

Through the years, Prescott remained adamant in his pursuit of revolutionary warfare. New methods of disabling the enemy became a difficult priority, but fearless diligence and national security propelled him onward. Research and experimentation were conducted in massive proportions despite limited financial allocations, and were deeply shrouded in secrecy. A labyrinth of confused means softened justifiable ends. He now stood on the brink of revolutionary discoveries, with his experimental research in its final stages. One more operation in New York and his findings would be complete. The culmination of years of planning would be a silent arsenal poised for absolute destruction, totally cloaked in a veil of enigma, understood only by an elite few.

Prescott felt an inner drive hurrying him along, passing him not from minute to minute but from destiny to history.

He parked his car in his assigned spot and stepped into the chilly air. The security guards posted at the building entrance took deliberate notice of his personal identification affixed to the lapel of his overcoat, then looked away. Prescott's heels clicked along the light green tile as he made his way down Corridor 'C' to his office. He entered his office and eased his coat onto a hanger and rested it on a hook behind his door. Closing the door, he withdrew a set of keys from a pocket of the coat and made his way to his desk. Unlocking the center draw with one key, Prescott then took another key and undid a lock hidden within the drawer causing a side drawer to snap open.

He removed a false bottom shelf from the side drawer and with a third key, unlocked a compartment which housed a folder marked "Night Shade." He untied a string that was wrapped around the folder and studied the typed pages which had been bound into a booklet. Retrieving a pen from a marble holder at the front of his desk, he began to jot down notes onto a legal pad.

Prescott was so engrossed in his work he hadn't noticed the sun had fully risen, bathing his office in total natural light. The parking lot had filled to capacity as employees filed into work. Sounds and activity emitting from the outer office went unnoticed as well.

He had filled nine pages of notes and questions as they related to the Night Shade report before a buzz on his intercom phone disturbed his concentration.

"Yes?" he said depressing a button, annoyed by the interruption.

"Good morning, Mister Prescott," came his secretary's voice.

"Yes?" he replied with impatience.

"If you're not in conference Mister Prescott, would you like coffee?"

"No," he said abruptly.

"Very well."

"Louise?"

"Yes."

"Don't disturb me again unless it's important. Understand?"

"Yes, Mister Prescott. I apologize."

"Another thing. Harmon Keller and John Tennley are scheduled to return from New York at one o'clock. When they arrive have them report to my office immediately."

"Yes sir. Anything else?"

"Not for now."

Before Louise could say anything else Prescott had disconnected her call.

Prescott swiveled his chair around to face the bright day. His eyes focused on the multi-colored trees surrounding the building, but their images didn't penetrate his thoughts. For more than two years little existed except his commitment, determination and drive to the project detailed on the pages he held in his hands.

The phone on his desk rang once more and he knew it was a direct interoffice call. He reached around, snapped the blinking button and spoke.

"Prescott."

"Prescott this is Hodge."

"Yes, sir?"

"Come to my office, on the double."

"Yes sir."

Prescott hung up the phone and combined his newly created notes with the Night Shade report and locked them up safely under the false bottom shelf.

He walked further down Corridor 'C' until he came to Hodge's outer office. Trudy Dobson was seated next to the door that lead to another short corridor and eventually to Hodge's office.

"Good morning Mister Prescott," the secretary said coldly.

"To see Ed," Prescott responded cryptically.

"You can go right through, Mister Hodge is waiting for you."

Prescott opened the first door without saying another word to the secretary and proceeded to Hodge's office.

It wasn't unusual to be called into an unscheduled meeting by a superior officer, but Prescott nevertheless tried to anticipate what it might be about. The name plate centered on the door read: "J. Edward Hodge." Prescott had worked under Hodge for eight years. When he was first assigned to his unit, Hodge was a GS-12. Since then he rose to become a GS-17, the equivalent of a two star general in the military.

Hodge stood six feet three inches tall, with broad, muscular shoulders. Born in Amarillo, Texas, Hodge later played football for Texas A & M. Over the years, he remained physically active and fit, he looked much younger than his years. His size and strength were imposing. When he spoke, he emitted a forcefulness that discouraged challenge.

Hodge had risen through the ranks of the Office of Strategic Services, the wartime predecessor to the CIA.

4

When the CIA was formed in 1947, Hodge made the transition easily.

Prescott knocked on the door and then entered. Hodge was standing with his back to the door looking out the window behind his desk. A large American flag stood in the corner of the room. Lining one wall were double book cases separated by the CIA emblem. Against the other wall was an eight foot couch with two chairs facing it and separated by a low glass table.

"Good morning sir." Prescott said standing rigidly before the desk.

"Good morning Emmet," Hodge said without turning. "Beautiful day," Hodge continued in a monotone.

"Yes sir. It is."

Hodge finally turned away from the window and looked at Prescott.

The two men stood facing each other and Prescott was able to detect an annoyance in Hodge's eyes.

There was a strange silence that existed between them as Hodge studied Prescott.

"Sit down, Emmet."

Prescott positioned himself erect in the chair as though responding to a direct order. Hodge stood for a moment, still silent, not moving. Finally he let himself down into his chair. He put his arms on the desk and leaned forward. Prescott noticed his large muscular hands clasped on the desk. Below them he saw the manila folder. It wasn't difficult to read upside down; the two words were immediately recognizable. Upon seeing them Prescott's anger was instantaneous. He felt an inner urge to jump out of the chair, grab the folder and tear it to threads.

Hodge looked directly at Prescott. There was a mission and purpose in his eyes. He was direct and straight forward, thinking of his words before speaking them.

"When I was sworn into the agency, I took a personal oath to do the best job I could do within certain boundaries," he started. "I have no false illusions about what we do and what we have to do, but there's a distinction between allegiance to the agency and responsibility to country. I know how easy it is to get wrapped up in this game, and with all the power and authority we command, how easy it is to let things get out of control...especially ourselves...our ego."

As Hodge spoke Prescott became angrier. He sensed the beginnings of a pious sermon he didn't want to hear. A myriad of feelings wheeled through him like hot spokes. His instinct was to strike out with an uncontrolled rage, but training kept him outwardly still.

"I go back to a time when the world was filled with inhumanity. What I witnessed in Europe was enough to last me ten lifetimes. But I have no way of conveying or imparting my observations and conclusions on anyone. All I can hope for is a unified clarity. This may sound contrived or overly moralistic, but believe me it's not. I want to take these misguided covert actions and crush them until nothing exists except purity and clarity."

Hodge raised his right arm with extended fingers and then curled them into a tight fist. He drove his hand down hard onto his desk.

"Enough!" he shouted. "Enough!" he shouted again and drove his fist down once more. The sound of the banging was like a clap of thunder and his voice reverberated throughout the room.

Prescott sat motionless, his acute anger struggling with his powers of restraint, as a sense of humiliation dug its way into his already swirling emotions.

"Where do you come off misappropriating contingency reserve funds?...Operating outside my knowledge?"

"What are you referring to?"

"What am I referring to? To this," he said pointing to the folder before him.

"You knew about our testing," Prescott defended.

"Not Night Shade! Not Night Shade!" he said waving the manila folder angrily in the air. "You never hinted about Night Shade!"

The face of Harmon Keller flashed in Prescott's mind. He was working on the logistics of operation Night Shade. He was aware of the delicacy of it, the need for secrecy. Prescott sensed Keller was opposed to the operation from its inception. But now, in cowardly fashion, he had reported to Hodge. Prescott felt a blast of adrenaline flood his arms. His hands tightened as though in some way he were exacting irreversible devastation on Keller.

Hodge rose from his chair and directed his attention out the window once more. The pastoral setting of the trees and the bright sunlight seemed to emphasize the difference between the serene beauty of nature and the absurd folly of man.

"I don't take exception to your efforts, only your methods and attitude. There are times when means don't justify ends," Hodge said.

There was a long pause as the angry GS-17 officer allowed himself time to regroup.

"I was among the troops that liberated Germany. I was a kid then but it wasn't difficult to understand what went on. I knew what happened in Dachau. The world knew what happened in Dachau, and we're all appalled by it! I read the data of the Naval Technical Mission."

Hodge turned from the window and looked through Prescott.

"This is not Dachau! I won't allow it!" he boomed.

Prescott sat motionless, a still but menacing bomb the instant before it exploded.

"That's an unfair parallel," Prescott said with restraint.

"Maybe so, but how far will you go?...What thresholds are you willing to cross for the sake of...of who knows what? When will your conscience or sense of justice finally step in and say that's enough? Or will it ever?"

"The Russians are involved in similar procedures..."

"I'm concerned with what they do, but I'm more concerned with what we do and how we do it. And what about Joe Emory?"

"What about him?"

"'What about him?'" Hodge screamed, "'What about him'?! He's dead! Killed by one of your experiments..."

"That was an accident of sorts..."

"Accident of sorts?"

"Yes. Emory volunteered. He had been taking ordinary, over-the-counter antihistamines for a simple cold. The mixture caused a problem, but we gave him the antidote and he was fine, everything was under control. We believe he became disoriented at night and accidentally fell over his balcony railing."

"Are you sure he wasn't hallucinating?"

"No. He was fine, responding well to the antidote."

Hodge kept staring at Prescott. It was impossible to conceal his disdain. He wanted to leap from the chair and drive his head into the floor, rip the arrogance from his face and crush his spirit. He secretly wished there were some sort of interdepartmental review board he could report him to, but structure dictated that reprimand was the sole responsibility of division chiefs.

Hodge felt consumed by frustration and anger from such irresponsibility. It was impossible to keep every subordinate on a leash or to uniform morality. But this was one operation he had the power to crush.

"As of this moment Operation Night Shade is over!...Understood?"

Prescott didn't respond.

"It's over!...That's an order! Cease and desist all maneuvers and spending. Redeploy all personnel! Understood?....Understood?

"Yes."

"I want all reports, notes, data, relating to Night Shade destroyed. I want everyone involved debriefed. I don't want this thing to come back to haunt us. Is that clear?"

"Yes."

"I want a follow-up report of detailed redeployment on my desk by o-eight hundred hours tomorrow...Is that clear?"

"Yes."

"And from now on, as long as I'm head of this division, I want to be apprised of every aspect of your work. And I want spending to be accounted for in greater detail...That's all, you can go now."

Prescott bolted from the chair and headed for his office. He felt himself giving in to his anger. He wanted to destroy anything in his path. He contemplated throwing his chair through a window or ripping his door from its hinges. Above all he wanted to kill Harmon Keller. As he passed his secretary she looked up and announced:

"Mister Prescott, Harmon Keller called and said they were delayed in New York, and he would be back in the office by this evening."

Prescott didn't respond. The mention of Keller's name resounded in him with an added fury and contempt. He continued into his office and stripped his coat from its hanger and stormed from the building. Along the way several people called to him, but Prescott was oblivious, submerged in blind rage. He started the engine of his car and drove through the gates. He picked up Interstate 495 and headed south to Arlington. The familiar highway passed before him in a blur as he recognized nothing, acknowledging only his own fermenting hatred.

Prescott drove his car into the driveway and brought it to a screeching halt. He jumped from the car and marched into his house kicking a chair and looking for something to blame.

"Keller! Keller! You're a dead man! You're a dead man!"

Prescott became consumed by anger and frustration, needing desperately to unleash his vengeance on Keller.

"You betrayed me! You fucking traitor! You betrayed me!"

Through his rage Prescott heard a noise behind him. He turned quickly to see his Doberman pincher approaching cautiously, instinctively aware of his master's anger. He crouched as Prescott approached him. Prescott's reaction was immediate.

"Keller! Keller!" he screamed.

He grabbed the animal around the neck with both hands and began to squeeze. The dog was stunned by the fury of his master. A sense of survival forced him to react, but the grip was overwhelming. The animal tried shaking the grip loose by tossing his head, but the more he moved, the tighter the grip.

Prescott looked into the eyes of the pathetic beast and growled. He drove his fingers deeper and tighter. Again the dog tried pushing Prescott away with his front paws but it had no leverage. It pivoted its hind legs but with nothing to push against with its front legs it was powerless, and finally faded from fright to acceptance. The strangulation grip was too much to bear. The bewildered animal was no longer able to support its own weight. Even as the dog went limp, Prescott kept squeezing with intense pressure. Thick foam cascaded from the corners of the dog's mouth as its eyes closed and life left its body.

"Keller! Keller!" he moaned as a wild delirium filled his eyes. Prescott loosened his grip slowly and let the dog drop to the floor with a thud. He stood looking down at the animal with no apparent remorse or relief. Prescott's body trembled; he felt weak. Beads of perspiration dripped from his forehead. A disquieting calm seemed to overtake him.

"I'm going to kill you Keller. If it's the last thing I do with my life, I'm going to kill you!"

TWO

15 years later

$\mathcal{H}$e measured cold by the impact it had upon his body. The greater his discomfort, the colder it was. Layers of battered, smelly clothing was a secondary line of defense against January and its wind. His primary defense was himself--his attitude. At times he refused to recognize the elements by concentrating on images that lived in his mind and revenge smoldered to a strange type of warmth. Other times his outward anger and rage overpowered whatever attacked and numbed his flesh.

His hands, set in badly ripped gloves and wrapped in cloth, were stuffed deep into the pockets of his over-sized coat. His pants, complete with human waste stains, were worn away at the cuffs where they scraped along the pavement. An old bath towel covered his head and ears, while a shapeless hat fell close to his angry eyes.

His skin was dark, made even darker by layers of inlaid dirt. On his left cheek and lower lip were open sores which refused to heal. Green mold crusted the upper portion of his teeth where they met the black line of his gums.

The stench which emitted from his mouth was no worse than the foul odor of his body. Appearing like a lumbering mutant, with an invisible weight bearing down on his shoulders, the dejected figure made his way up Forty-second Street. The street was fairly active with pedestrians. Steam poured upward through manhole covers in an attempt to escape to nowhere. Yellow cabs stopped to discharge fares in front of Grand Central Station while other fares were rushed away to posh restaurants or luxury apartments.

In spite of himself, the robust inviting aroma of roasting chestnuts and pretzels filled his nostrils. He stood for a moment downwind from the pushcart as a young executive-looking man bought his girlfriend a bag of chestnuts and a pretzel for himself. He waited, hoping the man would discard the partly eaten pretzel, but instead the couple proceeded toward Fifth Avenue.

The vendor put his hands into his pocket and swayed side to side as though trying to generate heat or to fan the charcoal that warmed larger stale pretzels and overly roasted chestnuts.

The street bum moved as close as he could to the pushcart to feel its warmth.

"Hey! You want somethin' pal?" the vendor said with a harsh voice.

The street bum looked hard into the vendor's eyes, as his hand slowly left his pocket and reached for the hatchet in the waist band of his battered pants.

"Gaw head! Gaw head! If you ain't buyin' move out!" the vendor continued.

From the corner of his eye the street bum noticed movement. Living wildly on the streets gave him an acute sense of observation. Without looking away from the vendor he was able to discern the movement as police. The two rookie policemen stopped before him without speaking. Their presence was a silent authority pressed into an unspoken command. The street bum was not intimidated but returned his hand into his pocket. A look of annoyance crossed the face of one of the policemen conveying disgust over another's misfortune. The other police officer turned toward the vendor and looked at the pushcart for a license.

"It's there," the vendor said pointing to the license displayed above the warm grill.

The policemen and the street bum turned and walked away at the same time.

Once out of earshot, the vendor muttered, "Fuckin' bums," referring to all three men.

As the street bum approached the entrance to Grand Central Station, opposite Vanderbilt Place, he paused and turned to the heavy wire mesh trash can and looked through it for something he may need for survival, a half-eaten sandwich or newspaper to wrap around his body for warmth. He pushed aside loose paper wrappers and retrieved a dried, useful copy of The New York Times. With the newspaper securely under his arm, he made his way into the station.

The newsstands, doughnut shops and candy stores had all been closed for the night. Few commuters milled about, only those who went for drinks after work and stayed long after the happy hour. The primary population was made up of displaced souls like himself.

The air in the station was thick and stale, not polluted, just synthetic as though it were made in a laboratory from inferior ingredients and laced with steel dust. As he walked, his eyes scanned the floor looking for lost change or a dropped wallet, gold earrings, anything of value. The few passing commuters paid him no attention, nor did the transit policeman. The street bum descended a staircase to the lower level of the station. He stood in the shadows of the ramp which leads to platforms where outgoing trains ushered passengers to warm beds and clean homes, away from absurd reality of the city. His suspicious eyes scanned the still but potentially hazardous environment. Lighting on the platform was unnaturally bleak; no sunshine ever invaded the area. The platform, walls and track beds stood dim and over the years seemed to have shriveled and dried from the lack of natural light and air.

The street bum made his way to the rear of the tunnel, opposite the passenger area. An intermittently placed light bulb gave off just enough light to guide his way. Following abandoned track he proceeded to a steel grate. Lifting the grate he made his way down a dark well which had a steel ladder bolted inside. Coming to the bottom, he accepted the absence of any form of light. He paused a moment to acclimate his eyes to the darkness and his senses to the insidious dungeon. He had long ago abandoned the thought of achieving a mild tolerance of his surroundings. There existed only an adopted indifference to any semblance of mankind.

He stood motionless as his eyes peered through the darkness. His ears strained as he heard the scratching sound of rat claws. The rats didn't frighten him as much as the wild cats. The rats were large, yet easy to detect. The cats were strong and silent, able to inflict serious harm. Fearlessness and the harsh environment brought out feline predator instincts. The man reluctantly felt like one of many species of animals locked together in cages of despair with little chance of escape.

Cautiously he continued to another ramp, then to another grate which he was able to discern more from memory than from light. Climbing down another cement tube he came to still another ramp which led to an aimless track where a train car had been abandoned years before. For him and the other inhabitants of the journeyless train it was a place the world and time forgot, a home for lost and displaced souls. What he previously had perceived as hell existed before him--fire displaced by cold. As he approached the car, muted sounds of shuffling and movement emitted from within; other residents feared they were discovered or would be attacked so they repositioned for better position. As he entered the car other suspicious eyes observed his movements but no one spoke. He proceeded to his usual spot and everyone relaxed knowing they were joined in their desolation and silent despair by one of their own. Total silence proceeded to settle over them and they were once again reclaimed by the darkness.

The smell of human waste and unbathed bodies repulsed him. An uncontrollable hostility for those around him, his environment and his own present condition struggled with an inner urge for vengeance and retaliation.

He let himself slide down the wall of the car and came to rest on the hard floor. Taking the newspaper from his coat pocket he began to unfold it and blanket his outstretched legs. What remained he placed under his coat with the illusion of protecting his chest.

Beside him lay a faceless image of himself, another form surrealistically distorted by chance and choice.

"Malcolm is that you?" uttered a voice.

Only ruffling paper and a graveyard cough responded.

"Malcolm is..."

"No!" interrupted the annoyed raspy voice.

The sound of shattering glass was heard off in the distance; the splintered end of a bottle of cheap wine.

From within the darkness a weak, mournful scream echoed in the tunnel. The scream lacked passion, strength, will. All elements of human demeanor had been extracted and consumed by the catacombs of horror. Above, the rumblings of trains exposed a blatant desire to escape the forbidding caverns.

The man ignored the train, the scream, the darkness, but beyond that he ignored himself. He knew he existed in a dimension that lacked reality and substance, personal recognition and regard. Survival was all that remained, but even that bore no logic and validity. A veil of abstract separation engulfed him. He was thrust into a physical world that stood apart from what lived in his mind. Two distinct existences, separated totally by different planes, yet, an uncontrollable disturbance antagonized both cores.

He angrily shaped newspaper into a ball and placed it under his head, using it as a pillow.

"Malcolm, you there?" the voice beside him called again.

"I told you I'm not Malcolm! I'm not Malcolm. My name is Harmon! Harmon! Not Malcolm! Don't call me Malcolm!"

"Harmon...do you have some extra paper for me?"

The tunnel went silent once more. Despair blanketed alienation while indifference fed upon rejection.

"Harmon...?"

"Don't call me Harmon!"

"But you said..."

"I said don't call me...don't speak to me!"

"All I want is some paper."

"Shut up! Shut up! The paper is mine! The paper belongs to me! Get your own paper and leave me alone!" Harmon's anger echoed in the tunnel piercing the darkness.

Harmon positioned himself close to the back wall and clung to the newspaper protecting his body. It was an illusionary comfort he chose to recognize.

Undaunted, the man next to him fumbled in the darkness, groping for Harmon's paper. His hand reached into the void, unmindful of the anger he knew existed within his partially invisible adversary. Whether fateful temptation or lack of individual concern, he pressed further into the ebony abyss. His hand poked into Harmon's shoulder infuriating him further.

"I said leave me alone!" Harmon scowled as he reached into his tattered coat and withdrew the hatchet. The nerves in his arms and legs caused him to shake uncontrollably. Destructive passion surged through his body like unharnessed electricity. Harmon scrambled to his knees and remained with the hatchet raised above his head. The blade was poised to descend upon anything within its range to deliver absolute punishment.

The darkness did not conceal the tunnel dweller, a dark, indiscernible mass moving before him. Harmon lived too long in the night not to be part of it. He felt a hand touch his chest, then he felt a burst of foul smelling breath on his face. Harmon's hand squeezed tightly on the handle of the hatchet and pushed the invading hand away abruptly.

"I need some paper, I'm cold."

"I said no!"

Harmon heard shuffling and then felt a sharp object cut through his coat and sting his chest. He moved to his left and felt a force pass his face.

"Give me some paper," the voice demanded.

Harmon didn't respond. He tried to reposition himself away from his antagonist. Once again he felt the sharp sting and realized he was being stabbed. His body continued to tremble violently; his bladder lost control and urine soaked his pants. The man lunged at him once more and Harmon's nervous energy found its way into his arm. Self-preservation overpowered him and survival became his only concern. With one swift stroke, he drove the hatchet through the darkness into the stranger's forehead. An unearthly shriek filled the tunnel. Warm blood immediately gushed onto Harmon's exposed fingers. The unseen figure fell backward and remained still and silent; waste effectively culminating into oblivion.

Harmon remained silent but allowed the rage to engulf him. Images of the past suddenly swirled in his mind; menacing faces antagonized him further.

Harmon rose to his feet and crouched near his fallen attacker. Raising the hatchet once more he drove it downward, hoping to transcend the present and landing it on the not too distant past with the hope of exacting some semblance of needed revenge. The blade seemed to have a life of its own as it ricocheted off the wall, sending a brief spark to glow in the night, and imbedding itself into his victim's cheek bone and jaw. Harmon looked at his own hand, still clutching the weapon, as though it were separate from himself. His arm had the familiar feeling of penetrating a weathered tree stump. Harmon pried the hatchet loose, confused and disoriented. The darkness that tried to own him had been instantly redesigned. He had met the challenge of the darkness and attained a misguided victory. A sense of freedom invaded his being, permeating every pore of his body. But struggling against him was an ambivalence that rendered his momentary victory shallow. The images of the past once again swelled within his mind--he suddenly knew there was much left for him to do.

Harmon thought he'd wait for daybreak to see his victim and face the judgment passed upon him. But then he realized there was no daybreak in this part of the

world. No sunshine, summer warmth, or spring fresh-
ness, only endless and unforgiving night, and a season
yet unnamed.

NIGHT SHADE

22

THREE

$\mathcal{E}$d Dennehey was executive director and coordinator of assignments for Public Broadcast News. His entire career was spent with the news, starting with the covering of the invasion of Normandy for the Stars and Stripes, then working as a freelance journalist for major newspapers in every large city that mattered. His career led him to the position of General Desk Editor of The Associated Press where he filed major news events for twenty years. The last ten years were spent at PBN where he worked for less money, but with more freedom to address issues in the way he felt the First Amendment was meant to be interpreted.

Dennehey was the quintessential behind-the-scenes news writer. His appearance differed dramatically from those who held anchor spots on national and public television stations. He lacked showmanship, marketability, and was hardly the type to be seen on the front pages of Gentleman's Quarterly. He was, however, a breed that closely resembled a salty, sea-faring captain whose wisdom and savvy reeked from every crack in his weary face. Dennehey wore shirts that were never pressed and ties that were worn as an annoying afterthought. Dennehey stood six feet four inches and, given his news savvy, when he spoke it was with insight and commanding conviction.

The smoke from his pipe filled the spacious but cluttered office. A mid-life roll hung over his belt, which he wore just above his crotch. His tie was loosely fitted around the open collar and knotted to one side, extending only to the third button of his shirt. His shirt sleeves were rolled to the elbows, a habit not easily discarded from his cub reporting days.

Seated before him was Mary Cello, a reporter who filed special assignments. Mary possessed a serious look which poured from her eyes. She wasn't hard or tough, just professional and serious. She was kind and compassionate yet rarely smiled, choosing to protect her personal sensitivity and vulnerability.

After graduating NYU with a degree in journalism, she started working as a copy editor on the city desk for PBN. Within five years Mary earned her way to her present position of special assignment editor with her own hour-long cable television spot.

On television, Mary smiled occasionally. When she did, it was a warm, engaging smile that easily exposed her vulnerability and enhanced her girlish appeal.

Dennehey observed Mary in a daughterly fashion, and at times had difficulty relating to her as a capable news reporter.

"Mary, I want you to do a follow-up special to the homeless piece you filed last May," Dennehey said holding the pipe close to his lips. "But this time not just the shelters."

"Funny you should suggest that, I've been thinking about an angle I'd like to bounce off you," she said trying to contain her excitement.

"What's that?"

"Suppose I live among them for a week. I mean, don't go home to shower or eat, just live off the streets as they do."

"That sounds good, but my gut reaction is telling me no. I'm sure it would give you an excellent perspective, but it could be dangerous...and I'm afraid of the fallout from viewers who will be screaming 'cheap shot.' You know what I'm saying here, like you're there for a week, they're there forever."

"Yes, I do."

"No matter how bad it gets for you, you have a back door to a warm, clean home. Get my point?"

"Yes. OK."

"Let's put that on hold right now. I'm more interested in a total picture without staged dramatics...Straight forward. Separate the runaway from the penniless, the substance abuser from the mentally incompetent. Make it a sixty minute piece. Track them from their repossessed homes or hospital releases to the streets. More specifically, I want something that is less visible and less known to the average citizen..."

"Like what?"

"Well most people see the bag person on the street. I want a report on the people who live below the street, what's not seen. Specifically dwellers in sewers, hideaway places in the pier, airports...ah, start with Grand Central. I want to know what's in their heads. Try to make me really understand what seems unnatural to comprehend."

"OK...Is homelessness becoming your personal crusade?"

"No...I just don't want the politicians to think the situation is acceptable. We'll do our part to keep up the pressure and inform the public."

"Do you think it will make a difference? Do you think the public cares?"

"No."

"The homeless problem is an important issue, but not a popular one. There are strong feelings and resentment on both sides."

"True, but Mary, I'm not going for ratings. Call Mike Nailen. He's commuter relations at Metro North. Here's his number," Dennehey said handing Mary a slip of paper.

"OK..."

"What kind of latitude do I have?"

"All you need. Just try not to make a pitch."

"It's hard to avoid."

"I know. Just make it so City Hall has to deal with their conscience."

"They have none."

"Then just call it the way it is. We'll see what happens after."

"Fine."

"Call Mike. When you set it up just let me know the schedule."

"Right, will do."

Mary left Dennehey's office and made her way down the hall to her cubical. She knew what Dennehey expected from the report, and she knew what she expected of herself. She wasn't thinking about an Emmy or a Pulitzer, she just wanted to retell a story that needed telling. Her adrenaline was pumping as her mind already thought of an approach and a governmental doorstep where she could lay blame. And maybe, just maybe, she could embarrass enough people that positive action would be taken.

Standing at her desk, she tapped Tyler's extension on her phone.

"Hacket," she heard after the second ring.

"Tyler?"

"Yes."

"Mary."

"Hi Mary. What's up?"

"Got something from Ed."

"A rush?"

"Kind of. Can you put me down for day after tomorrow?"

"Yes."

"I have to prepare for this one."

"What are we doing?"

"A story about homelessness. We'll need mostly interior shots. Starting with Grand Central. The tracks, tunnels, things like that. Then the airports, piers."

"How long a schedule?"

"I'm thinking three separate shoots."

"Fine, I'll have a crew ready. Daytime?"

"No night."

"Fine. How long a report?"

"So far it looks like an hour."

"No problem, just give me a schedule when I see you."

"Fine, thank you Tyler."

Mary depressed the phone's plunger, then punched in the number Dennehey had given her.

★★★

The American Airlines DC-10 touched down at Kennedy Airport at nine eighteen, twenty-two minutes late. Emmet Prescott, Jr. had mixed emotions about leaving Washington and the CIA, probably one of the few times in his life he felt any emotion beyond anger and hatred. Prescott was somewhat disoriented. The flight was long and. unnerving and the change from years of civil service to the private sector brought its own kind of transitional woes.

His retirement from the CIA was elective and planned, yet created some kind of strange doubt. The forfeiture of power and command decision-making was the most difficult aspect to leave. Prescott's adjustment was already abstract. He remained seated until the last passenger walked past him, then rose, alone as he disembarked the plane. He blended into the commuter crowd and headed to the terminal exit.

Immediately beyond the passenger gate Prescott spotted a limo driver holding a card which displayed his name. He approached the driver and spoke only when he was close to him.

"I'm Emmet Prescott," he said.

"Mister Prescott, hello sir, the car is right outside. Do you have any luggage?"

"Just my carry-on."

"Good. Here, let me take that for you sir," the driver said, reaching for the bag.

Prescott handed the driver the bag and followed him from the terminal to the car parked at the curb. The driver opened the back door for Prescott and then jumped into the front with the bag and drove out of the airport.

Prescott sat and watched through darkened glass as the city went by in block increments. It had been a long time since he had been in New York, but even now he felt a power over it, and a distinct indifference for it. His personal thoughts were those of resentment for the liberal attitude of the inner city mentality. He took exception to the allowances and excuses given to any bleeding heart group that cried for special treatment. He knew there were needy people but the emphasis seemed to go beyond them. The pressure self-serving groups brought to bear made it impossible for politicians and law enforcement officers to do their jobs. Wherever he looked he saw signs of lawlessness, lost political control and misdirection of justice. Inwardly he advocated more political strength and police might. He hoped a firm resolve would be exacted to reverse the trends which he felt could morally corrupt the city. He knew a political law and order hard line would give more direction than a pliable philosophy that could be bent and molded by any lobbying group. The conflicts that occupied his mind were personal thoughts which opposed political and social trends. His whole working career had been based on order and form, which, to his mind, were in direct opposition in this ungovernable city. His training and experience told him there was a better way, but it was not his battle to wage.

The limo stopped at a light at Sixty Third and Central Park West. A man in shabby clothing stepped off the curb and approached the windshield carrying a towel and a spray bottle of Windex. As he prepared to clean the window, the driver hit a button and automatically the car sprayed an even mist onto the windshield and the wipers proceeded to clean the area.

Upon seeing the would-be cleaner, a hint of anger stabbed in Prescott's stomach, but that was quickly dissipated when the driver cleverly foiled his attempt.

The limo pulled away from the light and Prescott could hear the disgruntled cleaner curse. At Sixty Fifth Street the limo stopped at the curb.

"Will there be anything else sir?" the driver asked.

"No. This is fine."

The driver quickly left the car and opened the door for Prescott.

"Good evening sir," the driver announced.

"Yeah," Prescott managed.

Prescott stood on the sidewalk as the car drove into the night. He turned and looked at the buildings lining the block, then at the park. In spite of his feelings for the city, a lucrative and prestigious job proved enticing and compromised his judgment. He had to live with his ambivalence and somehow find a way to conquer his trade-off.

The night air was cold and folded around him. His breath came out in puffs of white mist. He stood up the collar of his raincoat to cover his neck then slowly made his way into the building. The lobby was newly refurbished with marble floors, velour lounge furniture, plants and bright lighting. To the left of the lobby was a stucco archway that led to a hallway, elevators and the staircase. The lighting in the hallway was more subdued and the soft, relaxing sounds of piped music greeted his ears.

Prescott was anxious to get to his apartment, take a warm shower and make some business phone calls. He wasn't scheduled to start work for another week, but he wanted to have certain procedures in place and more importantly, he wanted to convey to his subordinates that he was on top of things and had high expectations. He pressed the "up" button and the elevator opened immediately. He slipped in and pressed "12." As the doors started to close, a figure emerged from the staircase and entered the elevator. The figure went to press a button, then turned to Prescott and slammed him against the wall. With his forearm pressed firmly into his chest and a knife at his throat, Prescott was immobile.

"Give me your fuckin' money now or die!" the man ordered.

Prescott was taken by surprise, and, thrown into a strange abyss. He was frightened but calm.

"OK," he said coldly.

"Now motherfucker!" the man said firmly and anxiously.

"OK here it is," Prescott said reaching for his wallet. "Nothing to get upset about. Consider the money yours. No problem. Take it easy."

As Prescott spoke he never showed signs of fear or anger. He just stared into the eyes of his assailant.

Prescott produced the wallet which his assailant tore from his hands.

"There's a lot in there," Prescott said in a calm, soothing voice.

"Shut the fuck up!"

"Whatever you say," Prescott said, disguising his feelings of defiance.

The assailant stuffed the wallet into his jacket pocket and quickly looked at the indicator light panel. With his attention misdirected, he eased his pressure on Prescott slightly but kept the knife pointed at his left eye.

Prescott repositioned himself on the wall and redistributed his weight evenly on both feet.

As the elevator came to a stop and the door opened, the mugger brought his arm back and slashed at Prescott's face. Prescott stepped within the arc of his assailant's arm and grabbed it at the forearm and elbow. With one quick violent motion he pushed the forearm away and the elbow toward him. The sound of breaking bones filled the confined quarters. The assailant screamed as the knife fell from his hand. He quickly grabbed Prescott around the throat with his other arm and began to choke him. Prescott drove the heel of his shoe into the assailant's shin. The bigger man fell backward against the wall. Prescott drove his own head backward hitting the man solidly on the chin. Prescott then twisted and forced his elbow into his attacker's solar plexus. A burst of air escaped the attacker's mouth as his strength seemed to leave his body.

Prescott quickly broke loose from his attacker's grasp and swung a powerful backhand, catching him on the temple with his knuckles. The man fell into the panel board and his hand hit the alarm button. Prescott stepped backward to gain room enough to deliver a kick. With one motion he jumped completely off the floor, the toe of his right foot smashing into the attacker's nose, causing the man to fall to the floor. Prescott could see blood covering the man's face and that his nose was disjointed. Prescott drove another powerful kick to the man's throat, rendering him helpless. He picked up the knife then quickly looked outside the elevator. Upon seeing no one, he stood astride the prone body. Contempt and anger filled his face. A controlled rage burned in his eyes.

"You motherfucker!" Prescott growled angrily.

He looked at the knife for a second and deliberately turned the cutting edge toward the attacker's head and aimed the point at his heart. Then with one powerful motion, he forced the blade deep into the assailant's chest until only the handle protruded from the man. The attacker's body jolted and began to quiver. His head bounced off the floor causing an erratic tapping sound. His hands felt frantically for the knife in a vain attempt to withdraw it and somehow remove the injury and restore his body to its normal condition. Then his arm raised up as though wanting to depress a button on the elevator panel, and flee through its open doors.

His arm began to lower slowly and a final gasp escaped from his throat. Blood oozed into the fabric of his shirt and his chest stopped heaving. His body became still and relaxed.

Prescott quickly withdrew a handkerchief from his pocket and wiped the handle of his fingerprints. He grabbed his attacker's hand and guided it around the handle and pressed an imprint onto it. He grabbed the dead man by the shoulder and turned him over making sure his arm stayed folded under his body.

The noise of the alarm finally brought some residents out into the hallway. Prescott turned and saw the frightened faces of several people. A quiet, reassuring calm exuded from him.

"Will someone please call the police. I've just been attacked," he said softly trying to sound defenseless.

At first the people didn't move. Distrust and morbid curiosity kept them immobile.

"Nine One One, please," Prescott said.

A middle-aged woman backed into her apartment and went to the phone.

Prescott bent down to retrieve his small piece of luggage. Upon grasping the handle he noticed blood had stained part of it. Once again anger invaded his stomach and contempt boiled in his eyes. He looked out to the hallway and noticed no one was watching him. With one quick motion he raised his leg and drove the heel of his shoe into the face of the corpse.

"You son of a bitch." He growled

Mary Cello sat in the van with the director/camera operator, Tyler Hacket. The crew also included tape operator, Bill Medley, gaffer Tom Barker, and Tony Armondo, the audio specialist who was driving the van to Grand Central Terminal.

The news crew had worked together on several projects in the past and had gained a respect for each other's ability. They worked well and felt at ease with their individual jobs. What they disliked universally was night assignments, not the subject. While each found reporting and recording the underbelly of society distasteful, that life style did hold a fascination over them. It was an alien existence that seemed to be in direct contrast to social behavior and human needs.

For Mary, understanding it became a challenge, being removed from it held solace. The crew sat silently, being jostled by the van's movements. Each was alone with their private mood, briefly isolated within the confines of individual thoughts.

"Mary," Tyler said, disturbing the silence.

"Yes?"

"I'd like to bounce my idea of shooting off you."

"What's that?"

"Well, I thought we'd shoot some film, in black and white, to get some effect. Give visual interest to the lead-in and maybe use it throughout to enhance the videotape footage."

"Great, it might underscore their separateness and alienation."

"We can pick up those shots as we go along. If need be we can even come back without you for more if we have to. Let's start with shooting tape of you in front of the station for your opening and closing commentary. Then we'll go into the tunnels. You report as we go along; your spontaneity will emphasize the reality. Is that in line with your concept?"

"Yes...Be sure to get some close-ups of these people. I'd like to show their expressions. What's in their eyes, the hopelessness, that kind of thing."

"No problem. Although some may run from us."

"Yeah, but some may not, they may have nothing more to care about."

"OK. Who's this guy we have to meet?"

"Mike Nailen, he's with Metro, he should be there by now."

The van came to a halt at the main entrance of Grand Central Station. Tony flipped down the visor displaying an official permit which would prevent a ticket or a tow.

As Mary stepped from the van, Mike Nailen was there to greet her.

"Mary Cello?" he asked.

"Yes."

"Hi, I'm Mike Nailen."

"Hi Mike, I'm grateful for this tour. It'll help enormously."

"My pleasure, Mary."

"This is Tyler Hacket, the director," she said as Hacket emerged.

"And our crew, Bill Medley, Tom Barker, and Tony Armondo," Mary said, indicating each.

"Hello gentlemen," Nailen said.

"OK, where do we go?" Mary asked.

"Well what would you have in mind?"

"I'd like to go into the bowels of the system. You know, where the commuter never goes and the public never sees. I'm sure there's a strange world beneath these streets."

"I'll say there is. Why don't we take it from the beginning?"

"Fine. We just need to quick shoot some commentary in the entrance before we get the interior shots."

"Good."

Mary positioned herself at the entrance to the station, holding a microphone. Tyler held the camera directly in front of her and Tom lighted the scene.

"Roll tape," Tyler ordered.

"We have speed," responded Tony.

"And action," directed Tyler.

"Good evening, I'm Mary Cello of Public Broadcast News. Tonight we're going to examine a problem facing not only New York, but every city in every state in the country...The problem is homelessness...A growing problem that has been labeled the Silent Shame."

Mary paused. She wanted her timing to be a dramatic tool. "The recognition of the homeless problem quietly began to surface into consciousness in the early nineteen eighties. The pictures of displaced farmers forced to uproot from land they had owned for generations, to an isolated figure sleeping on a subway grate, ushered in a new phenomenon...But who are the homeless? How many fill their ranks? A conservative estimate by the United States Department of Housing and Urban Development put the number at three hundred fifty thousand nationwide. But some feel that figure is dramatically low. In New York City alone there are believed to be forty thousand living on the streets, subways, airports and parks. Where do the homeless come from?...

"Decreasing availability of rentals for low-income families and burned out apartment houses surely feed the problem. Then we have newly arrived immigrants with no resources, recently released prisoners, alcoholics, drug users, and simply lazy people who wish to avoid work. Then there is the problem of the mentally ill...All contributing factors..."

A small curious crowd began to gather as Mary continued.

"According to professional estimates, nearly one third of all homeless individuals are mentally ill. In a survey of American cities, conducted one year ago by the United States Conference of Mayors, the percentage of mentally ill homeless ranged from sixty percent in Louisville, to forty-five percent in San Francisco, to twenty-five percent in New York...But why so many mentally ill homeless?...To know the reason for that, one must look at mental health professionals and administrators. They proposed that deinstitutionalization was the answer to budget cuts...It was not...and tonight you will see testimony to that misjudgment and failure."

Mary stopped her commentary and paused once more. She nodded to Tyler who announced, "Stop tape."

Tom flicked a switch and the spotlight faded. Bill let the tape run for another second then shut it off. The crowd suddenly became disinterested and continued on their way.

Tyler approached Mary.

"Sounds good."

"Thank you."

"I get the impression you're gonna hit hard with this."

"As hard as I can...Mike can we go into the tunnel now?" Mary asked.

"Sure Mary, let's go."

"OK. Bill and Tom, if we see any homeless we'll try to shoot--close-ups if possible. Tony at this point I don't think we'll need audio." Tyler instructed.

"Right."

Mary took out a small tape recorder to record her observations.

The group entered the station and grim solitude came over them. They felt as though they were entering a tomb for the living dead, a chamber of horrors fashioned from indifference and neglect with an epitaph written in abandonment and rejection.

"Valley of lost souls," Mike observed.

No one responded to Nailen's remark. They proceeded in abject silence, affected by the sad mosaic before them.

As they descended to the lower level of outbound commuter trains, a figure peered out from a wall separating the trains. Like a hunted animal, the man pressed back against the wall seeking cover. His look appeared frightened and suspicious. Tony shined a light at the man and Bill aimed his lens. The man ducked away and was gone.

"They appear to live with the cunning of an animal," Mike observed.

"Yes, they have to....Let's go back here Mary," Mike directed. "This takes us to the first area away from the commuters. This direction leads to what amounts to...catacombs," he said pointing into the distance.

As the group turned a corner they were met by a figure standing motionless and silent before them.

Tyler moved out in front cautiously and motioned for Tom and Bill to follow.

"Easy does it," Tyler said.

Bill started shooting video and suddenly the area was lit by Tom's bright spotlight. In the new light Bill was able to shoot his subject. He zoomed into a tight shot and the man remained still, mute.

Mary clicked on her recorder and quietly recorded her impressions.

"...Some show no concern; an etherized distrust. A cruel joke with no laughter, a deep pain with no cure."

Tyler slowly turned to Tony.

"Audio."

"Rolling."

"Hello," Mary said to the man.

The man just looked out from a very dark void.

"What's your name?" she pressed.

Looking at the man through the camera, Bill was able to gain a different perspective. The man's hopelessness appeared accentuated.

"What's your name?" Mary repeated.

The man looked at each member of the group as though they were specimens in a rare tank.

"Your name?" Mary said once more.

"Harmon," he replied slowly.

"Where are you from Harmon?"

"Nowhere," he said.

"Where are you going now?" Mary asked.

The vagrant remained silent, distant.

"Do you live down here, Harmon?" Mary asked.

"Careful, Mary," Tyler whispered.

"Do you live here?" Mary repeated, ignoring Tyler's concern.

Harmon was comatose. His eyes blinked as though to conceal his hopelessness for only an instant, but there was no relief. He turned slowly and headed toward the stairs which led to the street.

It took a long moment for any member of the group to move. Their universal reaction numbed their logic as their disbelief grew in intensity.

Mary brought up the collar of her coat in an attempt to protect herself from all sights and sounds. Bill toyed with his camera as an illusionary diversion from the reality surrounding him. Tyler wiped alway a claminess that had formed on his forehead.

"Let's go on Mike," Mary finally said.

The group descended a well to a platform. On the way down, Tyler instructed Tom to turn on the spotlight for visibility.

"I think if we descend to another platform we'll be able to see a core where they live." Mike announced.

"Let's do it," Mary said.

Down another tube to a platform the spotlight bathed an area unaccustomed to light. From within an abandoned train car--the same one Harmon had made his home--people scattered in fright.

"Oh my God!" Mary whispered in disbelief. "There must be fifty or sixty people here...The stench is unbelievable."

Tom panned the area with his spotlight and the camera followed. Mary turned on her recorder but was unable to express what she felt and saw.

"A political and social disgrace," Mike announced.

"I've seen a lot of shit, but this is awful," Tom said.

In a moment there was no movement. Everyone had hidden.

"God it stinks down here," Tony commented.

"That's human decay, there's somebody dead here," Tyler observed.

"Oh, no!" Mary reacted.

"Stay close everyone," Tyler commanded.

The group moved in unison, like commandos on a night raid, invading a fragile, frightened enemy.

Beyond them they noticed the abandoned rail car, the light reflecting off its broken glass and dull siding.

"How did that car get here?" Mary whispered.

"I don't know. That's a CT 120 sleeper. They've been out of service for fifty years...Maybe even longer," Mike responded. "There must have been an access rail to here. Somebody must have just parked it and forgot it," he continued.

The bright light revealed the essence of a horrible truth. One which the group found difficult to bear witness. The strange reality laid claim to their collective emotions: fear, anger, disbelief and a trace of guilt.

Tyler suddenly stopped and held out his arm, a signal for the rest to halt. The strange light caught a wild cat full face. Tyler had seen an angry house cat on its haunches before, but this was no ordinary house cat displaying normal anger. He was big and dirty. His eyes reflected a fearless evil. The light had frozen him but did not render him docile. A deep, menacing hiss escaped from the animal. He tensed, ready to strike, regardless of the size and number of his adversaries.

"The light's gonna blind him," Mary said.

"Fuck 'em, then maybe he won't be able to see us to attack," Tom responded.

"Don't walk toward him," Mike said.

"OK back up," Tyler said.

The group retreated and Tom moved the light away from the cat. From within the darkness they heard heavy thumping. The cat had probably been momentarily blinded, and in its panic and frenzy, crashed into walls.

Tyler moved into the rail car and noticed the debris that served as living quarters to many. There were papers, broken glass and cardboard boxes surrounding sections of seats. These were crudely made shelters in a world that defied shelter. Remnants of food and human waste were everywhere.

Tyler noticed the shapeless mound lying on the floor in a space between sections of seats.

"Tom give me some light over here," he ordered.

The lighting man moved cautiously into the car, concentrating the light to where Tyler was standing. Tyler reached into his jeans pocket and withdrew a handkerchief to protect his nose and mouth from the awful smell. There before his feet he saw the remains of what was once a human being.

"Damn!" came his muffled cry.

"What is it Tyler?"

"The guy's been killed."

"Oh no," Mary said.

"His face looks like it's been eaten away."

Mary fought valiantly and suppressed her urge to cry out. The scene incensed her, challenging her own definition of morality. She depressed the play/record button of her recorder and spoke.

"Surely as despair feeds upon despair, and horror begets horror, the human condition as we know it, ceases to exist." She commented as anger and disgust filled her voice. "Left in its wake is an inescapable abomination beyond comprehension, defying social and moral conscience. Down here few survive and fewer escape. But in a dark abandoned subway car, one man, blessed by mercy, did manage to escape."

FOUR

*L*ieutenant Lawrence Elroy arrived at Grand Central Station just as the PBN news van was leaving. His head turned up and down the impersonal street as a matter of habit, not with the hope of finding something new or welcoming.

There was a callous look on his face that was layered by years on the police force and the fate of his own life. His walk was mechanical and his attitude expressed impatience. He appeared to be a land baron who owned a part of the streets to which he really wanted no claim. He raised the collar of his leather coat to protect the back of his neck from the cold wind.

"What do we have patrolman?" he said to a policeman standing by the entrance of the station.

"Homicide, downstairs sir."

"Who was it?"

"Victim was a homeless male, no identification. This way sir," the patrolman said leading Elroy. As they walked through the main area of the station, Elroy could not ignore the degradation that had taken place in the station over the years. From an important commuter line to a squatters holding. It wasn't the transition that appalled him so much, it was the acceptance of the prevailing conditions. The descent of levels to the crime scene succeeded in underscoring the pessimism Elroy felt for society.

He shifted into his insulation mode which protected him from the decay of humanity. Over the years he became adept at conjuring up the needed numbness--too adept.

At the crime scene there were several policemen standing on the platform debating the best way to remove the deceased. In the old rail car was Doctor Michael Tippett of Forensic Medicine. Elroy looked at the surroundings and needed no dissertation as to the purpose of the area. His ability to conceal his disgust was evident.

"Who found the body?" Elroy asked one of the policemen.

"News crew "

"Was that the van I saw leaving?"

"PBN?"

"Yes."

"That was it."

"What were they doing down here?"

"Filming a documentary."

"About what?"

"The homeless."

Elroy made his way into the rail car but remained by the door. Doctor Tippett was in the process of completing his on-sight preliminary investigation when he looked up and saw Elroy.

"Larry," he acknowledged.

"Hi, Mike. What's it look like?"

"Not pretty. Guy's been dead for at least two days. He's been food for rats."

"How'd he buy it?"

"Gashed up pretty bad. I'll tell you when I'm done with the lab work. City gets worse and worse, Larry."

"Yeah."

"OK. I'm done here. Best way to get him up through the shaft is tie him onto the stretcher...fashion rope on the top and bottom and guide from the bottom," Tippett said to the policemen.

Two policemen placed the body bag onto the wooden stretcher and tied the body across the center of it. They placed rope through the hand holes on either end and lifted.

Elroy watched the body ascend, then spoke to the policeman who escorted him from the street.

"Did you get to speak to anyone down here?"

"Yes sir, we did manage to speak to three homeless; the best we got was incoherent."

"How about the reporters?"

"Nothing much there either. They spoke to one guy who they say looked spaced. That's about it."

"Who was the reporter?"

"Mary Cello, Public Broadcast News."

"Phone?"

"Yes sir, here," the patrolman said handing Elroy his note book.

"OK thanks...Anything else down here Mike?" the lieutenant asked.

"No Larry...I don't think we've gotta be told what happened here."

"Yeah. Give me the report anyway."

"You got it...You don't look good Larry. What's the matter?"

"Got a real bad headache. This smell isn't helping much."

"Well there isn't much more to be done down here, we can go now."

"OK, just fill me in Mike."

"Yes Lieutenant."

Elroy followed the same path back to the street. He never dreamed the air of the city would smell fresh, but compared to the tunnel he just emerged from, it felt like the Rockies after a spring rain.

He looked at the policeman's notes for Mary's number and punched it in on his car phone.

"PBN," came the voice.

"Mary Cello please."

"One moment please," the phone clicked to silence for a moment then another voice said:

"Assignments, Dennehey."

"Mary Cello please."

"Sorry, Mary's out of the office right now."

"My name is Lieutenant Larry Elroy of the Twenty-Ninth Precinct. Would you please have her return my call?"

"Yes Lieutenant I will. Would you like to tell me what this is about?"

Elroy paused for a moment, reluctant to answer.

"Please have her call me, Mr. Dennehey," Elroy said evasively.

Dennehey responded by hanging up the phone.

Elroy replaced his phone and grabbed the police car's radio. He pressed the cold plastic to his forehead in a vain attempt to relieve his headache. He then moved the mouthpiece to his lips, depressed a button and spoke.

"Dispatch," came a reply.

"Car eighteen, Lieutenant Elroy."

"Go ahead Lieutenant,"

"I'm leaving homicide scene at Grand Central and heading home, I'm not feeling well. If I receive a call from Mary Cello, give her my home number or get a phone number where I can call her back. Out."

"Mary Cello, copy Lieutenant."

Elroy drove cross town to Twelfth Avenue then turned and headed for Battery Park. A red light forced him to stop at the River Stage. Seated along the link fence was a string of street squatters huddled against the cold night air. At the corner were five more standing around a burning trash can, their hands hung over the flames as though they were in silent prayer to the patron saint of the fires of last hope.

For a moment Elroy tried to picture these people as they once were, young boys and girls, altar boys and cheerleaders, brothers, sisters, sons and daughters to other people. Perhaps at one time belonging, perhaps not, all now part of a coalition, befriending the fires in a trash can that won't burn much longer.

The light turned green and Elroy prepared to go. Standing next to his window was the face of a displaced sin of society. If the man's eyes could summon another look they would probably look pleading, but the stranger's eyes looked dead--hopelessly dead.

Elroy rolled down his window and handed the man a ten dollar bill and drove away.

The Trade Towers bounced out of the night like modern man's homage to Ozamandis. Elroy passed the towers and pulled into an underground garage of his Battery Park condo and took the elevator to the tenth floor. In the silence of the elevator he tried shaking the images of the homeless people but it clung to him like a clammy sweat. In his apartment he drew back curtains and looked out over the black Hudson River. A string of bright lights shone like a necklace along the Palisades. The view was pleasing, but did little for the feeling in his gut and the pain in his head.

Elroy's apartment was unusually neat for a single man, with no socks cluttering the floor, no sink filled with dirty dishes. The one bedroom apartment was decorated with modern furniture. Straight lines and no clutter. A beige leather couch, matching chair and glass table gave the illusion of empty space, and mirrors on the walls created a spacious, deep look. A Renoir print hung in the foyer and several Michael Atkinson prints covered other walls.

Elroy moved to his rack system and powered his CD player. After a couple of clicks, he heard an off key Bob Dylan singing about changing times.

He undressed and hung up his suit and took a long, warm shower. He let the water beat on his neck and shoulders in hopes of easing the pain. Emerging from the shower, he wrapped a thick, terry-cloth robe around his body and flattened his wet hair. The pain in his head had subsided slightly but lingered, like an echo.

Elroy poured himself a glass of apple juice, turned off the CD player, then clicked his remote to bring his television to life. He eased into the leather couch and ran the remote through the paces, checking in with the evening news shows, which made no mention of the slain man in Grand Central. Elroy slouched down in the couch, resting his head and began to doze. His mind replayed the fire burning in the can he saw earlier, then wandered to images of fire burning through a twisted car. He fought to redirect his thoughts away from the car to something pleasant. Old memories in need of diversion, old personal pains in search of acceptance. He recalled his trip to Paris. The Eiffel Tower stood out in his mind, and the sidewalk cafe where he ate with Lenore. Lenore, the disillusioned divorcée who also needed a period of adjustment, an escape from reality.

Elroy knew the relationship would never last, but he needed the misdirection of Paris for himself. He let the European setting and time take its course to relieve his trauma, but the further Elroy ran the more things remained unsettled.

In the distance he heard a noise shattering his thoughts and disturbing his rest. The noise sounded once more and Elroy tried to focus on it. The third time it sounded he realized it was the phone.

He staggered to the kitchen and picked it up before it rang again.

"Hello."

"Lieutenant Elroy please," came the voice.

"Yes."

"I'm Mary Cello, Public Broadcasting News.

"Oh yes, Mary. Thanks for calling."

"What was it you wanted Lieutenant?"

"I'm investigating the homicide in Grand Central earlier this evening and I wanted to speak to you about it."

"I'd be glad to help Lieutenant, but can it keep? I've had a bad night."

"Yes I'm sure you did, I'm sorry but I didn't mean tonight. Tomorrow?"

""Yes, that's fine. My office, nine o'clock?"

"Make it ten."

"Fine. Do you know where we're located?"

"No."

"Five oh five, Eighth Avenue, nineteenth floor."

"Got it. Ten o'clock."

"Good, see you at ten."

"Ten."

Elroy hung up the phone and jotted down the address. He walked back into the living room and picked up the glass he drank the juice from and brought it back into the kitchen and put it in the dishwasher.

He used the remote to turn the television to silence and went to bed.

The car fire, the Eiffel Tower, Lenore, and his headache all blended together briefly, but then succumbed to deep sleep.

★★★

Mary Cello's office was small and cluttered. On her desk were early editions of the New York Times, Washington Post and Chicago Sun Times. Piled neatly behind her were back issues of EXTRA--Fairness and Accuracy in Reporting. The issues of the Times and The Post were disheveled and certain articles in each paper were circled in red with certain paragraphs underlined.

Mary had put aside the papers and was keying into her PC. She studied the screen, wanting to complete her thoughts. Her fingers typed:

"...The laws as they pertain to the homeless, schizophrenic and psychotic are merely a tool to ensure their right to remain mentally ill. Laws regarding the mentally ill must be amended. Deinstitutionalization is an absolute failure and legislation should insure proper patient care and living facilities."

Mary paused and thought how ironic it was that by law a sick person thought to be mentally incapable was allowed to have their fate sealed by a loved one. Yet homeless mentally ill were excluded from that rationale. She thought of incorporating that idea into her commentary when the phone on her desk rang. It took several rings before she answered it.

"Mary Cello," she said not diverting her attention from the screen.

"Mary I have a Lieutenant Elroy here to see you."

Mary looked at her watch and remembered her ten o'clock appointment.

"Oh yes Louise, show him back."

The receptionist walked Elroy through a long corridor, several cubical offices and finally to Mary's office.

"In there Lieutenant," she indicated.

"Thank you...Mary Cello?"

"Yes. Lieutenant Elroy? Please come in. Sit down."

"Thank you...I hope I'm not disturbing you?"

"No, not at all, I'm just about finished."

Elroy couldn't help noticing how pretty Mary was. Dark long hair with big dark eyes. Delicate cheek bones and lips that seemed to be more comfortable whispering than speaking aloud. A checkered blouse clung to large full breasts.

"I won't take much of your time. I know it must have been awful to make such a discovery."

"It was. That was only part of it."

"I know what you mean. I was down in that tunnel also."

"Terrible comment of the human condition."

"Yes, makes you see how lucky we really are."

"Among other things....What can I help you with Lieutenant?"

"The obvious...ah...did you see anything, anyone unusual--you know how I mean that."

"Yes I do. To answer your question--no."

"Didn't find a gun, a bloody knife, anything?"

"No. How was he killed?"

"I don't know just yet, I'm waiting for the lab report...Obviously you were filming some kind of documentary."

"Yes, a piece on the homeless."

"Yeah, I figured that."

Elroy noticed Mary was looking directly into his eyes, not turning away. He felt she was monitoring his moves and measuring his impulses. Trying to look beyond his surface.

"Is that your commentary?" he asked motioning to the PC.

"Yes."

"I'm not too familiar with your news agency. I mean you're not prime time news."

"Hmmm," Mary chuckled. "Prime time, that's good. I like that. We like to think of ourselves as not main stream."

"What's the difference?"

"I guess you don't watch our news programs."

"No, I'm sorry."

"Try it. You may be surprised."

"You're a cable network?"

"Yes."

"When is your documentary going to air?"

"That depends on how fast we're able to put it together technically, what other scheduling commitments we have, that sort of thing."

"Public Broadcast News. Is that what it implies? Public?"

"Yes."

"Not sponsored?"

"No."

"Why not?"

"Manipulation, corporate control, we want to be totally responsible for content. I guess you can say we are an activist station with our assessments as to what things are really all about."

"What do you mean?"

"Well without corporate sponsorship or funding we're able to avoid any kind of censorship."

"Are you like PBS?"

"Not really. They have their own corporate sponsorship, so they are limited, not as much as network stations, but there are some restrictions."

"Sounds like you're in a position to create all sorts of controversy."

"Watch us, you'll see."

"OK I will...The subway...did your film crew happen to see anything? Or film anything?"

"No, not really. Other than some of the inhabitants there."

"Did any of them have bloody clothing?"

"We didn't notice. There was only one guy we did manage to speak to, but he was just...gone, out of it. That's all."

As she spoke, Elroy was taken in by her confidence. Mary appeared strong but not bitchy, professional but not discourteous and cold. And the way she looked into his eyes, he sensed an honesty and truthfulness about her, and a person who would expect no less in return.

"How much time and effort will you put into the investigation Lieutenant?"

Elroy was caught off guard by the question. He allowed a long moment to let her meaning register in his mind.

"Well, this will be difficult to canvas. It's not like we can go door to door in someone's neighborhood to get coherent observations. Those people are hard to pin down and to them there is no justice."

"That's not answering my question."

"I know what you mean, Mary. But a homeless person is just as important as a Park Avenue lawyer. I don't distinguish between the people, I respond to the crime."

"I'm sorry Lieutenant, I didn't mean to imply..."

"It's okay."

Elroy searched his mind, he wanted to prolong the conversation.

"What kind of impact will your documentary have?"

"I don't know. That's difficult to say. But like you respond to the crime, I respond to the condition. I have to expose the problem. I owe it to those people."

"It's a difficult situation. No easy answers."

"From our point of view it's an ethical question, but for them it's a lot more."

"I'm familiar with the position of victims. I've seen them for a long time," Elroy said.

"Those people are sheep living in a field with wolves. Everybody attacks them...Who do you think killed him?"

"Who would gain anything by killing him in the first place?"

"I suppose."

"Did you file a story on the murder?"

"No, but I'm going to incorporate it into my documentary. Maybe not that specific murder, but I will make mention of that phase of their plight."

"Was last night the first night you were down there?"

"Yes Lieutenant. Why?"

"Well, the coroner at the scene felt the guy was dead for at least two days."

"No, that was my first assigned location."

"Where else will you be filming, or is your documentary complete?"

"No, we'll be filming in the streets, airports, probably a shelter or two...Is this the only homeless homicide you're investigating or are there others?"

"Only one. I mean there are homeless killed every day, but this could be an isolated dispute over anything, or the beginning of a serial job. We have to wait and see for that."

"Will it be difficult to apprehend the killer?"

"Yes. Very. To be quite honest we probably won't get him. These kinds of killings are difficult for all the obvious reasons."

"Suppose it's a serial killer?"

"That's difficult too."

"How so?"

"Well, if you didn't happen to be there filming a documentary, the chances are good that body would have never been discovered. You know, it's not like a housewife or executive that gets killed, there's always somebody to know they're missing. But these people don't exist on any social rolls or census by name. Hordes of them could disappear and they probably wouldn't even get to change the census."

"Sad."

"Very."

"Where will you go from here Lieutenant?"

"Hopefully the lab will determine who the dead man was, then we check from there. But again, if he lived on the streets for any length of time he acquired new enemies--nameless like himself."

"I can see what you're up against."

"You too."

"Yes, which reminds me Lieutenant, I really have to get back to work. Unless there is something else?"

"No that's probably about it. Thank you for your time, Mary, I hope I didn't intrude."

"No, not at all."

"Listen if you remember anything, please call. You have my home number. If I'm out, just leave a message on my machine, I can get back to you."

"OK Lieutenant. I will."

"Thank you again, Mary."

"Can I walk you out?"

"No, that's alright, I'll find my way."

FIVE

The photo on the front page of The Daily News displayed a crumpled body lying on the floor of an elevator. The large bold headline above the picture read: "EXEC SLAYS ATTACKER"

Harmon was not interested in the news, only the paper it was written on. He made his way east on Broome Street toward the homeless shelter. He usually separated his staying time between various shelters, and locations on the street. He knew he didn't want to go back to Grand Central. Not because of the man he killed; his mind didn't respond to that consistently. At times he was beyond rational judgment and guilt. The incidents in his life mutated his thought process, propelling him beyond clarity and normal instinct into a world of psychotic revenge and paranoia. His normal personality and character traits were altered and reshaped into synthetic behavior. He had become a disease, a malignancy of social response.

Irresponsibility collided with indifference leaving in its wake an imbalance from which Harmon formed his conclusions. It was from this imbalance that he chose to spend the night in the shelter.

Perhaps the reporters he met had offered a greater threat, forcing him to reevaluate his conscience and rediscover his lost identity. At least for one more night he wanted to remain suspended in his world, defying his own logic, perpetuating self-delusions and bolstering his overwhelming impulse for revenge.

The shelter was a moderate improvement over the station. It wasn't the surroundings that created the despair, it was the human element. In the large room, beds were cramped together to imply unity, but nothing could down play the isolationism. The room had light, marginal heat and guarded cleanliness when compared to the tunnels, but there existed no absolution to the ingrained misery.

Harmon walked into a side room that housed a black and white television, several round tables and broken chairs. Pinned against one wall was a table with a coffee urn and a stack of styrofoam cups. A plaque on the wall read: "Lend a helping hand." Several residents were seated, their empty stares affixed in the direction of the television. News personalities addressed a catatonic audience. Unrelated information grazed their ears, defying the basic laws of communication.

"...residents of the west side neighborhood were asking building owners for increased security in the wake of the killing on Sixty-Fifth and Central Park West last night," the newscaster said. "In meetings with the building owners, residents expressed concern that increased drug and crack activity is creating a greater threat to their neighborhood. Residents demanded that a doorman be added to buildings that don't already have one. In addition, they requested a security guard be hired for each building to patrol the halls between the hours from eleven p.m. to five a.m....Sue..."

Harmon poured cold coffee into a cup and looked at it a long time before sipping it. His mind seemed focused on the dark liquid that formed tiny ripples in the confining cup. For an instant he felt disoriented and displaced, a stationary object outside himself surrounded by motion-- no sound, no light, only motion.

His hand folded in on the cup and he brought it to his lips. Not only was it cold, it was thick and bitter. Harmon looked at his feet and the floor. Gradually he began to reacquaint himself to the present and the surrealistic motion around him came to a halt. A grunt from one of the people in the room served as a factual reminder of his presence within his time and place. The sound of the television fell on his ears once more.

..."Police have identified the slain attacker as Michael Baylor. Baylor, 37, of East 128th Street had two prior convictions for assault and was currently in a drug Rehab program. Last night Baylor entered the building at 138 West Sixty-Third Street and attacked a pharmaceutical company executive who was identified as Emmet Prescott Junior"...

Harmon felt a hot jolt to his stomach as he quickly turned to the television. The image of Prescott sent shock waves over his entire body. The past had incredulously collided with the present to create a mega force explosion within Harmon. He listened intently.

"...Prescott was too distraught for comment. His lawyer told WPIX that Prescott was taking a mild sedative and under a doctor's care..." The news commentator turned to a colleague off camera and suddenly the two men were etched on the screen.

"Gerry what does it look like for the Giants?" he asked as glibly as though the previous story were the re-telling of an unrelated fable.

The screen displayed the sportscaster.

"The big story is the Giants. Their game with New England on Sunday is do or die...I'll have details after this..."

The screen swept to a bucket of ice cubes and a hand withdrawing a bottle of beer. Harmon reacted anxiously; he needed more information about Prescott.

"Sit down!" came a voice from behind Harmon.

Harmon remained immobile. Once more he seemed disoriented, not realizing he had walked to within two feet of the television.

"Sit down!" came another voice.

Harmon stepped away and backed out of the room. He made his way to his bed and sat at the foot of it. The image of Emmet Prescott exploded in his mind and caused his body to tremble. From across the expanse of time he reemerged to weave himself into the pattern of Harmon's own life. But Harmon knew Prescott had never really been out of his life. He carried reminders and effects of the relationship everywhere he went.

Harmon reached into his pocket for the newspaper. He examined the front page once more. Then turned into it. On page two he saw what he needed to know.

"...as Emmet Prescott Junior entered the elevator of his apartment building on Sixty-Third he was accosted by Baylor and robbed. According to police reports, a struggle broke out and Prescott, who had just arrived in New York from Washington, was knocked to the floor. As Baylor lunged at Prescott with the knife, he tripped over a small piece of Prescott's luggage, causing him to fall and fatally stab himself.

"Prescott was quoted by his attorney as saying the incident had been very upsetting and he was unable to speak to reporters. He even said he 'regretted what happened to Mister Baylor.' A doctor was summoned to sedate Prescott.

"Prescott, who had just been appointed to an executive position with Ryser Pharmaceuticals in New York said the incident was 'very frightening' but he did not think the city was as violent as his first night here might indicate."

Harmon threw the paper on the floor.

"Bullshit! Bullshit!" he said for no one in particular to hear.

" 'Upset' 'regretted' 'sedatives' you lying bastard you killed better people than that without as much as a second thought. They don't know you as I do Prescott."

Harmon stooped and retrieved the paper and reread a portion of the article. His fogged but astute mind picked out the gaps in logic and honesty he deemed obvious.

"I may be psychotic but I'm not dumb Prescott," he said aloud. "You manipulated them again. There's no mention that you worked for the CIA you deceptive bastard. No mention at all."

Harmon looked at the photo of the body and studied it for a long moment. Once again he threw the paper down and stomped it with his foot and angrily ground his heel into it, snarling as he twisted his foot.

"Tripped on your luggage and stabbed himself? Tripped on your luggage and stabbed himself? Stabbed himself? Dumb cops. Dumb cops. You murderer! Murderer! Murderer!"

"Shut up," someone in the room called out.

Harmon was oblivious to the command. He threw himself down on the bed as his rage fermented. He reached into his coat and felt the hatchet lodged in his pants. He squeezed it tightly trying to extract comfort and control from it. The sharp edge cut into his hand as he pressed in. His mouth sucked in air in deep, quick bursts.

"Can I have your paper?" a voice asked.

He recalled the same question from out of the past.

"...The paper is mine. The paper belongs to me!" he remembered he had said.

The dark images flashed in his mind. This time seen in a different light, recalled with greater detail.

The man stood in front of Harmon's bed looking down at him. Harmon's breathing was heavy, he was lost in his personal turmoil which rendered response impossible. The man suddenly stooped and picked up the newspaper not wanting to ask again.

"Get your own paper and leave me alone!" His own voice from the past continued to echo in his mind. He relived the sensation of the hatchet crashing into the faceless form. The past blended with the present as relief overtook him; he envisioned the hatchet being driven into Prescott. Again and again each measured and timed blow resounding an overdue justice. Pulverizing the face of deceit and the perpetrator of harm.

Harmon eased the grip on the hatchet as his breathing returned to normal. There was room enough in his damaged brain for a momentary glimpse of rationality. Revenge managed to blend briefly with a sense of guilt, as he realized he too had left a victim. This reality ultimately made it easy for him to purposefully decide to leave another.

"Prescott you're next. I'm going to get you."

SIX

$\mathcal{E}$lroy strolled from his car to police headquarters. He was oblivious to the light freezing rain that attacked him; Mary Cello still occupied his mind. She lingered with him like the remnants of a bluesy ballad.

He walked into his office and hung up his leather jacket on the coat rack. Several pink phone message slips were standing in the cradle of his phone. He went through them, the last one being Doctor Tippett, with a message to call him. Elroy looked at the Daily News on his desk. On page six he saw the article, reported by the Associated Press, of the murder. The two paragraph piece gave the impression it was an insignificant story filled with limited information and trying to invoke little concern.

From across the office, Captain Tim Reynolds emerged from his own office. Upon seeing Elroy he proceeded into his office. Reynolds was a no-nonsense, blunt individual who commanded the precinct with one philosophy: by the book. He had no tolerance for cops who made their own rules. Reynolds had worked with Elroy for the last twelve years and knew why he was one of the youngest men to ever make lieutenant.

"How you feeling Larry?" Reynolds asked.

"Not bad captain."

"Another headache?"

"Yeah."

"Bad?"

"It's gone now."

"That headache clinic in Montefiore can't help you?"

"They did captain. The medication helps."

"Well if you don't feel good today I want you home, understood?"

"Yes."

"What did you come up with that John Doe in Grand Central?"

"Not much. I've got a message to call Tippett, he may have something for me. I spoke with Mary Cello from PBN and they didn't have anything."

"Damn city's killing itself off and we can't keep up."

"Captain what do you know about the people at PBN?"

"Not much, they seem to be an alternative news agency, always at odds with network news and the papers. I think their radicals. Why?"

"I don't know."

"OK, Larry let me know how you make out with Tippett, if this is a case of one homeless killing another over a bottle of Mister Boston, I may reassign you."

"I'll get back to you captain."

Reynolds left the office and Elroy dialed Tippett's office number.

"Doctor Tippett's office."

"Trudy?"

"Yes?"

"Lieutenant Elroy...is he there?"

"Yes, hold on Lieutenant."

"Larry?"

"Hi Mike, I got a message to call you."

"Yes, Larry I've got an incomplete report for you. I thought you may want what I've got so far."

"Let's hear it."

"OK. Victim is male caucasian, five feet eight and a half inches tall. Death was caused by a blow to the left supra-orbital and infra-orbital margins and zygomatic bone..."

"What's that Mike?"

"In layman's terms it's the cheek bone and lower forehead. A second blow was delivered to the front ribcage rupturing the heart."

"What was the instrument?"

"Wedge shaped object--cleaver--small axe something like that, looks to be five inches in length."

"Anything else?"

"No, nothing that would lead to a suspect. At the time the victim had bronchial pneumonia, emphysema, liver damage and prostate cancer."

"Oh, my God."

"I'm running more tests on the brain. I may be able to tell if he suffered from some kind of mental illness."

"Got a name?"

"Not yet. I should have one by tomorrow, day after at the latest."

""You're a marvel, Mike."

"Well not really. Remember I said his face was eaten away by rats?"

"Yes."

"Well I was wrong. His face was eaten away by cats."

"Cats?"

"Yeah."

"How do you know?"

"Technology Lieutenant."

"I should have known."

"I was right about length of death--two days--forty-eight to...ahh no more than fifty-five hours, more like fifty."

"OK, Mike, anything else?"

"Just the name, soon as I have it you'll get it."

"Great. I'll hear from you."

"You bet."

Elroy hung up the phone and his instincts told him this was going to be another unsolved mystery. An unknown man going to his grave without a single mourner or a minor prayer. The thought pressed in on him like a cold compress. Suddenly the image of Mary Cello came to mind and the cut of loneliness bore a softer edge.

SEVEN

*H*armon stood outside Prescott's apartment building on the park side of the street. A molten sneer contorted his lips as unholy purpose burned in his eyes. He chose to remain removed from sight of the doorman who had been installed since the elevator attack. The doorman stood in the lobby behind the glass door.

Harmon tried to devise a way to gain entry to the building without being detected. Once inside he knew he should not study the directory or mailboxes in his effort to learn which floor and apartment were Prescott's. Harmon reasoned that Prescott may not have his name on the directory, and that he may use a postal box for his mail.

Harmon walked to the phone booth, deposited a coin and dialed.

"Information, Miss Olden."

"Miss Olden can I have the number of Emmet Prescott, Central Park West? It's a new listing."

"Hold for the number please."

Harmon heard a clicking, then synthesized speech.

"The number is 631-3811."

Harmon depressed the tongue and dialed.

"Hello."

"Mister Emmet Prescott?" he said trying to disguise his voice and speak coherently.

"Yes."

"Mister Prescott, I'm Bill Clayton of Manhattan Cable, our Services Department."

"Yes."

"I'm checking to verify an installation on a work order done in your apartment."

"That was done long before I moved in."

"Oh, OK, but was there not a reservice installation, to an existing designation, and not just a carry over."

"How was the reinstallation done?" Prescott asked.

"From our facility, I'm just calling to determine if your service was reinstalled."

"Yes it was."

"Was work and service completed to your satisfaction?"

"Yes."

"Good sir...and the reception?"

"Clear."

"Fine, and the apartment number there?"

There was a pause and Harmon froze. He knew Prescott was suspicious to a fault.

"What did you say your name was?" Prescott asked.

"Bill Clayton, sir."

"Well Mister Clayton if your people reinstalled the service you have my apartment number."

"Well yes we do sir, I just need for you to confirm it."

All Harmon heard was the emptiness close to his ear. He didn't breath or move. Everything around him came to an abrupt halt.

"Six eighteen." Prescott said reluctantly, after a while.

"Thank you sir. Have a nice evening."

Harmon stood in the phone booth and felt surges of emotional irony. Mental instability faded to conscious rage, then succumbed to apathy. His body trembled un-controllably, his expression ranged from quiet delirium to muted anger.

Harmon was ready to strike, but struggled with con-centration. It took time to formulate his thoughts. His ca-pabilities were mounting in small increments, while his resolve was encouraged by the lunacy of his mind as well as the normalcy of it.

The night and all the demons in it attacked him. He looked upon the apartment building as though it was his refuge, a salvation from all that haunted him.

The building had a green tunnel-like awning extend-ing from over the lobby to the curb. The covering offered protection and beckoned him.

Harmon paused, knowing he would be denied en-trance by the doorman. He waited, not knowing for what, while his inner struggle persisted.

The red brake lights of a taxicab puffed brightly as the car came to a halt at the curb. White smoke from the tailpipe danced in the wind and then disappeared into the night. The rear door opened and a passenger placed a large suitcase onto the sidewalk. He then emerged hold-ing another smaller suitcase in one hand and a bag with a long strap hung from his shoulder. The passenger closed the rear door and stepped to the front to hand the driver money. Suddenly the door to the building opened and the doorman walked out to retrieve the large suitcase.

Harmon didn't hesitate, he made his way into the lobby and headed quickly for the staircase which he spot-ted immediately. He climbed two steps at a time until he felt safely concealed within the stairwell. He continued up to the sixth floor where he stopped to catch his breath and waited for the pain in his legs to stop and his antici-pation to become tolerable.

He opened the door slightly and peered down both ends of the corridor. The hallway was deserted and quiet. Situated diagonally from the staircase door was room 618.

Harmon closed the door and pressed back against the cinder block wall. He started to shake his head violently as though to dislodge the ghosts of the past. But nothing seemed to help, there was no clear past, only a vague present, and predetermination pushed him toward a fateful future. A tin plate indicating the sixth floor was bent away from the wall on one end, and secured by a screw at the other. Harmon withdrew his hatchet and forced out the remaining screw and the plate fell into his hand. He then plied the piece of tin to test its flexibility and strength. He replaced the hatchet into the waistband of his pants and emerged from the stairwell. He again looked down the expanse of either ends of the corridor and stepped across the hall to 618.

Immediately his eyes went to the locks; an ordinary door lock and a dead bolt above it. Harmon knew if the dead bolt was secure he would not be able to gain entry, but his mind didn't allow itself to realize that obstacle. His hands started to tremble and his breathing became more pronounced. A cold sweat beaded above his lip and forehead.

"Prescott, Prescott, Prescott, Prescott," he began chanting for only himself to hear.

He stopped and put his ear to the door. There was no sound, no movement beyond it.

Maneuvering the sixth floor plate between the door and jam was easy. There was ample room and the plate provided the proper flexibility and strength. His hands were unable to feel the cylinder being forced back but the door opened slightly. His heart began pounding, the dead bolt was left undone. He quickly stepped into the apartment and withdrew his hatchet. He found himself in a large living room. A small table lamp was the only light in the room. The room itself was cluttered with mismatched furniture; magazines and plants were scattered about. Beyond the living room was another room with a television illuminating it. Harmon took a step in and noticed an opened roll-top desk. On the desk were pictures of people he had never seen before. A stack of mail rested in the center of the desk. He bent his head over and read the name of the addressee:

Ms. Miriam Ludlow
336 63rd Street
New York, N.Y.

A burst of anger ballooned within him. The ever distrusting Prescott had used deception to a clever end and once again Harmon had borne the brunt of his guile.

A door to an adjoining room opened and a woman dressed in flannel pajamas and a robe stepped out. Judging by her appearance, Harmon realized the woman had just emerged from a shower. Upon seeing the intruder her reaction was immediate. A scream that combined terror and panic filled the room. The shrill frightened Harmon who ran out of the apartment to the stairwell and down the stairs. The woman remained immobile, crying and screaming, pushed to an emotional brink. A neighbor's door flew open and a man wielding a baseball bat ran into the hallway.

"Miriam! Miriam!" he shouted as he entered the woman's apartment.

Harmon reached the lobby and quickly passed the doorman who was seated facing the entrance door. As he made his way across the street and into the park, a police car with a wailing siren and flashing lights stopped in front of the building.

Harmon wandered aimlessly in the darkness of the park, desperately trying to accept the effect of his defeat. His rage and anger intensified. A storm of demented conflict swirled in his mind. He was unable to render himself any form of comfort, control or consolation. He walked hurriedly in short bursts in all directions, aimless and forlorn. He finally fell to the cold hard grass and banged his fists until he cried.

★★★

It was eight a.m. when Prescott pushed the button of the elevator. After a moment he impatiently depressed the button once more but with greater force. He looked at his watch and mumbled something under his breath. A soft chime announced the arrival of the elevator. The doors opened and Prescott stepped in. Already in the elevator were two women who were standing against the side, away from the entrance. Both were dressed in business clothes and carrying attache cases.

Prescott raised his arm to depress the "Lobby" button but stopped in midair seeing it had already been depressed.

"It's really frightening," one of the women said to the other.

"But to enter her apartment the way he did. And why her?"

"Who knows?"

"I can't believe she didn't lock the deadbolt. That's the first thing I do."

"She forgot it, I guess."

"Forgot it. She won't ever forget it again, I bet."

"She's lucky he didn't kill her."

"But once he got in he had to know someone was home. What did he expect she was going to invite him to stay for coffee and cake?"

"Crazy."

"Was there a problem here ladies?" Prescott interrupted.

"Yes. Someone broke into an apartment."

"When?"

"Last night."

"I'd like to know how he got in," one woman pondered.

"Basement probably."

"Was anyone hurt?" Prescott asked.

"No."

"What time?" he asked.

"About ten, ten thirty."

"Where?" Prescott questioned again.

"Sixth floor...Six eighteen."

Prescott stared at the women; his eyes flashed suspicion but he remained stoic.

The elevator opened and Prescott held the door for the women. He walked to the lobby and asked the doorman to get him a cab. In twenty minutes Prescott entered the lobby of Ryser Pharmaceuticals. He walked past the receptionist who was seated under a giant chrome logo incorporating the letters R.P.

"Good morning, sir," the receptionist greeted.

"Morning," Prescott said without flashing a smile.

Prescott continued into his personal office and hung up his coat in a mahogany closet and placed his briefcase on the floor beside the desk. He sat in his high black leather chair and withdrew a phone book from a drawer. After turning several pages, his finger ran down a column of listings. He stopped at the one he was looking for and then proceeded to punch in the number.

"Manhattan Cable," came a voice after the seventh ring.

"Good morning, I'm calling to inquire if your company employs a Mister Bill Clayton. I believe he works in service or customer service, something like that."

"Sir, do you want Manhattan Cable?"

"Yes, Mister Clayton."

"I'm sorry sir, we have no Mister Clayton working for us."

"Are you sure?"

"Positive."

Prescott hung up the phone and his eyes looked out his window, focusing on nothing. A peculiar look blanked his face, like he saw shadows hiding behind shadows trying to conceal a mystery. He rested his elbows on the armrests of the chair and tapped the fingertips of both hands together. He had a strange sense, like there was something more to come. Perhaps a friend of his attacker in the elevator seeking revenge, perhaps not. In any event, Prescott told himself to be cautious.

EIGHT

$\mathcal{M}$ary Cello sat in the editing room of PBN watching images of herself and victims of homelessness on a video screen. Tyler Hacket had edited the many feet of video and incorporated it all into a fifty minute documentary. They watched in silence as the tape ended.

"What do you think Tyler?" she asked.

"Your reporting is powerful Mary. You say it all."

"Funny but I can't judge it. I'm too close to it."

"It's fine. I know you don't want to hear it, but it goes beyond Emmy--Maybe Pulitzer."

"You're right Tyler, I don't want to hear it. I don't want a prize at their expense."

"I know how you feel, but look at it this way; if you do get an Emmy it stands to reason your piece will wake up some sleepy politician who may exert some real energy to solve the problem."

"Thanks anyway Tyler, but you know and I know, that the only people who care about the Emmys are sponsors...and only for a season."

"Then why do you do it? Why do you risk your ass? It sure as hell ain't the pay."

"I guess somewhere down deep I hope I will make a difference. Focus enough attention on a problem to make it be dealt with and resolved."

"Then will you accept an Emmy?"

"Then I won't need one."

"OK. Let's get back to the tape. What I'm thinking of doing, Mary is this...you saw the lead-in, how we showed different homeless?"

"Yes."

"Well what I'm thinking is, that in the end when you say 'it's a problem that affects us all,' we superimpose a still image of the first guy we met in Grand Central..."

"Harmon?"

"Yes. even though we show him in the beginning of the piece. His face was the one that came through the best. The camera captured the true essence of the problem in his eyes. We show a tight shot and pan in. Now using one person in the end, instead of many as in the beginning, I'd like to convey a singular feeling, an attempt at personalizing. Sort of creating the feeling of isolation, in some way make the viewer identify to a singular unit. Do I explain myself well?"

"Yes. Very. Yes I like that idea."

"We show Harmon's face, hone in real tight until we get the image grainy. Like showing a human distortion. With that shot, lay down John Lennon's "Imagine" for music track, and finally roll white credits on a black background."

"Sounds good, but I think we should keep Harmon's face as a constant backdrop as the credits roll."

"Yes, better."

"Fine. How long will it take to complete?"

"When do you need it?"

"Dennehey wants to air week from yesterday."

"No problem."

"Good."

★★★

Lieutenant Elroy sat at his desk reading the arrest log of the day before. He wanted to acquaint himself with what had happened in his precinct's territory and let nothing escape his astute eye. Elroy was also interested and fascinated by statistics and criminal trends. For ten years he kept an ongoing log of murders, kidnappings and assaults. With the emphasis on murders. Over the years, he became concerned at the percentage increase in homicides as they related to themselves and the apprehension rate. According to his calculations, murders increased an average of thirty-two percent over the previous decade with an increase of forty-seven percent over the last half of that decade.

Percentage of arrests, unfortunately, ran well behind the rate of crimes, with an actual percentage decrease in arrests, particularly in the same five year period. But more disturbing was the rate of criminals who were convicted for crimes of murder a second time. The statistic, Elroy conceded, was much lower, but one which he felt should be one hundred percent in the negative column. Second offenders also pointed out to him an inherent fault in the judicial system. Elroy knew no law enforcement agency could prevent crime, only try to contain it, but according to his calculations, enforcement wasn't doing either.

As Elroy studied the roll, he heard a tap on his door. Looking up he saw a haggard looking patrolman who had just completed a late night tour of duty.

"Yes?" Elroy responded.

"Pardon me Lieutenant, but I just want to tell you something."

"Sure, come in, sit down."

The patrolman slumped into a chair in front of Elroy's desk.

"Rough night?" Elroy asked.

"I've had worse."

"What's on your mind, Billings?"

"Well Lieutenant, this may not mean anything, but I felt I should inform you about it."

"What's that?"

"Last night my partner and I responded to a break-in on Central Park West, at Sixty-Third Street..."

"Where that mugger was killed in the elevator?"

"Same building, but that's not what I'm getting at. We finally get the woman calmed down and she tells us that she was taking a shower, and when she came out, a stranger is standing in her living room like he belonged, real casual. She lets out a scream and he takes off."

"Yeah?"

"Well when we talk to her, there's not much she remembers. But she does say the guy was filthy."

"What do you mean?"

"Well the way she described it, he was homeless filthy."

"Interesting."

"That's what I thought. I know you're working on that homeless homicide in Grand Central. Lieutenant, one may have nothing at all to do with the other, but it did raise some thoughts to my mind at least."

"How so?"

"Well sir, what's a homeless guy doing in that building, on the sixth floor no less. There's something odd about him being there. It's like it's in the middle of nowhere. He can't escape to the roof or basement easily. You know what I mean?"

"Yes. How did he get into the building?"

"Don't know, there was a doorman there all night."

"How about the apartment itself?"

"Jimmied the front door. She forgot to lock the dead-bolt."

"After a guy gets killed in her building, she forgets to lock a lock?"

"Who knows? Go figure."

"It's like people ask for trouble."

"For sure...You think the guy just wandered in and was lost?"

"No chance."

"What else did she say?"

"Nothing much Lieutenant. It all happened so fast. She screamed and he took off. By the time we got there he was gone."

"Any other security in the building, aside from the doorman?"

"Just him. He confirmed seeing a bum-like man leaving in a hurry."

"He didn't stop the guy?"

"He was looking out the door, the guy came from behind and out in a split second."

"That's it?"

"Yes Lieutenant. As I said, it may not have anything at all to do with your homicide case, but I thought I'd let you know just the same. You never know."

"Thanks Billings, I appreciate it. What's the woman's name?"

"Miriam Ludlow...Six eighteen."

"OK, I'll let you know what I come up with. Thanks."

"Good Lieutenant."

Billings left Elroy sitting at his desk contemplating the likelihood of a connection between the murdered homeless victim and the attempted break-in of an apartment on the west side. Elroy knew in all probability there was nothing in common, but he remembered what he told Mary about doing all he could to solve the murder. He had to follow up on leads, no matter how improbable.

★★★

Elroy pulled up in front of the building on Sixty-Third and Central Park West and dropped his visor displaying the "On official business of New York Police" sign. He walked to the glass door and the doorman seemed to immediately know Elroy's occupation.

"Good morning," the doorman said.

"Good morning. I'm Lieutenant Elroy, New York Police," he said displaying his shield.

"Yes Lieutenant?"

"Were you on duty here last night?"

"No sir, I came on at eight this morning. I heard about the break-in."

"You did?"

"Yes."

"How do you figure the guy got in the building?"

"Maybe around back through a window. There are fire doors. There's a door that goes to the laundry room, one that goes to the basement. A storage door."

"Were those doors open?"

"No, they're supposed to be locked. And usually are. But you never know. Once a guy's in the building he could move around. People don't know everybody that lives here."

"Wouldn't they notice a guy who is real dirty?"

"Suppose so. But some of these people with all their money live like bums anyway. You'd be surprised what some of their apartments look like. Especially the ones with animals...Christ."

"OK, thanks. Where's the stairs?"

"Back to the left."

Elroy looked around the lobby as he made his way to the stairs. The elevator door opened and two kids resembling heavy metal rockers stepped through. Elroy didn't notice them, he was overcome by the feeling that invaded the pit of his stomach realizing the elevator was the sight of a recent death. The door automatically closed and Elroy turned away and walked through the door into the stairwell. He took the stairs down to the basement and walked through a corridor that led to a fire emergency door which was locked from inside. By depressing a long metal handle which read "Emergency Exit Only," it easily opened, rendering escape possible. Elroy opened the door and examined the outside which consisted of a flat steel door with no handles or key locks. A steel plate was also screwed into the door which covered the lock mechanism and double toggle bolted on the inside, making it almost impossible to jimmy the door open. Elroy let the door slam close forcibly by its own weight assuring him that entry from the door was unlikely.

He made his way up the stairs and read the wall plates indicating floor numbers. On the landing between the fifth and sixth floors he noticed the sixth floor plate lying on the floor. He continued up to the sixth floor and saw where the missing plate had been removed. Elroy emerged from the stairwell onto the sixth floor. He didn't have to be told that it was an unlikely area for an arbitrary break-in. He felt Billings was right. There was a high probability for suspicion.

Walking up and down the floor, his trained eye searched for any irregularities.

Approaching Miriam Ludlow's apartment, he noticed the chipped paint by the lock. He knocked on the door and in an instant saw an eye scrutinizing him through the peephole.

"Who is it?" came a voice.

"Lieutenant Elroy, New York Police," he said aiming his shield toward the hole. "We spoke earlier on the phone."

"Yes, just a second."

The sound of locks being undone shot into the hall-way and a chain allowed the door to open only slightly.

Elroy saw the face of a frightened woman framed by the door and jam with a chain running in front of her nose.

"Who are you?"

"Lieutenant Elroy, Ms. Ludlow," he said still display-ing his shield.

The door closed then reopened all the way, no longer confined by the chain.

"Come in Lieutenant."

"I'm sorry to disturb you Ms. Ludlow."

"It's quite alright. Please come in."

Before Elroy entered the apartment he noticed the in-side of the door jam.

"Do you mind?" he said examining it closely.

"No. Not at all. That's how he got in. He pushed something through it."

"Yes. Rudimentary but effective."

"Why would anyone want to break in here?"

"I don't know. It does seem rather unlikely."

"Yes...Sit down Lieutenant."

Miriam Ludlow was in her early fifties. She had short meticulously groomed pepper hair that covered her ears and was cropped evenly across her forehead. Her stare was direct and alert. Beneath her loose-fitting warm-up suit, Elroy noticed she was slender with firm and erect posture.

"Thank you, Ms. Ludlow."

"Miriam, please Lieutenant."

"Miriam."

"You know first the killing incident of that mugger in the elevator. Now this. It's too much."

"I know."

"Tell me Lieutenant..."

"Larry, please."

"...Larry, do you think there's a connection?"

"So far as we know at this point, I'd say no."

"That's what I thought."

"Miriam, let me ask you something. The day of the break-in were you out shopping, spending a lot of money?"

"No."

"How about at a bank or a cash machine withdrawing money?"

"No, I worked late, came in with groceries. Just small items, like milk, a loaf of bread and coffee."

"Did you take out a wallet in the store?"

"No Larry, I had ten dollars in my coat pocket. That's all."

"No one followed you home?"

"No, the doorman opened the door for me. Escorted me to the elevator. We spoke for a minute or so, and I came up."

"I hate to bring this up...but the lock."

"Oh God. I can't believe I was so careless. I don't know what was on my mind at the time. I'll never do that again."

"Those things happen, we all get mentally distracted at times....How long have you been living here, Miriam?"

"Fifteen years."

"Alone."

"Five of them."

"Ah, may...I ah..."

"Divorced."

"Thank you...How about your ex-husband, does he live around here?'

"Denver."

"How long?"

"Five years."

"Have you been dating recently?"

"Larry, do you have any idea what's out there to choose from? I'm sorry, I don't mean to make it sound like a sexist remark."

"It's alright, Miriam, I see it every day."

"Could you tell me anything about the intruder?""

"He looked like a homeless person. He did and he didn't."

"How do you mean that?"

"I don't know. It's hard to describe. I'm a fitness enthusiast and I can recognize a person in shape from one that's not. Ever notice a homeless person who doesn't eat or rest properly? They look lethargic. This man was dirty but fairly...ah energetic is the best way to describe it. When he turned to run he was quick...Oh God wait..."

"What is it, Miriam?"

"I just realized it, as he ran I noticed ah...ah...an axe or a hatchet in his hand."

"You did?"

"Yes. I just remembered, like my mind just saw it."

"Are you sure it was an axe?"

"Yes. Why?"

"Miriam do you mind if I make a call?"

"Go right ahead. There's the phone," she said pointing to the desk.

Elroy picked up the phone and tapped in Doctor Tippett's number.

"Can I get you coffee Larry?" Miriam asked.

"Yes, please."

"Medical Examiner," came the voice over the phone.

"Trudy is he there please?"

"Lieutenant Elroy?"

"Yes."

"Hold on one second."

As Elroy waited for Tippett, his eyes focused on the front door and tried to piece together the purpose of this vague intrusion.

"Yes, Larry?" came Tippett's voice returning Elroy's attention to his immediate purpose.

"Mike, I need a favor."

"Like what?"

"I'm at Three Thirty-six, Central Park West. The building on the corner of Sixty-third."

"Got it."

"Can you get here right away?"

"What do you have?"

"I need you to fine tooth something for me. Can you do it?"

"I'm on my way."

"Great."

Elroy replaced the phone and returned to the couch. Miriam brought in two cups of coffee, milk and sugar on a tray.

"How do you take it Larry?"

"Just some milk Miriam, real light."

"Larry, who's Doctor Tippett?"

"He's the medical examiner. The technical side of finding evidence."

"What's he coming here for?"

"Something I'd like him to check."

"Larry, I have a feeling there's something you're not telling me."

"What do you mean?"

"Why does ah...ah...a hobo risk coming into a building that has a doorman, come up to the sixth floor and single out my apartment? Especially at a time when there's sure to be someone home?"

"And then when he sees you...runs?"

"Something like that."

"I don't know Miriam."

"But you have some ideas?"

"Well it's more like something I have to check, with nothing specific in mind."

"Will you tell me when you find it?"

"Yes."

"Should I have reason for concern?"

"I tend to think not. My feeling is your intruder knew he was in the wrong place."

"That's what I hoped."

"But I would remember to lock your door from now on."

★★★

Harmon remained motionless on the cot in the homeless shelter, alone with his thoughts. The rough, dark-green blanket was pulled up over his clothes; his shoes rested under the bed. For the first time he had thought to remove his shoes and try to make himself comfortable and not be paranoid about someone stealing them. The duration of logical behavior was increasing. After his initial uncontrollable feelings after the break-in of the apartment, he felt beaten by Prescott, suffering a sense of defeat, humiliation and depression. All normal feelings to bear, he reasoned. He had to maintain his powers of reason long enough to formulate a plan. He knew he had to elevate himself from his present environment and return to his medication. Without it he was too unpredictable and unreasonable. To direct justice upon Prescott required all his cunning and guile, there was no room for illogical savagery. His actions must not be misguided by passion and a distorted mental state. With the medication, he knew he would be fine. But would he still seek revenge, or would he accept his fate and carry on with his life?

He struggled to maintain clarity, deciding to seek the medical help he relied on in the past. But with his renewed clarity, would he be able to accept the fact he killed someone? His thoughts caused him to shudder and quickly fade in and out, from terror to fear, anger to guilt. His inner conflict was consumed with morality, delusion, and triumph. He found himself fragmented by a battle to redefine the essence of his true self--a long obliterated commodity. Now was the time to escape from himself, his self-imposed prison. He had to break free and find the threads and patterns that remained of himself and weave them within the proper tapestry of his being. He owed it to himself, for all he had lost and all he hoped to regain.

NIGHT SHADE

NINE

*I*t was early afternoon when Lieutenant Elroy entered the basement of the Medical Examiner's building. He walked the long hallway to Doctor Tippett's office and entered after a quick knock.

"Hello Lieutenant," the receptionist said from her desk.

"Hi, Trudy. How's the family?"

"Fine. The kids are back to school now."

"They must love that."

"Well, I think they were ready to go back. How was your holiday?"

A sorrowful look passed over Elroy's face.

"Quiet. You know."

"I have a sister-in-law that would love to meet you Lieutenant. No one should be alone on holidays."

"The rich vegetarian with the overbite who carries multi-sized wedding rings in her purse?"

"You know her?"

"Don't you remember we were invited to the Halloween party at her house and she dressed as a Greek belly dancer? She walked around all night with the snake wrapped around her shoulders."

"Yes, I forgot you were there."

"I was."

"Yes and you wanted to shoot the snake."

"Not exactly, I really wanted to shoot her."

"Oh, Lieutenant, she's really a nice girl, needs a lot of attention...You have to admit she is colorful."

"Yeah, I'll give her that."

"Reconsider?"

"I'll get back to you."

"Good. I suppose you want to see Doctor Tippett?"

"Yes."

"He's in the lab," she said pointing to a room across the hall.

"Is he alone in there?" Elroy asked, referring to the dead bodies.

"Yes, he's doing forensic study from the break-in sight, that's all."

"Good. Thanks Trudy. Tell your sister-in-law I said hello."

"I will."

Elroy stepped across the hall to Tippett's laboratory, which was also the morgue. Elroy always experienced discomfort in this part of the building and avoided it at all costs. He walked through the door and noticed Tippett seated at his desk. Beyond the desk was a large bay window with blinds on the inner portion. On the other side of the window was the part of the laboratory set aside for autopsies and, adjacent to that, were the storage bins where the bodies were kept.

"Hi, Mike."

"Larry. How are you?"

"Fine."

The pungent smell of formaldehyde and other chemicals mixed with stale blood came together to make Elroy nauseated.

"I'm just finishing up here. I've got some interesting things to tell you."

"Good."

"First, the Grand Central victim."

"Yes?"

"One Thomas Bass."

Elroy took out a pad and pen and wrote down the name.

"OK."

"You might want to do some checking on him. I can tell you his fingerprints are on file with the state prison in Jolliet."

"Good work, Mike. Some day you have to show me how you do what you do."

"You don't want to know."

"I know I don't...What's next?"

"Miriam Ludlow's apartment."

"This sounds like it's gonna be good."

"More than you know...the plate you found...?"

"Sixth floor plate?"

"Yes. Definitely used to open her door..."

"Prints?"

"One. Checking on that. The wall the plate was removed from..."

"What about it?"

"Forced out with an axe or hatchet."

"How do you know it was an axe?"

"I used a laser probe and retrieved minute particles of steel that were found on the wall it was removed from, the door jam and the plate...Ready for this...They were the same particles that were in the head of Thomas Bass."

"What?"

"Yes."

"Incredible."

"That's what I said."

91

"And you're suggesting the same guy that killed Bass broke into Ludlow's apartment?"

"I'm saying the instrument used to kill Bass, was the same instrument used to extract the plate from the wall which in turn was used to pry open her door. I can prove that. I can't, at this point, prove it was the same guy."

"I'll be damned. She said it was a homeless looking guy who broke into her apartment, I have to assume it was a homeless guy that wasted Bass...Where's the connection?" Elroy questioned to himself.

"I told you it gets good."

"That print will be helpful."

"Soon as I get it I'll give it to you."

"There's gotta be a connection, Mike."

"Coincidence maybe."

"Nah, coincidence is the cop out we use when we can't find the link."

"Again, Larry we're assuming the guy that left the print is the same guy that broke into the apartment."

"Yes it's an assumption, but a safe one."

"But right now we can't prove that. I'm just thinking scientific, Larry."

"Yeah, I know, but something tells me this whole show will play itself out, and I'm just thinking instinct."

Elroy rose to leave.

"Anything else Mike?"

"That's it for now, Larry."

"Like always, good job, Mike, I appreciate it. Call me when you get that print made."

"You got it."

Elroy walked through the door marked National Crime Information Center. It was a small, cluttered office with two computer terminals, a modem and a laser printer. Seated before one green-tinted screen was a matronly woman keying in information. A second woman was wrestling with a long stream of paper as it was being printed out by the laser printer. She was an attractive woman with short blond hair and an obvious weakness for jewelry. Dozens of bracelets were cuffed to either wrist. There were rings on three fingers of each hand, rows of necklaces, and long dangling earrings. The jeweled woman turned as Elroy closed the door.

"Hello, Lieutenant," she said with a wide grin.

"Hi, Phyllis. How's it going?"

"Busy."

"Hi Margaret," Elroy said to the seated woman.

"Hello, Lieutenant," she responded turning from the screen.

"How's the grandkids, Margaret?"

"Oh dear, just fine. They were in from Seattle for the holidays."

"That must have been nice."

"It was beautiful."

"When did they go back?"

"Last week. They stayed for two weeks."

"Great. How's your daughter doing?"

"Fine, she loves it there. She's always after me to move there."

"That's nice, why don't you go?"

"I'm an east coast person...It's hard."

"Yes."

Margaret was the widow of a retired police captain who was killed trying to prevent a robbery of an elderly woman. The department offered her the job in N.C.I.C. and in a way she was carrying on what was her late husband's work, a connection difficult for Margaret to break.

"Well, if you go Margaret, we'll miss you."

"Thank you, Lieutenant."

"Does that mean I won't be getting my fruit cake at Christmas?"

"Don't worry, I'll still bake you a fruit cake no matter what...without rum."

"You're a queen Margaret."

"Oh go on."

"What can we do for you, Lieutenant?" Phyllis asked.

Elroy handed Phyllis a request for information form. As she reached for it her bracelets clanged together to sound an expensive chorus.

"Thomas Bass...Last known residence Jolliet State Prison," Elroy voiced the written information.

"Fine. High priority?"

"Well..."

"No problem, for you Lieutenant, anything. We'll get it out today, don't worry," she said with an inviting grin and a sparkle in her eyes.

"Thank you, Phyllis."

"I'll give you a call when we get confirmation."

"Great...Margaret you take care now. Say hello to your daughter.

"I will, thank you, Lieutenant, and you be careful."

"I will...Thanks again Phyllis."

"No problem, Lieutenant."

As Elroy closed the door behind him Phyllis walked to the unmanned terminal. She sat and pulled the chair close to the screen. Staring blankly at the blinking cursor for a moment, her mind appeared to be functioning in a different realm from her body.

"Oh that handsome man. What I wouldn't give..." she finally sighed.

"Now, now, Phyllis." said Margaret.

It was well past ten p.m. when Emmet Prescott left his office. He signed a log book at the security post in the lobby and stepped into the night. He paused a moment to breathe in the cold air then crouched into the rear of the limousine waiting at the curb.

Prescott pressed a button of the control panel in the armrest and a dark plexiglass partition slid down exposing the front of the vehicle.

"Yes sir?" the driver asked.

"Lincoln Center," Prescott ordered tersely and raised the dark glass once more.

The driver responded, and the black stretch drove away. Prescott tilted his head back onto the high portion of the seat. His eyes closed for a moment to shut out the sights and sounds of the city. He wanted to disconnect himself from everything except his own pulse. He swam within his own energy force, leaving behind anything insignificant and mortal. He concentrated on his own being and purpose, projecting himself beyond his definition of triviality and apathy. Visions of his upcoming meeting fueled him with determination and placated his individual need.

The car cruised to a stop behind a string of waiting limousines, poised to accept a jubilant after-theater crowd.

Prescott's eyes blinked open and were greeted to the sight of Lincoln Center bathed in bright light. A well dressed crowd filtered out onto the street after being treated to La Bohème.

Once again Prescott lowered the dark glass.

"Give me an hour," he said to the driver.

"Yes sir."

Prescott stepped from the car and walked among the opera crowd. After several minutes he crossed Columbus

Avenue and entered Hijia's Turkish Coffee House. His eyes scanned the crowded room until he saw a sole figure seated at a booth against a rear wall.

Prescott made his way to the back and slid across the cushioned bench.

"Hello Doug," Prescott said in a tired, unfriendly tone.

"Emmet," came the man's reply.

"Thanks for getting back to me so fast. I appreciate it."

Prescott threw a suspicious glance at the people seated around him and then returned his attention to the man seated before him.

Doug Hyatt was a freelance electronic surveillance expert and computer wiz. His bald, shiny head, dark rimmed glasses and two hundred and eighty pound frame stuffed into an untidy suit gave him the appearance of an unscrupulous southern politician. Hyatt's breathing was short and pronounced and each breath made a wheezing sound. Beyond his appearance, he remained an engaging southerner with a knack for befriending the right people. He met Prescott in the early seventies when the CIA needed its many forms of surveillance. Hyatt contracted himself primarily to the agency, but his clients also ranged from underworld crime bosses to oil cartel representatives.

"How's the coffee, Doug?"

"Not bad by New York standards."

"OK, what did you find out?" Prescott asked, not wanting to engage in small talk longer than he needed.

"First, Michael Baylor, the elevator accident victim."

"Yes?"

"Lone cowboy out riding the range. No connections to anyone we know, far as I can tell..." Hyatt stopped suddenly as a waiter approached the table.

"Can I get you anything else here?" the waiter interrupted.

"Yes," Hyatt beamed with an engaging superficial
smile.

"A second for me and one for my friend."

"Surely. Dark blend?"

"Exactly."

"Coming right up."

Hyatt waited until the waiter was gone before he
spoke.

"Unfortunate accident to Mister Baylor, but there's no
one upset about it."

"OK."

Your cable company phone call."

"What about it?"

"Made from a phone booth outside your apartment."

"Sure?"

"Absolutely...Emmet?"

"Yes?"

"That bit of info came high."

"How much."

"Five. I'm sorry..."

"It's quite alright. I'll make the deposit first thing tomorrow."

"Thank you."

"The break-in?"

"My inside guy tells me there's much interest there."

"How so?"

"Connection to a homicide."

"Where?"

"Some displaced person in Grand Central. No one to
speak of with no friends."

"Where's the fit?"

"Not yet, may come, may not. What I do know is they
found a finger mark at the site."

"And?"

"F.B.I. checking it out. But I don't think there's much to concern us there."

"OK. Let's turn to the bank account of our friend."

Hyatt went silent as the waiter arrived with the two cups of coffee.

"Will there be anything else?" he asked as he placed them on the table.

"Not for now, thank you," Hyatt responded with more of his patent phony grin.

Hyatt stirred the coffee and raised it to his lips and sipped. The steam from the hot liquid rose up to fog his glasses as the bitter taste assaulted his mouth.

"Good, better than the first...The account. No transaction for a year. Everything's going in, but nothing's coming out."

"How's he living?"

"Who knows. He hasn't shown up anywhere. He owns no appliances, and definitely no phone."

"How about the doctor, the medicine?"

"No visits, no prescription. Went bye-bye for a year now. Nothing anyplace."

"Interesting...Anything else?"

"No, sorry there's not more."

"Quite alright. What's the tab?"

"Seven fifty."

"Nothing for you?"

"No, I didn't do much this trip."

"Let me at least pay for the coffee."

The sun filtered into Elroy's office through the slats of the blinds. He could feel its warmth through the blue pin striped Yves St. Laurent suit. A pale blue shirt with an

English spread collar and French cuffs complimented the expensive looking suit.

The large manila envelope on his desk was marked "Lieutenant Lawrence Elroy--Information Request. Subject: Michael Baylor."

Elroy opened the envelope and read the limited information on the subject.

Michael Tyes Baylor. Born in Bolivar, Tennessee, date unknown. No schooling beyond sixth grade. No military service. Limited employment history. Remanded to Peoria Correctional Facility for boys for the term of one year from 1958 to 1959. From 1961 to 1968 incarcerated in Joliett State Prison for the offense of armed robbery. Partook of local prisoner release program from aforementioned institution. Invalid completion of program caused issue of a warrant for his rearrest.--End

Elroy studied the meager bio and derived more of a profile by what was not written. He knew there was no possible connection between Baylor and Miriam Ludlow. The thought of coincidence had suddenly seemed to be a likely possibility, but his mind tried to resist it. He knew the common denominator had to be the third party--the intruder.

He placed the open folder back on his desk and leaned back in his chair. His eyes closed and his mind began to sort through the vague maze of possibilities. At every conceivable turn there seemed to be a wall which resisted logic and possibilities. His thoughts tried to vault beyond the opaque barrier, but the inconsistencies rendered that leap difficult.

The short burst of his telephone interrupted him and cleared his mind from all thoughts which struggled for a connection. He opened his eyes and reached for the phone.

"Elroy," he said.

"Larry, Mike Tippet," came the voice.

"Yes, Mike."

"I got the print made from the Ludlow break-in."

"Great. Who do we have?"

"Harmon Keller."

"OK, Mike, now we have a place to go."

"Larry?"

Elroy sensed a shade of concern in Tippet's voice that seemed to dampen his enthusiasm.

"Yes, what's the matter, Mike?"

"Something's not right here, Larry."

"Why?"

"The guy Keller?"

"Yeah?"

"He's CIA."

"What?"

"You heard it right."

"Can't be."

"The print don't lie."

Elroy sat in disbelief. He knew he needed an open mind, but fantasy went beyond open-mindedness.

"F.B.I. came up with that?" Elroy asked.

"None other."

"But Miriam Ludlow said the guy looked homeless."

"I don't know what to make of it either, Larry."

Elroy went silent hoping something reasonable would pop into his mind.

"Got an address on Keller?"

"No."

"OK, I'll have to fill in with Keller. But what does he want with Miriam Ludlow?" Elroy asked rhetorically.

"Who knows?"

"And why the homeless routine?"

"I don't know, I just know what I got."

"Mike, I'm gonna hold this for now, I gotta think about this one."

"Fine, let me know if you need me, Larry."

"Thanks, Mike I will."

Elroy hung up the phone and shook his head in disbelief. He struggled to remind himself to remain open-minded.

★★★

The renting office was actually a one room apartment located in the lobby beyond the elevator and stairs. Elroy entered the room which was undecorated except for a desk, two chairs, and a steel file cabinet.

"Mister Daily?" Elroy said.

"Yes?"

"Lieutenant Elroy."

"Oh yes come in Lieutenant."

"Thank you for taking the time to see me."

"No problem...There seems to be a lot of interest in this building lately."

"Yes...Were you able to find that information I called about?"

"Yes, Lieutenant. I have a list...Where is it now?" Daily said to himself ruffling through a pile of papers on the desk. "Yes, here it is," he said handing Elroy several pages stapled together.

"Is this current, complete?"

"Yes, updated last week."

Elroy glanced through it.

"You'll notice the listings are by apartment number. Is there someone specific you're looking for?"

"Do you have a custodian on the premises?" Elroy asked ignoring Daily's question.

"Yes. Alex Hillerman. He's a resident...Lieutenant, does this have anything to do with the break-in to the Ludlow Apartment?"

"Yes...does Mister Hillerman have regular hours?"

"Usually nine a.m. to six p.m. However, he is on call beyond that."

"Does he have a work order sheet of some kind?"

"Yes, every job order carries its own listing by category and apartment number and is turned into this office at the end of every work day. But I can tell you there was nothing being done after hours for the last week."

"How about other workers. Painters, carpenters, electricians?"

"On occasion subcontractors are called in for big jobs that Mister Hillerman can't handle."

"Have there been any here recently?"

"None that were hired by this office in the last week. We also have a policy that we should be informed of any workers hired by tenants. It's a way to keep track as to who's coming and going from the building."

"Do the tenants usually follow policy and let you know if they are having outside contractors doing work for them?"

"Yes. But again, there was nothing being done recently."

"How about people moving in or out?"

"The last mover was three weeks ago, first floor unit."

"OK, you've been very helpful, Mister Daily."

"There seems to be more interest in the break-in than for the death we had in the elevator, Lieutenant. How come?"

"Good question. When I find out I'll let you know."

Elroy took the elevator to the sixth floor and knocked on Miriam Ludlow's door. He listened as shuffling and footsteps approached the inside of the door. He heard the peephole cover unlatch from the inside and saw distorted movement through the pinhole glass.

"Larry?" Miriam asked.

"Yes, Miriam. I'd like to speak with you."

"Just a second."

The peephole latch closed, then the dead bolt unlocked and the door came open.

"Won't you come in, Larry."

"Thank you, Miriam."

Elroy made his way into the living room and stood by the window.

"Won't you sit?"

"No, that's alright, Miriam, I'll only be a minute."

"What's up?"

"Miriam do you know anyone by the name of Harmon Keller?"

"No."

"Not at all?"

"Sorry, Larry. Why?"

"Just checking things...Let me ask you something. Is it possible your ex-husband might know him?"

"I doubt he knew him when I lived with him, but I can't speak for now."

"What kind of work does your former husband do?"

"Larry, there's something you're not telling me."

"Miriam, I hate to sound evasive, but there's nothing to tell. I'm just checking, please believe me."

"He's a dentist."

"His own practice?"

"Yes."

"Is it possible Harmon Keller was a patient of his?"

"I doubt it. I did the billing and I don't recall ever seeing or hearing that name...Why the interest in Harmon Keller?"

Elroy paused, not wanting to answer.

"Larry, I hate to sound suspicious, but I fear you're giving me reason to be."

"The floor plate used to break into your apartment contained a fingerprint belonging to someone named Harmon Keller."

"Is this Harmon Keller a criminal?"

Elroy walked to the sofa and sat down. Miriam's eyes followed his every movement.

"No," he responded after settling into the soft cushions.

"You seem hesitant, Larry, why?"

"No. No criminal record...He worked for the CIA."

"CIA?"

"Yes."

"You sure?"

"Yes."

"Well he sure didn't look like he worked for the CIA."

"There's no evidence it was Keller who broke in, only that he handled the plate...I'm making a circumstantial connection."

"I see."

"Do you know Alex Hillerman?"

"The janitor?"

"Yes."

"Certainly."

"Was it possibly him in your apartment...I mean you were obviously very frightened, and maybe in the..."

"Absolutely not. It wasn't Alex."

"OK...Let me ask you this, if I may?"

"Go ahead."

"Do you have any children?"

"Yes, a daughter. She's a premed student at U.C.L.A. And I'm sure she doesn't know Harmon Keller."

"No, she probably doesn't."

★★★

Elroy was reading through the renter's list when the elevator stopped at the tenth floor. He stepped from the elevator and walked slowly to his apartment. Putting the key into the lock, he swung the door wide and entered. He placed the list on the glass table in the living room and removed his coat. Easing onto the sofa he continued looking through the list and assured himself that Harmon Keller was not a resident, thus eliminating the possibility that he may have left the fingerprint. He knew the un-likelihood of that, but he was a stickler for detail and pos-sibilities.

After reading through the list, he placed it back on the table and hung up his coat in the foyer closet. Pro-ceeding into his bedroom, Elroy noticed the blinking red light on his phone answering machine and depressed the "play" button.

After a click and a rewinding sound the voice came from the speaker.

"Hi, Lieutenant, this is Mary Cello of PBN. If you're interested or at home tonight, the homeless piece is on at eight o'clock. Just wanted to tell you. Good luck with your investigation. Good night."

The machine clicked and rewound the tape again.

Elroy felt a warm feeling come over him. Since the day he met her she stayed on his mind as a pleasant memory. Elroy checked his watch and knew he had time to shower before the show. He took off his clothes and left them out so he could take them to the laundry the next day.

The shower was warm and relaxing but did nothing to relieve his preoccupation with his investigation. He toweled off and wrapped himself in a terry cloth robe. He threw himself on the couch, and tapped the remote. The images before him appeared superficial to what played out in his mind. Variations struggled with possibilities leaving him perplexed and unsure. He rested his head and tried to make sense of Harmon Keller. The best he could come up with was that Keller and the intruder in Miriam Ludlow's apartment were two different people. Then how did Keller's print get onto the plate he questioned. And why a homeless man on the sixth floor with an axe and the same axe that killed a vagrant?

An endless maze of "whys" curved through his mind. The strain of logic drained him, leaving him spent and tired.

Elroy's eyes began to close and his breathing became deep and slow. A light subtle sleep began to claim the complexity of his thoughts, relieving him of a certain burden. But the sanctity of sleep gave birth to burdens of a different kind. A dark wind began to invade his imagery, taking up everything in its path. Miriam Ludlow blended with a faceless Keller and a figure in tattered clothing blew by them. Ludlow's door remained locked, impervious to resistance. What truths were hidden behind it, what mysteries did it protect?

His mind shifted to the skeleton frame of a car being incinerated by fire. Wind and heat raising the flames in powerful bursts, creating an impersonal vengeance that attacked him. He stood motionless against the onslaught as silent screams filled his ears. The flames and the silence surrounded him, there was no escape, and no peace.

Elroy's head flinched, causing him to awaken abruptly. His heart began beating rapidly and his breathing had suddenly become quick and short. His skin felt clammy, and his body was warm and uncomfortable. He opened his robe and wiped his forehead.

The image of Mary Cello, already into her documentary, distracted him immediately. She looked different from the last time he saw her. Her hair matched the sophistication of her tailored business suit. She appeared purposeful without pleading, confident but not arrogant. She had command of herself and the camera. And above all, Elroy felt no interference between himself and her.

"...The picture is a broad one with many contributing factors and factions," she said. "During the late nineteen sixties and early nineteen seventies, many buildings in New York's Manhattan State Hospital closed and the patients were deinstitutionalized, adding to the number of homeless. Compounding the problem is gentrification of low-income housing and conversion to condominiums. Real estate brokers become one of the many players in the system. Power movers whose visions saw property as wealth; profit, as always, motivates beyond reason.

"The redevelopment of inner cities rose sharply. Low income housing gave way to highways, office buildings and convention centers. Changes in federal and state housing statutes made it unprofitable for landlords to maintain multiple dwellings, and many buildings were abandoned, yielded to vandals. The effects of those changes were far reaching from nineteen seventy to nineteen eighty-two. Over one million single-room units disappeared. And a good many of their original dwellers reappeared on streets, in subway tunnels, airport terminals or even in garbage dumpsters. Society's dredge that society refuses to accept."

Elroy became intrigued by Mary and her documentary. He was one member of society who didn't have to be told about the homeless, he saw the increasing heartbreak day to day on his job.

"...So it's easy to see how redevelopment, gentrification and deinstitutionalization became contributing factors to the problem. The mentally ill, as they left state hospitals with nowhere to go, and low-income people filled a city that didn't want them, didn't care for them.

"In an effort to shun responsibility, state mental hospitals created community mental health centers to bear the brunt of patient after-care, a form of deinstitutionalization. But only six point five percent of admissions into CMHC's were referred by state mental hospitals.

"Another point to consider is that for an eight year period from nineteen seventy through nineteen seventy-eight, there was a substantial decrease in admissions of patients diagnosed as being schizophrenic. This in itself does not necessarily reflect a neglect by CMHC's; it does, however, serve to increase the number of schizophrenics as homeless.

"The psychiatric community has long labored under the belief that schizophrenia and manic depression were a result of childhood experiences and strove to treat the problems through psychotherapy. A portion of the homeless problem is a direct result of that theory and one can safely say the psychiatric community has a failure of epic proportions on its hands. A statistic worth repeating is that approximately one-third of the homeless population suffer some form of mental illness."

A profound respect for Mary welled up in Elroy. He viewed her as some sort of hero, fighting for a basic human right of select people who had lost all will, reason and representation. She called attention to, and forced people to recognize an unexpected phenomenon and demanded justice. She no doubt gained medical and political enemies, but Elroy knew every cause was built in opposition.

The audio portion of the documentary went silent as the screen showed images of homeless men, women and children who have become woven into the dark fabric of Americana. Some were shown living in cardboard huts in empty lots, some sleeping over grates for warmth, some slumped in doorways, but all appeared hopeless and neglected. There was a close up shot of a victim sleeping on concrete steps. As the camera panned back revealing the broader picture, the steps were seen to be part of Saint Anthony's Catholic Church, somewhere in the city. Elroy felt a sort of poetic impact, a certain emotion void of definition. As articulate as Mary was and as deeply as her indictment cut, it was the images that carried the problem of the streets to the living rooms and hopefully to the conscience of the people.

Elroy wanted to applaud Mary for calling attention to something that needed recognition and resolve. Her concern was strong and her passion was direct and selfless.

"The problems of the homeless must be solved at the core," the documentary continued. "The substance abusers must be freed of the clutches of drugs and alcohol so they can function as a normal part of society. The unemployed must be productive and find new self-esteem and respect. And for the mentally ill, laws must be amended so those in need of treatment find it. Courts must not continue to allow hospitals to discharge patients to inadequate facilities. If it remains difficult to rehospitalize the mentally ill, then the law is condemning these people to an inescapable horror. Research must lead to treatment and ultimately rehabilitation.

"But in the final analysis, it comes down to you and me. If we demand this abomination cease, if we show unselfish concern and subscribe to the philosophy that none are free until all are free, then and only then, will the problem of the homeless be a problem no longer. Until then, it's a problem that will gain in complexity and ultimately mar our vision of humanity."

Elroy watched Mary's pretty face fade into a shot of one of the homeless. His pathetic look made Mary's words ring true. Elroy felt a strange kinship to the stranger, a connection that made him realize, at times we are all responsible.

Harmon stood outside the display window of a Radio Shack store. The large television showed his own image in a way he had never seen himself before. He studied his own pathetic appearance and wondered how he allowed himself to sink so low. He thought of Prescott and his vengeance, but ultimately he knew his lot was of his own doing. And now, he had to rely on himself to regain his pride and take command of his life. He would not allow himself to remain his own victim. There was help, he knew that, and he knew what was needed of himself to acquire that help. Harmon forced himself to concentrate on his goal. His facilities would not fail him. The road would be hard, but it was a road he must take. His hand reached up and circled an imaginary sphere, forming a tight fist around it. Within his grasp was his own fate, he vowed to hold it firm until his nightmare was completely over. His old ghosts set firmly into the distant past, recovery and renewal redesigned for his future.

On the west side, fate of another kind was taking shape, as coincidence fused with destiny. Emmet Prescott recognized the face he saw on his television. A mocking sneer broke out from his lips. His eyes scorched with a deep-rooted contempt. His chest heaved and his fists clenched with a powerful urge to destroy.

"Well, well, if it isn't Mister Bill Clayton of Manhattan Cable. You fucking parasite! Harmon Keller, the days left in your miserable, meaningless life are coming to a rapid close. I owned you, now I will destroy you."

Prescott walked into the kitchen and picked up the phone. He looked at his watch and knew it was only six o'clock in California. He dialed the number and hoped his party was in. After four rings he heard a deep voice.

"Yes?"

"Rayfer?"

"Yes."

"Do you know who this is?"

"Yes."

"I need you here to do something. Can you come?"

"When?"

"Tomorrow, day after."

"I'll be there tomorrow."

"You know where to find me?"

"Yes."

"Good. I want to close the book on Night Shade."

NIGHT SHADE

TEN

"Central Intelligence Agency," the voice said over the phone.

"Hello my name is Lawrence Elroy, I'm a detective with the New York Police Department."

"Yes, Lieutenant."

"I'm conducting an investigation and I would like some information on an employee."

"Certainly, hold on please, I'll transfer you to employment verification."

Elroy heard a click and then silence.

"Hello CIA, " came the voice of another woman.

"Yes. My name is Lieutenant Elroy with the New York Police Department, I'd like to have some information on an employee."

"Yes, Lieutenant, can I just have the spelling of your name."

Elroy frowned and shook his head trying to control his annoyance.

"E.L.R.O.Y., Lawrence."

"And the precinct there in New York, please."

Elroy remained calm not wanting to display his feelings.

"The six four."

"And your phone number please."

Elroy gave the woman his number, but was going to resist any other questions.

"Thank you, Lieutenant, please hold for employment verification."

There was another click and an unusually long silence. Elroy had the feeling they were conducting a brief investigation of their own on him. He turned in his chair and looked beyond his window to the gray day. Dark clouds and a fine rain combined to create a bleak day. Elroy turned away avoiding the negative effect he knew such a day would have on him.

"Employment verification. Can I help you Lieutenant?" came another voice which directed his thoughts away from the weather.

"Yes. I'd like some information on a Harmon Keller please."

"Harmon Keller? Is that K.E.L.L.E.R.?"

"Yes."

"OK, we employed Mister Keller, he is retired now."

"Can you tell me his capacity when he was within your employ?"

"I'm sorry Lieutenant. The only information I can supply is that he is or was employed by the CIA."

"But this is an official police investigation."

"I realize that Lieutenant, however, our policy is quite clear."

"Can you transfer me to the supervisor or commanding officer?"

"I'm sorry Lieutenant, that information is classified."

"Classified?"

"Yes, Lieutenant, I'm sorry."

"Well let me ask you this, can you tell me where Mister Keller retired to? Did he take a job in the corporate world?"

"I don't have that information, Lieutenant."

"If you did, would you pass it along to me?"

"Yes, only tenure within CIA employment is classified."

"Is there someone there who could tell me where Mister Keller may be now?"

"I'm sorry, Lieutenant we don't have that information. We only show Mister Keller as retired."

"Well can you tell me when he retired?"

"In December of nineteen eighty-five."

"And when he joined the CIA?"

"In June of nineteen sixty-eight."

"Thank you, you've been very helpful," Elroy said as he slammed the phone down.

"Cloak and dagger assholes."

Elroy picked himself up off his chair, and faced the dreary day. Annoyance became his defense against whatever affected him negatively. He knew he had to find Harmon Keller, but he also knew it was not going to be easy. Suddenly Mary Cello popped into his mind. He ostensibly wanted to call her and congratulate her for an excellent news feature but now his reasons compounded.

He turned to his desk and went through his Roledex stopping at Mary's number. He tapped it in and after the first ring it was answered.

"Public Broadcast News."

"Mary Cello please,"

"Hold on please."

Elroy didn't have to wait as long as he did with the CIA.

"Mary Cello," came her voice.

"Hi Mary, this is Lieutenant Elroy."

"Oh, hello Lieutenant."

"How are you, Mary?"

"Fine, how about yourself?"

"One of those days...Listen Mary I wanted to thank you for calling me and alerting me to your news broadcast."

"Oh that's alright. Did you get a chance to see it?"

"Yes, I did. And I just wanted to congratulate you about it."

"Thank you Lieutenant, but I didn't call you for that."

"I know."

Elroy struggled, trying to formulate his conversation.

"I just wanted to tell you it was really strong stuff. Very informative."

"Well it is a serious problem, and people need to be informed."

"Yes, I know. Ah...Mary I need to talk to you about something."

"Sure, Lieutenant, what is it?"

"Well something came up about the homicide in Grand Central and ah...well I just have to talk to you."

"Well I'll be in my office all day, just come by."

"Ah...yeah...well the thing is I'd rather talk to you privately and I'm going to be busy all day. How about tonight?"

"Sure, I'll be free. Just call me."

"Good. Ah I have an idea, if it's OK with you. Ah...I usually eat out, would you like to join me?"

There was a long pause and suddenly Elroy felt outside himself looking at his true motives. He wanted to hide within the silence but there was not enough cover.

"Seven o'clock," Mary finally said.

"Fine. That'll be fine. Where can I pick you up?"

"Seventy-Second Street just off Third. Two eleven."

"Got it. See you at seven?"

"Fine."

Elroy hung up the phone and turned toward the window once more. He suddenly felt unperturbed by the CIA and felt oblivious to the day that tried to mock him.

★★★

Third Avenue was alive with the usual New York crowd. Moviegoers, restaurant hounds, hustlers and shoppers, moving in related cadence. They brushed by each other in the form of a human kaleidoscope, similar patterns that mirror their universal disinterest.

Elroy turned right off the avenue at Seventy-Second and looked for a legal parking spot he knew he wasn't going to find.

He pulled into a restricted area and turned down the visor displaying the "Official Police Business" sign, and stepped out of the car. His eyes scanned the street which was lined on either side with early century brownstones and a continuous row of trees. Some trees had strings of tiny bright lights adorning their branches giving the block a holiday feel.

Elroy walked back toward Third Avenue until he spotted Mary's apartment. He climbed the stairs and rang the bell.

An outside light flashed on and Elroy saw Mary's smiling face looking at him through a small square window at the top of the door. He heard two locks being undone and the door swung open.

"Hello, Lieutenant."

"Hi, Mary."

"Oh come on in it's cold out there."

"Yeah, it is but it feels good," Elroy commented as he stepped into the warmth of her house.

"Were you able to park? I forgot to tell you it probably would be better to go into the lot on the corner. It's expensive, but it's convenient."

"That's alright I found a spot."

"Good."

Elroy expected the inside of the brownstone to be dark and stuffy. Instead the stately appearance of the interior was softened by modern furniture spaced to give an open, free, flowing feeling. A thick rug that covered oak floors and a chandelier gave total light without casting gloomy shadows. A fireplace in the middle of the living room gave off a soft glow and warmed the room.

"Very cozy in here," Elroy observed.

"Thank you."

"Rent must be a fortune."

"Not really, my father bought the building over thirty-five years ago and gave it to me."

"Very nice of him."

"Yeah, he's a gem. Sit down, Lieutenant we'll have a glass of wine before dinner."

"Thanks."

Elroy sat on the white leather couch, staring at the flame.

"White wine, Lieutenant?"

"Mary, if you don't mind, I'll take soda if you have it, I don't drink."

"Sure, what do you like?"

"Club soda is fine."

"Seltzer?"

"Good."

"I never really knew what the difference was."

"Between seltzer and club soda?"

"Yes."

"I don't either."

"Good, I'll give you what I have."

"Fine."

"Coming right up."

Mary walked into the kitchen and returned with the clear bubbly liquid.

"Fire feels good," Elroy observed.

"I always like a fireplace. I remember when I was a girl my mother and father had a cottage in Vermont we would go to in the wintertime, the fireplace was going all the time. I loved it then and still do. Funny how you get used to things."

"Yes. Here, let me pour that," Elroy said as he took the soda from Mary.

"Do you want me to pour you wine?" he asked.

"No, that's alright, I'll drink what you're having. How come you don't drink if you don't mind my asking?"

"Migraines. No alcohol."

"I see."

Elroy poured soda into two glasses and handed one to Mary.

"The best," he said raising his glass slightly.

"Yes."

They sipped their soda and Mary leaned forward to place hers on the table.

"So how'd the rest of your day go? When we spoke you sounded like you were having an off day?"

"It all worked out."

"They usually do.."

"Yes, I guess...Mary, talking about our conversation, I just want to repeat that I thought you did a fine job with the homeless report."

"Thank you."

"It's not just the reporting that was good, it was the intent, your purpose. Like you saw something wrong and tried to make it right."

"Well a lot of people were responsible for putting that piece together."

"I'm sure, but let me tell you something, I've been a policeman for just about fifteen years and have seen the homeless grow in numbers over that time and did absolutely nothing about it."

"Well I'm sure that's because you were busy trying to contain crime. You had a different function."

"Thanks anyway but as you said the problem belongs to all of us."

"Lieutenant do you..."

"Excuse me for interrupting, but please call me Larry."

"OK. Larry, as I was saying do you realize what would happen if people--all people--were to stand up and demand that government put an end to the homeless problem? The nuclear waste problem--all social injustice? Government would be forced to stop their politicking and get into the humanity business where it belongs."

"Mary, I think we realize that government can no longer govern, and humanity is not an issue they're interested in. Government deals in the abstract only. And most people can't be bothered or are uninformed."

"You're right, unfortunately."

"That's why there are people like you. You're our collective conscience. You tell us all when we're blowing it."

"I'm not a noble crusader, Larry, I'm just someone who likes to call attention to issues that need attention...And someone who also needs to get something to eat really soon. I'm starving."

"Fine," Elroy laughed. "Where would you like to go?"

"There's a nice Italian restaurant on Seventy-Third and Third."

"Sounds good."

"We'll walk."

"Fine. You better dress warm."

★★★

The restaurant was small, not trendy. Tables placed in close proximity to each other filled the center of the restaurant. Along the walls and lining the window on the Third Avenue side were booths with high tufted backs affording moderate privacy.

Although the restaurant was not crowded, Elroy elected to sit at a booth. A small glass lantern with a burning candle rested in the center of the table. The flickering light danced off Mary's face accentuating her soft, delicate contours. Elroy studied her as she read the menu.

"I know what I want," she said putting it down.

"Good."

The maitre d' who now doubled as waiter approached their table."

"Signora, what can I get for you?" he asked.

"The fish special."

"Ahh, bene, bene. And for you sir?"

"I'll have the same."

"Two fish specials. And to drink?"

"Club soda. Larry?" Mary asked.

"Two club sodas," Elroy said to the waiter.

"Bene, bene."

Elroy watched the waiter stroll away.

"That was simple."

"Yes, it was...So what did you have to tell me, Larry?" Mary asked.

"Oh, yeah," realizing he almost forgot, "the homicide. It seems to be getting real bizarre."

"How so?"

"Mary, at this point, I'm speaking off the record and in strictest confidence."

"Understood."

"Good...After you discovered the body, there was a break-in of a West Side apartment, apparently done by a homeless person. The weapon used in the killing at Grand Central was the same instrument used to dislodge a plate in a wall, which was used to jimmy the door of the break-in. Now the real intrigue is that we picked up a finger print off the plate that belongs to a retired CIA man."

"You're kidding."

"Wish I was. Now I'm not saying this CIA guy has anything to do with either crime, but the possibilities are interesting."

"I'll say. Did you find out the name of the dead man in Grand Central?"

"Yes, Thomas Bass."

"Any background on him?"

"Little, very little, but no CIA involvement."

"Sure?"

"As sure as we can be."

"How about the CIA man?"

"Harmon Keller."

Mary's eyes squinted as a puzzled look etched her face.

"What's the matter, Mary?"

"Harmon Keller"

"You know Him?"

"No, but when we were filming under Grand Central we came across a homeless man who told me his name was Harmon."

"Is that so. Did he give you his last name?"

"No...Could it be possible Harmon Keller is the same Harmon I met?"

"I don't know."

"What are the chances a retired CIA man becomes homeless and involved in a murder and a break-in?"

"It's a stretch of the imagination, but who knows."

"Did you learn anything about Harmon Keller?"

"I tried the CIA but they're stone walling me."

"I'm not surprised."

"All they told me is that he retired."

"How old is he?"

"I don't know, why?"

"Well if he's young, say not retirement age, then maybe there's something rotten in Denmark."

"Well I think he put in twenty years."

"Even at that he's probably still very young."

"Possibly."

"Where else can you go to find something out about Keller?"

"I was taking a long shot and going to ask you."

"Me?"

"Yes, I don't know why. I just thought...that maybe..."

"I'll check."

"Thanks, Mary."

The waiter reappeared and placed two glasses of club soda on the table.

"Thank you," Elroy said.

Elroy reached for the soda and sipped it.

"Mary, tell me about Public Broadcast News."

"Well, basically we're an agency who believe in investigating news rather than just reporting it."

"Isn't that what national networks do?"

"Yes and no. Mostly no. What you have to understand is that the networks are owned by big business: G.E., Westinghouse and the like. A company like G.E. is, among other things, in the nuclear business. Do you really think NBC can report honestly about the nuclear dangers as they relate to the environment? Not to mention political manipulation which at best is rampant."

"How do you avoid all that?"

"By being public. We rely on public funds only, and provide an alternative to regular network news.

"It must be expensive to run your station?"

"Very. We do get excellent public support. There is a community of people out there who think there is a need for alternate news. We don't broadcast twenty-four hours a day which helps to keep costs down. Also we own our broadcast signal and there are tremendous advantages there."

"You also run documentaries."

"Yes...We also air documentaries from other interest groups as well. That helps pay some of the freight. But basically we try to invigorate the First Amendment."

Mary was direct and her eyes never left Elroy's face.

"That's an awesome responsibility."

"I know. We try to keep that in mind every minute, but I'm sure it's no more than your responsibility."

"I guess."

"What will be your next step to find Bass' killer?"

"To be honest, Mary there isn't much. If I don't find Keller and if he's not involved, Bass becomes another fact of life in my job."

"That must frustrate you?"

"It does. Like you, I'm not a crusader, but some things should end differently than they do."

"Tell me, Larry, were you born in New York?"

"Yes."

"Lived here all your life?"

"California for three years. Vietnam for one."

"How was that one year?"

"An experience."

"Did you see much fighting?"

"Too much."

"I should tell you, while you were fighting there, I was protesting it here."

"Why am I not surprised? I told you Mary you're around to tell us when we're blowing it."

A shy smile crossed Mary's face and Elroy had an overpowering urge to reach for her face and bring it close to his so he could kiss her. It wasn't her plain beauty that moved him, it was something he couldn't see, something that was beyond him, out of reach. He wanted to say something, but speech for the moment was like something he hadn't learned. He remained mute, allowing himself to become engulfed in silent desire. But beyond what he felt, he sensed Mary's sudden silence had overtures all its own.

"Two fish specials," the waiter announced concealing an indescribable hush.

"Smells good," Mary commented.

"Enjoy," the waiter said. "Bono appetite."

Elroy looked at Mary's smiling face, joyful, not far from innocence, but not near vulnerability. There was no trace of false mystique or forced sophistication, just a plain desire for simple things.

"Mary I have something to confess to you."

"What's that?"

"Talking to you about the homicide was not the real reason I called you...I really wanted to take you to dinner, spend some time with you, get to know you."

Mary put down her fork and looked at Elroy. Her face displayed neither profound revelation nor an idiot's delight. She just remained contained within quiet, locked into a simple sincerity.

"I know, Larry."

★★★

Elroy sat on the white leather couch sipping coffee. Mary had removed her shoes and sat with her feet tucked under her. Flame from the fireplace provided the only light, and nullified the cold night beyond them. For reasons beyond his logic, Elroy dealt with a compendium of thoughts and feelings as they rushed through him, altering his perception. He was engrossed in a strange, enchanted land, one where he could escape the responsibility of his life and job for a brief moment, and ultimately put his trust in the night.

He put down his coffee and looked at Mary.

"Mary?" he said softly

"Yes?"

"This afternoon, on the phone. Why did you hesitate when I asked you to dinner?"

"Because I knew my decision ultimately would entail more than just dinner," she said with her usual directness.

Elroy watched her breathing become somewhat shorter and shallower. A pulse point in her throat began to pulsate noticeably. He moved his hand and gently clasped hers.

"Larry, I hope you understand what I mean."

"I think I do."

"You know, I can't say that when I first met you, you didn't appeal to me. Then I looked into your eyes and I saw a sadness there. A sadness that I don't think even you were safe from...It's funny, I immediately thought of you with a strange ambivalence. One part of you enticing, the other frightening. And then there was my own reaction and my own doubts...fears."

"It's funny but I had the feeling you were looking for something in my eyes."

"They show it all...What hurt you Larry?"

"Not now, some other time."

Elroy rose from the couch and walked to the fireplace. Housed on the mantel was a modern quartz clock, a brass planter with cascading ivy and a crystal dish with ordinary gambling dice. The dice seemed out of place with the decor and with Mary herself. He extended his hand downward to feel the fire's warmth.

"You know, Mary, the first time I met you, I had feelings of my own. You stayed with me, tucked somewhere like a fond memory or a shadow on my face...I was going round and round, no surprises, the loneliness and complacency balanced out. Then all of a sudden you came along and confused everything for me."

"So you pursued your feelings...or were they urges?"

"Whatever it was, they seemed to have a life of their own."

"Taking you along where ever they lead."

"In a sense, but not recklessly...taking nothing for granted."

"But I'm sure without caution, and without much too lose."

"I don't know."

"Why is it easier for a man, Larry?"

"I don't know that it is. We just pretend. Women cover it up better. In the end it all comes out even."

Mary leaned over and picked up her cup from the table and sipped her coffee.

"Cold. I hate cold coffee."

She put the cup back on the table and folded her arms across her breasts. She looked beyond Elroy to the fire.

"What are you thinking about?" he asked.

"Vermont. How uncluttered things were then."

"Mary we'll move slowly. Try to keep it loose and light. See what happens."

Mary's eyes moved from the fire to Elroy. She felt a surge of trust and confidence exude from him and his soft smile evoked an innocence that put all her fears to rest.

Elroy reached into the crystal dish and withdrew the dice.

"What are these for?" he asked, displaying them in the palm of his hand.

"Those?...When I get to know you better."

ELEVEN

The weather did not delay the landing of flight 702 from Los Angeles. The L1011 kicked up a thick spray from the runway as the wheels touched down and the wings disturbed the fluttering descent of light snow. The wide-body craft maneuvered easily to the arrivals gate and passengers began departing.

Rayfer was one of the last passengers to leave his seat. He looked down to assure himself he had left nothing behind, then continued past a smiling stewardess who thanked him for flying Delta.

In the time it took Rayfer to retrieve his luggage and leave the terminal, the snow had stopped and the sky began to brighten. He threw his suitcase into the back of a cab and settled in behind it.

"The Saint James Hotel in Manhattan," he announced to the cabbie.

The car pulled away from the curb delivering Rayfer on the last leg of a dark journey. A sense of cold excitement began to gather within him as his mission was slowly culminating with defined reality. The street-hard look in his eyes was frightening as he focused beyond the present. His attitude and demeanor discouraged challenge. He sat rigidly with his large stone-like hands cupped over his knee caps; his face was like stone, impervious to distraction.

Rayfer knew he was a device used for Prescott's personal desire, but in return he fulfilled a necessity warranted by his own needs. Their unholy alliance circumvented borders of reasonable trust and rational value where Rayfer viewed himself, not as a usable instrument, but more as a counterpart between himself and his deeds. He harbored no false illusions about himself and the dark persuasion he had for murder. Prescott was his own tool which allowed him to function within the limits of marginal protection and obscure purpose.

As the taxi moved along, Rayfer remembered how this relationship began. It was in Central America during Prescott's first overseas assignment. He was there ostensibly as an adviser for the Contras, and Rayfer was a soldier of fortune dabbling on the fringes of the drug trade. After a bar room altercation, Rayfer was arrested by the local police. In a jail cell crowded with local residents, drug dealers, pimps and murderers, Rayfer stood alone as the only foreigner. He was isolated and vulnerable, appearing to be the perfect prey to anyone enticed by outnumbering odds.

From within the group, a burly native with greasy hair and several missing teeth moved toward Rayfer. Thrown in the midst of a foreign culture, Rayfer recognized the universal language of contempt that expressed itself on the stranger's face.

"Americana puta!" the man announced.

Rayfer stood his ground, trying to defuse the impending menace by scowling at the blatant belligerence.

"Fuck you!" he growled back.

The latino threw a quick glance at a countryman standing at Rayfer's shoulder. Communication had been made which Rayfer knew was the silent command ordering his death. His only hope for survival was sudden, un-forgiving offense, a posture he was easily drawn too. With one swift, powerful motion, Rayfer drove his elbow up and backward catching the unseen adversary beside him in the throat. The blow was well placed and effective. The man gasped and fell to the floor, his trachea col-lapsed. Rayfer propelled his fist forward, landing a force-ful blow on the chin of the big man before him, causing him to stumble backward. As Rayfer charged, the man regained his footing and grabbed Rayfer by the shirt with both hands and ran with him, battering him into the iron bars that caged them.

The noise attracted the attention of the police. The apparent mismatch promised to entertain them and feed their appetite for violence and death.

Prescott happened to be in the police station negotiat-ing support for his own local operation. His organiza-tion's purpose was to cause disruption within the ranks of local military, gain a political representative of their choosing and subvert the delicate freedoms they prom-ised to uphold.

Prescott and the policemen watched as the greasy Latin man growled and pressed a strangle hold around Rayfer's throat.

There seemed to be a focused determination in Ray-fer's eyes that was chilling. He expressed no fear or terror, just a controlled ferocity that extended beyond anything Prescott had ever recognized. He studied Rayfer and be-came threatened and elated by his somber determination.

In a sense, Rayfer seemed to come out from within himself, and display a silent tenacity of unholy propor-tions. An evil resoluteness shown on his face. His eyes widened and his pupils constricted. His jaw muscles bulged as he clenched his teeth. He growled like an angry dog and stiffened the fingers of his right hand until they formed a flat, straight board-like weapon and drove it into the big man's chest.

Rayfer pushed into his esophagus causing the attacker to lose his ability to breathe. The man let go of Rayfer and grabbed for his own chest. Rayfer leaned back and brought his head and shoulders down quickly and forcibly. His forehead crashed into the bridge of the man's nose, breaking it instantly. Blood cascaded down, delighting Rayfer and providing him ample target to drive his palm up into his chin.

The sound of splintering teeth filled the cell as his lower jaw went through his tongue and crashed the upper portion of his mouth.

The man screamed and fell to one knee. Rayfer grabbed the man by the hair and forced him to the floor. With short powerful bursts, he repeatedly drove his head backward, crashing it into the hard cement floor rendering him unconscious. Blood from his nose and mouth covered his face. A slight pool gathered on the floor from the back of his head. Rayfer kneeled before his fallen adversary, whose body was limp.

With his fingertips, Rayfer raised the lid of the unconscious man's left eye to discover it had rolled back into his head and the pupil had dilated. There seemed to be no ability to recognize an imposing death or formulate any kind of human expression other than defeat. His breathing had become slower and shallower. His mouth opened slightly and Rayfer could see a portion of his tongue was missing, probably lodged in his throat.

Rayfer kept the eyelid forced up and formed a tight fist with the other hand. He slowly extended his pointing finger, and using it as a sturdy poker, drove it into and through the man's eye. Yellowish liquid mixed with blood gushed up, saturating Rayfer's fist. He felt the soft, smooth eye crush beneath his force and roll out and down his face. Rayfer maintained his single-mindedness, lost in demented reverie as he pumped his finger deeper into the cavity wanting to destroy the man's brain.

Blood bubbled up in the mouth of the victim as death choked in his throat. There was no more breathing and no pain to be felt. In an instant he was no longer victim or perpetrator, he merely passed from anonymity to death.

Rayfer absorbed himself in the totality of his deed, becoming one with his assault and its results. For an instant he felt no needs, nothing left to acquire or regain; he was now complete and placated, a satisfaction to his soul that was baptized in absolute darkness.

For the first time he heard the screams of the men in the cell. They were venting their horror and fear. They all pushed away from Rayfer trying to distance themselves from the demon in their midst.

The policeman from the other side of the bars drew a revolver and aimed at Rayfer. Prescott reached up and pulled the gun downward. The policeman turned and looked at Prescott. There was absurdity in his eyes, reflecting a horrible discovery and fearful admiration.

"No," Prescott whispered. "I want him."

The policeman lowered his gun, recognizing the frightening alliance that had just been formed. He understood, in an instant, the boundaries of terror that had just been drawn around him.

The cab stopped, transporting Rayfer to his present journey. He paid the fare and entered the hotel.

Once in his hotel room, Rayfer placed his suitcase on the bed and turned the rows of tiny numbers until the latches clicked open. He withdrew several pairs of pants with matching sweaters, as well as socks, underwear, and two pairs of shoes. One pair he placed under a chair, and the right shoe of the second pair he left on the bed. He withdrew a small black pouch containing toiletries, then proceeded to undress and take a warm shower. The water splashed off his lean, hard body relaxing him and removing a chill that had settled in close to his bones. He stepped from the shower and dried off. Through the mist Rayfer admired his body in the mirror. He tightened his fist and delighted as muscles in his arms became exaggerated and rigid and thick veins bulged under his skin.

He unzipped the black pouch and produced a hairbrush and brushed his hair straight back. He replaced the brush and picked out an item that resembled a very shortscrew driver attached to a large, flattened wing nut. He walked back into the bedroom and picked up the shoe off the bed. Forcing the blunt edge of the screwdriver-like instrument between the soul and upper portion of the shoe, he twisted firmly. The soul fell away from the body of the shoe and an E.R.N. Rostfrei knife fell onto the bed. Rayfer retrieved the weapon and walked to the telephone. He dialed a number and waited.

"Prescott," came the voice.

Rayfer pressed the button on the handle of the knife and a sleek eight inch blade shot straight out through the top. A demented smile parted his lips as he admired its mechanics, craftsmanship and potential for destruction. The purity and perfection of the Damascus Steel blade filled him with twisted delight.

"Your package has arrived," was all he said.

Doug Hyatt sat at his computer terminal and studied the amber screen flashing through the complicated series of overseas transactions at Citicorp's database. When the screen reached the end of the listings, Hyatt keyed in a code and watched the screen go blank, then serve up a list of domestic activity. He keyed in additional commands and information rolled up exposing the diverse activity of the bank. Confidential information revealed itself by the touch of certain keys. Hyatt appeared defiant and smug in the knowledge he was able to bypass the complicated electronic guards and gain access to the bank's database.

The intrusion proved easy for him once he knew the many design programs and codes. Access to that information had cost a great deal of money. Once paid, and the correct codes were in place, the rest was easy. He continued keying information until the screen beeped and stopped, isolating a single transaction.

Hyatt opened a notebook and wrote down information. He ran down the cursor on the transaction to the account of Harmon Keller in search of a home address. It showed one, and Hyatt recognized it as CIA headquarters in Langley, Virginia.

He leaned back in his chair and rubbed his eyes, content with his results. He delighted in his ability to invade the privacy of institutions and people, and not be detected. He garnered personal aggrandizement while displaying no concern or responsibility for the fate of Harmon Keller.

Hyatt leaned across his desk for the phone and dialed a number.

"Yes?" said the voice after one ring.

"We have bank activity."

"In what form?" the voice responded.

"A five thousand dollar withdrawal."

"When?"

"Yesterday."

"Hmm."

Hyatt removed his glasses and instantly the computer went blurry. He passed the palm of his hand down over his face in an effort to relieve the eye strain and fatigue.

He then replaced his glasses, blinked several times, as the screen returned into focus.

"Still no address?"

"No."

"How about the doctor, any movement there?"

"None. If he shows up there he may have to give a local address. I'll monitor him."

"Good. Keep me posted."

★★★

Harmon Keller had difficulty adjusting to the comforts of the hotel room. Everything seemed unfamiliar and threatening. He struggled, trying to equate himself to his surroundings. For the last year he had acclimated himself to living in the streets. Suddenly his environment was quiet, serene and clean. But within that serenity, Keller found distrust. His eyes darted around the room, unable to focus on anything. His body began to twitch and his head jerked as though trying to follow the flight of an erratic butterfly. He ran into a corner and curled up trying to protect himself from the cactus plant on the far side of the room which appeared to be poised for brutal attack.

"No! No!" he said to himself, struggling to maintain mental clarity.

He removed the coat that had not been off his body for months. Large sums of money fell from a pocket. He tried to concentrate on the money and realize its value.

"One hundred, two hundred," he counted, then looked at the plant, then the window and then the ceiling.

"Three hundred, three hundred fifty," he continued, returning his attention to the bills scattered on the floor.

He drew his legs closer to his body and reached up into the air with one hand as though to prevent the ceiling from falling onto his head. He held his arm aloft, rigid, then he suddenly withdrew it and cradled his chest with both arms, squeezing tightly.

"It's OK! It's OK!" he said to himself.

He swayed back and forth, resembling a holy man in silent prayer or an infant being rocked by an invisible hand.

"Hold on! Hold on!" he whispered, trying to encourage himself.

Keller tried to reaffirm within himself the need to gain control. An inner struggle waged, a duality of thought and purpose tore him in different directions. He was uncertain if it was fear of becoming normal and facing responsibility or the mental anguish that temporarily consumed him.

"Doctor Freeman will help," he told himself.

"Doctor Freeman...Doctor Freeman..."

The thought of the doctor prescribing medication served to remove his self-imposed panic.

"Doctor Freeman...Doctor Freeman..." he repeated for comfort and strength.

He uncurled himself from his fetal position and gathered in the money. He put it in piles on a table and stared at it. His body began to relax and his mind began to detail his actions. He needed to set into motion activity that would bring about his desired results. New clothes, a bath and food--good food--were his first objectives. But he also knew he couldn't trust his behavior without the medication. That was first. Or should he buy clothes first he wondered. Or perhaps a shave and a bath? Confusion began to settle in once more. A shower was first, he reasoned. But what would he do once he bought the clothes, shaved and ate? What would happen once the medication was represcribed? What would become of his life, he asked himself.

The questions tumbled in on him, trying to dislodge his quest for normalcy. He focused on Doctor Freeman, the anchor to keep secure in his personal quest. He struggled to keep positive images in his mind.

Keller threw himself on the bed and the silence of the room closed in on him. Noticeably absent were the sounds of rolling trains, the graveyard coughs, moans, screams and sighs of people held captive by desperation. Harmon had become accustomed to the sounds, but he vowed they were no longer going to be a part of him. He had gone too far and fallen too low. He had to seize control and reverse his decline. Ultimately he would have to deal with what lay beyond his personal nightmare. But for now he fought with the silence, the clean surroundings and himself. The only friendly face was the darkness. Keller hid within it, and there he found solace, familiarity and eventually, sleep.

TWELVE

Elroy sat opposite Mary in the lounge on the twenty-sixth floor of the Beekman Towers. In the center of the lounge, directly in front of the elevator, was a piano player/singer providing quiet, romantic music. Elroy and Mary sat at a tiny table on a far wall that was glass enclosed, which afforded an excellent view of the brilliantly lit city.

The sounds of clinking glasses, muted conversation and the piano faded into the background.

Elroy watched Mary closely and accepted the fact that she had filled all his senses. She appealed to every part of him, especially the anxious desire that she become a part of him. A commitment of lasting feeling, not merely a momentarily lustful accomplishment.

Elroy reached out and touched the back of her hand. Mary responded with a smile and turned her hand upward so she could hold his.

"You look very nice tonight," he commented.

"Thank you."

"Can I get you something else to drink?"

"No, I'm fine."

Mary noticed the look of Elroy's face had become softer from the first time she had met him--softer but still sad.

"Larry, I'm having a nice time."

"Good."

"You know, it seems so ridiculous that, here I am, a grown woman out with a man with an interesting background and all I have to say is something so simple."

"Mary we agreed no shop talk. Right?"

"Yes, but..."

"Mary it's what we're not saying that's important, we deal with minute details, and all kinds of nonsense constantly. I think we just need a break from it. I just want to sit here, hold your hand and...just...be."

"Be what?"

"With you. No social causes or unsolved crimes, just two people in the beginning of something they're both trying to feel their way through. That's all."

"Are you as jittery as I am?"

"Yes and no."

"Explain."

"No, because I already know what it is I want, and yes because I'm uncertain if I'll get it."

"What's that?"

"A commitment. An emotional commitment."

Elroy swirled the melting ice cubes around in his glass and replaced it on the table.

"Look Mary, I know you have your career, your causes and..and yourself. I have all that too, but there is room enough for you. I can handle you in my life. What's more I would like to be a positive factor in yours. Not for a night, or a few nights sprinkled through the year...something more."

"Are you sure of that?"

"I'm sure I want to try. No false starts, misguided intentions, just an honest shot....Mary, we live in a strange world, you never know what's going to happen from one day to the next. People are disposable, I don't want a brief run-through life...a throw-away romance. It goes against me. I like the relationship with staying power, guts. It makes me feel I've got something to count on."

"You know, my mother and father have a beautiful relationship. They were the only two people I've known that after being together for so many years never resented each other. They never forgot how to care. They're a personification of charm. I always wanted what they had...Vermont and all that goes with it."

"How come you never got it?"

"Never found a guy like my father. So I got involved with my career."

"You can have both, Mary."

"How?"

"Women do it all the time."

"Don't be silly, Larry. It's a lie women choose to live with. We can't do both successfully, especially if there are children involved. Our society hasn't evolved that far yet."

"That's surprising coming from you."

"How so?"

"Well, number one, you're a woman, and secondly, you obviously champion causes, equality."

"Let me bring you in on a little secret, Larry, there is no such things as equality. No matter how much we try to hide it, it's all a struggle for supremacy and dominance. From housewives to politicians. We will be allowed to go just so far and tolerated just so much. It all comes down to a game of manners...Hiding lust and exposing arrogance. There will always be discord between men and women no matter what the arena."

"Well I wouldn't publicize your feelings."

"Why not? I'm entitled to what I believe, and I'm not afraid of the facts...What I'm talking about has nothing at all to do with competence and the way things should really be, you understand?"

"No, I'm sure it doesn't."

"For the most part it's been men who've ruled the world and look where that's gotten us."

"Do you think women would have done a better job?"

"Yes Larry, they're the life givers. You must admit it would have been an interesting slant..."

"I'm afraid all this has taken us away from what we started to to say, Mary."

"No it hasn't. It's all basic individual needs. An appreciation of what it's all about. Standards."

Elroy felt as though he had gained a new perspective on Mary. In addition to being beautiful, she emerged as a woman with depth and individuality of thought. Independent yet accessible, courageous in human portions. And above all, sensual and reliable.

Elroy raised his hand slightly to gain the attention of the waiter.

"Anything else?" he asked as he approached the table.

Elroy looked at Mary, who paused for a moment then shook her head.

"Just the bill."

Mary was impressed and surprised with Elroy's apartment. She expected the stereotypical mess, with beer cans strewn about, and cheap, broken furnishings.

"Very nice," she commented.

"Thank you."

"How long have you lived here?"

"Five years, I moved from an apartment on Long Island."

"Is this a condo?"

"Yes."

Elroy helped Mary take off her coat and hung it up in the hall closet.

"Sit down Mary, feel comfortable. Can I get you something?"

"No. No thanks."

Mary walked to the window to be greeted by a view of the Statue of Liberty she had never seen before. It stood majestically in the middle of the harbor, adorned in bright light.

"It looks nice all lighted up," she said.

"Yeah, it is impressive."

"The city could be so beautiful, so beautiful."

"Deception at its finest," Elroy said from behind Mary.

He was standing close to her and for the first time smelled her perfume. It was light, almost undetectable. He breathed in and felt a pleasurable mixture of excitement and nervousness. He also noticed Mary's breathing was quicker.

Elroy had an overpowering urge to wrap his arms around Mary and hold her tight. Instead he put his hands gently upon her shoulders and kissed her neck. Mary turned and met Elroy's eyes. Her silent look expressed passion and trust, struggling with assurance and confidence. His hands circled around her waist and he pulled her close. Their heads moved closer, then stopped, a split second which equated to a final judgment. Mary then continued until they came together and kissed. Mary's mouth opened and Elroy could feel her nervously gasp for air. His hands spread across her back as she grabbed the back of his head. He felt her large breasts press

143

against his chest and he moved his whole body forward to feel every inch of her.

Elroy moved his hands and cupped her face, his lips kissed her cheeks, nose and forehead. Her eyes closed as though to shut in all her pleasure, and keep it personal and close.

"Mary, you're so beautiful," he said, choking on his own breath.

"Larry, Larry." she said with a sorrowful passion.

Elroy kissed her lips once more and hugged her. His heart pounded and he could feel her tremble, almost fall.

"God, I can't believe how you feel," he said as he brought his lips to her neck and down to the open part of her blouse. He kissed the fleshy part on the top of her breast and Mary reacted with a sudden gasp. Her fingers grabbed his hair and she pressed his head harder onto her breast.

A unique delirium caused Mary to lose sight of time and place. She was thrust into a world of blind submission, void of all thoughts she recognized, except a subliminal passion she didn't know existed. She thought she heard herself call his name once more, or was it simply an echo lodged somewhere in the caverns of her mind?

Mary's physical response and permission was an admission of a greater need, an acknowledgement of a deeper feeling.

Elroy lay bare his passion with the hope Mary would take it, hold and keep it in a special place between them for the rest of his life.

Elroy clasped Mary's hand gently behind her back, turned and led her into the bedroom. He watched as Mary, unashamed, shed her clothes. Her naked body was a beautiful extension of her face. She gracefully lowered herself onto his bed and reached up to embrace him. Elroy removed his clothing and moved gently and slowly, positioning himself between her outspread legs. He paused a moment. Their eyes burned together, fused by unspoken expressions. He lowered himself, penetrating her slowly. Her gasp attested to the communion of souls. He remained still as if wanting to freeze that instant for an eternity. He felt her legs wrap around his back and hold him purely. Her arms held his shoulders in an effort to bring him past her flesh into her spirit. A metaphysical baptism transcended delight and pleasure.

Mary's eyes never left Elroy's face and her expressions would not deny him the truth and honesty she subscribed to. There was nothing beyond him, not for just the moment, but for the rest of their lives.

Every movement, gesture and touch from Elroy was gentle and caring. He inwardly begged for acceptance and agonized within a delicate vulnerability. His eyes never left Mary's, he hoped they would convey what he found impossible to say. With each inward thrust he felt as though he was penetrating her being. With each outward movement he felt reborn, catapulted to a new existence. A renewal culminating in an indivisible union of spirit, mind and flesh. A totality, encompassing the whole of cosmic time, and forgiving all his mortal frailties. For Elroy, his life had instantly gained a new evaluation, all he was, all he had known and believed suddenly collided and perished into a new personal awareness.

"Mary..." he whispered trying desperately to relay his emotions.

"Yes, I know." she said intuitively.

Elroy knew there was nothing else to say. The communication and understanding that now existed between them was instinctive. They were on a threshold of a new and beautiful enlightenment.

Only in ecstacy did the raging passion subside. Mary brushed her fingertips along Elroy's forehead to wipe away his perspiration.

"You're sweating, Larry," she whispered in delight.

"God, I'm sorry."

"It's OK. Don't worry. Lie down," she said, gently pushing him onto his side.

Elroy rolled, but never let go of his hug, causing Mary to roll with him.

"You OK?" she asked.

"Fine...You?"

"Hmm," she acknowledged with a smile.

Elroy reexamined her face for a long time.

"You're beautiful," he finally observed.

Mary remained silent, her tension and nervousness were replaced by calm and satisfaction. With her fingertips she smoothed out his eyebrows and followed the contours of his face to his lips. Elroy kissed her hand and then her lips.

"Mary?"

"Hmm?"

"I feel better that that's out of the way."

"Me, too."

"I don't know about you, but I think we're gonna make it."

"I hope so."

"Ask me how I know."

"I don't have to."

Mary could feel his warm, even breathing on her face. He became placid and the glitter in his eyes became adoring.

"Larry?"

"Yes."

"You still look like you have sad eyes."

"Do I?"

"You do. If you want to avoid it, fine. But now's as good a time as any to start to know each other."

Elroy withdrew his arms from around her and propped himself up. He jabbed his elbow into the pillow and rested the side of his face on his hand.

"I guess I've been lonely...troubled."

"I can ease your loneliness."

"You already have."

"Troubled. By what?"

"Ghosts."

"What kind?"

Elroy took a deep breath and brought his free hand to Mary's breast. He caressed her nipple with his fingertips, trying to formulate his thoughts.

"Fire..." he said.

Elroy moved his head and kissed the softness of Mary's breast. He held it full in his hand and gently moved it across his face. His hand moved across her body and he held her tight.

"What kind of fire?" she whispered.

"Car...Car fire. I was waiting outside my apartment on Long Island...My mother and father were coming to pick me up for something...I don't remember what...

"They stopped for a light and a car came from behind...plowed into them...The gas tank ruptured...and...by the time I ran to them it was an inferno...Glass exploded."

"God."

"I tried to tell myself I was helpless..."

"You were."

"I don't know."

"Larry, you're not the kind of man who would let something like that happen to your parents and not try to save them."

"I should have done something."

"Like what?"

"I don't know, jump on the fire and try to smother it with my body."

"I knew a man like you would think of doing something like that."

"I should have, it would have been easier."

"They wouldn't have wanted you to do it."

"How can you be so sure?"

"I'm sure."

Elroy rolled onto his back and brought his arm across his forehead. His eyes looked at the ceiling and for the first time since the accident, Elroy felt a semblance of relief talking about it with Mary.

"It doesn't seem right."

"What's that?"

"There was a lawsuit and I got a lot of money. That's what enabled me to buy this place. It doesn't seem right...A profit made that way...I knew I couldn't stay on Long Island...I don't even go there anymore...So here I am."

"I'm sorry, Larry."

"Yeah, well..."

Elroy rose from the bed and walked into the living room. He looked down at the Statute of Liberty in time to see a barge floating aimlessly by in the silent water.

Mary came from behind him and pressed her breasts into his back and hugged him. She kissed the side of his face as he reached backward and grabbed her hips.

"The guilt is not yours to bear, Larry. Sorrow and grief is more than enough."

Elroy reached out and pressed his hand onto the cold windowpane. A thin veil of vapor formed on the glass in the pattern of his hand.

"Now wasn't the time to tell you, Mary."

Mary put her cheek onto his shoulder and felt his smooth skin.

"The dice," she said.

"The dice...on your mantle?"

"Those...When I was a little, girl, one, two years old, just as I was learning to speak. My father used them to teach me math."

"You're kidding," Elroy said smiling as he turned from the window.

"No...He taught me to add the spots. Five and two, six and one, three plus four. He used them to add, multiply and divide. Each toss became a different math problem."

"That's great. I don't believe it."

"Yeah. He also used a deck of cards for higher math-- eights, nines, tens. He also taught me colors, but that was no big deal, all they had was red and black."

"The man sounds creative."

"Yeah, he enjoyed it more than I did."

"He sounds like a stand-up guy."

"Yeah, well mostly he's my father...Can I make us a cup of coffee?"

"No, not for me. If you want one I'll get it."

"No. Do you have something for breakfast for us in the morning?"

"Are you staying the night?"

"That was my intention all along."

NIGHT SHADE

THIRTEEN

Harmon Keller sat in Doctor Freeman's waiting room trying to read the latest issue of Newsweek. The words seemed to be tripping on the page and his eyes tried to steady them. His mind and body were resistive to the imposed decorum they had to achieve. He had to remain still and lucid for a while longer--then he would be free of the nightmare.

Keller studied his hands; in spite of the showers some embedded dirt remained. He ran his hand along his face and the extreme roughness met with the dry skin causing a scraping sound. The new outer clothing looked fresh but somehow worn. Perhaps the fundamental neglect and abuse of his body over the past year was difficult to conceal. The pants looked baggy and his shirt did not tuck properly in them.

"Mister Keller," the nurse announced.

"Yes."

"This way please, Doctor Freeman will see you."

Keller rose and his jacket pulled across his rounded and slightly hunched shoulders causing it to look disproportionate to his torso and uneven at his buttocks.

"We haven't seen you in a while," the nurse said. "How have you been feeling?"

"OK," he responded with a shaky voice.

"Good, why don't you step in here," she said leading him to an examining room. "Doctor Freeman will be with you shortly."

"Thank you."

"Please remove your jacket and shirt."

The nurse closed the door behind her and Keller took off his jacket and shirt laying them on a chair. He walked to a sink and turned on the cold water. Putting his mouth to the faucet and began to drink voraciously. He wiped his mouth and looked up to see his image in the mirror above the sink. His hair was long and still somewhat oily. He ran his hands through it trying to make it look natural. The sores on his lip and forehead did not look as bad now that they were clean. His teeth, too, showed improvement since giving them some care.

The door opened and Doctor Freeman entered looking at a folder which contained Keller's medical history.

"Hello Harmon."

"Hi, Doctor Freeman."

The doctor looked up from the folder and tried to conceal his impression of Keller.

"So, how's things?"

"Not bad," he said, trying to steady his voice and body.

"Feeling fine?"

"Somewhat."

The doctor returned his attention to the folder and examined it for a moment. He finally closed it and rested it upon a table next to surgical pads and an assortment of first aid items.

"What can we do for you today, Harmon?"

"Doctor Freeman, I've not really been doing well," he answered tugging anxiously at the pockets of his pants.

"I can see that...Not taking your medication?"

"No."

"Harmon I told you never to stop taking it. Your susceptibilities were too much of a risk factor. You were to remain in touch with this office more often. According to the chart, you haven't been here in over a year."

"I know. I need your help."

"How can I help you, if you don't help yourself?"

"I don't know," he said as his anxiety grew.

"Don't worry, I'll help you now, take it easy," Freeman said, trying to take the edge off for Keller.

"Good."

"Just relax and we'll fix you up. But you have to remember Harmon, it doesn't stop just at today. You have to keep a vigilance on your condition."

"I know. I know."

"You adhere to my prescribed medication and you'll be fine. Sit here, let me examine you."

After a brief examination, Doctor Freeman was convinced his patient's vital organs were in good health. He knew instantly there was nutritional deterioration and a neurological setback, but the trauma was not irreversible.

"OK Harmon get dressed and come into my office."

After Keller dressed he entered the doctor's office. Freeman was sitting back in his chair with one foot perched on top of a lower drawer in his desk.

"Come in Harmon, close the door."

Keller closed the door and sat in a chair in front of Freeman. The doctor looked directly at Keller, pausing to chose his words.

"Harmon, I'm going to be very blunt. You and I have known each other very well. I know you have not been taking your thorazine for some time now. Don't you know you can not do without it?"

"Yes."

"I can only guess at what you've been experiencing unmedicated. I'm not here for that. If you want my help you have to take the medication as prescribed. Is that understood?"

"Yes...Doctor Freeman how long do I have to continue to take the medication?"

"I don't know, your situation was unique. It's hard to tell, but we won't worry about that now. It's the immediate I'm concerned with."

"OK."

"I can tell you haven't been eating well, sleeping well. Your personal hygiene is suspect and your physical condition is not what it should be. If you refuse to take the medication, Harmon, I have no recourse but to cease my professional availability to you. I want you well, you have to want that also."

"I do. I won't lapse. I just went off track for a while and it just kept getting worse, now I'm struggling to get my life in order.

"Fine. I want you to go home and get plenty of rest, eat well build yourself up. Take vitamins, I never tell my patients that, but in your case I'm breaking with tradition."

"OK."

"And come back in one month, I want to see you then. Make an appointment out front, it'll be put into the computer."

"Fine."

"Get this filled," he said handing Keller the prescription. "Need I say more about its importance?"

"No...Thank you doctor."

"One month."

"Yes."

Keller walked to the receptionist who was seated in front of a computer terminal.

"Patti, schedule Mister Keller for a return visit in one month," Freeman called out from his office.

"OK," she responded.

"Let's see, Mister Keller," she said keying a command and looking at her screen. "I have March twenty-seventh."

"Fine."

"We'll make you our first appointment--nine o'clock?"

"OK."

Pattie typed in the confirmation.

"A number where you can be reached during the day?"

"Carlyle Hotel, 744-1600."

"Fine. OK, hold it one second Mister Keller," she said as she waited for a printer to spit out a bill for the day's services.

★★★

The bar was crowded with boisterous, middle-management types enjoying a happy hour special. Loud laughter and conversation permeated the room and a thick cloud of cigarette smoke clung to the ceiling. The tables and booths along the side walls were occupied by people conducting quieter business of varying kinds.

Prescott sat opposite Rayfer and tried not to let his nervousness show. Rayfer was cold and unfriendly, seldom smiled and always searching for a weakness in someone. Prescott was well aware of Rayfer's ability and capacity for violence, and it made him uncomfortable. Rayfer was one of the few people who enjoyed the act of murder and his only allegiance was to his own nature. Rayfer was a psychotic, with an abnormal fixation for the ultimate power over someone. His background did not consist of any childhood psychological trauma. Prescott

suspected he was just a mental and social mutant who
channeled his particular attributes to his own advantage.

"It's been a long time Rayfer."

"Yes. How do you like being on the outside?"

"It's OK. I just find there's no clarity anywhere."

"In my business there is."

"Yes, I suppose so," Prescott chuckled nervously.

Prescott's eyes scanned the people at the bar more as
an effort to avoid Rayfer. He returned to his beer and
chugged it, hoping a stupor would supply him with
enough bravado to take the edge off his intimidation.

"So, loose ends finally tied?" Rayfer asked.

"Yes...For various reasons I had to wait this long."

"Your reasons are of no concern to me, I just care
about how it relates to me."

"There should be no level of difficulty in these."

"There's more than one?"

"Tennley and Keller."

"Fine."

"Tennley is a car dealer in Princeton, New Jersey...Tennley Auto Sales. He owns it...He hasn't changed
much, very predictable. You remember him?"

"Yes."

"Here's all the information you'll need on him,"
Prescott said, handing Rayfer an envelope.

"Keller I'm not sure about, we'll save him for last. I
want to savor his fate."

"Where is he?"

"Like I said, I'm not sure. I know he had a mental
breakdown of sorts and dropped out."

"And you can't find him?" Rayfer asked with a hint of
scorn.

"I will...I suspect he may have lost his grasp of reality.
He hasn't gone back to his home in Arlington. And he
hasn't touched his bank account for a year."

"Maybe he's already dead."

"No. I had some unpleasantness in the elevator of my building one night, and I suspect Keller may have been behind it."

"I heard about it. What makes you suspect Keller?"

"Because he showed up right after it."

"I thought you said you don't know where he is?"

"I don't. He's become a phantom, if you know what I mean. Hyatt's got his ear to the ground."

Rayfer sipped his beer and looked coldly at Prescott.

"Emmet, we worked together for a long time and got to know each other more through assumption and physiological profiles than anything else."

Prescott tried to remain detached as he nodded his head.

"I know the CIA had volumes on me, but there are things you can never get to know about someone through surveillance and evaluation of habits. We both knew what we were, but never the real essence of why."

"Rayfer, it seems to me we never really know the real essence of 'why' as you put it, about ourselves...And why are you so concerned about personalities now?"

"People are my business."

"Nonsense, we are our business. People serve as an expendable commodity for your nature, like nations serve the same for mine."

"Is that why you're going for Tennley and Keller, because there are no nations for you to take down?"

"Perhaps."

"Small tradeoff."

A hint of anger flashed in Prescott's eyes, but he remained calm, not wanting to challenge Rayfer's observation. Prescott sipped his beer once more and placed it on the table with force. Rayfer studied Prescott and the traces of a slight sneer formed on his face. Prescott turned his attention away from Rayfer to the executive-types standing around the bar.

"You see those pathetic fools at the bar working for some power broker hoping to be one themselves some day? Well, they spend their lives thinking they are driving forces, destined for corporate immortality. What they don't realize is that if their services are not needed for a bigger cause, they get crushed. They're allowed to function in a certain scheme; fire a secretary, layoff a controller, suck their own ways to a flimsy loft so they can piss in an imitation marble bathroom with brass fixtures. But what they don't realize is, the infrastructure will fuck them and they won't ever know they've been fucked. They will bend over for more and more and they will rise and fall like low class nations. Maneuvered and disposed as seen fit."

"I like my form of power better. Smaller scale, but the results are immediate, the satisfaction is spontaneous, exhilarating. I don't have to wait for years and varying political ideologies for my work to be assessed. I make my own history, on the spot."

"Well, I like my trophies to be continents. What I've done in the past helped allow this country to stay what it is. All the while I had to deal with the faggot radicals who kept an open forum for their sissy complaints. That was the thanks we got; uninformed accusations. The liberals are no better than fucking whores, they give away their cunts and asses for nothing. 'You can't do this because you'll hurt that. You shouldn't do that because you'll undo this,' they tell us. I say take all the fucking liberals, radicals, special interest groups and drown them all in the muddy Mississippi. It gets done our way and whoever don't see it that way, fuck 'em. That's why I retired, no more clarity. Things got too complex because there were too many interests involved. The world got too smart for its own good. Castro's got the right idea--not politically--just personally--you do it my way or get the fuck out. Control...order...established. Simply...clearly. What's better than that?"

Prescott finished his beer and the alcohol had sufficiently affected him. He was slow and his eyes squinted, combatting the smoke. He had lost a noticeable amount of muscle control and coordination as his head wobbled and his hand went to scratch his nose but landed on his cheek. He had become less intimidated; his speech wasn't slurred, but it lacked crispness and his thought process was also impaired.

"Tennley and Keller will restore clarity?"

"Yes."

"Why did you want him killed?"

"Keller?"

"No, Castro."

"Because at the time it made sense. Now, who the fuck knows?"

"And Keller, time doesn't affect his fate?"

"No! His disloyalty and weakness are unforgivable."

"He wasn't the only one."

The alcohol gave Prescott the courage to look coldly at Rayfer and detect his sarcasm and implication.

"What are you saying?"

"I just wondered about the trend."

"In every group you'll find defectors. It's no great re-evaluation of conscience or judicial enlightenment. They shouldn't have been there in the first place, that's all. They simply never understood the rules."

"There are no rules today, Emmet, it's all a matter of interpretation and what one can effectively hide behind."

"That's the problem, I'd rewrite the whole thing so there could be no misunderstanding."

"There'd be no opposition, either, right?"

"Right."

Rayfer finished his beer and rose.

"Well I'm glad for one thing," he said looking down at Prescott.

"What's that?"

"There will always be people like you, who keep people like me in demand...I'll let you know when I'm done in Princeton. Let me know about Keller."

FOURTEEN

It was almost dusk when Rayfer exited the New Jersey Turnpike and drove into Princeton. He checked into the Marriott Courtyard where he registered under his alias, Thomas Holden.

Alone in his room he drew the curtains shut and gained a sense of reverie from his bleak isolation. A strange hotel, in a strange town, unknown to unfamiliar people. The only person he knew was Tennley.

Rayfer walked slowly and deliberately within the confines of the room. He studied his surroundings as though to strike a mistrusting alliance, judging all things with his own perspective. He elected to touch nothing and leave no trace of himself. All things in his life were either useful or useless, equating, as they do, to his needs and desires, not appealing to his likes or dislikes.

Rayfer stood in front of a full length mirror examining his ominous image. The muted light softened his silhouette, obliterating detail and the sinister look in his eyes. But Rayfer could feel his dark personal obsession fusing together with his impending deed, creating an uncontrollable excitement.

He dangled the knife loosely from his fingertips and snapped the blade free from its handle. He viewed himself only within the context of his mission. One inseparable from the other, feeding off the other to create an overwhelming bond of purpose and need, consumed by intent.

Rayfer closed the door behind him and he stuffed the key into his pocket. He followed the route Prescott had outlined and found Tennley's house.

A corner split-level, concealed by thick pines and a high fence on the road side, rear and opposing side. The front remained partly obliterated by high shrubs and a full Japanese Maple tree. The lack of street lighting further concealed the house. The opposite side of the street consisted entirely of a row of newly constructed homes, making the area desolate and perfect for his needs.

Rayfer could see lights and activity through the bay window. He knew it was Tennley's wife, home alone.

He sat quietly undetected, the night covering him. His mind assessed the area and formulated his approach. He was in no rush; desire had to succumb to technicalities.

Within his rear view mirror he noticed approaching headlights. The car slowed and turned into the driveway. Rayfer watched as Tennley emerged from the car and opened one of the two car garage doors. Tennley re-entered the car and drove into the garage. Rayfer looked at his watch to check the time.

The garage door closed and the lights went out. Through the bay window, Rayfer could see Tennley enter what he believed to be the living room. He deduced there was a door leading from the garage to the house.

"John?" his wife called out from the kitchen.

"Yeah," Tennley responded walking through the living room.

"Home a little late tonight."

"Yeah, some last minute nonsense."

"What happened?"

"Damn service manager."

"Kelley?"

"Yeah, he scheduled a dozen recalls to be completed today and only eight rear seals came from the parts supplier, consequently I had four irate customers to soothe over."

"Why was there a mix-up?"

"Who knows? It's the things-will-fix-themselves principle. The only problem with that is I'm the fix-it broker."

"So what happened?"

"I now have four new cars on the road in lieu of free rental replacements. I wouldn't mind, but I'm not making money on the recall replacements."

"You need a better manager."

"What else is new?"

"John, I really don't have time to eat, I'm already late for my council meeting.

"Don't worry. Just go."

"I left dinner on the stove. All you have to do is put together a salad."

"I won't even eat, I ate late and my stomach is in knots."

"OK, just relax, I'll bring you back something."

"Don't bother, Gloria, I may be asleep by the time you get home."

"OK. I shouldn't be that late. Do you want me to put on some tea before I leave?"

"OK, just keep it low I want to take a shower first."

Gloria Tennley poured water into a tea kettle and put it on the stove. She threw her coat across her shoulders and darted out the living room door to the garage.

Rayfer saw the garage door open and Tennley's wife pull out of the driveway. His eyes followed her car until the lights disappeared into the night. He looked back at the house and the open door invitation. A bolt of temptation exploded within him. He realized he hadn't gained enough familiarity with the house and surroundings to attack, but he weighed that prematurity against the element of surprise. He further reasoned he had more than enough guile and strength to nullify the unexpected. He didn't know where Gloria Tennley was going or when she would return, but he knew Tennley was home alone, and there was no one nearby. The opportunity presented itself and Rayfer knew he had to respond.

He started his car and drove to the side street which ran along the side of Tennley's house. Shutting the engine, he walked to the foot of the fence and continued around the house, continually alert for potential witnesses. He came to the far side of the house, immediately adjacent to the open garage door. Looking out at the street, he saw no movement. The street was quiet and deserted. There was nothing to be seen beyond the far side of the property line except the continuation of the high trees. Rayfer couldn't ask for better cover.

He stepped into the garage and quickly stood on the bumper of Tennley's car and unscrewed the bulb rendering the garage dark. He stood motionless for a moment, acclimating his sight to the new environment.

He located the door leading to the living room and moved toward it. Leaning his head slightly, he listened for revealing noise beyond it. Once more he looked toward the street, but now he was well concealed by the car and one of the closed garage doors.

Rayfer turned the knob and opened the door slightly. A beam of light from the living room broke through the small opening and attacked his eyes. Rayfer ignored the light, using it only to see the entire living room and a portion of the kitchen beyond. He stepped into the room and locked the door from the inside. Quietly, he made his way through the room trying to avoid the window to the foot of the kitchen. Rayfer quickly evaluated the kitchen for other revealing windows, blind spots, or closed doors. Midway into the kitchen was an archway, opening into a foyer and eventually a dining room. In the center of the foyer was a staircase which Rayfer assumed led to bedrooms of the second floor. He heard movement from above and eased the Rostfrei from his jacket pocket and rolled it in his gloved hand until he felt a special unity with it. He gripped it gently, trusting the instrument to be his reliable accomplice in quenching an unusual thirst.

Rayfer moved to the foot of the stairs, deciding to ascend and attack.

Somewhere on the upper landing, light cast a moving shadow as Tennley walked about. A thick rug muffled his footsteps.

Rayfer maneuvered the knife to his fingertips and felt the button with his thumb. A mild delirium invaded his mind causing his body to appear light, floating in a realm of forbidden joy. He enjoyed the feeling, but didn't permit it to distract his awareness. He pressed the button softly and the blade responded, becoming an extension of an undesirable eroticism.

He put his foot to the first step, about to embark on one more journey to a land of deranged reason and human calamity. Behind him, out of the silence a shrill noise exploded his stupor. He turned quickly, poised for attack. His eyes searched the unfamiliar surroundings for a perpetrator to his scheme. His mind reacted quickly and determined the noise was the tea kettle he noticed on the stove. He heard the muffled footsteps above him become louder, conveying they were coming closer. Rayfer retreated into the kitchen and backed against a wall away from the foyer.

Tennley descended the stairs, his face revealing annoyance over a personal preoccupation. He walked into the kitchen past Rayfer. He remained oblivious to the intruder and unaware of his impending fate.

Assuming the boiling water could be used as an instrument of defense, Rayfer had to react quickly. He fell in behind Tennley and drove the bottom of his foot violently into Tennley's leg immediately behind the kneecap. The blow collapsed Tennley's leg, causing him to go crashing onto the floor. He tried to rise quickly but Rayfer delivered another well placed kick to Tennley's neck, causing him to emit guttural gasps and choke. In his panic, Tennley looked up and recognized Rayfer. Confusion, disbelief and pain fused together to render him helpless.

For an instant, he derived comfort from a familiar face connected to a distant past sent to help him in his agony, in the next he realized the real purpose of that face. Fear and terror overshadowed all other emotions. Tennley became wild, losing a sense of perception and rationale. He struggled once more, but Rayfer was purposeful, true to his perversion. He circled Tennley coldly, like a wild animal pursuing helpless prey, and delivered another kick, this one landing in his solar plexus. A burst of air lodged in his already closing throat and his struggle to breath became acute. He fell onto his back and rolled to one side. Rayfer stepped close to his head. Tennley tried to plead, but no words came. He reached for Rayfer's legs, but his attacker simply kicked his arms aside.

Rayfer passed the stiletto blade before Tennley's face. His eyes grew wide at the sight of it. He tried reaching, but Rayfer stepped beyond his grasp. A menacing sneer wrinkled Rayfer's upper lip, unbridled delight flamed in his eyes. Tennley tried to ignore his pain, he kicked, aiming for Rayfer's groin. The blow was weak and only grazed his thigh. A blast of anger coated Rayfer's face. He raised his leg and drove down hard onto Tennley's thigh muscle causing his leg to quiver violently and became useless. Rayfer then let his body drop, knee first, onto Tennley's chest. Tennley became lethargic. All fright and pain slowly seeped into unconsciousness and acceptance. He seemed strangely disconnected to the assault heaped upon him. Rayfer squeezed the handle of the knife, found the weak spot behind Tennley's right ear with its tip, and pulled it up sharply. Blood oozed from the slice and ran down Tennley's neck.

A slight sign of annoyance registered on Rayfer's face as he felt a twinge of disappointment that Tennley had passed beyond the ability to feel pain and experience danger. His victim deprived him of a personal pleasure. Blood cascaded freely from his head; his face winced and his mouth opened as though to scream. His body convulsed and his arms trembled uncontrollably.

With his free hand, Rayfer grabbed the other side of Tennley's face and pushed it further into the knife. He held the position until there was no more movement and expression from Tennley. He was still and totally silent. Rayfer knelt down to gain a close-up perspective of the face of death. His lips spread, under another circumstance it would have been a smile, now it was an impulse only he understood. Rayfer finally withdrew the blade and stood up to admire his work. He looked over his shoulder and realized the teapot was still whistling, a sound that for a while he had not heard. He walked slowly to the stove and shut off the flame. The pot responded by going silent.

Rayfer returned his attention to the lifeless body of Tennley. A calm blank look replaced all previous expression. He became satisfied beyond measure and temporarily at peace with all prior grievances.

He saw no reason to formulate an equation between Prescott and Tennley, all that needed focus was his own purpose, which was totally exclusive of other personal petty revenge.

"Fuck Night Shade!" he said. "I do this for me."

FIFTEEN

Mary Cello had spent most of the day sifting through documents and reports in PBN's archives trying to locate the elusive Harmon Keller. She followed the maze of references and cross references, investigative reports and interviews, dating back years before she joined the staff, only to discover a web of bureaucratic concealment and positional arrogance. Her findings were sensational, however, challenging belief, logic and morality.

She gathered several folders of information and slid them into her briefcase. Looking at her watch, she quickly reached for the phone and tapped in a number.

"Clip room," came a voice.

"Billy?"

"Yes."

"Mary Cello."

"Hi, Mary. What can I do for you?"

"Couple of weeks ago there was a killing on the west side, an exec killed a would-be mugger, can you find me the article in the News and Times and bring them to my office? I'll meet you there?"

"You got it."

"Good." Mary depressed the plunger of the phone briefly then dialed an outside number.

"Six twelve, Sergeant Philips."

"Lieutenant Elroy, please."

"Hold on."

Mary held the phone to her ear with her shoulder as she zippered her briefcase.

"Elroy."

"Hi, Larry."

"Hi, Mary. How are you?"

"Fine. How about you?"

"Good."

"Larry, listen, I'm in a rush now, but I did some research on Harmon Keller."

"Good. What did you find out?"

"I don't know, but whatever it is, I have to talk to you about it."

"You sound scared."

"I don't know if scared is the right word, but I have to see you."

"I'll be right over."

"No, I have the homeless coalition meeting tonight. I'm on my way there now."

"I'll pick you up."

"No, that's OK, I've already made arrangements. Larry, just meet me there."

"OK. I will."

"Bailey Hall on Spring Street. Do you...?"

"I know where it is. I'll be there in half an hour."

"Good. See you later."

Mary hung up the phone and slid her briefcase off the desk. Suddenly an ominous image of Keller flared in her mind, taking absolute control of her. He appeared vague, but no less suspicious, representing a faceless organization, capable of deception and treachery, and the reports she carried were a testament to their vast and sinister nature.

She gathered herself and walked to her office, unconsciously keeping the briefcase away from her body as though it contained a foul contaminant.

On her desk was the back issue of the Daily News with a note clipped to the front page.

"Mary, here's the paper with the article you needed. The Times did not carry the story. Billy."

Mary read the story carefully, then folded the paper and inserted it into her briefcase. She suddenly realized Elroy was right, she was harboring a fear which became acute, but not for herself; she was afraid for Elroy and his safety.

Bailey Hall was merely an empty warehouse on Spring Street in lower Manhattan. It was used for community meetings, part-time shelter for various reasons, and periodically served as a registration and voting poll facility.

The room made up the entire lower level of the seven story building which was built at the turn of the century. The lofts above the hall were occupied by people at a time when the building was condemned. Through creativity and hard work, the dwellers turned the living conditions from squalor into pleasant, clean places to live. The turnaround caused landlords to put pressure on the mayor to enact special housing legislation. The landlords wanted to profit from the renovations they themselves had been unwilling to perform and charge increased rents according to the new assessment structure. The people were bringing their own pressure to bear and the mayor was looking for a way out.

A collective low roar emitted from the pockets of people locked in passionate debate. An air of purpose and reform seemed to overtake the stagnant air of the room. With no windows and only two doors, the ventilation was inadequate. As a measure of security, one of the doors was bolted closed, never to be open. Rows of wooden folding chairs stretched the width of the hall, and one row of five chairs and a long table stood at the front facing them. On the wall behind the table was a banner which addressed the group's concern: INNER-CITY COALITION FOR ADEQUATE HOUSING.

Nate Ellerman, prime organizer of the group spotted Mary at the door and broke away from some people to greet her.

Nate had been a long-time friend to Mary and they worked together on occasions such as the protest of the United States involvement in Vietnam and nuclear armament buildup.

"Mary," he said, kissing her cheek.

"Hi, Nate."

"Thanks for coming."

"Anytime, you know that."

"I know. It seems that's all we've done over the years, Mary, is protest, try to raise awareness and stir consciousness."

"Yes, it does. I wish we'd run out of causes though."

"You know better. We're about to start, you ready?"

"Yes. Let's do it."

Nate led Mary through the crowd to the front table. He took her coat and hung it on a rack along the side. He walked to the center of the table and just stood silent a moment, waiting to be noticed and signaling a start to the meeting. Certain clumps of people spotted Nate and took seats and the noise gradually began to decrease.

"OK, can I have your attention!" Nate hollered to the rest. "Can I have your attention please. Please."

Slowly the talking stopped and everyone began to sit. Nate and Mary were joined at the front table by three other co-organizers of the meeting.

"Thank you," Nate announced when the hall was silent.

"I'm glad to see we have a good turnout tonight. And I'm glad to share your commitment for change and I also sense your optimism. I know we'll make a difference.

"Before we begin though, I'd like to introduce the people seated here with me. I know you know them all, but we'll do it anyway....Lester Abrahms, Michael Tilden, Boris Winkler from our Washington contingent, and friend, Mary Cello from Public Broadcast News, and me, I'm Nate Ellerman."

Applause rose up from the group which made Mary feel uncomfortable.

"Thank you, but save the applause for another time--a time when there are no people living on the streets of any city in this damn nation!"

A deafening roar rose up from the hall and Mary watched Nate. She pictured him as he was years younger, leading groups, protesting the war in Vietnam. He still knew how to excite a crowd, move them without manipulation. In a strange way, it all came back to her. A spirit that echoed through the years, a commitment to injustice, a personal crusade for positive change and the triumph of humanity.

The noise subsided slowly as Nate looked out to the crowd. His gaze circled the room and stopped at Mary. She smiled up at him and he knew it was not a smile of victory.

"OK. OK. As you all know in three weeks we are going to stage one of the biggest protest marches City Hall has ever seen. There will be simultaneous marches in Washington, Boston, Detroit, and Los Angeles. Boris

Winkler is here representing his group. From here we will go to Detroit to meet with those people and then on to LA where the organizers of each city will have a final meeting and rally. This will be one of the largest collective efforts, as we try to rid this nation of an unacceptable plague. There is much we need to discuss here and I think we should start tonight's agenda with Mary Cello.

"Mary," Nate said turning to her.

Applause rose once again and Mary stood up and stepped to where Nate was standing in the center of the table. She looked out at the crowd and tried to formulate her thoughts. As she surveyed the crowd she saw Elroy enter and take a seat in the rear.

"Thank you, Nate, co-organizers and you people for having me here...

"Earlier, Nate said to me that over the years it seems all we've done is protest, try to raise awareness and consciousness. Nate and I, and I'm sure many of you too, go back to a time when we stirred the public conscience over events in South East Asia. History still is uncertain if it was our protesting or something else that ended that fiasco. Well I'm here to say I'm certain what the reasons were..."

Loud applause broke into Mary's speech. She paused, focusing only on her thoughts and the message she needed to convey. She waited, looking into the crowd and beyond it.

"We made a difference then and we can do it again," she said over the applause. "But something tells me this is more difficult and we have to be careful in our approach.

"Marches run the risk of becoming media events and do little to dispel the fallacy that housing is a privilege earned, rather than a basic human right. Press coverage is divided into two camps: one that evokes sympathy and the other that blames victims. And, at all times, an uncaring government is perched squarely and steadfastly in the middle. Concerned only within the confines of rhetoric but not justifiable deed.

"Our government commands daily headlines, condemning human rights and atrocities in places such as South Africa or Central America, but is oblivious to their failure to protect a basic human right in this country. This is unacceptable. Totally unacceptable. And we will be here to tell the government just that.

"As I said in a recent television documentary, new legislation is needed...not to protect the people's rights to remain mentally incompetent, to choose a subway grate for a bed, to eat discarded remnants from garbage cans...but to show reason, compassion and justice. The government must also make an adequate financial commitment to those who are unemployed and have nowhere to go...Military spending must decrease dramatically. The cold war paranoia and general naivete of the fifties is over. We are all too aware today. Vietnam and Watergate have ushered in a new age of enlightenment and responsibility and we are going to hold politicians accountable for their actions. Their priorities and arrogance must change, especially since they have lost the ability to recognize their purpose. They must act in the best interest of the people as we see it, not the way they think it should be. In short, politicians must get out of the business of politics and get into the business of humanity...I will be using my office any way I can to reach that end. I support you in our collective endeavors, and this is a fight we can win. Thank you."

Mary stepped back as applause and cheers rang in her ears. Nate approached her and they embraced.

"That's the kind of inspiration we need. Beautiful," he said into her ear.

"God, how did the world get so messed up, Nate?"

"Who knows...I see it happening and I still can't explain it," He responded

★★★

Mary sat next to Elroy, feeling drained by her findings of the day. The exhilaration she felt from her involvement with the group slowly started to subside, leaving her quiet and tired.

She was curled up, her head resting on his chest. Elroy brushed hair away from her eyes and kissed her head.

"Mary, I can't believe how effective you were tonight. You should be proud of your contribution and commitment," he whispered.

"Thank you, Larry, but I realized something tonight. Awareness has a price and vigilance takes its toll. After a while you look for isolation...well not really isolation as much as solitude."

"Most efforts take a long time to exact change."

"I know, but right now all I want is a warm shower and sleep. Can I stay here with you tonight?"

"You're welcome to stay anytime, Mary. I never want you to leave," he responded. And, as she smiled, he asked, "What was it you had to tell me?"

"In my briefcase."

"Where is it?"

"I'll get it."

Mary sat up and reached over for her briefcase. She withdrew folders and placed them on the table. Her slow, lethargic mood quickly turned to quiet concern. Segments of distrust, suspicion, and mystery came together, dictating the look in her eyes, and regulating her level of anxiety.

"I have them in some sort of order. Here," she said, opening the first folder.

"There is little on Harmon Keller himself, but reading these reports, one has to assume he is a constant part of something. The name that does keep coming up is even more interesting."

"Who's that?"

"Emmet Prescott, Junior."

"That name is very familiar. Where do I know it from?"

"The exec who was involved in the attempted robbery on the west side..."

"OK yeah! The one in the elevator."

"Yes."

"He's CIA?"

"Yes."

"There was never a mention of that in the papers."

"I know. I have the paper here. I just read it. No mention at all. What does that tell you?"

"A lot. None of it good. Tell me about him."

"OK. His main area was chemicals and drug experimentation..."

"Interesting."

"It gets better. Operation Paper Clip started the whole thing in the early fifties. Prescott was too young to be CIA then, but it's a good reference point..."

"What was Paper Clip?"

"Basically it was a project supervised by the CIA to recruit hundreds of Nazi scientists who were involved with chemical and drug experiments during the war. The CIA wanted their data because they were looking for a truth drug, a mind control substance..."

"Yeah, I remember they were conveniently spared the Nuremberg Trials."

"Exactly. In any event, the experiments continued over the years as various different projects. Project MK-ULTRA was one that was established and that's the first time we see Prescott's name. MK-ULTRA was a highly secretive program that experimented with Seconal, Dexedrin, Pentothal Desoxyn and LSD. Even Strychnine, Tachrin, Neurokinin, Digitoxin, I can't even pronounce these names...They had a tremendous fascination with LSD."

"What was it all for?"

"Mostly mind control. But strychnine is a poison. Ahh...it says here tachrin induces vomiting and digitoxin induces a heart attack."

"I'm sure they had to prove it on people."

"I'm sure."

"Nice guys."

"To say the least."

"It looks like LSD was a cornerstone in their search for psychochemical weapons long before it became used in the hip counterculture. Here, read this," she said handing Elroy sheets of paper.

"This one," she said, pointing to the first sheet, "reports their indiscriminate use on unsuspecting citizens."

"Even on their staff at Christmas office parties?" Elroy questioned after reading.

"Yes. They were buying the stuff from a pharmaceutical company in Switzerland until they were able to reconstruct the compounds," Mary commented.

"Take a look at this, you might find this interesting," she continued handing Elroy more paper.

He read the report quickly.

"God...According to this, they experimented with prisoners, mental patients, foreigners, ethnic minorities in a public health service hospital in Lexington."

"Yes, but the facility was actually a penitentiary. It was only one the report mentions. Actually there were fifteen institutions where they did the same."

"It says inmates were given LSD every day to overcome tolerances and that the doses constantly increased. And if they volunteered they were given heroin and morphine."

"Yes. The CIA violated the Nuremberg code of ethics as it related to scientific research," Mary commented.

"I'm not too sure the inmates minded that so much."

"Probably not. But Lexington was designated specifically to cure heroin addicts."

"Brilliant...According to this," Elroy said reading another document, "...the CIA employed other organizations to conduct their experiments."

"Yes, they had go-betweens to hide behind."

Elroy sat back and continued reading.

"Look at this," he said. "Did you see this?"

"Which is that?"

"The institute in Canada that uses sleep therapy."

"Yes."

"You mean they actually put people to sleep for months at a time, then gave them electroshock treatments and doses of LSD?"

"Surprised?"

"You know, I knew they were a bizarre organization, even the police do things we're not supposed to, but this is ridiculous...And Prescott was behind it all?"

"I don't know if he was behind it all, but he was certainly involved...Here listen to this," Mary said, reading from a sheet of paper she held.

"San Francisco, Haight-Ashbury, Nineteen sixty-seven...remember?"

"I was in Vietnam then, but I know what you're talking about."

"The summer of love."

"Yes."

"Well a lot of LSD was laced with many contaminants. Among them was phencyclidine--PCP."

"Angel dust."

"Exactly. PCP was originally an animal tranquilizer, but servicemen were tested with it in the early fifties with vague results. The CIA stockpiled it, then conveniently set up laboratories in the Bay Area. They once again tested hallucinogenic drugs on unknowing citizens, but phased it out two or three years before the summer of love. Then suddenly in sixty-seven they started up again and reports indicate they were thought to be mixing in PCP and monitoring reactions."

"They weren't the only ones making the stuff though."

"Absolutely not. Drugs had always been a commodity everybody wanted a piece of, but the CIA was in the thick of it."

"Where's Keller when all this is going on?"

"Well, it was established he worked under Prescott, but that's about it. Other than him receiving a medical discharge almost two years ago, there's nothing."

Mary put the papers down and turned to Elroy.

"Larry, these reports go on and on naming different drugs and operations. But what frightens me is their ability, I mean they stop at nothing, and nothing means anything to them. That's why I'm afraid for you."

"Prescott and Keller are both out of the CIA now."

"Maybe so but...they still have that training, that mentality. That...that...oh I don't know. Look at the incident with Prescott and his attacker. Here, read this quote from him in the paper. He's upset he says. His tone is that of a naive farm boy. Does that sound like a man who has been doing what he's been doing for years? Or do his words ring false?"

"I agree."

"Now, can you believe the mugger really fell on his knife?"

"I don't know."

"Oh, Larry, if there's one thing you can say for a New York mugger, they are not that clumsy. You should know."

"Yeah, it does make it a little different...There's a footnote here that makes a reference to Night Shade. What's that?"

"I don't know. I checked, but there was nothing on file. I assume Night Shade was another experiment."

Elroy rose from the couch and walked to the window. His thoughts elsewhere, out of the present. He turned and looked at Mary.

"What's the matter?" she asked.

"Keller worked for Prescott..."

"Yes. Why?"

"Assume for a moment it was Keller who broke into Miriam Ludlow's apartment. She said the man had a hatchet or an axe in his hand. Obviously he was intent on destruction, and obviously he broke into the wrong apartment."

"What does it mean, Larry?"

"Well, I may know what it means...but not why."

Mary looked at Elroy trying to avoid the premonition that began to formulate in her mind. Her eyes displayed a forlorn concern and worry.

"You look tired, Mary, why don't you take that warm shower and let's get some sleep."

★★★

The hot water formed a pleasant mist which clung to the walls and ceiling, obscuring the mirror and hollowing the lights. It filled the room, making it feel like a soft dream with no discernable definition or coarse edges. Harsh reality stood lurking beyond the door, anticipating a moment yet to come, but for now it was forbidden to encroach upon the tranquil haze.

Mary stood directly under the cascading water, her hair wet, pressed down flat against her head and shoulders. Her eyelids fluttered, defending against the spray. Elroy held her close, his hands slowly following the contours of her hips and buttocks, caressing her through to her soul. He felt her whole body pressing into his skin, going beyond carnal sensuality and external desire. He brought her close so she could saturate him to the core and lay claim to his very existence.

Mary repositioned her left leg and wrapped it around his thigh. Her arms embraced his head drawing him onto her chest. She suddenly recognized a personal vulnerability she was unaware existed before she met him. Now, whether real or imaginary, all things became a threat and instinctively she tried to protect him from harm.

"Larry," she said on the brink of tears.

"Yes?"

"Be careful."

SIXTEEN

Night descended upon the city, touching off a tempered alliance between distrust and gaiety. The streets crawled with prowling villains eager for a score. Their alert eyes assessed potential victims; their cunning guaranteed ruthless assault at any unguarded moment. Faceless forms peddled flesh, as unholy partnerships waged disproportionate transactions, bartering souls for vice.

Bars and restaurants pulsated with an upbeat tempo. Lives undulated within vague rapture, embracing a spirit which imitated flight from general repression, as a unique symphony echoed a chord of human disparity.

Emmet Prescott was oblivious to the contrasts and the cold wind that slapped at him as he crossed Second Avenue. A lonely page of newspaper blew by his feet. His frame passed through vapor rising through a manhole cover, but all he focused on was the figure standing still on the opposite corner. He approached Rayfer, and they continued walking together in silence.

"How did it go in Princeton?" Prescott finally asked.

"Well."

"Problems?"

"None."

"Good."

Prescott withdrew an envelope from his pocket and handed it to Rayfer.

"That should cover it."

"Fine."

"You'll notice an address in there as well."

"OK."

"Hyatt came through, he tracked down Keller."

"He's a genius."

"Yes...the best."

"There's also Keller's doctor there...his address...that's where he showed up."

"Good."

"Tell me...how did Tennley behave?"

"Like most."

"Was he frightened? Did he plead?"

"Yes."

A slight sneer formed on Prescott's face and a sinister delight twinged in the pit of his stomach.

"How did the end come?"

"Blade...behind the ear."

Prescott envisioned the murder, incorporating his own perverse imagination. His inner visionary concept culminated the years of waiting.

"Beautiful...Beautiful....Was he able to resist?"

"He tried."

"Did he...?"

"He was no match. There was only one way for him to go."

"Fine. Fine...Thank you, Rayfer."

They continued walking in silence. Prescott remained engrossed with the satisfying result. He felt placated and relieved, his thirst for revenge quenched.

Rayfer touched the envelope containing the money; it allowed him the diversion he needed to conceal the disdain he felt for Prescott.

"I'm now anxious to see the final stage of this operation completed," Prescott finally announced.

"You will."

"Soon?"

"At the earliest possible convenience."

"Good."

"Tell me, Emmet, once this is done, what then?"

"That ends it."

"No, I mean what will you do?"

Prescott thought for a moment, then stopped walking. He turned and looked at Rayfer; his natural tentativeness toward Rayfer mixed with his own annoyance produced an immediate scorn he hoped would not be visible.

"What will you do?" Prescott countered.

With the help of the medication, Harmon Keller realigned his life. He ate and rested well, and exercised daily; his running increased to three miles a day. Evidence of his activity of the prior year was nonexistent. He gradually returned to a state of good health and environment. The temporary deficiencies he had imposed upon himself had not caused permanent physical damage and Keller relegated the time to a bad dream, on the verge of forgetfulness. Of that time, all that lingered in his mind was the man he attacked with his axe. Keller hoped that time would rearrange the memory of it as well.

Now that he began to stabilize, his truer nature rematerialized. He reflected on the past and tempered it with acceptance. The recollecting of Prescott lingered with passive ambivalence. New forms of thought restructured possible action and redefined approaches. He pondered the value of reprisal, reasoning it would only recommit him to the very thing he tried to escape. He welcomed a new beginning, one void of agitation and battles. The past would only manage to garner futility in the future.

Keller returned to his passion for reading classic French and Russian literature. Several books were on his night table, a New York Times rested on his bed. He had circled several ads for rental apartments and jobs. Hotel living had become comfortable, but expensive, and a steady job would complete his recovery.

He stood by the window, sipping orange juice. The bright sun streamed into his room. He felt its warmth penetrating his jogging suit and layered thermal under-wear. The warm sun soothed him; he felt calm, almost mesmerized. Reflections of the past were fragmented in his mind. Half-remembered faces tumbled together with forgotten names; all that remained was himself, and vague comprehension. He envisioned himself as a boy running through his father's farm in West Virginia. Behind him his sister shouting his name. He remembered racing her down hills by rolling like little barrels. At the bottom they would be dizzy and try to stand. They would run across the farm. "Harmon wait up," Linda would shout, "Wait up!" as she struggled in vain to catch him. Keller could see his sister's bright face and golden hair. Her laughter reverberated through the years. He can still see her and himself, the visions of two children, lost in a strange enchanted land, irrevocably changed by time and its consistent fickleness.

Time and distance blended irretrievably into the present with no traces of where it all went. He thought of his sister, now the only other surviving member of his family. She must be worried, he thought. It had been well over a year since he called her and he knew she had no way of knowing what had become of him.

He put the empty glass on the tray and raised his foot onto the chair and tied the lace of his sneaker. After his run he decided to call her.

★★★

Keller took long deep breaths of the cold air. He grabbed his leg at the top of the shinbone and brought his knee up to his chest. He repeated the procedure with his other leg. Content his legs were somewhat limber, he began walking at a brisk pace. After a block, he broke into a moderate trot. The air pushed against his face as his breath came out in white puffs. To him running was the true evaluation of a man. The limits his mind could push his body to, equated to the sum total of his accomplishments. Running was individual in structure. Time, distance and competition were merely outside measures.

Keller's breathing became deep, his heart pounded heavily and his legs and chest ached. He continued challenging the cold and ignoring his discomfort, seeking his personal best. People he passed appeared dazed; blank expressions filled their eyes. In the street, a car horn blared and tires screeched, someone shouted and the traffic continued to rush by. Bits of movement and expression formed a contrasting montage of impersonal proportions. Chaos struggled against the backdrop of numbness and Keller searched for his place within it all.

He felt the pavement hard against his feet, but he sensed the illusion of tall corn brushing against his arms. An imaginary open field lay endlessly before him, an ocean of grass flowing in the wind.

"Harmon, wait up!" Linda's voice echoed in his mind.

His pace quickened, he struggled in a desperate attempt to either run back in time or further away from the memory. He realized either direction bore its own level of distinct melodrama.

"Wait up!" he heard once more. The memory haunted him, yet filled him with delight.

★★★

Keller walked across the lobby of his hotel to the elevators. His eyes were tearing and his chest heaved. He felt perspiration dripping down his back, his body no longer affected by the cold.

The elevator doors opened and Keller stepped in. He depressed the "8" button and leaned back against the wall. Bending over at the waist he rested his palms upon his knees, supporting his torso. Long deep breaths escaped him as perspiration from his face fell onto the floor. The elevator ascended taking him to his floor.

The glass door to the lobby opened and Rayfer stepped in accompanied by a blast of cold air. He moved across the lobby slowly and stepped into the card shop.

"Hello," a matronly woman seated at the cash register said quietly as he entered.

"Hi," Rayfer responded, walking past her.

He made his way to a bookrack and reached for a book. From his vantage point he was able to see the entire lobby area and the elevators adjacent to the registration desk.

The lobby was deserted. For the moment the information and registration desks were unoccupied.

Rayfer took the book and approached the sales clerk.

"Will there be anything else?"

"No...What time do you close?" Rayfer asked.

"Seven during the week and five on the weekend."

"Fine."

Rayfer paid for the book and walked to the elevator. He surveyed his surroundings, making a mental note of all exits and staircases.

The elevator opened and Rayfer took it to the seventh floor. He left the elevator and took the stairs to the eighth floor where he opened the door slightly and peered into the hallway.

The corridor was narrow with a low ceiling. Lighting was adequate for his purpose. A maid had unlocked a linen closet and was placing clean towels onto her cleaning cart. On the other end a door of a room opened and a guest started walking toward the elevators.

Rayfer closed the door and waited until the man passed. He heard the elevator door open then close once again. Rayfer opened the door and walked into the hallway. The maid had disappeared, down another portion of the corridor, leaving the floor deserted. Rayfer started walking slowly down the hall until he spotted room 811. A level of excitement surfaced as he neared his prey. Beyond the door was Keller who, in turn, was only a means to appease his wicked instinct. He paused briefly, suppressing an urge to attack. His instinct to kill was overcome by his need for caution. He knew he had to wait, accepting the fact that planning was crucial, an intricate part to death which Rayfer savored because it bore its own brand of demented pleasure.

"You're mine, Keller," he growled quietly from the bottom of his throat. "You're mine."

Linda Carson sat in her den writing out checks for her monthly expenses. Her desk was strewn with papers, torn envelopes, a large folder containing her personal checks, and a calculator. The sunlight came through the glass facade which made up one entire wall of the room. In the center were French doors which opened to a flagstone patio. Some fifty feet beyond the patio was an in-ground pool covered with blue vinyl and a pile of dried leaves. A line of pine trees bordered the property creating privacy and a sense of seclusion.

Linda gently pushed her glasses off her nose and sipped tea. She put down her pen and directed her attention to the day beyond her window. Staring casually at the blue sky, she became momentarily lost in silent reflection.

She rose from her chair and walked to the French doors. A slight wind blew the leaves from the pool covering to a pile along a fence surrounding the entire pool.

A breath of melancholy was fanned on her by the barrenness of winter. The delicate harmony of nature presented a lonely contrast to the vibrancy and activity of summer. Winter seemed to form a perfect backdrop to the bleakness that for no apparent reason engulfed her.

The short burst of the phone ringing distracted her. Linda walked through the living room, placed her glasses on the desk and reached for the phone as it rang a second time.

"Hello," she said.

"Hi, honey," came her husband's voice.

"Hi, Paul. How are you?"

"Good. What are you doing?"

"Writing out some bills. Are you busy?"

"A little. How would you like to drive in and have lunch with me?"

"Now?"

"Yes."

"I thought you were going to have lunch with Gail for her birthday?"

"That's next Wednesday."

"Oh, that's right. OK, let's see, what time is it?" she said looking at her watch.

"It's twelve thirty. You could be here before one if you left now."

Suddenly Linda heard a beep in her phone.

"Paul, hold on, I've got another call."

She tapped the plunger of her phone once quickly, allowing her access to receive the second call.

"Hello," she said.

"Hello, Linda," came the voice. A wad of fear and excitement lumped simultaneously within her throat and stomach. She was displaced, unable to speak or breathe.

"Linda?" asked the voice again.

"Harmon?" she managed to whisper.

"Yes."

Linda felt a sudden burst of guarded memories and new fears. Her mind shifted, relentlessly unable to focus. Her reactions became emotional instincts. She wanted to scream, to vent a consuming worry she had carried for the last year. But she remained motionless, listening to the beating of her heart. Her breathing became short and quick.

"Harmon," she finally managed.

"Hello, Linda."

"Harmon, is it you?"

"Yes."

"God, Harmon are you all right?"

"Yes."

"Where have you been? I haven't heard from you for a year."

"It's a long story. I'm in New York now."

"New York?"

"Yes."

"Are you sure you're all right?"

"Yes, I'm fine. I'm fine."

"Why haven't I heard from you in over a year? It's not like you. Were you sick or something?"

"Well yes and no. I'm fine now. Trust me. Trust me....How are you?"

Linda was unable to respond, emotion obliterated her thoughts.

"Linda you OK?"

"Yes, I'm fine. It's just that I was so worried...and..."

"Hey, come on, I'm sorry I didn't call you sooner, but everything is ok...How's Paul?"

"He's fine. Harmon can you hold on I'm talking to him now. Don't go away. I'll be right back to you."

"OK."

Linda tapped the plunger once again.

"Paul?"

"Honey..."

"Paul, let me call you back. I'm talking to Harmon."

"Harmon?"

"Yes. I'll call you back."

"Fine."

Linda hit the plunger once again. She noticed her fingers were rigid and tense. She gripped the phone with uncommon intensity.

"Harmon?"

"I'm here, Linda."

"God, I was so worried about you."

"I kinda figured you were."

"For you not to call, I thought something awful happened to you."

"Well if it did, you know someone would have contacted you."

"Never mind. I called the CIA, they wouldn't tell me anything about you. Your friends didn't know where you were. I was going crazy, thinking the worst."

"I'm sorry, Linda, I can explain it all. I just wanted to tell you I'm OK and everything is working out...How's Laurie?"

"She's fine."

"How about yourself?"

"I'm OK. You know that during the winter, I don't get that involved with the horse club. I'm not as active, I get bored, then depressed a little."

"Isn't there anything else you can do?"

"Oh sure, but to be honest, I welcome the winter rest, I just have to deal with my reactions...Where are you working, Harmon?"

"I'm not."

"No job?"

"No. I'm living off my disability pension."

"Is it enough?"

"Sure, plenty, even by New York standards."

"Where in New York are you living?"

"In a hotel."

"Hotel?!"

"Yes, it's a long story, when I see you I'll explain it."

"Harmon?"

"Yes?"

"I received a call from Gloria Tennley last week."

"You're kidding."

"No."

"I didn't know you kept in touch. How's she doing? How's John?"

There was a long pause and Harmon knew the silence was a bad omen.

"Linda, what happened to John?"

"He was killed."

"Killed?"

"Yes."

"How?"

"Well...he was...murdered."

"Murdered?!"

"Yes. Gloria is distraught, obviously."

"What happened?"

"She went out for a while one night and when she came home she found him on the kitchen floor."

"Was it a burglary?"

"No. Nothing was missing."

"Was he shot?"

"No...God it's awful..."

"How was he killed?"

"Stabbed in the neck, head, I don't know."

Keller went cold. An abstract vision pressed through his mind. Suddenly all the progress and reevaluated thought of the past weeks became snagged into an inescapable web.

"Harmon?...Harmon?..."

"Yes?"

"What's it all about? Do you know something?"

"No, don't be silly. I just feel bad for John and Gloria," he said trying to be convincing.

"Gloria feels it was someone from the CIA. She asked about you. Wanted to know where you were."

"Why?"

"I don't know. I only know she didn't believe that I didn't know where you were. She made me think you knew something about it."

"Did she say that?"

"No, I just got the feeling."

"I'll call her."

"Harmon?..."

"Yes?"

"Why would the agency want to kill John?"

"Oh, be serious Linda."

"I am. Gloria is convinced. She said you and John were working on something secret, then he suddenly was sent to Central America and you went to Angola. Then you both got early medical retirement, and you disappear for a year and John gets killed."

"What does one have to do with the other?"

"I don't know. I just don't trust secrecy and your former employer."

"Well, don't worry. I'm fine and what happened to John is probably unrelated. We've both been retired for more than a year now."

"Well you have to realize we deal with distrust and it always makes things worse."

"Well don't worry. I'm going to rent a car and go see Gloria, then I'll take a flight to see you."

"OK, that would be great. It's been a long time."

"Yes it has. I want to get some of my stuff, do you still have that key?"

"Yes...Why?" Linda asked cautiously.

"No real reason, I just need some insurance policies and stocks."

"Sure?"

"Yes. Yes. Don't be so suspicious, Linda."

"If you say so."

"I say so. I'll probably be down to see you in two or three days."

"I'll look forward to it."

"Me too. Say hello to Paul and Laurie. I bet Laurie's getting so big."

"Senior in high school."

"Oh, don't tell me. I don't believe it."

"Yes, I know, strange isn't it?"

"To say the least...OK listen don't worry about anything Linda, I'll call you before I come, we'll sit and talk."

"Good, see you then. God it's been so good hearing your voice again."

"Yeah, I know, me too...See you in two days."

Linda hung up the phone and walked to her desk. She looked down at the papers and tried to free her mind of everything that caused her doubt and mistrust. An ambivalent smile crossed her face. No matter what her brother told her, she remained concerned and frightened and wished she wouldn't learn the things she was about the learn.

Keller watched from his window at the traffic below. He seemed far removed from its impersonal activity, disconnected by an individual problem which affected relativity and governed the world of isolationism. He wanted to affect the past by changing the future, but he knew the past demonstrated its own form of insidiousness by catching up to John Tennley. Keller also knew, he too was subject to the same trappings, and suddenly he became fearful.

SEVENTEEN

Elroy stepped off the elevator at the third floor of the Ryser Chemical building. He made his way down a hallway until he came to a receptionist area. The area was relatively quiet and bright. The low murmur from the heating ducts provided a constant muted sound, while florescent lighting created an artificial botanical environment for the many potted plants that stood by the receptionist's desk.

"Can I help you?" the receptionist asked as Elroy moved to her desk.

"Yes. I'd like to see Mister Prescott please."

"Is he expecting you?"

"Yes, I called earlier. My name is Lawrence Elroy."

"Oh, yes Mister Elroy, one moment please."

The receptionist reached for her phone and pressed an intercom button.

"Mister Elroy to see you," she said after a slight pause.

Elroy could hear Prescott's voice from where he stood.

"Would you follow me please, Mister Elroy," she said rising from behind her desk.

Elroy followed her through a door and into a dark stately office. The room was in total contrast to the reception area. Although there were ceiling-to-floor windows, thick, heavy drapes prevented total sunlight from entering. There were no plants and no pictures on the walls. A black leather couch seemed to grow out of one wall like a fungus and the large mahogany desk Prescott sat at was disproportionate to the size of the room. There were two wooden chairs at the foot of the desk which appeared scaled down in relationship to the desk.

Prescott's chair was black, matching the leather couch, but with an unusually high back, and the seat appeared raised unusually high. In an instant Elroy knew anyone seated in the chair before the desk would be positioned much lower than Prescott, overpowered by the size of his desk and the exaggerated height of Prescott's chair.

"Mister Elroy," the receptionist announced and then quickly left, closing the door behind her.

"Come in Mister Elroy," Prescott barked. "Sit down."

"I know you're very busy, so I won't take much of your time. I won't even sit."

A suspicious look immediately filled Prescott's face. He knew Elroy had recognized the disadvantaging ploy of the chairs. He felt a minor defeat and was unable to disguise his disdain. The sphere of battle had immediately been formed between them. Prescott didn't respond, but his belligerence was evident.

"I just want to ask you some questions."

Prescott didn't move or respond. He just waited in icy silence.

"Mister Prescott do you know Harmon Keller?"

"I did."

"In what capacity?"

"Why Sergeant?"

Elroy was too streetwise not to recognize Prescott's arrogance and antagonism. For an instant he wanted to end the questioning by driving his fist into his face.

"Lieutenant Elroy, not Sergeant...What was the capacity?" Elroy said, jockeying for position.

"He worked for me," Prescott said deliberately, not apologizing for the mistake in rank.

"In the CIA?"

A look of total anger was Prescott's new expression. If Elroy's instincts were correct, he expected Prescott to leap across the table like a wounded bear.

"Yes."

"Can you describe the nature of the work he was involved in?"

"I'm sorry, that's classified."

"Have you seen him recently?"

"I'm retired from the CIA."

"Have you seen him recently?" Elroy repeated, trying to override Prescott's evasiveness.

"No."

"When did you see him last?"

"Perhaps two years ago."

Elroy knew Prescott wasn't going to offer more information than necessary. He just hoped he could rely on its authenticity.

"Two years. Is that how long you've been away from the CIA?"

"No."

"How long have you been retired from them?"

"I thought you wanted to talk about Keller."

"I do. I'm just trying to fill in the two year gap."

"Two years ago he was reassigned to Angola."

"Under your command?"

"No, a reassignment in command also."

"He served in Angola for two years?"

"No."

"How long?"

"One year."

"Then what?"

"In Angola he contracted malaria and took early medical retirement."

"You haven't seen him since he was assigned in Angola?"

"That's what I said."

Elroy's eyes burned with a controlled fury. His direct stare never left Prescott's. It was a silent confrontation of wills.

"Where does he live?"

"No idea."

"Where did he live when he worked for you?"

"Virginia."

"Langley?"

"Manassas."

"Does he have any family?"

"Look, you're taking up too much of my time. What's this all about?"

"It's about official police business."

"Can't you find another way to conduct your official business?"

"I most certainly can."

"Without threatening to take me to headquarters."

"That's not what I had in mind."

Prescott sensed an impending assault. He rose silently and leaned across the desk. A vein in his forehead protruded and he snarled like a bull about to charge.

"Is that a threat?" he growled.

Elroy's hands folded to hard fists. He stepped closer to the desk, prepared to walk through it to get at Prescott.

"It's what you make it."

"I don't like your manner Lieutenant."

"I don't give a fuck what you like or don't! I don't give a fuck how much time I take either! I just want answers! Does he have family?"

Prescott stood stone-like, unmoved by challenge, impervious to intimidation. He briefly balanced contempt within omission, arrogantly defying Elroy and his authority. He was resolved to give no quarter and prepared for any occurrence.

"Family? Does he have any?" Elroy snarled.

Prescott simmered, wanting to explode. He had assumed a posture he was prepared to defend, but he also recognized the marked futility. His best way out was a strategic retreat.

"Sister," he said with a cold, harsh sneer.

"Married?"

"Um hum," Prescott uttered.

"Married name?"

"Carson."

"Living in Virginia?"

"Prince William at the time."

Elroy heard himself asking how to contact the sister, but he was not willing to deal with the air of superiority with which Prescott was likely to respond.

"What's her husband's first name?"

"How should I know?"

"Because the CIA makes it their business to know everything."

"I'm not CIA now."

"Oh no?...Thank you Mister Prescott, I'll be in touch," Elroy said in a tone that implied threat.

"Anytime," Prescott responded.

Elroy made his way out of the office, past the receptionist, to the elevator. He started to lose control of his pent up anger and punched at the "down" button. Prescott's antagonistic, insipid attitude was the perfect ingredient for an adversarial confrontation. A chemical reaction that was the foundation of a challenge.

Inside the elevator Elroy glanced down and envisioned Michael Baylor's bloody body. He had no doubt Baylor tried to mug Prescott, but now he was equally certain Prescott murdered him vigilante style.

★★★

Gloria Tennley displayed tremendous restraint. The loss of her husband was devastating; the brutality and invasion to her home was frightening and the effects were evident. Her slender body was now frail. Her once sharp facial features had suddenly become drawn and hollow. She sat opposite Keller, filled with grief and horror which ran together and wildly formed accusation.

"Gloria...I'm sorry. I know how you must feel."

"No you don't...The CIA kills for its own purposes, but never is it concerned with the effect it has on a human level. You don't know it because you don't understand it."

Keller accepted her scorn and didn't try to defend himself or persuade her otherwise, mainly because he knew she was right. He sat silently, giving her anger a chance to subside.

"You're right, Gloria, I don't know what it's like, but I am sorry. John was a friend."

"I'm sorry too, John always said you were different...you had a conscience. It's just that I lumped you in with the rest of them."

"What makes you think John was killed by CIA?"

"Come on Harmon, look at it. The worst enemy John made since he left the agency was a disgruntled customer whose car wasn't cleaned properly."

"Was he in contact with anyone from the agency since he left?"

"No. You were the only one, and we haven't seen you for a year."

"Yes, well..."

"They must have been watching us for a long time. They must have known every Wednesday night I attended a Ladies Auxiliary meeting...They just picked this one," she said, bravely suppressing her tears.

Keller reached across to Gloria and squeezed her hand gently. He wanted to know more about the murder, but didn't know how to ask.

"How's Tommy?"

"Fine," she said as a minute trace of a smile crossed her. lips.

"He flew in from Okinawa. He's a great comfort."

"I'm not surprised, John was proud of him, you both did a good job in raising him."

"Thank you, it was easy, Tommy had a great disposition."

"Is he going to career with the Navy?"

"Yes."

"That's good. That's good."

Gloria reached for a tissue on the table by her knees. She patted her eyes and wiped her nose. She rolled the moist tissue up in a ball and kept it in her clenched fist.

"Harmon what happened two years ago?"

"What are you referring to?"

"Immediately after Ed Hodge died you were sent abruptly to Angola and John to San Salvador...I knew something was wrong. John was upset about it. It was something that seemed unplanned and out of context with normal operations."

"Did he say anything about that?"

"Anything he said, I'm sure you knew. He spoke more to you than to me....He did allude to the fact that

Emmet Prescott was responsible and was making it a punishment assignment."

"Did he say that specifically?"

"No. He didn't want to worry me. But I felt John and yourself were purposefully put into a dangerous environment...Like it was punishment for something."

"Like what?"

"I don't know. I know you had fallen from grace with Emmet Prescott."

Suddenly Gloria stopped and looked suspiciously at Keller. "Why are you asking me this Harmon?"

"I don't know. I'm trying to figure it all out myself."

"You make me feel that I'm right about the agency being behind it."

"I don't know."

"Why did Prescott turn against both of you?"

"I don't know that he did."

"Don't play CIA games with me Harmon, I've lost too much, I deserve more."

"Yes you do."

"John said as long as Ed Hodge was around things were contained. What control was he able to exert?"

"He was a decent man."

"And Prescott was not?"

"No."

"He took over from Hodge?"

"Yes, he did."

"So when Hodge died, you and John lost his protection?"

"Yes."

"From what?"

"Gloria, that was all a long time ago. It was about departmental policies, it wouldn't carry over to now, not with these results."

"How can you be so sure? To some men killing is a game. Time is no element and reason doesn't factor in. It all has to do with their own mental deformity, and who can gauge that?"

"That's true, but the men in the agency didn't deal in petty revenge."

"Who are you trying to convince, me or yourself...Look Harmon, psychotics are everywhere, look at the world."

Keller lowered his eyes in defeat.

"Don't think I'm naive, Harmon, I never was, it's just now, I'm bitter and angry, and I want to know why my husband was killed."

"I wish I could give you that answer, Gloria."

"I'm sure you could open some doors to the past that would give me some ideas."

"I'm sure I could, but that would be his life's work, not this."

"Harmon?"

"Yes?"

"What was Night Shade?"

"Night Shade?"

"Yes."

"Did John talk about it?"

"He mentioned it."

"Night Shade was a code name for an operation we were involved in. But that was years ago...When we were in New York."

"That was fifteen years ago."

"More like seventeen. I don't see how that would have any bearing."

"I don't either. I remember John saying he and you were involved in an operation years ago that was abruptly brought to a halt. Years later I heard the term

Night Shade and assumed all the trouble started from that."

"We took some heat, but it was normal departmental problems."

"Was Prescott involved in it?"

"Yes, John and I worked under him then."

"Did Prescott reassign you and John?"

"Well there are many factors in reassignments."

"Did Prescott reassign you?"

"Well..."

"Tell me straight."

"Yes."

"Why?"

"He was a vindictive man."

"Vindictive enough to kill John?"

Keller paused as a lifelong association with Prescott flashed in his mind. The question caused abstract thoughts to race through a maze of knowledge and search for a simple truth. But in the end, Keller knew, truth delivered more pain than consolation.

"I don't know...I really don't know."

★★★

Keller elected to drive the rented car to his sister's house. He pushed through Delaware and Washington heading toward Virginia. The area was familiar to him and conjured up a melancholy that slumped in on his heart. His mind assembled vague fragments from the past which constructed a sphere of awfulness around him. So much had engulfed him that he was unable to separate himself from the pillage of disillusionment that surrounded him. It sounded a deafening bell, numbing his senses and obliterating excuses, leaving reason out there, but nowhere to be found.

Keller struggled with his inability to tell Gloria about Night Shade. Was it a pretext to protect her from a painful truth and terrifying probability, or was he imprisoned by the code of duty that still kept him blind, successfully stripping him of his own identity, morality, and sense of justice? Was he so securely woven into the tapestry of deceit, that no matter how desperately he tried, he could never completely absolve himself? He wondered.

He agonized more with his own thought and intentions than he did with the probability that Prescott had killed John. But that too flooded cracks and formed streams of possibilities. If Prescott killed Tennley was it really an old vendetta? Was it possible Prescott entombed it for so many years, excavating it at a time when torment vaulted the boundary of sensibility? At times Keller thought it was totally absurd, at other times he was able to see the possibility. Keller knew after Ed Hodge died a new season had suddenly opened and there was no one to know the motive. Keller reexamined the nature of the assignments to Angola and El Salvador at a time when danger was at a premium. His own physical condition was all Prescott's doing, he knew, and it all coincided with Hodge's death. And now that Tennley and Prescott were no longer members of the CIA, there was no visible connection. The crime could be perfect.

If it all went beyond Keller's speculation, he reasoned his own fate had been determined as well. For the past year he knew he was untraceable, but now that he resurfaced, Prescott could easily track him down. A new threat soaked Keller throughout which warranted an old pattern of caution be resurrected and practiced. Once again he reevaluated his purpose and determined that his past would not set him free.

Elroy lay face down on his bed. His hand reached around to his neck and he massaged it gently. The room was dark and quiet, his sensitivity to light and noise was acute. He rolled side to side trying to imbed his face into the pillow in hopes of becoming one with its softness which, in turn, would help him transcend his pain.

"Can I get you something, Larry?" Mary whispered.

"No."

"God, you seem to be in so much pain."

"Mary, why don't you leave, I don't want you to see me like this."

"Don't be silly. Is there anything you can take?"

"I already did."

"Isn't it helping?"

"Yes."

"God, what would you be like without medication?" she asked.

"Dead."

"I've never known anyone who suffered migraines."

Elroy's response was in the form of a muffled moan. He gathered the ends of the pillow with both hands and curved it around his head in a vain attempt to suffocate his pain. Mary reached down and massaged the area of the neck Elroy's hand had left. She began massaging his shoulders and the base of his spine.

"I heard somewhere to relieve a headache, massage the base of the spine...Is that helping?"

"No."

Mary rubbed his body in an effort to relieve the pain or to distract his mind. After a while she reached down and removed Elroy's shoes and socks. She then reached around him and unbuckled his belt and removed his pants.

"Mary..."

"Shh. I just want to make you comfortable so you can rest."

She retrieved an extra blanket from the closet and draped it over his partly naked body. She kicked off her shoes and removed her clothing and slipped into a white terry cloth robe. She lay on her side close to Elroy's body, gently embedding her fingertips into his neck.

"Get better Larry. Get better," she whispered and kissed the back of his head.

Elroy tried to respond, but he was distracted by pain and ultimately overcome with sleep.

Mary rose silently from the bed and walked into the kitchen to boil water for tea. She thought of watching television but quickly dismissed the idea fearing the noise would disturb Elroy. She sank into the couch and folded her hands around the cup and sipped. The quiet of Elroy's apartment filled her with a strange delight which combined with her sense of concern for him. She felt intrinsically akin to her surroundings, not from an exterior point of reference, but more from the core. Mary defined her presence with a new and bright meaning. Elroy had awakened passions long dormant in her which evoked new personal dimensions and a sense of belonging. There were newly discovered enrichments that encompassed human alliances and not just academics or causes she was used to. She felt alive because her instinct for protection was rekindled and needed. Her being had purpose, her affections met with personal reward...and her love...her love she thought defied comprehension and analysis. All she knew was that her optimism and desire were on the verge of preparedness, perched high, eager and hopeful.

She put the empty cup on the table and walked quietly into the bedroom. Elroy was curled up and only his face protruded from the blanket. Within the dark room, Mary was able to see the pain and distortion etched on his face. She lowered herself onto the bed and curved herself around him. Throughout the night she heard him moan and felt him toss, trying to rid himself of the pain. Her sleep was light and unrestful as she tried to guard him against an unforgiving malady.

The morning light flooded the living room, while only residual light found its way into the bedroom. It was an unbalanced dawn that reflected an imperfect night.

Mary was groggy and unrefreshed as she went into the shower. When she emerged Elroy was standing in the kitchen. He looked haggard and weak. Through the robe Mary could see he looked thinner. His face was ashen and his eyes squinted and were watery.

"You OK?" she asked.

"Yes," he responded weakly and hoarsely.

"Do you get those things often?"

"Sometimes."

"Can I make you something to eat?"

"No."

"But you didn't eat all of yesterday."

"I probably won't eat today either."

"How come?"

"Sick."

"To your stomach?"

"Yes."

"How about coffee?"

"No, just water."

"You're thirsty?"

"Yes, every time I get a migraine I get so thirsty."

"How about juice?"

"I think there's apple juice in the refrigerator."

"I'll get it."

Mary walked toward the kitchen but stopped before Elroy. She threw her arms around him and held him close.

"Are you sure you're all right?" she whispered in his ear.

"Yes."

"God, you had me worried."

"I'm sorry."

"Don't be silly, I'm sorry you were sick...Why don't you shower, I'll get the juice."

"OK."

Mary watched as Elroy dragged himself into the bathroom. His shoulders were rounded and hunched making him appear older and frail.

She poured the juice and made him a piece of dry toast. She made herself coffee and sat at the table and waited. When Elroy walked into the kitchen he was refreshed, but still sickly.

"Did the shower help you?"

"A little."

"I made you some dry toast."

"Thanks, Mary."

Elroy sipped his juice and nibbled the toast.

"Larry, what brings these headaches on?"

"Oh, foods, tension, body chemistry."

"How long have you been getting them?"

"Ten years."

"My...how do you stand it?"

"Becomes part of life."

"Well, just sit and relax."

Elroy struggled to get into the chair. The effort seemed to take his remaining energy.

"I met with mysterious Mister Prescott yesterday," he said.

"Oh, to locate Harmon Keller?"

"Yes."

"And...?"

"Emmet Prescott is real dark, dirty water."

"How so?"

"Reading his comments in the paper after that assault, and my confrontation with him yesterday, I thought they were two different guys. He's not capable of remorse, not like he tried to project in the paper."

"Was he belligerent?"

"He went beyond belligerence...menacing was more like it."

"Was he menacing to you?"

"He tried."

"What else?"

"I'm sure he lied about how Baylor checked out."

"Accidentally falling on the knife?"

"Yes."

"Will you reopen the case?"

"No."

"Why?"

"Because I checked it out with Tippett and he said that based on the knife entry it would be easy to prove he fell on it."

"How?"

"Because the cutting edge of the blade was directed toward his neck and the way his arm folded under his body support the accident theory. An inept lawyer could win the point easily."

"But we know differently."

"True, but proving it is something else. Baylor had traces of drugs in his system. Tippett said that could have disoriented him. He was a heavy man and the force of the fall could have definitely resulted in the fatal wound...There were only Baylor's fingerprints on the knife, and then of course there were only two witnesses, and one is dead."

"So Prescott gets off."

"Prescott gets off...yes," Elroy confirmed.

"More juice?" Mary asked.

"Just a little."

As Mary leaned forward and poured the juice into El-roy's glass, she noticed the look of frustration in his eyes.

"So what did you learn about Keller?"

"There's bad blood between Prescott and Keller."

"Did he tell you that?"

"No."

"Then how do you know?"

"I just know. His attitude told me."

"Did he know where Keller was?"

"No."

"Sure?"

Yes. If he knew he would have fingered him. That, or maybe he would like to find him himself."

"To settle a score?"

"Could be...Could very well be."

"OK, now what?"

"I don't know. We wait. If Keller shows up, we talk to him. I've checked with Manassas motor vehicle, he has a current license not due for renewal for another year and a half."

"Is that where he lived?"

"Yes."

"How about car insurance, registration?"

"No car registered. No outstanding summons. Nothing."

"Any family?"

"Yes, a sister, I was surprised Prescott told me that."

"Where does she live?"

"In Prince William, Virginia. Her married name is Carson, I'm checking that out."

"Funny how things interrelate."

"Yes."

"More toast?"

"No, I can't finish this, thanks."

"Larry, you have to eat."

"I will, when I feel better."

"What do you think you'll learn when you find Keller?"

"I don't know, but I'm sure he's going to be more open about Prescott than Prescott was about Keller."

"Do you think Prescott knows that Keller broke into an apartment in his building?"

"If it was Keller who broke into the apartment, that becomes an interesting question."

"Larry?"

"What?"

"If there is bad blood between Prescott and Keller, and obviously Prescott has questionable capabilities, please be careful. I'm afraid you'll get caught in the middle."

Mary exposed her vulnerability and Elroy was touched by her concern.

"I will...Thanks."

"I don't want to sound like a worrier, but it's hard being with a cop...a cop I care about. You give danger a new meaning."

"Don't worry, Mary, I've been doing this for a long time, I can take care of myself."

"I know, I just...worry, that's all."

"Thanks. And thanks for last night, you didn't have to stay."

"I wanted to."

★★★

Keller sat in the car for a long time just looking at his sister's house. A light snow began to accumulate on the roof and gently blanketed the lawn around the house.

The street was quiet and his tire marks were the only disruption to the sea of white. The serene setting evoked a strange melancholy that contrasted the inner turmoil which consumed him. His mind tripped back through time, trying to gain a perspective that would give reason to the changes that had transpired in his life. He determined there could be no rationale, only acceptance, no explanation, only the attrition of time itself.

Linda Carson looked through her window at the strange car parked in front of her house. She noticed the out-of-state license plate and assumed it was her brother. She opened the front door and stood behind the glass storm door.

Keller noticed she hadn't changed at all since he saw her last. Even from the distance, she appeared comfortable, at ease with her surroundings and position. Her gracefulness tended to conceal any shortcomings her life encountered. It was a majestic display of manipulation for the sake of peaceful coexistence. He suddenly remembered it was a trait so eloquently mastered by his mother.

Linda recognized Keller the instant he stepped from the car. She opened the door and proceeded cautiously through the snow to greet him. There were no words, only a long embrace. For the moment, conversation would somehow threaten the joy of their reunion. As he held her, he was able to feel the accumulation of her anguish transforming into the culmination of her relief. Her breath puffed out in white clouds, snow mingling with her hair and the knit of her sweater.

"You're gonna catch cold," he said awkwardly, trying to gain a level of triviality.

"I thought you were going to call me when you flew in," she answered.

"I decided to drive."

"In this weather?"

"Flying's worse."

"Come on in. I was about to make some lunch."

Keller turned and had better footing than Linda. He took two steps and was immediately ahead of her.

"Wait up," she said, trying to gain stable footing.

Keller turned and took hold of her arm and supported her up the walk. They kicked the snow off their shoes and put them on a rug in the foyer.

"Give me your coat," Linda said as Keller took it off.

She hung it up in the hall closet and they proceeded through the foyer to a large room that was a combination of kitchen, living room and dining room. It was bright and airy, uncluttered by heavy furnishings.

"You redecorated since I was here last," Keller observed.

"Yes, opened everything up, extended the patio."

"Ahh, I see you put in a pool," Keller said, looking through the living room window.

"Yes, last summer, I'm glad we did."

Linda stood beside her brother, studying the lines of his face. She detected signs of strain, abuse and neglect.

"How have you been feeling?" she asked, deliberate in her questions and attitude.

"Fine."

"Sit down. You must be tired from driving."

"Actually it wasn't bad, I made good time. The snow wasn't a factor...I had forgotten how beautiful this part of the country was," he said, letting himself down onto the couch.

"So why did you wind up in New York?"

"I don't know, it seemed like a good idea at the time."

"Where are you living?"

"Well actually I'm living in a hotel now, but I got an apartment that I'll be moving into as soon as I get back. I probably won't even unpack."

"The hotel must be expensive."

"It is, that's why I'm getting out. The apartment is a one bedroom condo with an option to buy."

"Are you working?"

"No, but I've got a couple of things going, there's a good opportunity in Dallas I may be looking into."

"Good...What have you been doing in the meantime?"

"Well I have that disability pension, been living off that."

"Yes, you mentioned that. Harmon you look sickly, are you sure you are alright?"

"Yes, don't worry. I was sick for a while but I'm fine now, believe me. How's Paul's practice?"

"Fine, he's doing well."

"And Laurie?"

"Doing real well. We're in the process of choosing a college."

"Great. What are you looking at?"

"I think Georgetown."

"Fine choice...Will she be home soon?"

"No she's out of town this week on a student exchange program."

"I'm sorry I missed her."

"God, Harmon I'm so glad to see you."

"Yeah, me too. It's been a long year."

"Hungry?"

"No, but I'll take coffee."

"Great."

Linda stood up and walked into the kitchen.

"What time does Paul get home?" Keller shouted after Linda.

"Tonight about seven. He'll be glad to see you."

Keller followed Linda into the kitchen and leaned up against a cabinet.

"Does he still have that notion to sail to the Caribbean?"

"Sure does. After Laurie's done with college we may."

"You too?"

"I don't know, might be fun."

"But you've always been a land person, born on a farm."

"It's only a trip."

"I guess...I went to see Gloria Tennley."

"Oh, how's she doing?"

"As well as can be expected."

Linda reached into a cupboard and withdrew two cups and placed them on the table. Keller's eyes glanced at the counter and noticed an envelope with his name printed across it.

"Is that my key?" he asked pointing to the envelope.

"Yes."

Keller took the envelope and folded it into his pocket.

"What did she have to say?"

"Nothing much, she's shocked, confused."

"She blames Emmet Prescott," Linda said.

"She told you that?"

"Yes...Did she say anything to you?"

"She mentioned his name."

"What do you think, do you think he had anything to do with it?"

"I don't know Linda...it's...it's hard to say."

"But you think the possibility is there?"

Linda confronted the ghost that haunted Keller's mind. He was less resistive and more open with her.

"Yes."

"Why?"

"I don't know."

"Yes you do."

Keller studied his sister whose smooth exterior had suddenly turned coarse from worry. She looked at him with examining eyes that made him uncomfortable. He noticed the coffeemaker had filled the pot. He reached for the handle and walked to the table and poured coffee into the two cups.

"Yes I do."

"Does that key have anything to do with it?"

"Yes."

A cold frightened chill passed through Linda. The key which had been in her presence for a year had suddenly become ominous, establishing a sinister life of its own.

"How are you involved, Harmon?" she asked.

"By being Prescott's enemy."

"So you're saying he's going to kill you next?"

"I don't know...Maybe."

"God, Harmon there's got to be something you can do."

"Like what?"

"Go to the police, tell them...that...that Prescott killed Tennley."

"They won't be able to prove it."

"Fine, but if you call attention to him, he may be inclined to leave you alone. Once he knows the police suspect him in one murder he'll be foolish to commit another."

"You really don't understand Prescott."

"I guess I don't. I do know you have to protect yourself some way."

"I know that."

Linda opened the refrigerator and withdrew milk. She poured some into her cup and then in Keller's.

"Sugar?"

"No thanks."

"Harmon, I'm scared. I never trusted Prescott. You never told me anything about him, but I remember meeting him and never trusting him...How can one man be allowed to ruin so many lives...John, Gloria, now you, me...and God knows who else."

"Listen, Linda, we may be blowing this thing way out of proportion."

"Are we? Tell me in a way that I can truly believe...Tell me."

"I can't."

Linda put the cup to her mouth to try and hide her quivering lips. Tears filled her eyes and her serene world had quickly become threatened by dark forces. There seemed to be a pattern in her life that always fluctuated between peace and disorder. The cycle was now in motion, counteracting the tranquility which she distrusted because of its foreboding.

"You're right about one thing though," Linda said composing herself. "I don't know Prescott, but I'm learning about him very quickly."

"That may be our defense."

"What's that?"

"He's predictable, so we can prepare, be alert."

"Will that key help you prepare?"

"I don't know, Linda, I really don't."

"Why don't you stay here a few days, I'd feel better if you were here."

"I think I will. If the weather doesn't get too bad we'll take a ride down to our old farm."

"Oh, that would be beautiful."

★★★

Rayfer pulled the hood of his jogging suit over his head and tucked the ends of the towel into the sides of it, covering the lower portion of his face. He walked through the lobby and took the elevator to the eighth floor. He proceeded to Keller's room and stood by the door, pretending to search through his pocket for a key.

"Oh, no!" he said loud enough for the maid several doors down to hear.

"Excuse me ma'am," he said to the woman through the towel he now held in front of his face as he pretended to wipe his brow.

"Yes?"

"Have you cleaned in my room?"

"Yes. It's done already."

"I can't believe it. I locked myself out and all I ran out with was a ten dollar bill," he said showing her the bill as a lure.

"Would you want me to let you in?" she asked.

"Would you mind? I can't believe I was so careless."

"Not at all. I'm always locking my car keys in the car."

The maid walked toward Rayfer and unlocked the door.

"Thank you," he said, still attempting to conceal his face with the towel.

"Sure," the maid said, pushing the door open.

Rayfer handed the maid the ten dollar bill and stepped into the room.

"Thank you," she said as the door closed in front of her.

Once inside, Rayfer's demeanor instantly changed from the helplessness he projected to the maid. His persona became alert, cunning, he moved through the room with controlled aggression. From monitoring the room, he knew Keller had been gone for two days, but being figuratively close ignited a flame of primeval destruction in him. His rancor was excessive, but did not hinder his potential for professional effectiveness. He was the embodiment of boiling hot water running through a cold copper pipe.

He approached a pair of running shoes lying next to a chair. A menacing scowl occupied his face, as an absurd pleasure toyed with his aggression. He moved toward them and proceeded to grind his foot forcibly, trying to drive the shoes through the carpet.

Rayfer assessed the sum total of all things as insignificant. The sanctity of survival was viewed from his singular vision with loathsome indifference. Everything to Rayfer was inconsequential; therefore, nothing was important. Destruction by way of superiority remained the purest form of judgment. It was within this context that Rayfer functioned, with the feeling of total omnipotence.

He studied the room and felt delight that the bed was situated far enough away from the door. His plan would be to enter while Keller slept, and the positioning of the furniture would make it difficult for his sleeping prey to be awakened by approaching footsteps.

Rayfer walked to the window and looked at the bleak day. A clap of thunder smashed into the room, proclaiming disapproval to Rayfer's intentions. He was oblivious to sound, distraction, all that consumed him was his own intent. He picked up the telephone and dialed the hotel front desk.

"Yes, can I help you please?" he heard.

"This is Harmon Keller in eight sixteen."

"Yes, Mister Keller?"

"I seem to have misplaced my room key, can you supply another?"

"Certainly, if you stop by the front desk. I'd be happy to provide you with another."

"Fine. Thank you, but one thing, I'm unable to leave my room just now, can you please have someone send it up to me?"

"Of course I'll get a bellman to bring it to you."

"Thank you."

"Mister Keller, I'm afraid we will have to charge you for the lost key and ask for a five dollar deposit for the second."

"That's no problem."

"Fine, a bellman will bring it to you shortly."

"Thank you."

Rayfer hung up the phone and unlocked the door. He placed eight dollars on the dresser and waited. His planning was going better than he expected, no force of opposition or quirk of interference appeared pitted against him. Ease of operation was never distrusted, only welcomed as a bonus to his labors.

The soft knock on the door concluded one more phase of his planning. It built upon his strategy for the unexpected.

Rayfer walked into the bathroom which was by the door. He put on the light and started running water in the sink. There was another knock, only louder.

"Its open, come in," Rayfer said, hiding behind the partially opened bathroom door.

"Bellman sir, I have a key."

"Yeah, great, you can put it on the dresser. There's five bucks for the deposit, three's for you."

"Thank you sir."

The bellman placed the key down and put the money in his pocket. "Would you want a receipt for the key sir?"

"No, don't worry about it, I'll square up when I check out."

"Very well sir. Have a nice day."

"Thank you."

When Rayfer heard the door close, he shut off the water and turned out the light. He proceeded to the dresser and stared down at the key. The harmless looking instrument would soon unlock a destructive menace. Rayfer put the key into his pocket. Now all that remained was a silent entrance, late at night, when Keller was asleep. He felt a strange power over Keller, an advantage and dominance that would pass so mercilessly beyond the boundaries of misery and pain.

FRANK PRETE

EIGHTEEN

Keller walked into the Farmers' Bank of Virginia and stood for a moment studying the surroundings. There were no familiar faces and modernization briefly caused him to question if he was in the right place. The branch office no longer resembled a personal, small town bank. Polished mahogany teller cages with brass decorative bars were replaced by obtrusive granite bunkers, separating teller and customer. Thick plexiglass shielding mounted upon stone block represented a pronounced distrust. There were three tellers conducting transactions from within their individual vaults with small lines of customers. Loan officers were on a platform area, to the side of the tellers' cages. The bank was fairly busy but library-quiet.

Keller walked to a receptionist who looked up as he approached.

"Can I help you?" she asked.

"Yes, I would like to get into my safety deposit box."

"Certainly. Do you have your key?"

"Yes."

"Fine. If you follow me, I will show you to the deposit vault."

She turned to a man sitting next to her and announced, "Jeff, safety deposit customer, answer my phone."

The man said, "OK," without looking up.

The woman then took a set of keys from her desk and led Keller through an alcove away from the main banking area. She approached the door that was merely a row of bars and unlocked it.

The main vault consisted of rows of smaller safes which extended from the floor to the top of the vault which was eight feet high. An isle separated two walls of boxes, and resting beside one row was a sturdy stool used for access to the higher safes.

"There you are sir," she said swinging the door open. "Will you need assistance?" she asked.

"No, I can manage, thank you."

"If you need privacy, there is an enclosed area in the rear of the vault with a tiny desk which you can rest your deposit box on."

"Thanks."

The woman stepped away from the door and allowed Keller his privacy.

The rows of safes were indicated alphabetically and numerically. Keller looked at the key which was numbered "J275", then found the "J" row and followed that to "275". which was eye level. He inserted the key and opened the safe. Keller grabbed the handle of a steel inner box and slid it out. He held the box from the bottom and raised the long lid. Looking inside, he saw the brown envelope where he had placed it a lifetime ago. He reached in and lifted the envelope and tucked it under his arm. He replaced the box into the safe and locked it. Quickly he glanced around him, displaying an age old distrust. Confident no one was in the vault, he proceeded to open the envelope and withdrew its contents. The past quickly flooded the present, entrapping him in a cycle of deceit, as he reread the heading he had originally typed years earlier:

NIGHT SHADE:

CLASSIFIED/CONFIDENTIAL

Keller opened the folder and scanned the typed information. Dormant images flared in his mind, reconstructed from memory and idealism. The passing of time neither softened nor enhanced his philosophy. What burned in his conscience was not left for the judgment of history, it was merely his to assess and bear. What did evoke emotional response, was the vague recollection of another time, not of innocence lost, but one of simple passage. Keller replaced the papers in the envelope and left the bank.

He and his sister were able to visit the farm of their youth the day before, but Keller wanted to be there one more time. It was just before sunset when he finally arrived. He parked on the shoulder of Route 101 which bordered the southwest portion of the farm. He climbed a moderate hill and looked out over the field. From his vantage point he was able to see the house and barn, melancholy blotches of remembrance rising from the dry amber earth. Unlike the bank, nothing on the farm had changed but proportion. The house, barn and field seemed smaller than he remembered from his youth. Their quiet stillness withstood the lifetime of echoes that rang in his ears. Isolated and aloof, they stood sturdy and erect, unscathed by time, unmoved through memory, remaining as a testament to the virtue of stability and consolation.

Keller felt an unusual kinship to the house and land. A kinship that remained locked in the recesses of his mind, unlikely to hear the chimes of expression, for fear the past would cast judgment and make folly of the sardonic present.

The sun sunk mournfully behind the horizon, a misty twilight gathered up and surrounded Keller. His figure was dark and defined, silhouetted against the bleak sky. He lingered long enough for the memory to hurt, then turned and descended the hill, realizing there was nothing more he could do. All that remained for Keller was tempered acceptance of where he was and who he had become. He left the farm and headed toward New York, driving headlong into a rendezvous with destiny.

It was just before midnight when Keller arrived in New York. He passed through the Lincoln Tunnel and navigated the lively streets until he came to the hotel. He parked in the hotel parking lot, weary from the thoughts that drained him, and tired from the long trip. He left his suitcase in the trunk of the car knowing he was going to check out in the morning and move into his apartment.

The lobby of the hotel was unusually busy for the time of night. A sign welcomed the New York Chapter of Building Tradesmen--Local 912. Their convention or contingent of negotiators spilled out from the main ballroom. The handful of people in the lobby were talkative but calm. Bits of conversation whizzed by Keller as he made his way to the elevator. The hallway of the eighth floor displayed more activity than the lobby. Beyond Keller's room were two adjoining suites and two opposing suites, each filled with negotiators. Their doors were open and the atmosphere was a combination of business meetings and party celebration. Keller felt a sudden surge of annoyance anticipating the unusual noise would filter into his room and disturb him.

Unlocking the door, Keller stepped into the room. The sounds in the hallway became muffled, almost inaudible, once he closed the door. He kicked off his shoes and threw his coat on a chair. He was anxious to take a warm shower and get a good night's sleep.

The shower was hot as it hit his body. Keller lowered his head and let the water splash at his neck hoping it would relieve the tension there. He closed his eyes and rolled his head from side to side. Obscure images flashed in his mind. A wheat field blown by an unseen wind lightly veiled a distant farm house. A lone figure resembling Emmet Prescott appeared on the porch. His presence projected a clear, menacing purpose. Keller quickly opened his eyes as the water attacked them. The visions in his mind rose up from a dubious alliance and a misguided understanding gone horribly awry. Keller knew that Prescott was an inescapable ghost that eventually had to be reckoned with, not to alter the past, but in some way to free the future.

Keller emerged from the shower with a towel wrapped around his waist. He felt refreshed but the shower did little to relieve his preoccupation. He opened the bathroom door and the mist from the shower did not advance beyond the boundary of the bathroom. Accompanying his entry into the bedroom, the phone rang, startling him.

"Hello," Keller said softly.

"Aaron?" asked the strange voice.

"No, I think you have the wrong number."

"This is not Aaron Levy's room?"

"No, it is not."

"I'm sorry to disturb you," the voice said, and then Keller heard a click and a blank whine in his ear.

He replaced the phone and went to bed.

A thin smile formed on Rayfer's lips as he hung up the phone. The sound of Keller's familiar voice excited him. His prey had returned, he was nearby. Rayfer remained prone on the bed fully clothed. The room was dark, concealing his image and his intentions.

★★★

Rayfer looked at his watch as he stood in the stairwell outside Keller's room. He felt confident he had given Keller enough time to be in a deep sleep, and the minimum noise he would make opening the door should not disturb him. In his left hand he held the key to the room, in his right, the Rostfrei knife. He anticipated no unforseen problem from Keller, but in the event there was, he maintained the same posture of confidence and level of offense as he had for John Tennley. He felt no strain or negative tension, believing his exploit would be achieved simply.

Rayfer opened the door and stepped into the hall, his plan coming down to the final phase. Low muffled voices and clanging glass distracted him immediately. He turned to the direction of the sounds. Activity emitted from within two suites whose doors were open; instantly Rayfer had to deal with the unexpected. A minor intrusion forced him to reevaluate his position. His mind calculated his options. Should he abort his operation and wait for a more opportune moment?

He continued walking toward Keller's room slowly, he needed more time for evaluation. His mind quickly calculated his options, and leaving was a safe alternative. The further away from the suites he walked, the fainter the conversation became. He was certain the level of noise by Keller's room would be nonexistent. He remained calm, in control, defying anything to upset his plan. Rayfer could not afford to become careless; he didn't want to rush opening Keller's door. The more patient he remained, the quieter it would render his entry. Silence and surprise were the cornerstone of his attack.

From behind, Rayfer heard someone step into the hall. He turned slightly and looked over his shoulder to see three indistinguishable figures standing as unwitting centurions, guarding against an unseen, impending evil. They spoke among themselves, remaining unmindful of Rayfer, yet acknowledging his presence. Rayfer was forced to continue beyond Keller's room, trying to project an air of belonging within the hotel. As he passed the room, feelings of anger rose to an excess. The strangers' presence deprived him of a need he relied on.

He felt consumed by defeat and disappointed by circumstance. Rayfer quickly tried to console himself with the thought there would be another opportunity. He vowed his next attempt would meet with consummation and the devastation would serve to justify and appease this minor setback.

NIGHT SHADE

NINETEEN

Keller stood surveying the room, making sure he left nothing of his behind. He was anxious to leave the hotel and move into his apartment. The transition was symbolic of his positive direction and attested to his formal recovery. He had traveled a strange, irreverent road which at one point showed no promise or hope. Now he stood entrenched in the throes of righting his listing life, intent on reclaiming his proper identity and passing a threshold which seemed impossible a short time ago.

He bent down to pick up his suitcase which contained the balance of his belongings, and left the room.

Keller stepped into the elevator and watched as the doors closed before his face, exposing his vague reflection in the polished chrome. His stature projected a state of well-being which assured him that all which had passed was committed to memory, but not exposed to judgment and fault. His future would be subject to the powers of choice and reaction, and the forces of chance and fate.

Keller walked across the lobby and rested his suitcase before the lobby desk.

"Checking out," he said placing the key on the desk.

"Certainly," the clerk said, taking the key and noticing the number. He then walked to a green computer screen.

233

He typed in some information and a nearby printer began to spit out information. The clerk ripped the printed paper along a perforated edge and walked back to Keller.

"Did you have an enjoyable stay, Mister Keller?"

"Yes, thank you."

"Good. Here's your bill Mister Keller," he announced.

Keller took the bill and glanced at it for the amount. He went into his pocket and produced a pack of bills folded in half. He began to count out the proper amount and dropped the bills on the print out.

"Was everything satisfactory, Mister Keller?"

"Yes."

The clerk reached for the currency and the bill as something strange caught Keller's eye.

"Hold it," he said reaching for the bill.

"What's this?" Keller asked.

"What's that?"

"Duplicate key five dollars?"

"Yes sir, your second key."

"I only have one."

"I'm sorry sir, there was a second key issued."

"To my room?"

"Yes, Mister Keller. If you recall, the other day you had called from your room requesting a replacement to a lost key. I remember because I took the call."

"I called?"

"Yes sir."

"And how was I given that key?"

"A bellman came to your room."

Keller became perplexed. He didn't remember seeing a second key anywhere.

"To my room?"

"Yes sir."

Suddenly Keller felt an overpowering violation. Someone had been in his room pretending to be him. A definite intrusion into his privacy, but an intrusion for what purpose? Keller knew nothing had been taken, there was nothing of value. Disconnected thoughts swirled in his head. Inconsistencies blended within oddities, inducing a state of confusion. Within the disorder, John Tennley flashed in his mind.

Keller wondered if Tennley's murder was a precursor to his own fate. There was no doubt the crass manner of intrusion had the imprint of Emmet Prescott, and therein he realized was the vein of complicity. Keller knew he had been located and the hunt was drawing to a close. He could no longer afford to be uncertain and hesitant about his pursuers.

"OK," Keller said handing the bill to the clerk.

The clerk took the money and handed Keller change. Keller left the hotel with a new awareness and aggression. He made his way into the garage of the hotel. Tension and concern preoccupied his mind. He knew he had to defend against an assault that was imminent. He knew Prescott would not stop because his addiction for power, dominance and revenge were the cornerstones of his existence. He possessed a psychotic, insatiable sense of retribution.

Keller wondered how he would come. As he opened the car door he thought of a bomb. He put his suitcase on the rear seat and slowly eased himself into the driver's seat. He was tentative about putting the key into the ignition.

"Keys," he thought to himself. The key to his hotel room was in the hands of a murderer. Yes he thought, an assassin would enter when he was taking a shower or was sound asleep. His life snuffed out in a cowardly way, without a chance at self-defense. Was the key to his life in his own hands? In a sense he felt if the car were armed with a bomb he could take delight in knowing it was he himself who chose to turn the key and end it all. In a morbid way he would deny Prescott or a hired assassin the privilege of seeing him die.

Keller took a deep breath, trying to control his racing heart and trembling hands. Even though he was seated and still, he sensed himself falling backwards, tumbling down a dark shaft. There was nowhere to turn and nothing to see or hear. All that existed was his own nervousness crashing inside him. All that remained was a simple turn of a key.

Keller gripped the wheel with one hand and squeezed the key between his thumb and the side of his pointing finger. Caution struggled with paranoia. Keller knew he had to preserve one and prevent the other.

"Fuck it!" he said boldly aloud and turned the key. The engine started with its usual moan but somehow sounded more exaggerated, as though it were in the middle of an echo chamber. The tension had caused Keller's body to become taunt, his leg rigid and his foot jamming the gas pedal to the floor. The engine roared angrily at full throttle, but the car remained a benign inanimate object, staying safely within the bounds of its own explosive power.

It took Keller a long moment to gain his composure and remove his foot from the pedal. Once again, he became aware of himself, seated, still, no feelings of falling, only relief that would take more time to be fully realized.

Keller looked around quickly and drove out of the parking lot, temporarily eluding an approaching force, dark and sinister and prepared to kill.

Elroy finished dialing and sat back in his chair, using his shoulder to hold the phone to his ear. After the third ring he heard a woman's voice.

"Hello."

"Hello," Elroy responded. "Linda Carson, please."

"This is she."

"Mrs. Carson, my name is Lawrence Elroy of the New York Police Department."

"God, what is it, what's the matter?" she said, fright and terror governing her actions.

"It's nothing Mrs. Carson, I was informed you were the sister of Harmon Keller..."

"What's happened to Harmon?" she shrieked.

"Nothing, nothing at all. I don't mean to alarm you, it's only a routine investigation."

"Are you certain Harmon is not hurt?"

"Mrs. Carson, I don't know your brother or where he is, I was hoping you could tell me."

Linda's terror mixed with suspicion. She became cautious while trying to overcome her fears.

"Who did you say you were?" she asked.

"Lieutenant Lawrence Elroy, New York Police."

"How can I be sure?"

Elroy began to adopt suspicions of his own. Linda's reactions seemed to ignite an already existing concern.

"You don't. But please believe me, I am a police lieutenant. Six, one, two precinct in New York...You can call New York information for our telephone number and dial us direct."

"Who's your commanding officer?"

"Captain Reynolds."

"Why should I call you?...Why do I want to talk with you?"

"Mrs. Carson, I am just trying to locate your brother to ask him a few simple questions relating to an insignificant matter, that's all."

Linda wanted to hang up, but she reasoned if the caller were really a policeman she would mention John Tennley's murder in hopes it would protect Harmon.

"Well, I will not say another word until I'm convinced you are who you say you are."

"I don't blame you at all. Please, Mrs. Carson do as I suggest, call New York information, they will give you our number here, that should convince you."

"OK," Linda said and hung up the phone.

Elroy left his office for Captain Reynolds'."

"Captain?" Elroy said entering the office.

"Yes Lieutenant, what's up?"

"I just spoke with the sister of the murder, break-in suspect."

"Yes?"

"She's going to call here because she wants to verify it is a police investigation."

"OK. But why was she suspicious about it not being an investigation?"

"I don't know. She seemed to have overreacted...She was overly cautious."

"Like she's hiding something?"

"Something, I don't know what. But my guess is she'll call you first to verify."

"OK."

The phone on Reynolds' desk rang.

"Probably her now," Elroy said.

"Captain Reynolds," he said into the mouthpiece.

"Is this police precinct 612?" the voice asked.

"Yes it is," Reynolds said.

He looked at Elroy and motioned with his head to indicate the caller was Linda Carson.

Elroy listened as Reynolds answered a question she asked.

"Yes Lieutenant Elroy does work in the police precinct."

Elroy watched as Reynolds sat listening to Linda.

"True, he is conducting an investigation."

Reynolds paused again.

"Well, I think it would be better if Lieutenant Elroy explained it to you. It is his investigation."

"I certainly can. Would you hold on, I'll transfer your call to him," the captain said.

He depressed the hold button and held out the phone for Elroy.

"She wants to speak with you. I thought it best if she didn't know you were in my office."

"OK."

Elroy pressed the blinking button and spoke.

"Lieutenant Elroy."

"Lieutenant, this is Linda Carson."

"Hello, Mrs. Carson."

"I'm sorry to act so distrusting, but it pays to be cautious."

"Absolutely, I don't blame you, Mrs. Carson."

"Can you tell me what this is about Lieutenant? Why do you want to speak with Harmon?"

"Well to be very honest I'm investigating a felony which your brother may be able to help me with."

"How so?...Can you be more specific?"

Elroy thought quickly. He didn't want to mention the murder in Grand Central.

"There was a break-in in my precinct and a preliminary investigation reveals your brother may know the person or persons who were responsible. I would just like to ask him about it to learn what he knows."

"Was the break-in in Princeton, New Jersey?" Linda blurted out.

"Princeton? No not at all. I have no jurisdiction in Princeton."

"Do you know of a murder in Princeton?"

"No, I don't but...What are you trying to tell me, Mrs. Carson?"

"Emmet Prescott."

Elroy froze, his eyes caught Reynolds' who saw his expression become rigid.

"What about Emmet Prescott?" he asked, his voice reflecting his surprise.

"Do you know him?" Linda asked.

"Yes, I do."

"Are you his friend?"

"I met him only once and I can assure you, Mister Prescott is no friend of mine."

"How did you get to meet him?"

Elroy's first reaction was not to answer, but his instincts told him to play along.

"Well to be honest, Mrs. Carson, I went to Mister Prescott to find your brother."

"Then you know Harmon worked for Prescott?"

"Yes, I do."

"Do you know John Tennley worked for Prescott also?"

"Who's John Tennley?"

"I suggest you contact Princeton police."

"Why?"

"Because John Tennley was murdered last week."

Elroy paused for a moment. His instincts told him he was about to uncover a storeroom full of secrets.

"I'm sorry Mrs. Carson, what are you trying to tell me?"

"I don't know...I don't know, Lieutenant. I'm afraid for my brother, that's all I know."

"OK, Mrs. Carson let's get all this in perspective. How does Mister Telly..."

"Tennley, John."

"OK, how does John Tennley fit into all this?" Elroy asked as he scribbled Tennley's name on a piece of paper.

"He and Harmon worked under Prescott. Now Tennley's dead and I'm afraid for Harmon."

"You say Princeton, New Jersey?" Elroy confirmed.

"Yes...Where John lived."

"Were Harmon and Tennley good friends?"

"Yes."

"And now you're suggesting Prescott may know something about Mister Tennley's death?"

There was a long pause; Linda didn't respond. She was becoming hesitant about saying something she had no proof of.

"Mrs. Carson?"

"Ask Gloria," she blurted out.

"Who's Gloria?"

"John Tennley's widow...Princeton police may know something also."

"I will check with Gloria Tennley, but a homicide in Princeton is outside of my jurisdiction..."

"Murder is murder and police are police," Linda interrupted. "You should help one another," she continued.

"That's true, and often times we do and as I said I will check into it. But let me ask you something if I may."

"Certainly."

"Does Harmon have any information about Mister Tennley?"

"I don't know, he's still CIA-minded."

"Well can I contact him?"

Linda paused once more, she had to collect her thoughts.

"I'll talk to Harmon, if he has any information, I'll have him call you."

"Mrs. Carson, it would be better if I contacted him. Won't you...?"

"I'll speak to him first, that's the way it has to be Lieutenant."

"Fine, Mrs. Carson, in the meantime I'll contact Princeton police and Gloria Tennley."

"I can give you Gloria's phone number."

"That will be fine, what is it?"

Elroy wrote down the phone number as Linda dictated it to him.

"That's two oh one area code," she concluded.

"Right, got it. Thank you Mrs. Carson, and please have Harmon contact me as soon as possible, especially if you feel he's in any kind of danger. We will be able to help him."

"I hope so, that's why I mentioned John."

"OK, thank you Mrs. Carson," Elroy said and depressed the phone's plunger with his finger for a moment, then dialed an intraprecinct extension.

"What was that all about?" Reynolds asked.

"A homicide in Princeton," Elroy responded into the phone as he waited for a response to his call. "That may connect..."

"Communications Department, Alice Worlley speaking."

"Alice, this is Lieutenant Elroy."

"Yes, Lieutenant?"

"Alice, I'd like you to contact Princeton, New Jersey police and have the precinct involved teletype all information on a homicide of John Tennley. That's T.E.N.N.L.E.Y."

"First name John, regular spelling?" she repeated to clarify.

"John, yes...No address...Alice this is A.S.A.P."

"Will do, Lieutenant, I'll have the information on your desk as soon as it comes in."

"Thanks Alice, appreciate it."

Elroy hung up the phone and diverted his attention to Reynolds.

"These guys have a grudge match going on," he announced.

"Who's that?"

"Prescott, Keller and now a dead guy named John Tennley. Keller's sister thinks Prescott put Tennley down for the count."

"How does she think that?"

"No idea, but I'm gonna find out, And if she's right Prescott and Keller are definitely going to shoot it out in the dark."

"We don't need three-piece suits thinking this precinct is the OK Corral...Maybe Prescott could use a tail."

"I don't think Prescott's doing his own dirty work. I've got to get to Keller, he's key."

"How so?"

"Prescott's definitely not talking about anything. He's one of those brassy elite that think laws don't govern him and nothing touches him. Keller, on the other hand, may be on the retreat, but I've got a feeling he's coming out commando style. A break-in of an apartment where Prescott lives was probably pulled off by Keller in some kind of hobo disguise. My guess is he tried to ice Prescott but just made the wrong apartment."

"Why don't you pitch a tent around Prescott and wait for Keller to show up at camp?"

"That might be a way out, but I'm afraid of showing my hand any more than I already have. And don't forget these guys wrote the book on surveillance...No, I want to come from that bastard Prescott's blind side.

"Fine. Any idea why these super sports are playing cowboy and Indian?"

"Who knows...like anything else it probably comes down to ego."

"You think Tennley's wife might be able to throw some light?"

"Yeah, she obviously knows something. I've got to call. I may take a trip to see her."

"When you're down there don't let Princeton P.D. hold out anything they've found. I want you informed, I don't want you getting suckered by these guys."

"I won't.

"OK, let me know when you're going and try to keep in close contact with me."

Elroy understood the captain's comment to be an extension to the look of concern he plainly saw on his face. It was the unspoken, but ever present fear fellow cops adopt as a way of life and share as a burden.

But Elroy didn't have to be told to be careful. He met Prescott once and suspected him to be a man of dubious capabilities. Although Elroy's posture would be reactive rather than aggressive, he felt confident. He just hoped there would be a margin in which to maneuver within any kind of assault.

TWENTY

Forty-second Street and Fifth Avenue pulsated with life. Its brash aura was distinct and personal, with its own mood and temperment not unlike the people who cut hasty paths through it.

There was a hard symmetry between the personality of the street and the people--where indifference abounded and alienation prevailed. The large stone lions perched high above the street at the entrance of the library seemed to display it best. Within their rigid stillness, one could almost interpret their silence not as prideful protector, but more as arrogant observer. They stood witness to a unique wasteland, while maintaining a stony indifference.

Harmon Keller blended in with the people. For the first time since his recovery he was able to observe them in their daily journeys to jobs, meetings, and whatever brought them away from personal relaxation and enjoyment.

He studied their faces as they rushed by him and he came to realize why, when he was sick and dirty, no one ever stopped to offer him loose change or even a sympathetic glance.

On the east side corner, Keller noticed a teenaged girl screaming angrily at a boy her own age. Her arms flailed before his face as he tried to appear disinterested through his own anger. He attempted to walk away from her, but she stepped into his path. Her voice was angry and hurt. The boy tried once more to side-step her, attempting to quell an aggravated condition, but she prevented him. Suddenly a level of containment had been breached as he reached up to her head, grabbed a hand full of hair, and threw her to the ground. The girl resembled a large stuffed doll as she hit the concrete. She quickly rose up and continued hollering, her hurt and anger accompanied by humiliation and defenselessness.

Keller turned from the fighting couple and noticed people walking past them just as casually as though they were among the many waiting impatiently to cross the street.

Keller did not become disinterested toward the absurd ballet being fought in the street, he just remained focused on his own intent.

He had to remain alert and cautious, sharp to a precise edge. Doug Hyatt's call earlier in the week had reinforced that. His familiar voice reverberated from a far-off past, struggling to remain friendly and pertinent with the present. There was an attempt at slight pleasantries, but his tone for the most part was ominous and foreboding. His conversation was brief and evasive, saying they should meet to discuss something of vital interest to Keller.

Hyatt was secretive, but Keller didn't have to be told the reason or urgency behind the proposed meeting. The mere fact Hyatt had tracked him explained volumes, with only one already known conclusion. He remembered Hyatt from the CIA days when they worked together. Hyatt was on the payroll as a consultant. An independent who worked all sides of the street for any paying customer. All that held his interest or earned his allegiance were electronics and money. He was a genius with anything run by chips or diodes. He saw the application of technology as an enormous life of its own, beating invisibly within endless arteries which he was able to manipulate and control. The money was something that fed his greed and insecurity. He lived miserly in a perverted sense, hoarding money for neither enjoyment nor pleasure, present or future. Collecting currency was merely a formality, void of the passion or beauty of possessing art or butterflies.

Keller's caution suspected Hyatt of being part of an assassination plot, but his reason told him Hyatt was a mercenary, interested only in lucrative gain, not calculating consequences to reach that end.

In spite of his insight, Keller did not abandon his caution. He told Hyatt he would call him in three days and choose a meeting place only one hour before the meeting. Hyatt understood the planning and agreed.

The library crowd was a mixture of students interested in research, tourists gawking in awe, and some people trying to stay warm.

Keller took precautions to give himself a different appearance. His hair was shorter than usual, matted down with a sparing amount of Vaseline and styled differently than he had worn it most of his adult life. A three day growth of beard changed the contours of his face slightly, and thin framed wire glasses gave him the appearance of an older foreign exchange student. He turned the large collar of his leather bomber jacket up to conceal the back of his head and a portion of his profile. He wore dark colored clothing and his hands hung casually at his sides, trying not to project anything that would be outstanding or noticeable.

He arrived at the library at noon and stuffed himself into a public phone booth to dial the number Hyatt had given him.

"Yes?" came Hyatt's voice.

From the sound of traffic on Hyatt's end, Keller knew he reached his car phone.

"Public library," was all Keller said.

"OK."

"When you come in, go to the information desk, get a building layout."

"Then what?"

"Just do that."

"Fine. I can be there in thirty-five minutes."

Keller heard the click, then stepped from the phone booth and looked at his watch.

He proceeded to the information desk and gathered up a handful of gate-fold flyers that contained historical information of the library and the building's layout. He walked away from the desk, and wrote "D.O.U.G." on the top right hand corner of six flyers. He unfolded the flyers to the diagram portion and circled "Catalog Room 315."

The catalog room was further broken down into sections, or research chambers. Keller made an "X" below "315N" on the flyer which corresponded to one of the chambers. The area he denoted was set back in the catalog room, well concealed from any main area. He inserted the flyers back into their display slots making sure "D.O.U.G." was visible. He climbed the circular staircase to the second floor and positioned himself under a marble archway. From his vantage point he could look down at everyone entering or leaving the building through the Fifth Avenue entrance.

The main entrance was roped off so that only one door was available for entering, while the large revolving doors and smaller side door were utilized for exiting only. This setup made the monitoring of everyone entering much easier. He was also in a position to see the information desk, which he observed periodically to insure no one took the flyers he had marked.

Thirty minutes after the phone call Doug Hyatt stepped into the lobby of the library. Keller watched as he paused for a second to unbutton his coat and remove his hat. As Hyatt made his way to the information desk, Keller started walking toward the staircase on the opposite side of the lobby, keeping his eye on the entrance at all times.

Hyatt paused at the desk and looked around until he saw the flyer with his name. He withdrew the flyer and opened it to discover the "circle" and the "X." Keller watched as Hyatt ascended the circular staircase, following the cryptic instructions. Keller then proceeded to the information desk to retrieve the remaining flyers he had written on, and then followed Hyatt. He stopped on the second floor gallery and looked down to the main lobby and the staircase. Certain there was no one following Hyatt, he proceeded to the third floor. Keller paused outside the Catalog Room 315 for a final look behind him, then quickly ducked into the large hall.

The catalog room was actually made up of four adjoining rooms. The right half of the first room was a spacious area filled with lanes of tables strung with rows of personal computers. The left half was filled with higher tables and small bronze lamps spaced intermittently on them. The walls of the room were a series of shelves crowded with books which enclosed the entire area. Eight or ten feet off the ground was a balcony and the continuation of the mountain of books.

Keller walked through the first room where it led to a passageway and three other adjoining rooms. At the foot of the passageway was the security post and the employees' room. To the left and right were two reading rooms identical to the first room. Keller looked right and knew Hyatt was in the furthermost portion of the larger room.

Keller made his way through the north main reading room until he came to 315N--U.S. History, Local History and Genealogy Division.

Proceeding slowly into the room, he noticed Hyatt alone looking intently at a book. Keller paused for a moment knowing this was the last time he would be able to exercise caution before making contact.

From the corner of his eye, Hyatt noticed a figure standing at the door watching him. As he turned his attention to the figure, it took him a moment to recognize Keller. When he did, a broad, hollow smile crossed his lips. Keller remained uncertain; the two men stood watching each other, neither moved.

Keller's eyes quickly sized up Hyatt and the area around him. He moved toward him in the remote event he tried to attack, he would be close enough to defend himself. Keller approached, stepping beyond him, then turned to keep his back to a bookshelf and his gaze at the only entrance into the room.

"Hello, Harmon. How have you been?" Hyatt whispered.

Keller didn't respond; his eyes were affixed to the entrance way.

"I'm alone, Harmon, don't worry," Hyatt said recognizing Keller's anxiety.

"Yes, I'm sure you are."

Hyatt paused until he felt Keller was no longer suspicious.

"It's been a long time, you look different," Hyatt finally said. "I had trouble recognizing you."

"Time changes everything."

"True. You look better for the wear."

"Yeah."

"What have you been doing since retiring?"

"Vacationing," Keller said, trying to hide his sarcasm.

"Good for you. You look tanned and relaxed."

Keller looked hard into Hyatt's eyes, a scowling reaction to his insincerity.

"What was it you had to tell me?" Keller asked, avoiding the lie.

Hyatt now looked around, trying to convince himself the ongoing negotiations were done in private.

"My information is very important to you."

Hyatt paused, allowing time for his meaning to become clear.

Keller searched into his jacket pocket and withdrew the envelope. Hyatt fingered its contents, following the contours and thickness of the money.

"It's all there," Keller said with a hard voice.

"Good."

Keller watched as Hyatt quickly shoved the envelope into the front pocket of his pants. A look of greed and satisfaction danced in his eyes.

"So how have you been doing?"

"What's on your mind?" Keller asked not wanting to be social.

"Some old friends have shown renewed interest as to your whereabouts," Hyatt said.

"What friends?"

"One, Mister Prescott."

"Tell me something I don't know."

"Mister Rayfer."

"Rayfer?" Keller reacted with a combination of anger and fear.

"None other."

"Rayfer...I should have guessed."

"I don't mean to alarm you, but I feel you should know what interest you still hold with Prescott."

"Yeah."

"Mister Prescott also has an interest in efficiency, the kind Rayfer is so very capable of providing."

"Yes...Was it Rayfer who demonstrated that efficiency on John Tennley?"

"You know the things that don't concern me are kept from me."

"Right...What did concern you about me?"

"Just where you are."

"Hyatt, you always were a slimy little man."

"Harmon, there's no need for that. I had a job to do and I did it. I didn't have to ring you up to tell you what I'm telling you."

"And that makes you a nice guy?"

"No, but it does give you a way out...Realize too, Harmon, I myself am in a great deal of jeopardy should my client learn of this meeting."

"Where can I find Rayfer?"

"He'll find you."

"Like he did in the hotel?"

"Yes..."

An elderly woman walked into the room and moved toward them, searching for a book. Keller and Hyatt went silent as they studied her movements. She moved next to Hyatt and searched for a book brushing against his shoulder.

"Oh excuse me," she whispered.

"Quite alright," he responded with an artificial grin.

The woman took the book and walked to a table and sat. Hyatt returned his attention to Keller. The two men resumed in the mood that had engulfed them before the minor interruption.

"Look, I'm giving you a good chance," Hyatt said. "You know Rayfer, how he operates, and above all, you know he will be the one. The rest is up to you. And as far as my actions are concerned, it all comes down to point of view."

"Yeah...right."

"Well consider this, if you emerge victorious, you will realize I had a hand in it--I helped you..."

"You tip Prescott off to where I am for a price, then you come to me for a cash bonus. How is that help? You're the one who wins and without having to make a stand."

"Mister Prescott will find you with me or without me. With me, you know how he's coming. Without me, you're a headline waiting to be printed. I suggest you reevaluate your position before you condemn me...And by taking no stand, I betray no one."

"Especially not yourself."

"Harmon, I came to help you. My interference does have a price, yes. But let's not bring personalities or absurd ethics to bear. You have something much more at stake. And if the outcome is not favorable, what difference will it all make in the end?"

Keller went silent at the confirmation that his death was being considered in immediate terms. A hateful force, determined to enable its own will and give no quarter, was proceeding in silent motion.

Keller felt displaced, transported beyond the boundaries of the library and its controlled silence. He sunk into deep isolation where he remained threatened and insecure.

Hyatt buttoned his coat and put on his hat. He smoothed the front of his coat and patted his pockets as though feeling for car keys or an imaginary pair of gloves. He looked at the books around him, stacked evenly on the shelves. A librarian entered the room, returning several books to their shelves.

Turning back to Keller, he saw abject desolation in his eyes. Hyatt felt a momentary concern for him. Not sympathy or remorse, only a passing interest for the outcome to his situation.

"Harmon...I wish you well," Hyatt said with an uncharacteristic hint of sincerity. Then he casually walked away, leaving Keller alone to reckon with his fear and to struggle with the uncertainty of his own fate.

★★★

The night rolled in on Keller more solemnly than ever before. Even when he lived on the streets, he recognized the distinction, that night was painted in surrealism, brushed more to an overstated horror than an impending, ultimate disaster. Perhaps then it was his abandonment of reality, or the notion there was little that remained to lose.

Now that his life rebounded, all threats became real, and his own preservation had once again become paramount.

Keller sat up in bed envisioning Rayfer standing behind every closed door, or walking out from deep shadows, prepared to inflict his brand of devastation. He felt Rayfer's intense eyes watching him from secluded places, his ominous presence, prepared, capable and unforgiving.

Awareness for Keller was only part of his defense. He knew he needed to nullify the surprise, and then try to match Rayfer's forceful aggression, if not his cold instincts.

Keller thought of ways to trap or defend against Rayfer, but the means at his disposal were limited. He no longer had access to an army of cohorts equipped with an array of technology and resources. He was all there was, and the only way he saw to get Rayfer was to be his own decoy. Lure him into a situation that would pit them against each other on reasonably equal terms. Keller knew he had to bring Rayfer into an arena where his attack would not be so sudden and final.

Keller rose from the bed and walked to the window. He saw the endless display of lights which adorned the city. The visual image of his reflection that superimposed itself in the glass tended to isolate and accentuate his personal drama. He tried to ease his mind, but in spite of his efforts, Keller could neither withdraw into peaceful seclusion nor absorb himself in fanciful delusion. The forces of irony were ever present, about to move in and strike a mark of their own.

Keller turned from the window and opened a closet door in his bedroom. He took down a small piece of luggage from a shelf and laid it on the bed. He undid the clasps and raised the lid. Reaching into an inner zippered pouch, he withdrew a small case and opened it. He reached and felt the contours of the Smith and Wesson .38. His finger rested on the trigger and his hand wrapped around its handle. A look of determination blended with disgust and took command of his face. His inner feelings pressed together, forming an unfamiliar emotion. His mind tried to equate it to the moment he drove an axe into the face of a fellow homeless person a long time ago. But there was no comparison or equation to draw on. In his entire lifetime there was nothing to resemble his present feeling. In the final analysis, it was not so much his fear of death as his fear of Rayfer.

Keller knew he could not allow himself to be intimidated. He could let nothing hinder his necessary response to Rayfer. He looked at the gun in his hand and felt a sense of strength and support. He brought his arm up un-

til it was parallel to the floor and aimed it into an unknown void. His eyes squinted, his jaw clenched, and his
stomach hardened. His entire persona focused on his target.

He saw Rayfer's face in his mind. The past was now
making a turn and heading full circle, coming toward
him like an unstoppable train. He had hoped for time, but
there was none. He maneuvered for escape, but there was
no room. Keller knew he could not capitulate, all that remained was a head-on collision with only one survivor.

"Come on Rayfer," he growled, as contempt and anger masked his fear. "Whenever you're ready!"

✲✲✲

Rayfer watched from his car as Keller climbed the
steps to the Sixty-Third Street YMCA. He had followed
him there on several occasions. When Keller disappeared
into the building, Rayfer stepped from his car wearing a
jogging suit and carrying an Adidas sport bag.

It was early Sunday morning and the street was serene and deserted. There were few cars parked on the
street and no bikes were chained to the steel post in front
of the building. Rayfer knew the recreation area of the "Y"
would be unpopulated and quiet for the time of day. As
he walked into the old building, he noticed a displaced
soul slumped in a torn chair in the lounge area to the
right of the entrance. A security guard appeared lethargic
as he leaned against the wall, unconcerned with anything
around him. It was too early for anyone to be on guard
for anything.

The main lobby was dirty and papers were strewn
about and areas of missing tiles blotched the floor. Rayfer
bent down and picked up a piece of paper and folded it
into quarters. He walked to the elevators which were op-

posite the lounge area and depressed a sticky button. The elevator opened and Rayfer stepped in and pressed "2."

The building was a multi-level structure which housed locker rooms on the second floor. A basketball court and running track, two weight rooms, and an aerobics room were located on the fourth floor. Business offices and living quarters were above that for the displaced, transient or thrifty. A steam room and sauna were located below the locker rooms. This area could be considered a half level, connected to the other floors by a small staircase.

Rayfer exited the elevator on the second floor and walked slowly toward the locker room. As he approached a check point just outside the locker room, he raised the piece of paper he had picked up off the floor to indicate to the attendant he was displaying a membership card. The attendant's eyes just flashed at Rayfer as he remained engrossed in a telephone conversation.

The locker room was divided into three sections with each section having its own maze of individual lockers.

The first section was separated from the other two by a shower/bathroom and one of the two adjoining rooms jutted out making an "L" shape of the entire locker area.

Rayfer stepped into the first area and proceeded immediately to an available locker. He opened the door silently and stood behind it in an attempt to hide himself from anyone who may pass by. From his vantage point he was able to look over the top of the door and observe anyone leaving the locker room going to the gym area, but he was unable to detect anyone descending the small staircase to the sauna or steam room. There was another entrance way for that purpose that was between the three areas and beyond Rayfer's view.

Rayfer unzipped his gym bag and withdrew two towels which were the only contents. One he placed over his head and tucked into the neck portion of his jacket, and the other he rolled and curved around his neck.

Off in the distance, Rayfer heard the clanging of what sounded like two lockers. He judged the sound to be coming from each of the two rooms. He stood motionless, listening for what he couldn't see. He knew one was Keller, but he had to concern himself with the other as well. There were the muffled sounds of indiscriminate shuffling, then a cough. Suddenly a locker door slammed, followed by the sound of sneakers gripping the floor, walking toward him. Rayfer watched intently as a muscular black man walked by, presumably on his way to a weight lifting workout.

Rayfer knew there was only one person left in the inner locker room, and that person was Keller. He reached into his jacket pocket and produced the Rostfrei knife. He held it comfortably in his right hand as it sent a surge of excitement through his whole body.

Rayfer closed the door of the locker and walked toward the inner locker room, using an aisle that was parallel to the main aisle. He wanted to insure the secrecy of his presence until the last possible second.

As he neared the end of the lockers, he heard the door to the sauna/steam room open, then close. He continued through the room until he came to the main aisle. The rooms were completely silent, indicating Keller had gone to one of the rooms below, but he walked into the locker room nonetheless. He proceeded cautiously, listening for the slightest sound. If Keller was there he would attack; the locker room was a perfect place, well concealed with varying possibilities for exits to choose from.

He moved like a silent tiger through the aisles only to discover Keller was gone. He left the locker rooms and proceeded to the steam room, an area with only one escape route, much more concealed than the locker rooms.

As Rayfer stepped through the door, Keller remained frozen with his back pressed against the cold tile of the bathroom that separated the locker areas. He knew Rayfer had been following him. Keller tried to spring a trap of his own, so he opened and closed the door to the sauna and hid in the bathroom, hoping to create the proper illusion for Rayfer to follow. From within the bathroom, he was able to look through the space between the stall portion and the wall and see the doorway to the steam/sauna room clearly, without being seen from the hallway. But as the figure passed before him, he was unable to distinguish the face clearly because of the towels. But the fact he went into the inner locker rooms first, led Keller to believe it was Rayfer being his usual cautious self. And judging from his physical appearance, Keller was almost certain his instincts were correct.

Being so close to Rayfer, and under the circumstances, Keller wanted to bolt from the building and run away. Escape into the city and hide. The fear he felt had suddenly become pronounced, confusing his mind and controlling his body. His throat closed, breathing became difficult. His heart no longer beat rhythmically, instead it was one long moan on the verge of bursting. His arms and legs were weak and cold sweat oozed from every pore in his body. For an instant he was tempted to walk, oblivious to the danger, down to the steam room and have Rayfer put an end to his overwhelming fear and relieve him of the great challenge facing him.

He had succeeded in trapping Rayfer, an advantage he could not forfeit. But the advantage was really not his to enjoy. He had no tendency for murder even though it was masked behind the veil of survival. But there were few choices, Rayfer had to be confronted.

Keller held the gun at his side and a towel concealed the weapon. He walked through the door and down the stairs. At the bottom of the stairs was a short dingy corridor, which led to several more steps leading to a pool for children. Midway down the corridor was a door which opened to the sauna/steam room. Keller quickly climbed the steps to the children's pool and tried to open the door. The knob didn't turn in his hand which meant the only remaining place Rayfer could be was in the steam/sauna area. He paused for an instant, not willing to take the initiative to make a move. He hoped Rayfer would emerge from the room and force the issue. His fear grew as he knew he had approached the point where his being would meet its destiny.

Keller descended the steps and entered the steam room area. Again there was a small corridor which led to a small alcove at the foot of the steam room and sauna. With the exception of a low, long bench bolted to the floor, the area was barren. The steam room was to the right and a large window provided a view into it. Keller threw the towel away and raised the gun to his hip. He walked in front of the glass and noticed thick steam filling the room which made a clear view impossible. Entrance into the room was via a doorway on the other side of the room, beyond Keller's view. On that side of the room was still another small corridor which lead to shower stalls. He knew the door to the room was open as steam found its way into the open area. Directly in front of him was the doorway to the sauna. A small window in the redwood door showed there was no light on in the sauna.

Keller moved slowly, assuming Rayfer was either hiding behind the door to the steam room or in the sauna. The probability of his being in the steam room was unlikely, although he could be behind the door, thus explaining why it was open. A sudden thought fanned his already exaggerated fear; what if Rayfer had somehow gotten behind him? There was no way to protect his rear. He relied on all his senses to detect any movement. The soft sound of steam filled the area, handicapping him slightly. Because of the heat and humidity, his body began sweating profusely. He proceeded cautiously to the end of the steam room which led to the corridor and a view of the open door. As he drew closer, the steam became thicker, shrouding him in mist, but not concealing him from harm. He inched closer to the edge of the steam room, his eyes peered through the mist. On the floor, stuffed under the door, was a towel which caused the door to remain open, concealing the shower stalls beyond it. Instantly, he knew Rayfer was not in that area. He turned quickly to the sauna. The instant he turned he heard a loud explosion; the door of the sauna swung open, hitting him flush in his body and the side of his face. The impact caused the glass to shatter and a piece of wood to break off the door. The force of the blow knocked Keller backward, forcing him to fall over the small bench. As he fell, his head struck the wall and his gun was knocked from his hand.

Rayfer charged from the sauna like a vengeful bull. His eyes were glazed with ruin, and the knife in his hand accompanied his intent. Rayfer knew his time was short. His kill would have to be swift, there would be time later to recall his pleasure.

Keller was wedged with his back against the wall and his legs over the bench. As Rayfer charged, Keller brought his right foot up quickly and as powerfully as possible to kick Rayfer in the scrotum. The blow inflicted just enough pain to stop him suddenly and give Keller enough time to get to a kneeling position.

Rayfer's rage had suddenly become tainted with insult. He sneered and he lunged forward, intent on driving the blade deep into Keller's eye. But at the same instant he dove forward, Keller leaned away and scrambled to his feet. The sharp point of the knife only succeeded in cutting the mist. In a clean sweeping motion he thrusted the knife sideways, hoping to stab Keller with his second stroke. Keller rolled to his right, far enough away from the second stab. He stood instantly and stepped backward, out from behind the bench. His mind was blank but rushed, he didn't know where the gun had fallen and couldn't think of a way to defend against the attack. He had a desire to run, but there was nowhere to go. He stepped backward against the sauna door. As he moved across it, he felt the broken piece of wood. He reached behind him and ripped it cleanly from the door. It was a molding that wasn't sturdy, but came to a sharp point. He whipped frantically at Rayfer who had become increasingly angry that he had allowed Keller to retaliate to such an extent.

Keller thought of running into the steam room and closing the door behind him to gain time. But the door, which opened outward and had the towel under it, would provide its own obstacle. He stood face-to-face with Rayfer. The steam still gathered around him, but he no longer felt it. His body was hot, but he felt cold; his heart raced, but he remained still, poised on the brink of diaster. Time lapsed into stillness and reality blended into confusion. All he could think of was escape.

Rayfer jabbed the blade toward Keller's heart. The point of the blade stopped just short of its target because Keller had driven the point of the longer piece of wood into Rayfer's neck. The retaliation rendered Rayfer's assault ineffective. The wood pierced Rayfer's neck; blood trickled from the wound and anger consumed him. His professional capabilities had given way to his natural rage. He became obsessed, stabbing and thrashing uncontrollably.

The knife either cut through his warm-up suit into his flesh or, passed violently through the mist. Keller responded with the same action, but driven by a different motivation. He backed up, swinging and jabbing the stick. He aimed for Rayfer's eyes while trying to keep away from certain doom.

He backed into the small corridor adjacent to the steam room and hit the door. It became free from the towel and continued opening as he continued backward. When he cleared the door it started to close, Keller grabbed it by the side and flung it in Rayfer's direction. Rayfer stepped back, allowing the door to slam and then ran after Keller who had turned and run into the shower.

Keller became frantic, he had run out of places to go. He was familiar with the area and quickly reached for a glass soap dispenser fastened to the wall and ripped it free. As Rayfer ran in, Keller threw the dispenser, hitting him on the chest. The glass broke as it hit the tile floor and liquid soap covered the area by Rayfer's feet. The object caused Rayfer to pause a second and Keller reached for a second dispenser. When he turned to take it off the wall, Rayfer charged at Keller, but the liquid soap caused him to slip to one knee. Keller reacted and ran to kick Rayfer's face. Rayfer blocked the kick and managed to tackle Keller to the floor. Rayfer quickly jumped on him, but found Keller was gripping the hand holding the knife with both hands.

Rayfer tried to put all his weight into a downward motion, but his feet kept slipping on the soap.

With his free hand, Rayfer squeezed Keller's throat. The pain to Keller was considerable, but it left Rayfer with little leverage. Keller rolled his body forcibly to the right causing Rayfer to roll to the side of him. He quickly threw his own weight on Rayfer and forced the arm with the knife to the floor.

Rayfer reached up and tried to insert his thumb into Keller's eye. Keller moved his head away, and in so doing, compromised the strength he had over the hand with the knife.

Keller jumped up quickly and fell backward, hitting the shower handle and causing the water to shower down. Rayfer was quick to rise, but Keller kicked him, knocking him against the wall. As Keller approached, Rayfer lashed out, aiming the knife into his chest. Keller managed to deflect a portion of the force, but not entirely. The blade penetrated his shoulder. Keller screamed, then grabbed Rayfer and threw him against the shower wall. He put his palm under Rayfer's chin and drove his head into the hard tile wall. There was a loud thud as Rayfer became dazed. Water showered down on his body.

Keller stepped back and noticed a black electrical wire running along the ceiling to a lone light bulb. He quickly jumped up and grabbed the loose wire and pulled it down. The wire broke free as did the cheap porcelain fixture connected to it. Keller snapped the wire and fixture like a whip at Rayfer's face. The bulb broke on his chin and a jagged end of the fixture became caught in the zipper of his jacket. Water began hitting the exposed wire on the inside of the fixture, sending electricity through Rayfer's body. He stood erect and began to quiver. A small puff of smoke began to emit from Rayfer's chest where the bare wire touched him. A dome of black began to spread, discoloring his tanned skin. His arms were rigid at his sides. He could neither run nor fall, he was trapped by a force beyond his own rule. The exposed wire continued to spark, as the water descended upon it.

The images he had of his victims at the instant of their deaths had suddenly been witnessed from a different perspective. The intimate association with which he had harbored such a perverted obsession toward them, was now his alone to experience from within. Personal and unique, total and far-reaching, and granting him a deep, unusual satisfaction.

Keller noticed the strange, disbelieving look that had come over Rayfer's face. Was it the same look the homeless man had the instant Keller drove the axe into him? He wondered.

Keller watched as Rayfer succumbed indifferently to his own fate. There was no escape for Rayfer. The ruthless life he chose had finally taken ultimate control of him, a vindication by the ultimate equality that affects all things.

Time and place became a blur for Keller. The pain to his shoulder and his bleeding were insignificant for the moment. Nothing existed except the strange, momentary gratification brought on by a sense of relief. He met and overcame just one more of the many demons of his life that temporarily sought to destroy him.

He turned and walked away, exhausted and disgusted. For now, the battle had been won, but beyond his ability to think, and overriding his condition, he knew, that Prescott still remained.

NIGHT SHADE

TWENTY-ONE

Lieutenant Elroy double-parked behind four patrol cars. There were two policemen standing on the steps of the YMCA as Elroy approached the building.

"Hello Lieutenant," they said.

"Hi. What do we have?" Elroy responded.

"Homicide victim. Downstairs," one of them responded.

The patrolman opened the door and Elroy followed. In the lobby there was an unusual sense of excitement as people responded to the presence of the police. Word had spread among the people that a murder had taken place and they expressed the usual blend of morbid curiosity and perverted interest. Their collective interests were kept quiet and hidden as they observed police activity from a suspicious silence.

Elroy and the policeman walked into the elevator and the patrolman depressed the "2" button. They stood silently as the doors closed.

"Who responded to the call?" Elroy asked.

"Car nine. Billings and Saunders. Me and my partner showed up last."

"Find anything?"

"No. We looked around. Nothing to find."

"Did someone contact the medical examiner's office?"

"Yes sir, Billings did."

"Good. I'm surprised the newspeople are not here yet."

"They'll be here any minute, I'm sure."

"When they come, keep them outside. I don't want them screwing around here just yet."

"Got it."

The elevator door opened and the two men stepped out.

"This way Lieutenant."

As Elroy walked down the corridor, he noticed one police officer talking to someone and taking notes. Another officer stood in front of the door leading to the sauna/steam room preventing unauthorized personnel from entering.

"Lieutenant," the officer said as Elroy approached.

"Hi, Marty...Downstairs?"

"Yeah, right through here," he responded opening the door.

Elroy descended the stairs and walked into the area. The room was humid and hot, the walls covered with a thin film of moisture. Three policemen and three employees of the Y stood in the outer area.

"Hello Lieutenant," one policeman said.

"Hello, Mike. I understand we have some trouble here?"

"Yes Lieutenant. As you can see, looks like a fight broke out here and ended in the shower over in the back."

"Yes," Elroy said studying the broken sauna door.

"You were here first, Mike?"

"Yes I was."

"Who found the body?"

"Gentleman over there," the officer pointed to one of the employees.

"He's supervisor of security. Do you want to take over Lieutenant?"

"No, Mike, do what you're doing. I heard the call and drove by. Just give me a report tomorrow."

"Yes sir."

"How did he buy it?" Elroy asked.

"The killer ripped an electrical cord from the ceiling and stuffed it into the guy's jacket in the shower."

"What did we find on the victim?" Elroy asked.

"Nothing. I'm waiting for the medical examiner."

"Good work, Mike."

"Thank you Lieutenant."

"Was anyone else around?"

"It was early, only one other member, he didn't see anybody but he did hear someone in the locker room. But he went upstairs, and that was it."

"Who are these guys?" Elroy asked referring to the three employees standing beyond them looking very nervous.

"Jeffrey Sutter, he's the security supervisor."

"The guy that found the body?"

"Yes sir."

"The other two guys?"

"One's Brian Brown, he's security at the check point to the locker. The last guy is Keith Bottic, he's member services director. He wasn't here at the time, but came over when he got a call."

"OK. Don't all members have to check in or sign in when they use the facility?"

"Yes, but Brown didn't see the victim come in."

"Is there another way into the locker area?"

"Not from the elevators, no. He had to pass that check point. Personally sir, I think the kid is lying."

Elroy looked at Mike, a good cop with all the right instincts, and Elroy believed him.

269

"Let's get him alone."

"Right."

Elroy walked into the shower area where he was able to see Rayfer sprawled on the floor. The light fixture was now resting harmlessly on his chest with the electricity disconnected. He approached the lifeless body and crouched down before it. In all the violent murders Elroy had seen, he was always amazed by the tranquil and serene look of the victims. Horrible wounds notwithstanding, there was never any indication in their eyes of the trauma that preceded their deaths. This observation led him to suspect there was more peace in death, than in life.

Elroy looked closely at the body and noticed a very small portion of the knife protruding from under his leg. He pushed Rayfer's leg, exposing the entire knife and picked it up by the point of the blade.

Elroy studied the knife, appreciating its craftsmanship and quality and carefully read the name stamped into the blade. He replaced the knife and felt Rayfer's pocket. In one jacket pocket he found a blank piece of wet paper folded in quarters. He patted at the second pocket and heard the jingling of keys. Elroy unzipped the pocket and withdrew two sets of keys. One set was car keys bound with a key ring that advertised "Hertz Rent A Car". The second set was an individual key with a "St. James Hotel" identifying emblem and the number "1038" stamped into the key.

Elroy put the keys into his own pocket and stood up. As he turned to leave, officer Mike Billings entered with the security guard.

"Lieutenant, this is Brian Brown," Billings announced.

"Hello, Brian."

"Hi, man."

"Lieutenant, Brian was the security guard at the locker check point and he doesn't remember seeing the victim enter the locker room," Billings announced.

"Is that so?" Elroy asked looking into Brian's eyes.

"That's right," he responded uncomfortably.

In an instant Elroy knew Billings was right; he sensed the guard was hiding something.

"Brian, let me ask you something...What's your job here?"

"I check all the members' cards as they come in. Make sure the picture on the card is the guy."

"You mean the membership cards have their pictures?"

"Yeah, like your driver's license."

"OK...And you check all members that come in?"

"Yeah. Sometimes I run their bar code through our computer."

"So then there must be a record of every member who comes in on any given day?"

"Yeah."

"And you check every identification card?"

"Yup," Brian said and moved more uncomfortably.

"Let me ask you something else Brian...suppose you get busy and there's a line of people waiting to get in and they didn't want to wait, would some members just walk by and flash their membership cards?"

"They're not supposta."

"Yeah, but do they?"

"Yeah."

"What would happen if your boss saw that, would he come down on you?"

"Yeah...hard."

"Lose your job maybe?"

"Maybe."

"Did this guy walk by and flash his membership card?" Elroy asked directly, going to Rayfer.

Brian didn't respond, he just looked nervously behind him toward the corridor.

"Sunday morning, everything's slow, peaceful, a perfect time to overlook something right? Nobody expects this to happen," Elroy said.

"Man, please don't tell my boss...With this gone down, I'm history for sure," the guard confessed.

"He won't hear from us."

"Oh, man, that's cool. I'm sorry, I didn't do my job really."

"Too late now. What can you tell us about him and the other two guys that came in?"

"There was two guys before him. First guy was a brother, I ran his card through the machine, the second guy, I didn't. I'm gonna catch heat just for that."

"You don't remember his name?"

"No man, I really didn't even look at the card. Seven o'clock on Sunday morning...it's...slow, man, like you said who expects this?"

"Yeah I know...Will you be able to remember the second guy?"

"I don't know, maybe."

Elroy paused and looked at the worried security guard.

"Man, I feel like everything's coming down on me like...like I'm the only key," he continued.

"Don't worry, just think hard, if you remember anything get back to us."

"Yeah, OK, man I will. And thanks man, I still ain't outa this yet."

"Don't worry you didn't kill him."

Elroy waited for Brian to leave.

"Good call, Mike."

"If he would have recorded that bar code we'd be in pretty good shape."

"Yeah, I know. What were you able to find out?"

"Well, Sutter found the guy being fried and shut the power and then made his calls. Nine one one, then his boss. Once he left here, he was afraid to come back. No real help."

"What did Bottic have to say?"

"Not much, other than tell me there are five thousand nine hundred twenty-two members to the exercise facility. Slightly over fifteen hundred are women."

"That might narrow it down...OK what else?"

"There are one hundred fifty permanent residents here, some from Julliard rent. Outpatients from Sloan Kettering and their families."

"Any transients?"

"Some."

"Of those that live here do they use the exercise facilities?"

"Yes, some."

"A lot of possibilities."

"If you ask me, Lieutenant, with all the gays here, I think it was a homosexual affair that went bad."

"I don't think so, I think it was a lot more."

"How so?"

"This guy was traveling light, no ID, nothing. I think he came in specifically for one victim."

"A hit that turned around?"

"That's my guess. Did you see the knife under his body?"

"Yes. Looks like a switch blade."

"E.R.N. Rostfrei, no better precision instrument. The blade, if my guess serves me, is Damascus steel, the best money can buy. A guy who kills for a living would want something that good."

"Why, if he's a hit man, doesn't he come in with a gun--one shot real quick and leave without the possibility of a struggle?"

"Some guys like the feel of death close up. It has its own kind of power. Steel penetrating flesh turns some guys on."

"Real sick."

"No doubt."

"OK, so who's the other guy then?"

"The missing bar code."

"Yeah...Damn that kid."

"Yeah...Listen Mike, get me a list of all the members who use this place and the people who live here."

"Right."

"Keep in touch with traffic, get the name of every owner of every car that gets a summons within a five block radius running for the next week."

"Fine, Lieutenant."

"Make it ten blocks. I'm especially interested in rented cars...Hertz."

"Will do."

"And naturally, when the medical examiner gets a make on this guy tell me."

"Fine. Anything else?"

"Yeah...Good job."

"Thanks Lieutenant."

★★★

Elroy drove through the streets of Manhattan, trying to shake a nagging thought. It hung onto him like a half-remembered secret, or an obscure vision. Something in his gut was making an association, something he couldn't see, challenging his premonition and exciting his curiosity.

He reached for his car phone and dialed a number.

"Hello," came Mary's voice after several rings.

"Good morning," he said.

"Hi, Larry, where are you? I just called your apartment."

"I'm in the car, on my way to see you. Is that alright?"

"Of course, don't be silly...I'll make us some breakfast."

"Mary, would you mind if we go out, I have something to do."

"That sounds good too."

"Great, I'll be there in fifteen minutes, is that enough time?"

"I'm ready now."

"Fine, see you then."

"OK."

Elroy hung up the phone and thought of Mary. She occupied his mind with a feeling of friendship and reliability. She was the bridge between his person and his life. He always felt welcome in her world, with no barriers or sense of privacy invaded. He felt a warm sense of traditionalism with her, one promising never to wear thin.

When he pulled in front of her house, she was standing on the sidewalk. He quickly leaned across the passenger seat and opened the door. Mary swayed in and immediately kissed him.

"Good morning," she said.

"Hi, Mary. Weren't you cold standing out there?"

"No, it felt good, cold but no wind."

"How do you feel?"

"Fine, yourself?"

"Yeah, good."

"Where did you go so early this morning?"

"Homicide at the Sixty-Third Street Y."

"Oh, no. What was it?"

"I don't know, but I think I have a way of finding out."

"How?"

"Hotel key in his pocket."

"Which hotel?"

"Saint James."

"We going there now?"

"Feel like it?"

"Sure, why not?"

"Good. I'll buy you breakfast later."

"OK."

✱✱✱

Elroy parked in a "No Parking" zone and turned down the sun visor displaying an "Official Police Business" sign. He and Mary left the car and walked into the hotel.

The lobby of the hotel was expensively decorated with Italian marble tables and painted Pairpoint lamps. A Simon Willard mahogany tall-case clock stood in one corner and a double staircase with thick red velvet carpeting led to a large reception room where a stately portrait of George III stood master over it all.

Mary paused for a moment to look around. She turned to Elroy with a look of disbelief in her eyes.

"You found a murder victim at the Sixty-Third Street Y?" she asked.

"Yes," Elroy said, recognizing Mary's suspicions.

"The Y is at least forty blocks away from here..."

"Three...Forty-three."

"Compared to this, it's on the other side of the world."

"I know."

"I'm sure they have a gym here, with showers and a sauna...clean too."

"Your reporter instincts are great, Mary."

"Then why go there?

"I hope to find out."

"Can I help you please?" the concierge asked from behind the desk as Elroy approached.

"Yes," Elroy responded displaying his identification. "Lieutenant Lawrence Elroy, New York police."

"Yes, Lieutenant, how can I help you?"

"I would like the name of the person who is in room ten thirty-eight. This is official police business."

"Certainly sir, one minute please."

The concierge leaned down to a computer and keyed in information. It took a second for the screen to display the information which he wrote on a piece of hotel letterhead.

He looked up and handed the paper to Elroy.

"Thomas Holden, 13 Citrus Drive, Tampa, Florida," he said.

"Great. When did he check in?"

The concierge looked at the screen once again and called out, "The second of the month."

"That makes it three weeks."

"Yes sir, it does."

"Thank you. I have to get into his room."

"I'll call up for you sir."

"That won't be necessary."

"Shall I...?"

"I'll take it from here, thank you," Elroy interrupted and turned and led Mary to the elevators.

The ride in the elevator was smooth and quiet; Elroy felt the luxury everywhere.

"Mary, maybe you should wait downstairs."

"Why?"

"Well suppose there's trouble?"

"Larry, the guy that rented that room is not coming back, what trouble could there be?"

"I don't know, I shouldn't have taken you along."

"Don't be silly, besides I may be able to see something for you."

The elevator came to a stop and Elroy led Mary off. They walked down the hall until they reached room 1038. Elroy put his ear to the door and listened for movement from within. He then inserted the key, turned the lock, and pushed the door wide open. Standing outside for a moment, he scanned the room and became convinced it was vacant.

"Give me a minute," he said to Mary and stepped in.

Mary waited a moment then entered behind Elroy.

The room had not been made up, but it still was not terribly unkempt. Mary looked around and felt somewhat uncomfortable over trespassing into someone's privacy even though that person was dead.

"Damn!" Elroy said.

"What is it, Larry?"

"Look at this," he said, looking at an airline ticket on a dresser.

"Yeah, so?"

"California."

"Yes, Los Angeles, what's wrong with that?"

"The clerk said the guy, Holden, was from Florida. My guess is he's from California and he's not Holden."

"Then who is he?"

"Good question."

Mary walked around the bed to the night table and opened the drawer. She withdrew a piece of paper that was on top of the Gideons Bible.

"Larry, look at this."

"What?" he said and walked toward her.

"Doctor Freedman, phone number and address."

"Good girl, that should help."

Elroy opened the closet door and looked in pockets of all the clothes. All he found was a roll of money totalling five thousand, three hundred, eighty dollars.

"Nice piece of pocket change."

"For sure."

Elroy rolled up the money and replaced it into the pocket where he had taken it from. He pulled down a piece of luggage and opened it on the bed. Inside he found a billfold with a valid driver's license issued to Thomas Holden of 13 Citrus Drive, Tampa, Florida.

"Look at this, Mary."

"Yes, maybe he is Thomas Holden and he's going to California from here."

Elroy went to the phone and dialed a number. He waited for someone to answer.

"Bet a dinner," he said to Mary.

"I'll settle for breakfast."

"You're hungry right?"

"I just need to eat, I'm a little uneasy."

"OK, we'll...Yes this is Lieutenant Elroy," he said abruptly into the phone. "I'm at the Saint James hotel. Please get someone from the medical examiner's office here. Room ten thirty-eight."

"Yes Lieutenant."

"Also send someone from the property clerk's office."

"Yes."

"And one other thing, check Tampa motor vehicles for a Thomas Holden. 13 Citrus Drive. That's Holden...Thomas."

"Yes."

"Get back to me here when you find that information please."

"Yes."

Elroy hung up the phone, then immediately picked it up again.

"Front desk?" he said

"Yes," came the reply.

"This is Lieutenant Elroy."

"Yes Lieutenant, can I help you again?"

"Yes, can you put together a list of phone calls made from Mister Holden's phone and bring it to me as soon as possible?"

"Yes sir. Are you in Mister Holden's room now?"

"Yes, I am."

"I will have that information for you immediately sir."

"Thank you."

Elroy hung up the phone and searched his mind, trying not to overlook any procedure.

"You know, Larry, there's something strange here," Mary observed, disturbing his concentration.

"What's that?"

"Holden, or whatever his name is, has been here for three weeks and aside from his driver's license, there's nothing with his name on it. No travelers checks, no Blue Cross card, nothing. Only clothes. No books, no magazines, pictures, nothing livable, nothing with a personal touch. You know what I mean?"

"What does that tell you, Mary?"

"Scary, that's what that tells me."

"I see suspicion all around here, Mary. This has all the watermarks of an invisible man, up to no good. A phantom man, here on an unholy mission..."

"Larry, you're scaring me."

"I'm sorry."

"Suppose the name is a fake, then what?"

"Check doctor, what's his name?"

"Freeman."

"Yes, see what he can tell me. If not, get a make on his fingerprints."

"That should tell you."

"I hope so."

The phone behind Elroy rang, startling Mary. Elroy picked it up and listened.

"Yes this is Elroy," he answered.

Mary watched his face as he kept the phone to his ear. By the look in his eyes, she knew the news was disturbing him. He turned to look at Mary, detecting her uneasiness.

"OK, thank you," Elroy said.

"No, that's all. That's all I needed to know."

Elroy hung up the phone, as a look of slight dejection crossed his face. He studied Mary and recognized uneasiness laced with fear. In spite of his investigation, he wanted to protect her.

"Mary, as soon as the desk clerk comes, we'll leave," he said, walking toward her, touching her shoulder.

"What was that call?" she asked.

"My office."

"And?"

"Thomas Holden, three in Tampa, all retirees, none with Citrus Drive addresses."

"This guy's a fake?"

"This guy's a fake, yes."

There was a soft knock on the door and Elroy went to open it. Standing outside was the desk clerk and another man.

"I'm sorry Lieutenant," he said, "This is Mister Wellsworth, he's the manager. I took the liberty of bringing him along. I hope you understand."

"Yes, it's OK."

"Thank you. Here's the information you requested," he said and handed Elroy an envelope.

"May we come in Lieutenant?" Wellsworth asked.

"At this point I would ask that you did not."

"Is there some problem with Mister Holden?"

"We are checking that possibility. There will be people from my office here shortly and when they're finished you can enter."

"At this point, would it be a safe assumption to consider the room vacant?"

"When my people leave, that would be a safe assumption, yes."

"Thank you Lieutenant, if there's anything else we can do for you please let us know."

"I will, thank you for your cooperation."

Elroy closed the door and opened the envelope the clerk had given him and studied its contents.

"What is it?" Mary asked.

"One phone call, the day he arrived."

"To whom?"

"I don't know. I'm about to find out."

Elroy started for the phone, but stopped when he heard another knock on the door. He quickly turned and opened it. Standing there was Ed Barrett from the medical examiner's office. Barrett looked as though he had been wakened from a sound sleep and rushed to dress and leave his house.

"Hi Lieutenant," Barrett said.

"Hi, Eddie."

"What's going on this morning Lieutenant? Our office got a call to go to the Y uptown real pronto, now here."

"Yeah, real busy. Did Tippett go to the Y?"

"On Sunday? Come on Lieutenant. I just left there and was a block away when I got a call on my car phone."

"This shouldn't take long, when you're done you can take the rest of the weekend off."

"Weekends? I'm just looking for six straight hours, that's all."

"You should have been a veterinarian, Eddie."

"Yeah, I know probably still not too late."

"Come on in...Eddie say hello to Mary Cello. Mary, Eddie Barrett from the medical examiner's office."

"Hi, Eddie."

"Hi, Mary."

Elroy walked to the telephone and dialed another number. From behind him he heard Barrett ask Mary if she was the news reporter on PBN.

Elroy spoke into the phone, giving the number he was reading off the paper to the police telephone information operator.

"Checking Lieutenant, please hold," the operator said.

He listened as Barrett and Mary were making friendly conversation. Through the phone, he heard the clicking of a computer keyboard.

"Still checking, Lieutenant," the operator said again.

"Thank you."

Barrett had put the bag containing his equipment on the bed.

"Whose room is this Lieutenant?" Barrett asked.

"The guy at the Y."

"What would you want me to do here that they couldn't do there Lieutenant?"

"I just need to know who he is."

"No ID on the guy at the Y?"

"None."

"Check the register?"

"False name," Mary responded.

"Once they print him, we'll probably learn who he is..."

"Yes, I'm here," Elroy said into the phone.

"The destination is an extension within a main trunk line Lieutenant," the police operator said.

"OK can you tell me who the main trunk line belongs to?"

"Yes Lieutenant...Ryser Pharmaceutical Corporation."

"What!?" Elroy shouted.

Mary and Barrett turned their attention to Elroy.

"Are you sure about that?" Elroy asked.

"Yes, Lieutenant."

"OK. Thank you very much."

Elroy slammed down the phone.

"Damn!" he shouted.

"What is it Larry?" Mary asked.

"I should have known," Elroy said, recalling his earlier instincts.

"What, Larry?"

"Prescott! That damn Prescott!"

"What about him?" Mary asked.

"Eddie, I don't think we'll need you here much longer. You'll be able to take your six hours off," he said, ignoring Mary's questions.

"I think I know what's going on Mary," he finally said to her, his tone hard, but not angry.

"Alias Thomas Holden made one phone call the day he checked in here," he continued. "To Emmet Prescott."

"Are you sure?" Mary asked.

"Holden called Ryser Pharmaceuticals, it had to be to Prescott."

"Why do you think Prescott?"

"My guess is Holden was contracted to kill Harmon Keller, who incidentally, is probably a registered member at the Y. Unless he's using an alias too."

"If he is registered under his real name, then you'll finally be able to find him," Mary commented.

"Maybe. If Keller had something to do with Holden, he probably won't be hanging around."

"So, if he runs, he'll be proving your theory?"

"Safe bet...Eddie, you mind staying here until the property clerk people get here? I'm going back to the Y to see if Keller is registered there."

"You bet Lieutenant."

★★★

Harmon Keller knew he had to move fast. He had no false illusions about who was pursuing him now. In addition to another hired assassin Prescott would enlist, the police were sure to discover his identity. He went over in his mind the evidence they could follow. The guard at the Y may remember him, fingerprints he left, especially on the wood from the sauna door, perhaps eyewitnesses he didn't see. The police were not a major concern to Keller, he knew killing Rayfer was a case of self-defense, but his instincts were to outpace all pursuers. His major obstacle was Prescott.

The wound to Keller's shoulder was still painful, but the bleeding had stopped. He managed to pack all his clothes and leave his apartment. Once again he was on the run, feeling like a fugitive being chased by the shadows of his own relentless fate.

He distanced himself from the city, searching for a quiet haven that would provide him shelter and seclusion. He needed time to hide, recover and plan. He weaved his way up the Henry Hudson to the Cross Westchester and Hutchinson Parkways. At Rye, he traveled Westchester Avenue until he entered the parking lot of the Rye Town Hilton. The hotel was recessed into the tree-filled landscape of the county, and not visible from the road. Keller felt isolated as he entered the quiet lobby.

A small restaurant to the right of the entrance was sparse of diners. At the far end of the lobby, an elderly man sat before a large fireplace, staring blankly at the dancing flames. For an instant, Keller became envious of the man and his apparent tranquility and exclusion from harm. An employee in a green uniform walked across the floor, pushing an empty luggage rack. The employee performed a trouble-free task, void of danger and threat. The simple peacefulness of the two men dramatically contrasted with Keller's turmoil. It intensified his own situation and called attention, with unflinching clarity, to his dilemma. For an instant, he felt a loathsome contempt for the CIA, and in particular for Emmet Prescott, a reckless force, intent on a deadly rivalry, allowing no alternatives, only conclusions.

As the bellman passed Keller, he smiled and continued through a corridor, disappearing into one of the ballrooms.

The check-in procedure seemed slow, irritating Keller's already unnerving condition. He tried to suppress his impatience and trauma. The pain in his shoulder was worse than ever; the urge to scream and relieve the anxiety that consumed him was overwhelming. The quietness and serenity of his surroundings suddenly were no longer soothing and protective. He needed to escape.

The desk clerk concluded the registration procedure and handed Keller the key.

"Room two thirty-two, sir. Can I have the bellman take your luggage?"

"No, that's alright."

"Fine. If you go to your right, to the corridor, and then go left, you'll find the elevators just beyond the pool area. Room two thirty-two will be on the second floor. Thank you and have a nice stay."

Keller took the key and followed the directions. He hurried into his room and pulled off his coat. He threw himself onto the bed, and an exasperated sigh escaped him. The sound filled the room and echoed in his ears. He heard firsthand the proof of his struggle and guilt. His eyes closed tightly in an attempt to shut out the world. His mind offered him little peace as it recalled the events of the day. Indiscriminate images disrupted his conscience and assaulted his values. He felt vile and hostile; the victory over Rayfer offered him no justification or redemption. He felt trapped, realizing his options were simply kill or be killed, and neither was a solution. He felt submerged in a wasteland that engulfed his younger ideology, which he no longer recognized, and a future which had no certainty. He became angry that his life slipped into a maze of upheaval. Blaming Prescott was easy, but he tried to examine his own complicity. Minute vignettes of his life juxtaposed themselves in his mind, giving him no answers or solutions. More importantly, he had to find a way out, discover a lifeline to his own peace of mind.

Thoughts became difficult and vague for Keller. The silence and darkness of the room blended to form a blanket that covered him. He floated down into a much needed sleep. There would be time to formulate his approach in the light of day.

The thick terry cloth robe fell off Emmet Prescott's knees, exposing his naked body. He sat slouched with his head resting on the back portion of the sofa, his legs spread apart. His left hand squeezed his testicles with undue pressure as his right hand stroked his blood-gorged penis. His squinted eyes and his face expressed a perverse sexual passion. The room was illuminated only by the light of the television, the only sound was his own harsh breathing. Prescott watched the images that were projected through his video player; the volume was turned off.

The scene was of three people in a barren, shabby room, the walls of which were windowless and dirty. A bare light bulb hung from the ceiling, but there was obviously a great source of unseen lighting filling the room. The floor was covered with a dark linoleum that was curled at the edges and worn in the middle. In the center of the room was a large, crudely made frame, resembling a door frame. Two pieces of two by four wood were attached to each corner forming an X within the frame. Standing within the frame, and tied spread eagle to each end of the cross member, was a man. Except for two dog choker chains wrapped around his neck, a thick belt around his waist and rope twined tightly around his penis and testicles, he was naked.

The other two members of the trio were sinister looking women. Each wore black high heel boots that extended to their knees and leather skirts that fit from their waists to the bottom of their buttocks. Fitting snugly from their waists to under their breasts was a leather corset with small chains attached to the locks that were fastened to the sides of the corsets. One woman was heavier, with large breasts, and a tattoo of a snake circling her left nipple. The other woman was smaller, but harder looking. The cheeks of her face were pockmarked, and she was missing a tooth on the lower front portion of her mouth. There was no gentleness in her eyes, only an old sadness that converted to a deep rooted anger.

Prescott watched her and knew by her appearance and actions, she was a stone-hard drug user.

The two women appeared to be taunting and humiliating the man. Prescott preferred no sound as he found greater eroticism in the visuals only. On occasion, he supplied his own dialogue, which was best suited for his own particular perversion.

The two women each reached for an end of the dog choker chains and pulled, cutting off a controlled amount of air into the man's lungs.

"Yes! Yes!" Prescott growled as though something choked him, restricting normal speech.

The man on the screen tried to move away from the pain, but his pleasure was evident. The women let go of the chain, restoring proper air flow into his lungs.

From somewhere off camera the smaller woman produced a very large safety pin. She unclasped the pointy part and bent the pin until it was in the form of an "L." The man's eyes widened in forced fright as he anticipated its use. The two women smiled at each other as they each carefully licked the pin. The heavier woman grabbed the left side of the man's chest and formed a fleshy ball. The man started to shake his head, but the smaller woman slapped him hard.

"Again! Again!" Prescott growled.

The smaller woman smiled and brought the point of the pin close to the man's nipple and in one short motion drove it through.

The man let out a silent scream, and started to thrust his lower body back and forth.

"MMM, MMM, MMM," Prescott moaned in forbidden delight.

The camera panned down to the man's erect penis. The pain obviously delighted him in a strange way. The heavier woman stepped in front of the man, blocking him from view of the camera. She untied his hands and he fell to his knees before her. Both women faced each other, ignoring the man, and hugged. Then they turned toward the camera and a serious resentful look etched their faces.

They suddenly appeared disconnected and unaffected by what they had just done. The words "The End" were superimposed over the women and the screen went black. The video player automatically clicked off when the tape reached its end and the television screen became snowy. Prescott remained seated for a while, lost in his personal form of pleasure.

His hands pulled away from his body, leaving him exhausted, but not fulfilled.

He slowly reached for the video remote and switched it off, automatically reverting the television to regular programming. Prescott depressed the volume button and the fading chorus from a Pepsi-Cola ad filled the room.

The next face Prescott saw was that of an anchor woman for the late Sunday news.

"Earlier today police were called to the Sixty-Third Street YMCA to investigate what they believe to be a possible murder," she said in a matter-of-fact tone.

Prescott rose from the sofa to withdraw the video cassette from its player.

"The man was found, fully clothed, in a shower stall. There were bruises about his face and neck, but a preliminary investigation has revealed that the probable cause of death was due to electrocution. A live electrical cord from the room's lighting system had been deliberately attached to him...The male caucasian has been tentatively identified as Thomas Holden of Tampa, Florida..."

Prescott froze, his eyes widened, and his attention became riveted to the television in a much different fashion than earlier.

"Police have no clues to the crime, and because of the early morning hour, there were no other members using the athletic portion of the facility," the news commentator concluded.

The news caused Prescott to become instantly enraged. He knew Thomas Holden was an alias used by Rayfer, and he used a Tampa, Florida address. Was it the same Holden, Prescott thought. He looked intently at the news broadcaster, but she reported on a different subject. There was no other information. The report created a myriad of speculations in his mind. Was it Keller who killed Rayfer, he questioned, through his anger? If so, how? The electrical cord was merely a tool, not an explanation. Rayfer was too much a professional to succumb to such results, Prescott reasoned. Where is Keller now, he thought. It had to be Keller, unbelievable as it was, it had to be.

Prescott walked into the small kitchen and poured himself a cup of coffee. He stared at the glass pot in his firm grip, and his mind began to focus.

Prescott found it difficult to comprehend Keller beating Rayfer, there had to be more to it.

A sense of urgency mixed with his rage. He knew it was ultimately coming down to Keller and himself. A confrontation he suddenly regretted postponing. The years had become nonexistent, bridged only by an unfulfilled covenant that Prescott swore would soon meet with timely justification.

"You got in my way once before...This is the last time you little fuck!" he said aloud, and threw the coffee pot against the wall.

TWENTY-TWO

Elroy didn't bother to knock on Doctor Freedman's door. He just pushed it open and stepped into the empty waiting room. A young receptionist dressed in nurses' whites looked up from her desk.

"Good morning, can I help you?" she asked with a schoolgirl smile.

"Yes," Elroy responded, approaching her desk.

"I'm Lieutenant Elroy, New York Police. Is Doctor Freedman in?"

"No, I'm sorry. He doesn't have office hours on Mondays here."

"Where is Doctor Freedman?"

"He is in his Mount Sinai office."

"I see."

"What is this in reference to Lieutenant, perhaps I can help?"

"Maybe you can, does Doctor Freedman have a patient named, or does he know a Thomas Holden?"

"The name doesn't sound familiar, but I'll check," she said as she turned to a computer beside her. "As for Doctor Freedman knowing him personally, I really can't answer that."

She typed in the name and the screen remained blank. "Are you spelling that H.O.L.D.E.N?"

"Yes."

"No, I'm sorry Lieutenant, he's not a patient, I didn't think so."

"How about Harmon Keller?"

"Yes, Mister Keller, I know."

"He is a patient?"

"Yes."

"Was he here recently?"

"I can tell you in a second," she said and started to type. The nurse suddenly stopped and turned to look at Elroy; a veil of concern covered her face. "You know Lieutenant, I'm not sure it's ethical to divulge this information."

"This is an official police investigation. I can legally seize Doctor Freedman's patient list; however, I don't have the time and I really hoped you would cooperate."

The nurse sat motionless for a moment, contemplating her options. "Is there a problem with Mister Keller?"

"To be perfectly honest, I really don't know. I would just like to speak with him."

"Why come here?"

"Because I know Mister Keller is a patient of Doctor Freedman, and I need a little background. Believe me, I only need to speak with Mister Keller."

"OK," the nurse said and finished typing his name into the computer."Here it is," she said.

"Yes," Elroy said looking at the screen. He noticed the address was listed as the Carlyle Hotel. "Is that a new address for Mister Keller?" Elroy asked.

"He was last here two months ago. That was the address he gave us."

"How long has Mister Keller been a patient?"

The nurse eyes scanned the screen. "He first came in two years ago."

"What was he being treated for?"

"It says malaria."

"Malaria?"

"Yes, Mister Keller had been working somewhere in Africa at the time when he became infected."

"Then he came to Doctor Freedman?"

"Yes."

"How often did he come?"

"In the beginning he was coming once a week, for three months."

Elroy continued studying the screen.

"According to that," he said, pointing toward the monitor, "he stopped coming all of last year and only continued two months ago."

"Yes...Oh, it says here he was due to come in last month, the twenty-seventh."

"Did he?"

"No."

"Any reason?"

"None."

"And he is being treated for malaria?"

"Yes."

"Is Mister Keller scheduled for a visit soon?"

"Other than the missed appointment last month, no."

"I see...OK...By the way, what's that?" Elroy asked.

"What Lieutenant?"

"Thorazine," he said, pointing to the lower left portion of the screen.

"His medication."

"OK. I think you've helped me quite a bit, thank you."

"You're quite welcome, Lieutenant."

"One thing...If Mister Keller calls for an appointment, would you kindly call me and let me know?"

"Lieutenant, I think it would be best if you take that issue up with Doctor Freedman. I gave you this information, and that seems alright, but what you're asking is something else. I hope you understand."

"Yes, you're right. I'll call Doctor Freedman. I'll talk to him about it. Thank you."

Elroy left the office haunted by obscure questions. The closer he got to Keller, the deeper he submerged himself into shadows. Keller's evasiveness seemed to be by choice, designed with purpose and need in mind. Was he cautious and calculating, or frightened and guilty, Elroy wondered. Elroy sensed a wall of secrecy neatly concealing Keller's actions and motives. But Elroy knew time was running out for Keller; he would crack the enigma that seemed to shroud him. And once he did, he was certain to find the ghost of Emmet Prescott.

Elroy drove into the police garage and hurried to his office. Waiting for him was Officer Mike Billings and Doctor Tippett.

"Good morning," he said.

"Hello Lieutenant."

"Larry."

"Sorry I'm late."

"It's OK."

Elroy took off his coat and put it on his coat rack.

"OK," he said sitting into his seat, "Billings what do we have?"

"Lieutenant, there were sixty-seven summonses issued within a ten block area of the Y, and thirty-two tows."

"OK."

"Of the sixty-seven, one was a Hertz rental registered to Thomas Holden."

Elroy looked at Billings. There was no surprise in his eyes.

"I figured you would not be interested in the other sixty-six, so I followed up Holden's rental."

"Good."

"The car had been towed to the police pound, and I checked it out personally."

"And?"

"Clean. The guy rented the car three weeks ago, and there's not even a cigarette butt in the ash trays. No maps, no scrap paper, nothing. Not even gum wrappers."

"OK. How about Keller?"

"Obtained a search warrant of the premises that was listed with the Y records, and checked his place out. Looks like he left in a hurry, took all his clothes, hasn't been back."

"Pulling twenty-four hour surveillance?"

"Yes sir."

Elroy leaned back in his chair and rubbed his eyes.

"Any feedback from the people at his apartment?"

"Spoke to the rental agent, all the transactions were in cash. One and a half months security, first month upfront. That's it, only one meeting, that was the last they saw of him."

"Damn, these guys don't leave trails."

"They all went to the same school," Tippett said.

"Don't tell me."

"Yes, Thomas Holden is a mystery man."

"Prints didn't come up with anything?"

"No, nothing."

"I can't believe it!" Elroy said showing annoyance.

"How about teeth?"

"So far nothing. I wouldn't count on it Larry."

"Yeah, I know. This guy was a hired pro. A no name."

"There was nothing on the guy. He was obviously in an altercation. Some bruises on his body were caused by wood from the sauna door. Death was by electrocution. That's the tale of the tape."

"Damn," Elroy said and stared off into space.

"All phantoms, Holden a hit man from nowhere with no traceable prints or teeth. Prescott an arrogant runt who won't say anything and Keller, all I know about him is he had malaria and takes thorazine."

"Thorazine?" Tippett asked.

"Yes."

"For malaria?"

"Yes, why?"

"Not for malaria."

"No?"

"Absolutely not."

"For what then?"

"Well...for schizophrenia mainly...severe depression."

"Schizo...are you sure?"

"Trust me."

"Hmm, why would his doctor prescribe...something's wrong here."

"Are you sure it was thorazine?"

"Yes, I saw the medication listed myself."

"Then maybe it's not malaria."

"No the nurse said malaria, and that was listed there also."

"Well it's the wrong cure for the wrong disease, Larry," Tippett concluded.

"That's for sure...What do you make of it, Mike?"

"No idea Lieutenant."

"OK then what can you tell me about schizophrenia?"

"Well it's a mental disorder with a biochemical basis."

"Biochemical basis?"

"Yes."

Elroy's mind recalled Mary telling him Prescott was involved in biochemical testing with the CIA.

"It's completely plausible that high potencies of certain biochemicals produced through metabolic dysfunction of the human organism may cause psychotic disturbances."

"What can happen in these disturbances?"

"Intense color perception, hallucination, depersonalization, intense anxiety, paranoia, and in some cases catatonic manifestations."

"Alright, let me ask you this. Is it possible for a person in a schizophrenic state to lose sight of reality to such a degree that they become dysfunctional in everyday society and just wander about living in the streets?"

"Absolutely. A large number of homeless are schizophrenic...Why?"

Elroy didn't hear Tippett's question. The images of a homeless person breaking into Miriam Ludlow's apartment occupied his mind. Suddenly the questions were becoming defined. Did Prescott purposely cause Keller to get sick by some chemical application? If so, it seems reasonable, Keller was trying to seek revenge on Prescott that night and for some reason just went into the wrong apartment. All reasonable questions and possibilities were leading to only one question--why?

"What you're saying then, is there are chemicals that can cause schizophrenia?" Elroy clarified.

"More exactly there are chemicals that can produce the exact symptoms of schizophrenia, yes."

"And thorazine would be the drug to counteract those symptoms?"

"Among others, yes."

"Mike that helped out a lot, thanks."

"What's going on, Larry?" Tippett asked.

"I don't know yet."

"Do you still want surveillance on Keller?" Billings asked.

"Yes. Tail Emmet Prescott too, I'll give you the information later, but this guy's real slick so become invisible."

"OK. What else Lieutenant?"

"That's it for now. Thanks for all your help."

Tippett and Billings rose from their chairs and left Elroy's office. Elroy reached across his desk to his Rolodex and turned it until he came to Gloria Tennley's name and dialed her number.

After the third ring he heard a timid, "Hello."

"Gloria Tennley please."

"This is she."

"Mrs. Tennley, my name is Lieutenant Elroy from the New York City Police."

"Yes, Lieutenant."

"I recently spoke with Linda Carson..."

"Yes, she told me," Gloria interrupted.

"I'd like to express my sorrow for your husband."

"Thank you, Lieutenant, your thoughts are appreciated. How can I help you?"

"I'm conducting an investigation here in New York that may have some relevance with Mister Tennley."

"Does it have to do with Emmet Prescott?"

"Mrs. Tennley, I really can't say much over the phone, can I possibly come to see you tomorrow?"

There was a long pause. Gloria Tennley struggled with apprehension and distrust.

"Mrs. Tennley..." Elroy said, breaking the silence.

"Fine."

"Good, thank you. Say ten a.m.?"

"Yes."

"Thank you, I'll see you then."

Elroy hung up and twisted his Rolodex once more until he saw Linda Carson's name. He dialed her number.

"Hello, this is Linda. I'm not able to come to the phone right now, but if you leave your name and number, I'll get to you as soon as possible."

Elroy waited for the beep and then spoke.

"Linda this is Lieutenant Elroy from New York City Police. I would like to speak with you as soon as possible regarding a matter that is very important to you. I intend to be in Prince William some time in the early to mid afternoon tomorrow. If you will not be home, please call me tonight at my home. Thank you."

Elroy gave Linda his home number, hung up, and dialed an interoffice number.

"Sergeant Taylor," he heard.

"Sergeant, this is Lieutenant Elroy. Is Marty Franich there?"

"No Lieutenant, he had to fly to Rykers."

"Is his schedule open for tomorrow?"

"Hold on, I'll check."

Elroy heard Taylor shuffle through papers.

"Lieutenant, according to this he has no scheduling tomorrow."

"Good, put me down for nine a.m. tomorrow. I need the helicopter to take me to Princeton, New Jersey, then on to Prince William, Virginia."

"Princeton, Prince William, OK got it."

"Thank you."

Elroy hung up the phone and sat back in his chair. Gloria Tennley and Linda Carson were two women, he felt, who would be able to bring him closer to the awful alliance between Tennley, Keller, Prescott, and hopefully Thomas Holden. Through knowledge would come understanding, and Elroy hoped to gain much needed understanding before any more players got killed.

Elroy laid on the floor of Mary's house with his back to the fireplace. He could feel the heat through the blanket that covered his naked body. The warmth relaxed him, making him drowsy. His head rested on the pillow and his arms were wrapped around Mary. She had her face pressed against his chest and her eyes were closed, but she was not asleep. Elroy let his finger tips follow the contours of her body from her shoulder down to her buttocks and back again.

"Hmm, that feels good," she whispered.

Elroy continued without responding. He felt warm puffs of breath from Mary's mouth billowing onto his chest. Elroy recognized them as an early hint of her passion. He leaned forward and kissed the top of her head. Mary traced a wet line with her tongue, from his nipple to his neck where she gently bit on a mouth full of flesh and began to suck. In one fluid motion, she rose from under the blanket, forcing Elroy onto his back. She straddled his lower body with her legs and laid on him.

"I love you, Larry," she whispered in his ear.

Elroy wrapped his arms around her, gripping her buttocks with both hands and pressed her close to him.

"I love you too."

She rocked back and forth, feeling content being cradled in his arms.

"Oh, you feel so good," she said.

Mary leaned upward and supported her weight on both her palms, and studied Elroy's face. His eyes focused on her, but she sensed they looked beyond her.

"What's bothering you, Larry?" she asked.

"Nothing."

"Keller?"

"Yes."

"He didn't show up at his apartment?"

"No, not yet."

"You think he killed Holden?"

"Probably."

"What do you do now?"

"Hope he shows up soon. I can't keep my men watching his apartment much longer."

"How about Prescott?"

"Same thing...Some day those two guys are going to collide, I just want to try and stop it."

"Some things you can't prevent, Larry."

"I know."

Mary eased off Elroy and repositioned herself at his side. Her arms fell across his chest and she reached out to feel the warmth of the flames. She pulled her hand back and touched Elroy's face. His stare was riveted on the ceiling, immovable, disconnected.

"Hey," she whispered.

"Yes?" he answered, turning his attention toward her.

"Don't worry about it. They're going to do whatever it is they have to. If they want to waste their lives over some petty outdated jealousy, that's their failure."

"I guess so."

"But you're still going to worry, right?"

"Well basically I'm going to see Gloria Tennley and Linda Carson tomorrow."

"Where?"

"Jersey, Virginia."

"You taking the police helicopter?"

"Yes. I should be back tomorrow night."

"Will they be able to help?"

"I hope so, I really do."

Mary became mesmerized by the flames. They captured her attention, taking her mind away from everything. After a while she turned her attention back to Elroy. She leaned up and kissed his cheek. He half smiled but his stare never left the ceiling.

"Want coffee?" she asked.

"Do you mind?" he responded.

Mary knew instantly what Elroy meant. His mind was too preoccupied to make love.

"No, that's alright."

★★★

It was five minutes to nine when Elroy walked into the outer office of the police heliport. Marty Franich was standing off to the side sipping coffee and going over some papers. The room was dirty and unkept. The large windows that faced the pad were stained and streaked; the room was an expression of functionalism and neglect, resembling a tiny state unemployment office.

"Hello Marty," Elroy said, approaching him.

"Good morning Lieutenant."

"How's it look for flying?"

"Good now, might be tricky later on."

"Weather?"

"Yeah, potential storm system coming out of the Rockies, heading our way at five miles per hour. Too soon to tell, but I'm tracking it."

"OK why don't we get going then."

"Fine. According to this request sheet you want Princeton, New Jersey and Prince William, Virginia."

"That's right."

"Which one first?"

"Princeton."

"OK. What's the exact destination?"

"Lodi Road, Princeton."

Franich removed a map of streets from his pocket and turned pages. His eyes scanned a myriad of crisscrosses and references.

"Lodi...no that's not it," he said more to himself. "Lodi Road, OK, here we are. Lodi Road," he said, seeing the street fit within the scale of the map.

"OK Lieutenant we have a choice, we can land in Princeton Airport or Police Barracks in Princeton. The airport is closer to Route 206, which will bring you roughly four or five miles closer to your destination."

"How far is Lodi Road from the airport?"

Franich looked at the map and made some quick calculations in his head. "Looks like five to seven miles."

"OK, let's get going. I'll be able to get a car there."

Elroy and Franich walked out onto the pad. The air was cold, but there was no wind blowing. Elroy looked up at the sky and became concerned at the gray overcast that had the potential of becoming a problem.

They entered the craft and buckled their safety belts. A slight nervousness gnawed at Elroy's stomach; Franich was calm as he functioned routinely.

"I still don't understand how these things fly," Elroy commented.

"Neither do I, Lieutenant."

Franich turned to see a pale, frightened look that found its way to Elroy's face.

"Relax, Lieutenant, pilot humor."

Elroy tried to nod his head in agreement, but instead he just gripped his kneecaps tightly. The initial whining sound of the rotor motors gave way to a deafening roar. Franich checked instruments and gauges of the craft and flicked several switches. He pulled on a throttle and the craft began to rise.

"Here we go," Franich shouted.

The helicopter lifted from the pad and raced into the sky, leaving the city behind.

Harmon Keller's eyes blinked open, responding to the sunlight that filtered into his room. The restless thoughts that haunted his mind caused him to snap up from bed as though awaking abruptly from a cruel nightmare. His body was clammy, coated with a film of perspiration. He felt disoriented; an unrestful sleep gave way to a rude awakening. His mind was foggy and it took him a moment to adjust and realize the reason he felt so poorly. He looked at his shoulder to reassess the harm caused by the stab. A small scab formed at the point of contact and there was circular discoloration that resembled a nasty bruise. He moved his shoulder slightly to ascertain its function. There was residual, pain but nothing he couldn't bear. He eased himself back down on the bed as the thoughts of his mind drowned out all connection to his body. Illusion struggled with reality which caused an inner conflict to his own morality and justice. He lay there trying to take solace in the fact that killing Rayfer was an act of self-defense. But the intruding sense of guilt offered no consolation. At one point in his life he worked side-by-side with men like Rayfer; now was no time to allow himself the luxury to believe he was anything different.

Keller rolled out of bed and placed his feet onto the rug-lined floor. His legs were unsteady and his mouth felt as though he had been sucking on a copper penny. There was a distinct notion of outrage that permeated his senses. The overall weight which fell in on him was not easily shed.

Keller walked into the bathroom and turned on the water. He let a puddle accumulate into his cupped hands and then splashed it onto his face. The water was cool, but not refreshing. He stood slumped over with his elbows resting on the sink, staring at the water swirling down the drain. Keller let his mind wander, searching for a brief refuge, trying in vain to escape into a world he knew no longer existed for him. He recognized his own passage over thresholds from which there was no excuse and no return. He picked up his head and looked at his reflection in the mirror. There was something uniquely different in his face, something he had never seen before. Beyond the glaring strain and inner anxiety was a murky unfamiliarity. For the first time in his life he saw something in himself he had never seen before. Had Rayfer brought out a dark side to himself, he wondered. Or did killing him push him into an alien world, exposing a sinister, vile instinct which had been lying dormant? He knew his actions could not withstand truthful self-examination. His own complicity blistered his soul, indicting his actions and convicting his pretense. Keller recognized the inescapable fact that Rayfer and Prescott were part of the same infirmity which in turn had contaminated his own life. Escape and deliverance now seemed like an indifferent voyage. There was no more running because now the pursuer was Keller himself.

Keller left the bathroom and walked back into the bedroom. He approached the bed and let himself sit gently on the edge. He looked at the telephone for a long moment, then slowly reached for it. He tapped in his sister's number on the keypad, secretly wanting to hear a familiar, friendly voice, one which could offer kindness, gentleness and forgiveness.

"Hello," he heard her say in her sweet, understanding voice.

"Linda," he said tentatively.

"Harmon, is that you?" her voice now becoming urgent and excitable.

"Yes."

"Harmon are you all right?"

"Yes. I'm all right."

"You don't sound it. Something's wrong, where are you?"

"In New York."

"Are you home? I tried calling your new apartment all night."

"I didn't go home last night, I..." Keller stopped.

"There's someone looking for you," she blurted out.

"For me? Who?"

"A Lieutenant Elroy from the New York City Police Department."

"New York City Police?"

"Yes."

"Did he say what it was about?"

"No, he left a message on my answering machine. I was out."

"Asking for me?"

"Yes...I had spoken to him once before."

"Once before..."

"Yes."

"What about?"

"John Tennley."

"John Tennley? How does he get into that?"

"I was hoping you could tell me."

Keller fell silent. He wished he could just confess to all that had encumbered him, the way he had done so many times before when they were children on the farm. But the passing of time complicated the simplest of abilities. The loss of clarity obliterated innocence and confined him to a desperate reclusiveness.

"Harmon?"

"Yes?"

"What's going on?"

"I don't really know...Why is he investigating Tennley?"

"I don't know that he is. He had called here once before asking for you, he didn't know about John then...I just mentioned it."

"And he called back again?"

"Yes."

"When?"

"I got the message early evening, it was probably late afternoon."

Keller's mind worked in quick segments, questioning, confirming his suspicions.

"How did he hear of me?" he asked.

"Through Prescott, I think."

"Prescott?"

"Yes."

"When did he first contact you?"

"The day after you were here, he was investigating a break-in."

"A break-in?" Keller questioned in disbelief.

"That's what he had said."

Once again Keller was tormented by his thoughts. How did the police connect him to the break-in.

"When did he call the second time?" Keller asked.

"Had to be sometime yesterday afternoon."

Keller knew by the timing of the call he was suspected of killing Rayfer. For once he was amazed at the efficiency of police investigation. Or perhaps Prescott had obliged them with the information he knew to be true.

"Harmon, what's going on?"

Keller felt an inner sense of defeat, but still tried to think of a way out.

"Harmon?"

"Yes?"

"What's going on?"

"I really don't know yet Linda, but when Lieutenant, what's his name?"

"Elroy."

"OK, when Elroy gets there, tell him I'll call him when he gets back to New York. I'll answer all his questions then."

"When will I get to see you, Harmon?"

"I'll call you after I talk with Elroy."

"I want to come up and see you now, Harmon."

"No Linda, that won't be necessary." His comment betrayed his need for her support, further perpetrating his personal denial. "Let me first see why Elroy is looking for me."

"Do you have to ask him why he's looking for you?" she asked, with a hint of incrimination in her voice.

The question took Keller by surprise.

"No...I just have to present my side of things, that's all," he responded truthfully.

"Where can I reach you Harmon?"

"I'll call you Linda...I'll call you."

Keller listened to the lonely silence that bonded him to his sister. He could easily picture her concern and envision her piercing eyes, not turning away, but looking straight ahead for truth. He sensed her familiar pose, with tightly pressed lips on the edge of anguish refusing to quiver or yield. He could also feel her quiet strength; she was capable and reliant enough for two.

"Harmon?"

"Yes?"

"Take care of yourself."

"I will."

"We're all that's left of our family."

"I know."

"I love you."

"Yes...I love you also."

Keller hung up the phone and reclined on the bed. His exhaustion obliterated his anger and fear and his desolation had quickly succumbed to resignation. Keller folded his forearm across his eyes in an effort to shut out reality. He recognized a cloud of justice which had somewhere gathered, about to descend upon him. There was no avoiding its vast sweep and unstoppable determination. Inwardly Keller felt a sense of relief, as a day of reckoning, long overdue, was about to call in all debts. The debts which chiefly concerned him were not those of his own making so much as those which were Emmet Prescott's to finally pay.

Keller rolled off the bed and pulled out the top drawer of the night table. He withdrew a telephone book and rifled through the pages. He suddenly stopped, then turned individual pages. When he found the address he was looking for, he merely made a mental note of it.

He knew approaching Prescott would have unpredictable results. He had to ensure there would be someone left who would represent the truth.

NIGHT SHADE

TWENTY-THREE

The helicopter eased onto the helipad at Princeton Airport as a Crescent 106 bore down a runway and cut a path into the gray day. Lieutenant Elroy undid the buckle of his safety belt freeing himself from the seat.

"Marty, I'll probably be gone most of the morning. I'll try to be back before noon," Elroy announced.

"Good deal Lieutenant, I'll hang around."

"I'll meet you in the terminal later."

Elroy stepped from the craft and walked to the airport terminal. There were few travelers and most of the terminal's occupants were airport personnel and rental car agents.

Elroy completed the transaction for the rental car and with the street map Marty had provided him, he was able to find Gloria Tennley's house with little problem.

Elroy stepped from the car and approached the house tentatively. He felt a guarded sense of repugnance which his profession had honed in him whenever he stood at the scene of a homicide. Before he was able to depress the button for the bell, Gloria Tennley had opened an inner door. From the other side of the glass outer door, she stood looking at Elroy with infinitely sad eyes.

"Lieutenant Elroy?" she asked.

"Yes. Mrs. Tennley?"

"Come in Lieutenant," she said, unlocking the storm door.

"I hope I'm not disturbing you."

"No, not at all."

Gloria led Elroy into a cozy living room which was decorated in Early American style. "Sit here Lieutenant," she said and pointed to a floral pattern high backed couch. "I was about to have some tea, would you like some?"

"If it's not much trouble."

"None at all, I have it made already. Excuse me while I get it."

Gloria left the room leaving Elroy alone with a strange silence that surrounded him. His eyes scanned the room, focusing mostly on photographs that were placed atop two end tables and several which lined the fireplace mantle. Each picture depicted a happy family in various stages of growth. One picture, closest to Elroy, was of Gloria appearing much younger, seated under a tree with a man Elroy assumed was her husband. She was dressed in plaid slacks and a bulky sweater. Her knees were bent toward her chin, her arms folded around them. The man was seated by her side, his arm around her shoulders. A pile of fallen autumn leaves, deliberately placed, covered his outstretched legs. He was youthful, with a boyish grin.

The photo was taken for them alone to cherish through the years, without the remote possibility of it ever being seen on a particular day by a New York City policeman. Their combined smiles reflected a better time, one which made it impossible to predict this fateful moment in the future.

Gloria reentered the room carrying a tray with steaming cups and a tiny pitcher of milk and sugar. She placed the tray on the table and put the cup in front of him.

"I don't know how you want it Lieutenant."

"Plain is fine, thank you."

Elroy leaned forward and picked up the cup. He took a sip and replaced it onto the table.

"Mrs. Tennley, I'm sorry about your husband," he said softly.

"Thank you Lieutenant."

"Is that him?" Elroy said, pointing to the autumn picture.

"Yes, we were living in Arlington when that was taken."

"When John was working for the CIA?"

"Yes."

"Did he discuss his work?"

"Rarely, when he did it was mundane, irrelevant talk."

"You know Harmon Keller?"

"Yes, he and John were co-workers and good friends."

"Did they know each other before joining the agency?"

"No, they met within the first year after recruitment."

"They got along well?"

"Very well. Harmon was often at my house; dinner breakfast, he never married."

"And you knew Linda?"

"Yes, very sincere woman. She and Harmon were born on a farm...earthy kind of people."

"Is that so?"

"Yes...Harmon always reminded me of a man out of place working for the CIA."

"How so?"

"Farmboy, simple background, he seemed somehow to be outside his element."

"I see. How about Emmet Prescott?"

At the sound of the name, Gloria went stiff. A cold angry look flipped onto her face as though recalling dreaded personal violation. "What about him?"

"What can you tell me about him?"

"He is a cruel and evil man."

"What can you base that observation on?"

"He killed my husband, that's evil. He waited years to do it, that's cruel."

"Why would he want to kill your husband?"

"An old grudge that Harmon Keller could explain."

"I'm seeing his sister later today; as of yet I haven't been able to speak with Harmon."

"When you do, I'm sure he will be able to give you a better insight as to why Prescott killed John."

"So your feeling is that whatever the reason, it stemmed from the time he worked for Prescott in the CIA?"

"Yes."

"Any particular time period?"

"I don't know exactly, but it was at least fifteen years ago. When John and Harmon were constantly traveling to New York."

"What makes you feel it was then?"

"Because John began acting differently then."

"How so?"

"He appeared frightened. For as long as I've known John he was never frightened about anything. He was then."

"Frightened of Prescott?"

"No, not Prescott, something else."

"What?"

"I don't know, whenever I broached the subject with him he simply denied it. That was his way of dealing with things."

"And then what happen?"

"What do you mean?"

"This feeling of being frightened, how did it resolve itself?"

"The assignment in New York ended and that seemed to be the end of it."

"Was John subject to any kind of reprimand or de-partmental action over the assignment in New York?"

"No, but years later he was subpoenaed by a senate subcommittee headed by Senator Church in Washington regarding some form of biological and chemical testing."

"Testing by the CIA?"

"Yes, as I recall the Air Force was involved as well...Hoffman-La Roche. It was all part of their investi-gation."

"How long after the New York operation was the senate investigation?"

"Oh, perhaps four or five years, I believe."

"Was there a connection between his assignment in New York and the Church Committee hearings?"

"He testified that there wasn't."

"Did Harmon Keller testify?"

"Yes."

"Prescott?"

"Yes."

"They too said the same thing?"

"Yes."

"Was there a connection?"

"I don't know."

"What, if anything, does Linda Carson know about all of this?"

"Probably very little. John didn't speak much about it to me and we were married."

"So what happened some fifteen years ago is the basis of your suspicion that Prescott was responsible for John's death?"

A slight spark of anger lighted in Gloria's eyes. Elroy's comment represented a negative insinuation.

"Lieutenant, I know as a policeman you're more comfortable with proof, but I didn't live all those years with John and not develop a sense of things. Even though he spoke little of his activities, I'm not a naive woman. You too should know how things work."

"Yes I do, and because I do, I hope you will understand when I say I have become cynical."

"I understand. I just don't understand what it will take to convince you."

"I'd feel comfortable with a motive."

"As I said, see Harmon."

"Had your husband seen either Prescott or Keller recently?"

"No. He hadn't seen Prescott for several years, nor had he seen Harmon for a year or so."

"I see."

Elroy felt a strange wave of inertia pass over him, he was moving ahead, but going nowhere. Harmon Keller was his ticket to ride, but he remained hidden behind a wall of evasiveness. Elroy reached for his cup of tea. He needed to clear the bitter taste of frustration from his mouth.

"It's probably cold Lieutenant. Can I get you a fresh cup?"

"No, that's alright, this is fine...Let me ask you something, Gloria, did you ever hear the name, Thomas Holden?"

"Holden, no."

"It was more than likely an alias. John never referred to it?"

"No Lieutenant, I never heard the name, why?"

"It was just a name that came up, no real reason."

Elroy knew there was nothing further he was going to learn from Gloria. She had obviously been kept in the dark about many aspects of her husband's work. Elroy realized he had confided to Mary more about his work and personal life than John had probably done in all the years he was married to Gloria. The thought of Mary filled him with a comfort that overrode his frustration. He needed to be with her, but first he had to see Linda Carson.

"Gloria, I want you to know I'm going to do everything I can to find out what's going on. I've been trying to contact Harmon Keller but that hasn't been easy. I'm on my way to Virginia to see Linda Carson. If anything, I'm hoping she will be able to tell me where I can find Harmon. I will keep you informed as to how my investigation goes."

"Thank you Lieutenant, that's good of you."

Elroy rose from the couch and trained his stare down into her eyes. He had been aware of Gloria's pain, anger and grief all along, but now it registered to him in a different way. She looked so small and defenseless seated, like a withdrawing victim, not just a witness.

As Gloria followed Elroy to the door, he felt a need to offer more, to be more than just a questioning cop with no quick solutions. He opened the door and then turned to look at her. Amid her anguish and vulnerability she remained restrained and composed.

"Gloria," he said, "if you are correct about Prescott, I'll pursue him to the end. It can not change what's happened, but I hope there is some consolation in bringing him to justice."

"Thank you Lieutenant, it will make me feel better."

"Goodbye," was all Elroy said as he left the house.

Elroy drove to the airport. The wind whistled as it slid past the car, not disturbing the bits of disconnected information that burst in his head. The Church Committee's investigation into chemical and biological testing consumed his thoughts. Testing what, where he wondered. Prescott now works for a chemical company. What does that mean, if anything? Mary told him Prescott was involved with some sort of chemical operation in the CIA. Was it all connected, Elroy wondered. Would it be logical for Prescott to wait so many years to settle an old grudge? Not likely, but maybe it wasn't an old beef, Elroy reasoned. Something recent, unrelated to agency business. The hungry and the hunted involved in a footless chase to nowhere.

Whatever teetered on Elroy's thought process or fanned his fires of reason, all came down to Keller. What did he and Tennley do to incur Prescott's wrath? What did they do that warranted a senate investigation? Only Keller could provide the answers. He would be able to supply an insight, but Elroy knew that Keller had deeds of his own that needed concealment.

Elroy made a quick turn off the road and kicked up a cloud of dust as he stopped the rented car in front of a telephone booth on the side of the road.

He jumped out of the car and stepped briskly to the phone. Reaching into his wallet, he withdrew a telephone credit card and punched in a slew of numbers and waited.

"PBN."

"Mary Cello, please."

"One moment please."

Elroy heard a click then listened impatiently to a long pause.

"Mary Cello," he finally heard.

"Mary, Larry."

"Hi babe, where are you?"

"Jersey. Listen Mary I'm in a hurry and I need your help."

"Sure."

"There was a senate committee hearing back in the early to mid seventies, I need to know what it was about. What can you do for me?"

"Who chaired it?"

"Church, Frank Church."

"What was he investigating?"

"Chemical testing by the CIA."

"Does this have anything to do with Prescott and Keller?"

"It might, Tennley also."

"I'll check our archives, but I have a feeling I'll get more from the library."

"I hate to impose, but can you find out something for me by tonight?"

"No problem."

"Listen, I'm on my way back to the airport and then to Virginia. I'll stop by when I get back tonight."

"Good, I'll have something for you by then."

"Thanks Mary, I really appreciate it."

"Don't be silly, just be careful. Have a safe trip."

Elroy hung up the phone and hurried back to the airport. He drove into the parking lot and returned the rented car. Marty Franich was seated in the lounge and waved for Elroy's attention when he saw him. Elroy's pace was quick. He felt his excitement mount as he was drawing close to an answer to a riddle.

"Marty," Elroy said.

"Hey Lieutenant, that was quick," Franich said, looking at his watch.

"Yeah."

"How'd it go?"

"So, so."

"You, still wanna go to Virginia?"

"Yeah, why?"

"There's a storm system heading for the area. We can get there, but forget about leaving."

"I've got to get there Marty."

"Can it wait a coupla days?"

"Probably, but I can't."

"OK then, let's go, the longer we wait, the worse it is."

Mary walked down the hall to the archive/reference room of PBN. She opened the door and stood staring at the rows of bookshelves crammed with books and reference material. The room was windowless, with only one door. The giant cinder block storeroom was silent, restricting sound from penetrating its thick walls. There was a musty smell of fermenting paper that permeated the area. Above each aisle was a line of recessed lighting. A short segment in the fluorescent string blinked dimly, adding an eerie pulse.

The shelves filled all the available space and were interconnected and bolted to the floor and to each other at the top. At the head of each aisle, affixed to the book shelves was a tag identifying the source of information and reference matter contained in the respective aisle. She walked to an aisle that was tagged "Government Hearings I", the "I" indicating there were other aisles dedicated to the topic. The first tag was subheaded "Senate Hearings 1970 through 1980". Mary proceeded down the aisle until she saw volumes of "The Annals of America". She reached for one displaying "1975" on the spine and turned to "C" in the index. There her eyes scanned down the listings until she saw "Church, Frank," listed on page 276.

At the designated page she began reading about a senate select subcommittee under Chairman Frank Church studying illegal intelligence activities. The committee found gross violations of privacy of American citizens through covert action designed to discredit the activities of individuals and groups. Harassment and blatant invasion of privacy were disturbing, but not new revelations to Mary. She knew Elroy was looking for other information as well.

Mary returned the book and began walking toward another area of the room.

"Hi, Mary," came the voice of Ed Dennehey catching her by surprise.

"Oh, Ed, you scared me," she said jumping slightly.

"Sorry, Mary. What are you looking for?" he asked.

"Trying to find a bit of information a senate committee was working on."

"Which committee?"

"Church."

"When?"

"I don't know, seventy-four, seventy-five."

"Regarding what?"

"Chemical testing."

"Where? By whom?"

"New York. CIA."

A beam of concern and worry bolted from Dennehey's eyes.

"What are you working on Mary?"

"It's for a friend of mine."

"Sure?"

"Yes, Why?"

"Just asking."

Mary saw the concern in Dennehey's eyes.

"Something's bothering you, Ed."

"I always get leery when I hear CIA that's all."

"Why?"

"Nasty bastards."

"You know something about testing in New York?"

"Yes, I covered the story then."

"Tell me about it."

Dennehey was hesitant to speak. He was protective, trying to spare Mary the sting of reality.

"Ed?" Mary asked, trying to break his silence.

"Testing was done in the sixties," he said reluctantly. "The Church Committee came some years later. It was the fall of seventy-five, if my memory serves me." Dennehey looked up at the failing light and made a mental note to have the bulb changed. "It was part of a twenty year long project...Operation MK Naomi...Like a bunch of kids playing a secret game, they had dumb code names for everything."

"Yeah, go ahead."

"They developed poisons that could cause deadly diseases in humans and systems for destroying crops. The toxin was made from shellfish and cobra venom. It was a whole new slant on warfare. Biochemical war..."

"Germ warfare is not new. Indians were exposed to smallpox, World War One had its share of gasses, not to mention Vietnam."

"That's true, but this testing was carried out in the subways of New York. The poisonous gas was used as a means of assessing threat of an invasion to passengers. They used citizens as lab rats, determining the ease of dissemination and methods of delivery. No concern was given to them as people. No one cared about the effects it would have on personal health, if it threatened lives. Remember these were experiments with no known outcome. God only knows how many citizens were exposed to diseased gasses. How many got sick and died. They used the subways to assess the city's susceptibility and

vulnerability to an attack. They also gauged what an of-
fensive attack would be like."

"No one was aware of the testing?"

"The U.S. Public Health Service was involved with
producing the poison. They provided the raw toxin to an
Army corps of scientists. But city officials, transit authori-
ties and above all the citizens were unaware anything
was going on. Probably only interested in fare hikes. As I
said, the Church Committee didn't hear about it until
years later."

"Was it a deadly toxin?"

"Very. A gram could kill five thousand people. By the
time the Church Committee investigated it, there was no
way of determining how many people died as a result of
it. Colby was the director then and he testified that the
CIA records were too incomplete to make any determination as to the effects."

"Convenient."

"Of course...Colby also used the term 'disease carrying' gases in his testimony. No one in the Church Committee picked up on it. To me poison and disease were
two different things."

"So there was more going on than just the shellfish
and cobra venom?"

"Yes."

"How did they get the toxins into the subways?"

"They threw bulbs containing the toxins onto the
tracks. When the trains came, they monitored the wind
dispersement and found the trains suck the poison air in
all directions."

Mary shook her head in disbelief.

"Nixon ordered the toxin destroyed, but he never followed up, and middle-level CIA people never complied.
They felt the shellfish was not a chemical weapon. They

just did what they wanted to do, and still do," Dennehey continued.

"Do you remember if there was any fallout with agents of the CIA over this?"

"No, why?"

"Just wondering."

"Mary if you would like to know more, I can recommend some good books."

"Yes. I would. Is there anything I could pick up from The Times microfilm?"

"Yes, it was covered by The Times, but the committee itself had to negotiate with executive officials about what information would be provided and how it would be handled."

"Why?"

"Why else?"

"National security," she answered sarcastically.

"Bingo."

"OK, I think I'll take a look anyway. Thanks, Ed, you've been very helpful."

"Mary?"

"Yes?"

"This friend, ahh, any particular reason he's interested in this?"

"The friend's a cop who needs background information."

"OK...I hope you don't mind my asking?"

"No. I'm glad you did."

"The Times will give you more if you need information right away."

"I do."

"Then check them out."

"I'll go do that right now. Thanks, Ed."

Mary turned and walked out of the room and headed to the Records Room where New York Times microfilm was kept. Dennehey stepped out into the hall and watched as she walked away. The crusty look of an old newsman weathered by torrents of injustice began to scale away. Concern uprooted the years of cynicism that had imbedded themselves in every line and crack of his face. His concern had little to do with the possibility of an immediate danger. He was regretful that Mary's idealism may be damaged as she exposed vile truths she would be powerless to correct.

Dennehey began to walk in the opposite direction from Mary. His head was bowed, his eyes staring blankly at the floor. Approaching him was Bill Medley, one of the cameramen from PBN.

"Hi, Ed," Medley said as he passed.

Dennehey was unresponsive, continued on, truly not hearing anything. The hollow sound of his heels clicking onto the floor echoed in his head. He harbored no other thoughts, only blank expression.

TWENTY-FOUR

Mary darted out of the PBN building and stood at the curb with raised hand in hopes of attracting the attention of a cab.

The weather caused the evening rush hour traffic to become slower and angrier than usual. As people rushed by her, she was able to sense their undulating impatience and need to be in a warm dry place, sequestered for the night. She too was somewhat anxious to be home. She had spent a good part of the day going through microfilm of past issues of The New York Times and had information to convey to Elroy. In part, The Times added little to what Dennehey had told her, but it did substantiate his memory.

A vacant cab stopped in front of Mary and she opened the back door and climbed in. The car was warm and spacious, but a stale odor resembling wet cloth and diesel fuel filled her nose. The cabby, appearing oblivious to the odor and the menacing traffic, made a notation on a clipboard, then lowered the lever which started the fare meter. After Mary announced her destination, the cab merged into the traffic, becoming just another link in a long caravan that moved in forced succession.

Mary was tired and just wanted to remain still and quiet, removed from the aggression and pace around her. She hoped the cabby was not talkative.

Mary settled comfortably in the seat, glad to be off the cold street. She arranged her coat over her knees and pulled her briefcase across the seat, resting it on her lap. She folded her hands over the cool leather in an attempt to protect the notes she had made for Elroy. Her mind was preoccupied with thoughts of him, interspersed with what she had learned earlier. Disgust for the blatant misuse of power mingled with concern for Elroy's safety. Both were becoming exaggerated by an invading fatigue. She rested her head on the back portion of the seat, trying to block everything from her mind. She closed her eyes in an attempt to isolate herself from the hurried confusion of which she was, reluctantly, a part. For the brief time she was in the cab, she wanted to focus on nothing, float above everything that tried to pull her down.

Mary soon became unaware of the weather and the noise. All she felt was the movement of the car, the stop and go. Eventually the rocking motion lulled her into a light relaxation. Soon she became aware of nothing but her own breathing, inattentive to the things around her, especially the car that had been parked at the curb, purposely waiting for her as she emerged from work. The engine was running, but she didn't hear it or notice the driver who was paying icy attention to her every movement. She didn't focus on his quick response to follow the cab as it left with her aboard.

Through the jerky traffic, the car followed closely behind.

The cab turned sharply, tossing Mary to one side and disturbing her self-imposed silence. Her eyes opened to recognize her street and house.

"Here we are," the cab driver announced.

Mary looked at the fare registered on the meter and withdrew money from her purse. She paid the driver, stepped from the cab and began climbing the stairs to her brownstone. Home, she thought, and the warm, quiet privacy that goes along with it. As the cab pulled away, the car that followed parked opposite Mary's house. Again, unknown to Mary, the driver watched her closely. She removed keys from her purse and unlocked the outer door. The sound of her ringing phone caused her to rush. She stepped quickly to the second door and unlocked it quickly. With her foot, she kicked the door closed, but not forcefully enough for it to close properly and lock.

Mary ran through her living room to the phone in the kitchen.

"Hello," she said, trying to catch her breath.

"Mary?"

"Hi, Larry."

"You all right, you sound out of breath?"

"I'm OK, I just came in, had to run for the phone. Where are you?"

"Virginia, the weather grounded me."

"I figured that. Is it that bad there?"

"Not so much now. But it was earlier, there's no way I could have gotten back."

"Just as well, I'd rather you were safe."

"We plan to leave first thing in the morning."

"Good...How did your day go?"

"Not bad, not good."

"Were you able to see Gloria and Linda?"

"Yes."

"What did they have to say?"

"Gloria Tennley thinks she knows who killed her husband, but doesn't know why. She and Linda Carson don't know too much about what John and Harmon were involved in, so it's tough. How did you make out?"

"OK, I guess. Tennley and Keller were involved in some sort of chemical testing in New York subways some years ago. I didn't get to do all the research I wanted, but it's a starting point."

"Chemical testing? Gloria Tennley said the same thing. Testing like what?"

"Trying to determine what impact poisonous gases would have on New Yorkers in the event of an enemy attack."

"Enemies? What enemies?"

"Take your pick."

"The only enemies we have are those guys themselves. Who are they trying to kid?"

"You're starting to sound like a radical, Larry."

"Yeah, what were they doing? What kind of poison?"

"Well basically they were using a poison they made from shellfish and extracted cobra venom. Releasing it in the subways, letting the trains disperse it into the air."

"You're kidding me."

"No."

"Anybody die from it?"

"Nobody knows for sure. It wasn't found out until years later. No way to determine who died from what."

"You can rest assured they know."

"Maybe that's why there's a grudge, somebody wants to do some talking."

"It's a possibility. But with those lunatics you never know."

"I have some notes I took from The New York Times, it's all true."

"Show me tomorrow, OK?"

"I will."

"How about their testimony to the Church Committee, anything?"

"No, the microfilm I saw today didn't mention them at all. That's why I want to do some more research."

"OK, I'll pass by your office in the morning, show me what you have."

"OK."

"Did you have dinner yet?" Elroy asked.

"No, I just got in. I was going to make something for us, now I'll just have a sandwich. How about yourself?"

"Me and Marty had something at the hotel."

Mary didn't hear the car door open and close outside her house. Nor was she able to see the stranger who had been following her up the steps to her front door and had silently forced his way past the outer door.

"What are you doing now?"

"About to shower and relax. I'm trying to go over what Gloria and Linda said, see if I missed anything."

"Who does Gloria feel killed her husband?"

"Prescott."

"Oh?"

"Yeah, those guys definitely have a secret."

"How about Linda?"

"She's in a strange position. She wants to protect her brother, but she really doesn't know who to protect him from."

"Did they know about the chemical testing?"

"No, but they knew about the Church Committee hearings. Gloria did mention that whatever trouble existed between John and Prescott started sometime ago when he was shuttling back and forth to New York."

"In nineteen seventy?"

"Yes."

"That's about when all that testing was going on."

"Interesting."

"Do you think there's a connection?"

"Could be."

"Why don't you talk to Prescott about it?"

"No. Prescott won't admit to anything, especially if he had Tennley killed. He's not about to bring attention close to himself."

"That's true."

"Mary, did those clippings indicate how the Church Committee found out about the testing?"

"No."

"How about any internal dissension?"

"Within the CIA?"

"Yes."

"The paper didn't mention it...Why?"

"Just looking for something."

"Well at least we have an idea as to what may have started the problem."

"Possibly. Yes, but there's something missing."

"Like what?"

"Let's say Gloria Tennley's right, that whatever bad blood existed between John and Prescott stemmed from the days of that testing,"

"Yes."

"Why wait all these years to even it up? Especially since they haven't seen each other in years."

"How do you know that?"

"Gloria said so."

"So what is it you're implying?"

"Nothing really, I'm just trying to make sense of it all."

"Based on what you're saying, there really doesn't seem to be a case against Prescott."

"Exactly."

"How about a case against Keller?"

"Could very well be, although Gloria said Keller and John were friends."

"It gets confusing."

"For sure."

"Larry, why don't you give it a rest, clear your mind and think about it when you're fresh."

"Good idea."

"If you were here, I'd give you a great massage, relax you."

"Sounds great. I wish we were able to fly back tonight, I miss you."

"Me too. Tomorrow night I'll cook, we'll stay in."

"That has a nice sound to it."

"Yes, I kinda like it myself."

"Mary, I'll see you in your office tomorrow."

Mary replaced the phone and kicked off her shoes and let them stay where they tumbled. She took off her coat and scarf and started to walk toward the front closet with them draped over her arm. Entering the living room, she noticed the inner door had not fully closed. She quickly remembered not kicking the door hard enough for it to lock automatically. As she approached the door, she noticed a dark figure through the stippled glass. The figure lurked in the foyer between the two doors. Mary tried to deal calmly with the sudden fear that exploded within her. She thought of running to the kitchen to get a knife or reaching for the poker by the fireplace, but oddly enough she stood motionless, unable to resort to violence.

She moved slowly and silently toward the door, attempting to slam it shut. Her heart pounded and her throat began to close. She was suddenly struck with the strange image of seeing herself from outside herself. Her view was of a helpless girl; then her father crossed her mind. She would never see him again, she feared. Genuine fright oozed from every pore. The urge to scream became a dire necessity.

As she inched closer to the door, she saw the figure moving closer to it also. She stood before it, about to slam it shut and give herself the illusion of protection. Through the small opening of the door, she saw eyes looking at her. They were strange, silently communicating aggression and violence, filled with purpose and intensity.

She reached to slam the door. The invading stranger reached forward in an attempt to push it open.

"Mary?" the stranger whispered.

The realization that the perpetrator knew her name filled Mary with a despicable fright.

"No wait, Mary. I'm here to speak to you. I mean you no harm," the voice continued.

Mary took no chances as she tried to force the door closed. There was a loud, solid thump as it crashed into the stranger's foot which was between the door and its jam. The loud crash displayed to Mary just how forcefully she tried to close the door.

"Mary, please," the stranger pleaded.

"Who are you?" she forced.

"I need to speak with you."

Mary braced her shoulder against the thick wood trim of the door, prepared to force it shut.

"Who are you? What do you want?" she nearly pleaded.

"My name is Harmon Keller. I need to speak with you."

Mary froze, at the mention of the name.

"Harmon Keller?"

"Yes."

"What do you want?"

"I need to speak to you. Please trust me."

Mary paused for a moment, not in an attempt to think but more to regain her thinking ability. Instinctively, she stepped away from the door and swung it open. Keller stood motionless in the hall, knowing he had gained a minimum of her confidence. He treaded cautiously, not wanting to dislodge Mary's fragile trust.

"You're a reporter, I need to speak with you."

Mary stood bravely facing him, but still frightened.

"Why don't you just call me at my office? Why do you sneak into my home?"

"I apologize, but I'm in trouble and I'm afraid you may be watched."

"By whom?"

"I don't know. I just don't trust anyone anymore."

"What is this all about?"

"May I come in?"

"You already have," Mary answered angrily.

"I'm sorry. I just didn't know of a better way."

Mary studied his eyes. Beyond their grim determination was familiarity, one reminiscent of a vague horror she remembered from an unexplainable region. "I know you," she observed cryptically.

"Yes."

"From where?"

"The tunnels, beneath Grand Central Station."

"Yes!" Mary said, astonishment blending with fear. The video of the homeless quickly came to mind as she saw the eyes that bore so much hopelessness and despair. Now, here, under different circumstances much of the same look was still present.

"I filmed you."

"Yes."

"What were you doing there?"

"Living."

"You were different then."

"Not much."

"What happened?"

"It's a long story...Can we sit down?"

Mary was tentative and guarded, but her reporter's curiosity overruled her caution. She backed into the living room, acknowledging Keller's entrance. He moved slowly and closed the door quietly. He was deliberate, keeping a reassuring distance between them. He appeared uncomfortable, almost frightened as he entered her home.

"Mary...forgive my intrusion. Believe me, I don't mean to frighten you."

Mary looked at Keller with less suspicion as fragmented thoughts shot through her mind. Was Keller a suspected murderer or defender of his own life? How and why was he, at one point in time, among the destitute of the world? She wished Elroy had not been forced to stay in Virginia. If he hadn't, he would be walking through the door shortly and relieve her fear.

"So what is it you have to talk to me about?" she asked.

Keller unbuttoned his coat and purposely sat in the chair furthest from Mary. She placed her coat and scarf on the couch and sat next to them.

"Where do I begin," Keller thought aloud.

"You can start by telling me not who you are, but what you are."

Keller's look turned to surprise and suspicion.

"You seem to know something about me."

"Your name has come up."

"Oh?"

"CIA or ex-CIA?"

"How do you...?"

"Insignificant how I know."

Keller saw the look of determination set deep in Mary's eyes. She was no longer frightened and her defense was in her directness.

"Ex...Ex-CIA."

"Good...That's a start. What else?"

"What else do you want to know?"

"You can tell me about John Tennley, Operation Naomi."

"You know about them?"

"Just a little. Tell me more."

"I didn't expect you'd know all this. Are you investigating me, or...?"

"What I'm doing is of no consequence to you. I just need answers."

Keller held her in his sights, observing her as stone-like, not about to forfeit her position.

"I'll get to John in a minute," he conceded. "First, some background information. MK Naomi was a secret operation to test the effect chemical and biological warfare would have on a given enemy."

"You mean an effect it would have on us in the event of an attack?"

"Mary, what you don't understand is that all testing is done with aggression in mind. This government really cares little for citizens. National security becomes the false catchall phrase for an elusive, larger issue. It's an uncommon ground, vaguely marked by disillusionment and paranoia. Might is considered the first line to maintaining that illusion and might should never be misconstrued with defense, only aggression."

"So we tested our vulnerability, figuring it would also be an enemy's?"

"Exactly...Weakness is always the key to defeat."

"Why the subways with shellfish and cobra venom?"

"That was just part of it. A very small part."

"What else?"

Keller reached into the inside of his coat and withdrew the folder. He rose quietly and walked toward Mary, dropping the folder on the table before her. She looked at the large block letters on the cover which read:

OPERATION NIGHT SHADE
CLASSIFIED/CONFIDENTIAL

Keller turned and stepped to the lifeless fireplace and stared at the dark pit. Mary reached for the folder and opened it.

"Emmet Prescott's pet project," Keller announced blankly.

"The cobra venom was nothing compared to that. The subways were only one area. Tunnels, turnpikes, from vans, planes, boats, infectious bacteria spewing out all over. Sophisticated...Secret...What a mess."

Mary sat motionless, watching Keller. He appeared like a man in need of spiritual cleansing, an absolution through confession, a baptism by the fires of speech.

"Prescott wasn't involved in all of it, but when he took over he went crazy. First there were the tunnels...Twenty-eight miles of tunnels. Holland, Lincoln, filled with genetically-altered bacteria. We sprayed many miles of The Pennsylvania Turnpike also. The Air Force was used to spray Dade County, Florida with a bacteria that caused whooping cough to raise three thousand percent. Boats were used in San Francisco Harbor. Up and down the bay for days contaminating the city. It was an open market for chemical testing."

"You mean you contaminated whole cities."

"Yes."

"With what?"

"In New York we used bacillus globigii, aspergillus fumigatus, spraying out from a customized Volkswagen."

"Spraying?"

"Yes, like an aerosol."

"What did it do?"

"It was an uncommon sporadic that caused asthmatic attacks, ear infections, who knows what else."

"And in Pennsylvania?"

"Same thing...In San Francisco, a converted fishing boat saturated the air with serratia marcesens which caused urinary infections, heart trouble, various blood conditions, pneumonia...It lowered people's resistance and killed them."

"That is inhumane."

"We didn't see it that way then."

"You should have."

"I know."

"Why though?"

"There is always someone figuring new ways of killing populations of people. After World War Two, biochemicals became the silent arsenal. Atomic power was getting all the attention, but the chemicals were worse by far."

"Why?"

"Their devastation was not as evident...it was silent. The world had more to fear from chemical biological warfare than bombs. The scientists were genetically altering bacteria, giving birth to a host of new viruses and diseases that could obliterate mankind. It's a runaway phenomena with no antidote."

Keller paused. He seemed sullen, regretful. His words rekindled an anger and disbelief long dormant in the recesses of his past. Now he found himself laden with guilt and seeking forgiveness.

"Lowered resistance?" Mary asked.

Keller turned from the fireplace. The meaning behind her question had not gone unnoticed.

"Yes. Genetically altered bacteria back then, probably similar alterations of which are producing the immune deficiency syndrome of today."

"You, Tennley and Prescott were involved in all of it?"

"Just the New York operation. Prescott gave the orders. Tennley and I worked out the logistics. We worked with a team of scientists from Fort Detrick in Frederick, Maryland. That's where most of this stuff was produced...Tell me, how do you know John Tennley?" he asked, almost as an afterthought.

"I don't know him, I just know a little of what's going on...Did you think what you were doing was wrong?"

"Not at the time. Not until Night Shade."

Mary looked at the folder in her hand quickly. She didn't want to stop and read it now.

"Explain Night Shade to me."

"Prescott wasn't able to conceptualize the effect of the shellfish and cobra venom because people weren't dropping dead instantly. He needed to see more. We had what we called GB and UK-- nerve gasses."

Mary looked down at the folder and saw on page three:

GB chemical compound

$CH_3 [C_3H_7O] F PO$

Keller turned to look at Mary.

"I see it here, but it's been a long time since I took any Chemistry 101. What's the compound?"

"It's nasty. GB and UK work by inhibiting a key enzyme needed to control muscle movement. That's how it kills. The enzyme is known as acetylcholinesterase or ACHE. It's all a complex process of nature, but at millions of junctions in the nervous system, a body-produced chemical known as acetylcholine transmits nerve signals. Upon receiving a signal, it moves across the junction and activates muscles or nerve cells on the opposite side. After activation has taken place, the body releases ACHE to neutralize or destroy the buildup of acetylcholine. When the nerve agents enter the system, they immediately inhibit the production of ACHE, thus the body loses an important control over the transmissions of acetylcholine and in effect, strangles its own vital organs. It's horrible. The voluntary muscles go into a state of vibration and become paralyzed. The heart slows and there is a paralysis of the respiratory muscles. Death by asphyxia every time...no exceptions."

"And Prescott wanted to flood the subways with GB and UK?"

"Yes. That's when Tennley and myself realized Prescott was deranged."

"Did Prescott know the effect of GB?"

"Of course. He was an expert on chemicals and their compounds. He experimented with another agent, Joe Emory. Joe was a friend of mine and Tennley's. Prescott had somehow infected Joe with crystallized LSD. He became psychotic with delusions of persecution. Prescott arranged to have him check into the Chestnut Lodge, a sanitarium in Rockville, Maryland. The place was staffed with CIA-cleared psychiatrists. It was full of CIA personnel suffering from similar disorders. Anyway, Joe threw himself from the window that night and died. There was a cover-up, everything was erased and his widow was never told the truth."

"Did you ever approach Prescott and apprise him of the effects it would have?"

"Yes, but he insisted the amount and the dispersement would not produce fatal effects. We disagreed, but he ordered us."

"Then what happened?"

"We blew the whistle on Prescott. The report you have in your hand went to Ed Hodge who was a GS-17 at the time."

"Prescott's superior?"

"Yes."

"Is that why there's bad blood between you and Prescott?"

"Yes...I'm sure he killed Tennley because of it."

"But this all started years ago and Tennley was recently killed."

"You seem to know a lot about us, Mary."

Mary ignored the question. She could not tell Keller how she came to know so much. "Would Prescott carry the grudge that long?" Mary continued.

"Obviously you don't know Emmet Prescott."

"No I don't."

"He's psychotic, a very deranged individual. In his own way he felt betrayed by Tennley and myself, completely overlooking the consequences of his plan. Our allegiance was not to Prescott then. Believe me, Tennley and I became very worried over Night Shade. There was no way we could have allowed it. Luckily Hodge saw it that way too."

"If Prescott killed Tennley why did he wait so long?"

"Hodge was around, he was our shield. When he died, Tennley and myself were doomed. Prescott waited until he was retired from the agency. His life became very dull to him at that point. You have to understand his mentality and ego. There were no challenges for him anymore and his sense of revenge was probably consuming."

"And he killed Tennley?"

"I'm sure of it."

"And you?...Did he try to kill you?"

"Twice...Once he used quinuclidinyl Benzilate or BZ. He concocted a way to vaporize it into my house. BZ inhibits the production of a chemical substance that facilitates the transfer of messages along the nerve endings, thereby disrupting my normal perceptual patterns. In the beginning, I had headaches, disorientation, auditory and visual hallucinations and maniacal behavior. Usually the effect of BZ lasts only several days, but with me it was different. It played havoc with my brain chemistry. The psychoactive substance produced a psychotic disturbance through some sort of metabolic dysfunction. My schizophrenia was brought on by a biochemical indoctrination."

"So when I happened upon you in the tunnels you were sick, still suffering the effects of exposure to those chemicals?"

"Yes."

"How long were you living there?"

"A year or so. I don't remember exactly."

Mary paused, becoming afraid of her next line of questioning.

"Harmon, did you know a man named Thomas Bass?"

"No, why?"

"He was a murder victim we found the day I saw you."

Keller bowed his head and turned once more to the fireplace. Though there was no flame, he felt the heat of hell burn through to his conscience. A silent indictment pressed in on him, imprisoning his soul.

"Bass?" he whispered.

"Yes."

"We argued over a piece of newspaper. It was dark. He struck out at me. His knife tore at my coat, I hit him with my axe."

Keller's hands covered his face as though to hide his shame. "A piece of newspaper...We fought over a piece of newspaper...God was it that bad? When segments of mankind become that desperate, there's no hope for any of us," Keller continued.

Mary allowed Keller the dignity of his own ethics. She sat in respectful silence, withholding all judgments.

"I'm sorry, Mary, where were we?" Keller said, lapsing away from his self-inflicted indictment.

"Prescott."

"Yes, as long as I take my medication, I'm all right, but he's the reason for it."

"Harmon, do you know a man named Thomas Holden?"

Keller turned sharply and glared at Mary. His look renewed the fright she felt earlier.

"His name is not Thomas Holden. It's Alex Rayfer. A hired assassin. And how do you know about him?"

"I'm a reporter, I follow stories."

"Why do I somehow feel this is a police investigation?"

"Harmon, you came to me remember?...Did you kill Alex Rayfer?"

"That doesn't seem like a story a reporter of your standing would know about."

"How do you know what kind of story I would cover?"

"Because the CIA has been monitoring PBN for years. All organizations that do the kind of investigative reporting you do and are free from any guidelines were of interest to us. That's why I didn't want to come to your office. I had to follow you home from work. I couldn't take the chance."

"I know about the type of monitoring the CIA and FBI does. Other than it being an invasion of privacy which infringes on fundamental freedom, I'm not concerned with that now. Tell me about Thomas, rather, about Alex Rayfer."

Keller studied Mary, measuring her own level of distrust. His reluctance to answer was monitored only by his suspicion.

"Alex Rayfer was one of those secret tools used by us. Known only to a select few. He was hired out in strict confidence to do select work. He wasn't an employee of the CIA, just a budgeting factor paid for under operating expenses, like a private limousine. He was exclusively on Prescott's expense account. He and Prescott made a strange combination, they fed each other's violent perversity. When I found out Tennley was killed, then I learned Rayfer was coming for me, it all came together..."

"Do you know for a fact Rayfer killed Tennley?"

"Yes, but without proof."

"How did you learn Rayfer was coming for you?"

"Through someone who's only in for the money. Anyway when I knew Rayfer was coming, I laid a trap."

"Did he attack you at the Y?"

"Yes. I thought I could catch him by surprise, but he was good at what he did. I got lucky."

"Why didn't you go to the police with the Alex Rayfer thing?"

"Because there's no connection between Prescott and him."

"How about someone else at the Agency?"

"Out of the question. Very few people there knew Rayfer even existed. Those who did wouldn't come out against Prescott."

"So because of Night Shade, Prescott is looking for revenge?"

"No, not exactly. Prescott blends the extreme properties of obsession. His mind does not see outside his own decisions. His capabilities are vast. He has a deranged sense of justice. Not that it doesn't have to do with Night Shade. That was doomed from the start. It only has to do with Prescott and what he wants. And there's no force that can dissuade him. It's what drives him, gives him life. And after Rayfer's failed attempt on me, he's suddenly gone mad, madder than he is normally."

"So why did you come to see me?"

"Because I'm probably the only one who can tell you what this is all about."

"Why not go to the police?"

"I told you, I don't trust anyone."

"But the police can help."

"You don't understand. No one can help."

"What do you mean?"

"What do you think?"

"You're going for Prescott yourself."

"If he wins, at least I know I've left enough behind that may bring him down."

"Of all you've told me there's no proof. How can he be brought down? This is all hearsay."

"That's why I chose you. You are an investigative reporter and this is no ordinary act of revenge or defense. The implications are immense. I feel better knowing you're after Prescott than the police."

"That's ridiculous."

"Maybe, but that's how I see it."

"That's single-mindedness, like Prescott."

"Maybe beneath it all we're the same. I tend to think not, but at the point where there's no way out, logic gives way to instinct."

Mary sensed the futility in Keller's plight and in her own ability to detract him from his intentions. She saw the focus of destiny about to converge between Keller and Prescott. Whisking another human drama by the unrecorded annals of humanity. The unnoticed act of hate and revenge or, as Keller believes, madness. Maybe that's why the world is the way it is, Mary thought. It's a good enough reason as any.

"Mary?" Keller said. "I hope I don't put you into a dangerous or awkward situation. I come to you because...well I guess I trust you. I don't trust people, but you seem different. What I said about Rayfer and, ah, Bass, that's between us."

"I'm not making any promises. I'll see what I can do, what feels right. You came to me because of yourself and your own sense of revenge. If you die trying to kill Prescott, you know I'll try for him in another way. That gives you comfort; it does little to undo what's happened to Tennley, his wife, and all the innocent people your organization thinks so little of. Chemical testing, covert wars, invasion of privacy. You jeopardize the very essence of this nation's freedom, the freedom you claim to protect."

"I'm sorry you feel that way."

"I'm sorry I'm made to feel that way about all of it...For once, try to do it differently. Go to the police."

"I can't, Mary. I can't."

"Why not? You set up Rayfer, now try to set up Prescott. Try to get him to confess to Tennley."

"How?"

"I don't know, there's got to be a way. You said you're different than Prescott. Prove it. You haven't gotten to the point of no way out yet, so be logical."

"You still believe in a legal justice."

"I have to. So do you, or else you wouldn't be here now."

"I thought you said I was here for revenge."

"For yourself yes, but for Prescott, justice."

Keller pondered the reasoning that had been presented him. In a theoretical sense there was no disputing it. But reality bore colors of a different fabric. He had to weigh the opposing factors and decide which to exercise. But hovering between the two alleys of contention was

349

Prescott. Keller knew that he would not bring to bear alternate modes of resolve. His choice would be clear and concise and strictly one-dimensional.

"Mary, he knows I got Rayfer. He's prepared for anything, and not about to allow himself to be trapped."

"I understand, but try."

"You don't understand."

"I understand revenge is not the way out."

"Neither is capitulation."

"Your way, one of you, or maybe even both of you, won't come out of it. My way, you may be able to get him."

"That's not going to be easy."

"I know."

Keller paused, realizing he was not going to convince Mary.

"I'll try," he said finally.

"That's good enough for me. Meanwhile, I'll try to get background on Prescott."

"OK. Good luck."

"Good luck to you too."

"I hope your way is right."

Twenty-Five

Mary spent most of the morning sequestered in her office. She had been up all night reading through the Night Shade report Keller had given her, trying to comprehend the ramifications of what he had confessed. The knowledge burdened her. She wondered how the information would impact on her relationship with Elroy. Part of what was said to her should be kept confidential, yet Elroy needed to know the context.

Night Shade was not the integral part of Elroy's case. He was primarily concerned with the murder of Thomas Bass. Mary had no difficulty presenting Elroy with background information. After all, she'd made no promises to Keller. But divulging Bass' murderer was another matter. She pondered where she should draw the line between what information she could and could not ethically divulge. She always suspected that her source confidentiality would be tested, but she had no way of knowing it would be on such a personal level.

In one brief conversation, she had been pitted between her professional sanctity and her unrelated emotions. The two were poles apart, yet bound on an individual course poised for collision.

She tried to postpone the thought of any impending implication her knowledge would have and focus only on Operation Night Shade.

Some of the technical terms within the report were alien to her, but she was able to understand the mechanics behind the operation. What was impossible to comprehend was the logic and lack of morality. The arrogance of the initiators enraged her, transforming enlightenment into cynicism.

Mary focused on their insensitivity and indifference. Their actions went unchallenged and when finally questioned, she believed they responded with omnipotence and indignation. They believed their means served the greater good, and any opposing factors were insignificant.

Beyond what Keller had said, the report added little except for giving exact locations and personnel involved. As she reexamined the results, she realized they were assessed in the short term and nowhere was there any indication that there was concern for the innocent victims. Their findings did little to bolster a sound defense or reaffirm a national dominance which left her believing it was all an unfair trade-off.

From within her thoughts she heard the soft knock on her door. She picked up her head and took a deep breath.

"Come in," she announced hesitantly.

Elroy opened the door and stepped into her office. His face looked haggard and tired, but his eyes were bright, reflecting a gladness upon seeing Mary.

"Hi Mary," he said.

"Hi, Larry."

Mary rose from behind her desk and walked to greet him. As they kissed, she could feel his hands grasping hers firmly, a controlled response she recognized as a deeper expression. She too harbored her own underlying need. All she wanted to do was fall into his arms and re-side there. She felt frightened and threatened, but hoped that in spite of what she could or could not tell him, he would always allow her that comfort in that special place.

Elroy sensed her disturbance, appearing distant and guarded. He let go of her hands, but watched her curiously.

"How was the trip back, Larry?" she asked.

"No problems. How are you?"

Mary didn't answer. She stepped behind Elroy and closed the door. She moved back to her desk and sat down.

"You all right?" Elroy asked.

Mary looked into his eyes, making no attempt to conceal her turmoil.

"No," she responded.

"What's the matter?"

"We'll talk about it later."

"Mary, tell me now."

"Later...Here's the information I picked up from back issues of The Times.

Elroy looked through Mary's handwritten notes, hoping to piece together the missing links. He was startled by what he read, but his interests were in other bits of information which could help him solve a homicide.

"There's nothing there on Keller or Prescott, just the operation itself," Mary observed.

"Hmm, hmm. They really did this?"

"Yes."

Elroy continued flipping through the pages, quickly reading bits of information.

"There's no mention of anyone ever being held accountable. No involvement of Prescott."

"I know."

"According to these notes, they keep referring to 'safe' testing..."

"Yes..."

"What determined safe?"

"They just wanted to minimize their efforts or cover them up."

"Is that it?"

"No...Read this, you might find it more informative, Larry," she said, handing Elroy the Night Shade folder.

"What's this?"

"A more detailed explanation of the operation."

Elroy opened the folder and began reading. His attention was quickly absorbed in the report. He saw chemical names he couldn't pronounce and names of people, Emmet Prescott among them.

"Here we go, Prescott's responsible for the planning," he announced.

"Yes."

"According to this, Keller and Tennley were involved in the logistics, preparation...GB, nerve gas," he read aloud from the report.

"You know about that?"

"In Vietnam we saw a film of its effect, nasty stuff. Where did you get this Mary?" he asked.

"From Harmon Keller."

Elroy looked up. Surprise and anger filled his eyes.

"Harmon Keller?" he shouted.

"Yes."

"Where did you see him?"

Mary hesitated, afraid to speak.

"Mary, where did you see him?" Elroy repeated.

"He came to my house."

"What?" Elroy closed the folder and rolled it into a tight tube."What was he doing at your house? What did he want?"

"To tell me about Night Shade."

"Why you?"

"He remembered me from the homeless report I did."

"What do you mean, remembered you?"

"You remember the closing shot, the homeless guy we panned in on...his eyes?"

"Yes."

"That was Keller."

"That was Keller?"

"Yes."

"What was he doing there?"

"He was homeless at the time and by sheer coincidence he was there when we were."

"Was he actually homeless?"

"Yes."

"How come a working guy making good money winds up homeless?"

"It's a strange story."

"Tell me about it."

"Well you read the report. That's the beginning of it. Prescott had devised this plan to fill the subways of New York with nerve gas. Keller and Tennley were to arrange the logistics, but the more they knew of the effects the gas would have, the less they wanted to go through with it. In essence, Keller and Tennley opposed Prescott. They made mention of this phase of the operation to Prescott's superior and Prescott never forgot it...To get even with Keller, he administered a chemical that manifested itself as schizophrenia."

"That makes sense, Mike Tippett told me the medication he was getting from his doctor was for schizophrenia. But I thought one was born with that disease."

"According to Keller, it's biological, in his case brought on by 'BZ' he called it, and his own body's reaction."

"That explains Keller breaking into Miriam Ludlow's apartment."

"I guess."

"He just had the wrong one."

"Obviously."

"So why after all these years do these guys come gunning for each other?"

"That's what I wanted to know, but Keller said I had to know Prescott to understand that."

"All right, after Tennley, he went for Keller?"

"Yes. Prescott hired an assassin..."

"Thomas Holden?"

"Yes, really Alex Rayfer."

"Good, now we're getting somewhere. Rayfer killed Tennley?"

"Keller believes so."

"What happened at the Y?"

"According to Keller, he knew Rayfer was following him; he was prepared. It was a case of self-defense."

"How did he know Rayfer was following him?"

"He didn't say."

Elroy leaned back in the chair and tapped his chin with the rolled folder.

"What's bothering you, Larry?" Mary questioned.

"Something's not right."

"Like what?"

"I don't know, Keller."

"What about him?"

"I'd like to believe him only because I don't like Prescott, but that's not enough."

"It's enough for Keller. He's going for Prescott."

"How?"

"I asked him to go to the police, try to set up Prescott."

"What did he say?"

"Very difficult, apparently Prescott is very cunning, nobody's fool."

"Yeah, that's my impression too, but who's to say he killed Rayfer in self-defense? Maybe he's looking to set you up so when he kills Prescott it all looks like there's a reasonable cause."

"Why bring exposure to himself by contacting me?"

"Why? He knows I'm suspecting him for Thomas Holden, or Rayfer, maybe he's hoping for an elaborate scheme to pull off a hoax and get himself free."

"I doubt it."

"He was living in the tunnel when Thomas Bass was killed, right?"

Mary remained silent. She feared what would follow.

"Did he confess to killing Bass?"

The question made her tremble, she wanted to cry.

"Why aren t you answering me, Mary?"

"I can't."

"Why?"

Mary faced off Elroy. The challenge was before her, but she wanted to run away, into the next room or any place that would take her away from the problem.

"Mary this is a police investigation, don't hide behind professional immunity," he continued.

"I'm sorry, Larry."

"Mary you're not a priest in a confessional."

"I know that."

"There's something more at stake here."

"I'm not sure there is. He's not a mass murderer about to strike again..."

"He's about to kill Prescott and no matter what, Prescott deserves my protection," he interrupted.

"You don't need me to protect Prescott."

"That's true, but Keller is probably a murderer and you're making him out to be a victim."

"It's not what he is that's in question...It's what I am."

"I don't agree with your liberalism. You see what I've seen in the streets over the years and sometimes in the pit of my stomach I wish there were only one rule, get the criminal no matter what."

"Oh, come on, Larry, you don't really believe that."

"I don't know, it's just that deep down I realize there's too much margin. The wrong people are getting away with things they shouldn't."

"You have got to have a balance."

"Look Mary, I'm not here to argue about the virtues of liberal politics versus the threat to a free society. I'm just looking to find a killer and serve justice. It's my job."

"I know that, Larry, but I have a job also, and if I say anything to you, I compromise every news reporter and their privileged information. No matter how unjust that may seem to you, it's something I can't do and it's killing me. How do you think I feel? I'm caught between a theoretical ethic and a real emotion. If something I say can keep you from harm, then the hell with the ethic. If I betray that ethic for a personal cause, how do I continue to function in my work? Do I live a lie, or regret a truth? Either way I lose...I can only hope it all comes out right."

Elroy released his grip on the folder, allowing it to seek its original shape. He placed it on Mary's desk and it unfolded to form only a quarter moon.

He rose from the chair and walked across the room until he was next to Mary. He saw her eyes watching his every movement. They reflected a frightened vulnerability, threatened but unflinching, causing him to feel inspired by her resistance. Elroy diverted his attention to her personal computer. It displayed a paragraph without a title and a sentence left unfinished. An amber cursor blinked where Mary had left off, representing her midthought and the machine's own heart beat.

"What are you working on?" he asked, hoping to dispel some tension.

"A story."

"What about?"

"Government neglect."

"What kind of neglect?"

"Every kind."

"That'll be a long story."

"I know."

Elroy reached down to the keyboard and tapped the space bar causing the cursor to jump to the right. He started to read the screen, but the thoughts didn't register in his mind.

"Mary...?"

"What?"

"I respect your point of view. I wouldn't dream of making you do something that went against your ethics, I don't have that right...I wouldn't want it done to me. As for my safety, don't worry about it, they're preoccupied with each other and won't see me coming."

Mary's eyes filled with a tear as a flood of relief cascaded down her face. She suddenly felt light; the burden had been lifted from her. She floated up from her chair and threw her arms around Elroy's neck and pressed against his face.

"I'll get to talk to Keller and bring down Prescott if he's guilty, that's for sure," Elroy continued.

"Thank you, Larry."

"For what? There's something more important here. I can't forget who I am Mary. I'm a cop. But I'm also a man who loves you. One will never interfere with the other."

Mary was speechless, responding with a soft kiss to Elroy's neck and a hard kiss to his lips. His arms went around to her back and she could feel him crush her into him.

"I missed you last night," he said.

"Me too."

"I had trouble sleeping."

"Why don't you go home and rest."

"Later, I have to go back to work now."

"Don't push yourself, you look tired."

"I'm OK."

Mary looked into Elroy's face to reacquaint herself with his good looks and sturdy features. She reached up to remove an eye lash that had fallen onto his cheek. Then she ran her fingertips down his face and across his lips. His skin was smooth and hard, somehow reflecting his personality.

"I can tell you Keller is scared and on the run," Mary commented.

"I'm sure he is."

"He's also a lot like you."

"How so?"

"Gentle by nature, but aggressive and determined when pushed into a corner. He's like a guy who's too far from home who would prefer to avoid a confrontation, but he appears capable if trouble comes his way."

"He's got to be more than capable to meet Prescott. But then again he had to have something to take out Rayfer. Thanks Mary, I'll keep that in mind, it helps a lot."

"No it doesn't, but thanks anyway."

A slight smirk wrinkled the corners of Elroy's lips, a reaction to being exposed to Mary's candor.

"Did you tell him we knew each other?" Elroy asked.

"No...You think I should have?"

"I don't know that it makes a difference."

Elroy kissed Mary on the forehead and stepped backward.

"Mary, I have to go now."

"Take care of yourself, Larry."

TWENTY-SIX

Emmet Prescott placed his briefcase on the floor out-side his apartment and produced a key from his pocket to lock the door. His eyes suspiciously scanned the dimly lit corridor in both directions, looking for any signs of Keller. All he thought of was Keller, constantly trying to predict his method of approach. At first sight of him, Prescott was prepared and determined to strike. He was confident that his quick reactions would nullify any sur-prise.

He walked to the elevator and pressed the button. He positioned himself to the side of the doors, electing not to stand directly in front of them. When the doors opened, he waited until they were about to close before he stepped in. Once inside the elevator, he assumed a posi-tion to the side of the opening.

In the lobby, he looked through the glass door at the vehicles parked to the front and rear of his car, making sure no one was in them and the car would be able to drive away quickly. Prescott paid for a service whereby each morning a valet would start his car and have it parked in front of the building, waiting. This was an al-ternate he utilized when he elected not to use the com-pany limousine.

The doorman opened the door for Prescott as he approached.

"Good morning sir," the doorman said.

Prescott just grunted as he passed the man and stepped into the cold morning air. The attendant driving Prescott's car recognized him and quickly climbed from the warm car and kept the door open. Prescott darted across the sidewalk and ducked into the driver's seat. He quickly looked around the car as the attendant closed the door, isolating him behind darkly tinted windows.

Prescott was alone, hidden within a vain executive privacy, temporarily invisible to the outside world. No one could see the deep grimace of his face which displayed anger for having to live defensively and feeling hunted. Prescott drove away quickly. As the car pulled away from the curb, an unmarked police car followed.

Alice De Giess was a recent police academy graduate Elroy had assigned to follow Prescott. She was a tough no-nonsense woman who scored within the top ten percent of her graduating class. Elroy felt a woman officer would not be as conspicuous and Alice was the best for the job.

The traffic was light for that time of the morning which made it easy for Alice to tail Prescott. She drove with one hand on the wheel and with the other she drank coffee from a Thermos cup with a slit in the lid. She appeared focused and confident, totally engrossed in her assignment.

Prescott barreled through the city streets and finally slowed in front of Ryser Chemical Corporation. He turned sharply and continued down into the underground garage.

He passed the security post and continued up the ramp to the first level and parked in his assigned spot close to the elevator.

Alice proceeded beyond the garage and parked on the opposite side of the street. She sat observing the entrance way and   finished her coffee. After a while, she stepped from the car and walked to the garage. She proceeded down a two-way ramp which led into the belly of the building. Fluorescent lights lined the low ceiling, filling the alley-like cavities with surreal light. In the far corner of the garage, she noticed several parked limos. Adjacent to the limousine parking area was a security post manned by two staff guards. The post was glass enclosed and a faint eerie blue light from rows of video monitors bathed its interior. Alice reasoned the entire garage was under electronic surveillance.

Alice returned to her car. From where she was positioned she could maintain surveillance on the lobby of Ryser Chemical and the entrance way to the garage. She sat and waited, the part of the job she disliked most.

Harmon Keller could no longer live with the sinking feeling in his soul, a mood initiated by Prescott but not exclusively dependent upon him. He had to cut away from it no matter what the repercussion. Prescott represented an evil presence which could no longer be allowed to bring him down. Keller had to pass through to his own imminent future. His transition would be dependent upon his action and determination. And if everything went according to plan, it would be a final confrontation which would ultimately free him from a terrible grip.

Keller had been following Prescott for a week, trying to determine his vulnerability. He had searched for an area where Prescott could be drawn into a confrontation, with police nearby to witness what he hoped would be a confession. It would be difficult, but there was a way. If

Prescott would not be duped into making the confession, at least he would have some protection from the police. But for it to happen, everything had to go right. He played it over and over in his mind, trying to see its flaws and hoping any miscues would not be fatal. There were many intangibles and variables. The biggest was Prescott. How would he react? Would he sense a set-up? Would his angry personality cause him to make a mistake, or would he be coy and evasive? Keller guessed killing Rayfer had infuriated Prescott. He hoped he would remain rash and belligerent.

Keller locked the hotel room door and made his way down the corridor. The floral carpet was thick beneath his feet, rendering his footsteps quiet. The soothing music which emitted from speakers on the walls did nothing to ease his restless mind. As he passed the pool area, bright sunshine shown brilliantly through the glass that enclosed it. He felt the sun's warmth and squinted at its brilliance. He paused and looked at the shimmering blue water and lush foliage.

A boy of ten or so paddled in shallow water as his mother looked on from a chaise lounge. It was a scene out of time and place with the season beyond the surrounding glass. Keller's reflection in the glass superimposed itself over the boy in the water, creating, a strange blend of illusion and reality. Keller remembered the peaceful summer days of his childhood. He pictured himself as a boy, idly passing warm lazy days, resting in tall grass beside the pond he would swim in. He longed for those carefree days when all that touched him was a soft August breeze and all he pondered were the shapes of clouds. That time was gone, never to be re-traveled. Now he lived between the memory and the pain, sorrow and self-pity, all begging for balance and resolution.

Keller couldn't allow his mind to trip back in time or to be momentarily introspective. Such a lapse would serve only to compromise his defenses. He took one last look at the boy, turned his head, and continued on.

★★★

Lieutenant Elroy sat at his desk at the end of an uneventful day. Alice De Giess had phoned in once to report she was watching Prescott and that he hadn't left his office all day. He was about to pick up the phone and call Mary when it rang. He punched the blinking button and answered the call.

"Lieutenant Elroy," he said.

"Lieutenant?"

"Yes?"

"This is Harmon Keller."

Elroy felt a bolt of surprise flare up in his body.

"Hello, Harmon, I'm glad you called," Elroy said struggling to be casual.

"My sister tells me that you are looking to ask me some questions, Lieutenant."

"Yes, I am."

"Concerning?"

"I'd much rather discuss them in person. Is there a place we can meet?"

"No, I'm afraid not."

"It would be in your best interest if we did."

Keller went silent and Elroy sensed he was either trying to be strategic or about to hang up. Elroy was afraid of losing him.

"Harmon?" Elroy said.

"I'm here."

"I could come to see you. Where are you?"

"On the road. Let me ask you something, Lieutenant. Do you suspect me of something?"

"There are questions I think only you can answer...that would clear up some things, that's all."

"It would help if I knew what they were...Please be honest with me."

"Just some questions."

"You didn't travel all the way to Virginia to see my sister just for a few questions. Please don't be vague."

Elroy suddenly went silent, trying to buy time to access his position.

"They're questions regarding people and incidents," he finally answered. "Miriam Ludlow. Thomas Bass. Thomas Holden. John Tennley. Emmet Prescott."

"I see."

"Can you tell me if you know these people?"

"I know John Tennley, Prescott, Thomas Holden, but his real name is Alex Rayfer."

"Alex Rayfer was found dead at a YMCA in Manhattan. Can you tell me anything about that?"

Keller didn't respond. He knew he was going to eventually be asked about that, but he had never prepared to answer properly.

"Harmon?"

"Yes."

"Alex Rayfer...Can you tell me something about why he was killed?"

"No...I'd rather not make any comment."

"Can I interpret that as meaning that you have some knowledge?"

"Lieutenant, what I will tell you is that all your questions will be answered in time."

"When?"

"Tonight."

"Oh?"

"Can you be available about seven?"

"Yes. Where?"

"I'll call you later."

"Harmon this is not the way I do things..."

"I'm sorry, Lieutenant, it has to be this way."

"Why?"

"Because there are many implications...things you don't understand."

"Well let's discuss them, I'm sure we can come to an understanding."

"I really don't have time now. Can I call you at this number later?"

"Yes, what time?"

"Six or seven."

"And if I don't hear from you?"

"You will."

"What will happen then?"

"I'll talk with you later and answer your questions. You'll have to trust me, Lieutenant."

"Why should I?"

"Because I ask you to."

"Look Keller, I don't know you..."

"I know...It's your choice, Lieutenant. We all have choices even though they're limited and difficult. I'll call you later."

Elroy hung up the phone and wished he had put a trace on the call. He sat back in his chair and rubbed his forehead. He felt the early stages of a migraine and hoped it would not interfere with whatever Keller had planned. He reached for the phone again to call Mary to inform her he would be working late.

It was late afternoon when Harmon Keller drove into the garage of Ryser Chemical Company. He descended the ramp slowly and switched on the blinker indicating to a traffic guard that he wanted to turn into the "visitors" parking area. The guard quickly looked to be certain there was no opposing traffic, then waved Keller on.

He proceeded slowly to the left of the security post, through a passageway which lead to a ramp. Keller followed the ramp which ascended to either a small parking area to the side and behind the security post, or to a ramp that connected the four parking levels.

The visitors parking was separated from the employees parking by geometrically opposing ramps, making it difficult to cross over except on the fourth level where there was a narrow passageway which connected them. Once through that passageway, a car could descend a ramp; however, it would be going against traffic. The fourth level was designed purposely to accommodate excessive volume from the employee side.

Unlike the parking for employees, the first level of the visitors area was nearly deserted. Keller parked the car and turned off the engine. The sound of the car faded into the dark veins of the garage leaving a hollow silence. Keller felt desolate in the quiet setting. For a time he was reluctant to move, unwilling to jostle the air around him. He closed his eyes and inhaled deeply, filling his lungs with stale air, hoping it would calm the nervousness that sparked through his body like an arc of electricity. What he had to do needed a raw anger, void of hesitancy and second thought. He wished he was not under the balancing influence of his medication. Without it, he would have the crazed edge needed to get him through.

He looked in the rear view mirror and recognized the fright in his eyes. Secretly he wondered if perhaps there were another way. For an instant, in his dank seclusion, he smelled the inviting lure of retreat. But he held firm, realizing there was no other refuge.

He stepped from the car and checked his suit in the glass of the door. He wanted to convince himself he had the proper executive appearance. Blending in with the work force was his first line of assurance.

Keller walked to the elevator which accessed all levels of the parking lot. It was a dual-ended door which opened on the opposite side at the lobby level.

In the lobby, there was a short tunnel-like corridor with one automatic locking door which opened into the rear of the lobby. Above the door, and trained directly at the elevator, was a video camera which Keller had noticed before and knew was monitored by a secondary security post which was located in a small, inconspicuous office to the extreme left of the main lobby.

As Keller emerged from the elevator, an electric eye opened the door to the lobby and he continued in as though he was just another executive on his way to a board meeting.

He crossed the lobby to the public telephones adjacent to the main entrance. Activity in the lobby was sparse, a delivery man approached the information desk seeking directions to the loading dock; three executive looking men were standing around talking. Keller sensed his presence was not even noticed.

He deposited a coin and dialed a number.

"Lieutenant Elroy," came the voice.

"Lieutenant?"

"Yes?"

"This is Harmon Keller."

"Yes, Harmon what is it?"

"Can you get to the security office in the garage area of Ryser Chemical Company?"

"Ryser Chemical?"

"Yes."

"Emmet Prescott's office?"

"Yes."

"And do what?"

"Just wait there."

"Wait for what? Harmon what's going on?"

"I need to put things in order and this is the only way I know how."

"Well what's going to happen?"

"I don't know, I hope something that clears everything up."

"Everything like what?"

"John Tennley, Alex Rayfer."

"Why can't that be cleared up between you and me?"

"I really wish it was that simple Lieutenant...Believe me, I wish it was."

Elroy listened carefully to Keller's voice and detected a tone that reflected concern, doubt and fear.

"Are you putting yourself on the line?"

"Yes."

"Let me stretch for Prescott myself."

"No Lieutenant, that won't work."

"Why not?"

"You won't be able to connect him to Rayfer, that relationship is too concealed. You could prove he knew Tennley, but that's it. You need me to flush him out."

"And if you don't?"

"Then we do it your way."

"Which means what to you?"

"I'm not thinking that far."

Keller's eyes scanned the lobby. He noticed a woman had joined the three executives who seemed to be smiling more because of her presence. The delivery man had gone and a security guard had positioned himself in front of the information desk making conversation with the receptionist.

Keller heard the woman executive say: "...right this way," and watched her lead the group to the elevator.

One executive turned to the receptionist and smiled. She smiled back.

"Keller?" Elroy's voice asked, returning Keller's attention.

"Yes?"

"I need to know how prepared Prescott is going to be."

"No preparation. Just his reaction, that's all. And that's the way I need it to be."

Elroy was dissatisfied and slightly distrusting, but he had to follow Keller's lead.

"OK, we'll do it your way for now."

"Lieutenant, something else...if Prescott sees police or their cars hanging around he may not bite."

"I'll be alone, don't worry. I'm leaving now," Elroy concluded and hung up the phone.

Keller walked back to the elevator that took him to the level where his car was parked. He entered his car nonchalantly, suspecting his movements were being monitored by security. Inside the car, he felt a certain relief that his plan was going well and comforted that Elroy was about to be present.

Keller started the car and drove up the ramp to the fourth level. He continued around to the ramp that connected to the employees parking and hesitated. For Keller, the ramp would present the first obstacle. If he were monitored going down, which was the opposite direction, he ran the likelihood of being approached by security. Although he was prepared, he preferred to remain unseen and concentrate his efforts on Prescott. Checking the time on a digital readout, he knew in just a few minutes the parking lot would become alive with people.

Keller continued slowly to the ramp and descended, trusting the ramp remained invisible to the camera, but the level was not. Once he came to the landing he preformed a broken U-turn and directed the car in the proper position. He noticed the elevator doors open and two carloads of people converged onto the level and fanned out for their cars.

One by one the engines fired up, filling the garage with exhaust fumes and a monotonic roar.

Sporadically, cars emerged from their spots, each wanting to be first down the ramp and away from the building.

Keller fell in line and became part of the slow moving caravan which snaked its way into the night. The descent was stop and go which Keller knew was being governed by the traffic guard at the exit point, allowing the levels to mesh into each other.

Reaching the first level, Keller broke rank and drove into the parking area. He continued until he spotted Prescott's car and parked in front of it, separated only by the distance of the driving lane. He turned off the engine and waited. After a while, he became confident security had not seen his cross over, but his anxiety began to mount as he knew he was coming close to an overdue showdown.

He quickly scanned the parking level and noticed there were only a handful of cars that still remained. Above the elevator, built into the ceiling, was a dark half-sphere which housed the video security camera. It was placed far enough from where Keller was parked to assure him it could not record the interior of his car, especially in the ambient lighting. He also noticed the dull metal piping that protruded from the side of the elevator which ran from the floor into the ceiling, but paid it little attention.

Keller settled into the seat and drew a deep breath and concentrated on the elevator door, trying to prepare for the fate that would soon emerge. His readiness was suspect, the outcome uncertain. All he hoped was that the overdue justice would finally be doled out to Prescott, and somewhere within the maze of it all, there would be justice for himself.

★★★

Because of the exiting traffic, Elroy couldn't drive into the Ryser garage. The entrance was temporarily converted to a one-way exit. He found a parking spot beyond the building and walked back to the garage.

The merging of the employee traffic into the general traffic was challenging at best. Horns blared from irate drivers and every car refused to yield a precious inch of street in the event another car would gain a merging lead.

In the garage, Elroy felt removed from the harsh ballet being played in the street above him. Little noise drifted down into the cavern that now surrounded him. He felt suddenly transposed from confusion to isolation, where whatever was going to happen would be a drama unseen from the street. What transpired there was of concern only to itself and oblivious and uncaring to anything else. He felt alone, apprehensive and somewhat frightened. His head was beginning to throb beyond endurance. His whole body was weak and sickly. Quiet and sleep were what he needed, but freedom from pain more so.

He opened the door to the security post and walked in. A lone guard was seated in a Naugahyde swivel chair listening to a radio, staring into the distance. When Elroy approached, the guard turned in the chair and rose.

"Can I help you?"

"Yes," Elroy responded, displaying his police shield for the guard to see.

373

"My name is Lieutenant Elroy, New York Police. I'm conducting an investigation."

"On what?"

"Right now that's confidential. I'm following a lead that brought me here, I may have to remain here for a while."

"Is there anything you want me to do?"

"No. Are you the only security guard here?"

"No, Bob Daily is directing traffic up top."

"Has everyone left the building?"

"Mostly. You see them all on their way out. There are some stragglers left."

"When does the building usually empty?"

"Figure by six, six-thirty it's usually deserted."

"How about the executives?"

"There's always one or two who stay later, but not much."

"Is this place secure all night?"

"Yes. At nine we close off both entrances to the parking garage and the only available spaces are what's immediately around this security post."

"Who mans it?"

"Me. My relief comes in at twelve."

"Any other security?"

"In the main lobby, one guard."

"Any cleaning people come in?"

"Yes, we have a company that comes in."

"Through where?"

"Always through the main lobby."

"What time?"

"Nine or so."

"Anyone else usually come into the building?"

"No. If there is, we have to have prior notification; if not, they don't get in."

"Suppose it's someone you know?"

"If it's someone we know they're aware of the rules, it's our job to enforce them."

"OK...Ever have somebody try to break in here?"

"I've been here ten years and nothing...Easy job."

"Sounds it. Where do these ramps lead?" Elroy asked, pointing out the window.

"To the upper levels. This way," the guard said, pointing right. This is visitors parking, the other way is for employees."

"Any other way in or out?"

"No. What you see in front of you is it."

Elroy looked at the row of monitors as the guard studied Elroy's face.

"You look sick Lieutenant, you all right?"

"I'll be ok...What do those screens show?"

The guard turned to look at the monitors.

"The various parking levels. Different sections of each. There are four cameras per level. And one monitors the entrance.

"I see...What's that control for?" Elroy asked, pointing to a key-lock pad with red knobs and a row of toggle switches.

"That's for the security gates, we unlock the pad which engages the mechanism, then throw the switches for the particular gate we want to open or close."

"OK...Listen, can I come around and sit a while?"

"Sure. Can I get you something?"

"No. I just need to sit, I got a real bad headache."

"Go ahead relax. I used to get bad headaches years ago. I was in my own business. Since I'm working, nothing. I tell you Lieutenant it's all stress. It'll kill you."

The guard looked at his watch then at the existing traffic. He walked to a monitor that showed the top level of the parking lot. It was deserted, with no cars on either the visitors or employees sides. He reached for a toggle switch and threw it down. The gate that separated the parking areas responded and came down slowly.

Elroy sat in the chair and put his face into his hands and dug his fingertips into his forehead and massaged firmly trying to force the pain out the other side of his head. His palms were clammy and a foul nausea rolled up in his throat. He leaned involuntarily to the left, about to fall, but stopped himself by anchoring his arms to the rests of the chair.

His eyes squinted dramatically as he peered through the window of the office. The line of cars had all successfully and without incident blended into the larger veins of traffic. Very few people remained in the office building, but Elroy felt Prescott and Keller were there somewhere poised in the shadows of the past, about to be propelled full circle by the forces of revenge and hate.

Keller snapped to attention as the elevator doors opened with a thud, shattering an uneasy silence. His eyes widened as two executives emerged. Their ties were undone and their shirt collars unbuttoned. They paused briefly in front of the elevator and spoke. Their voices seemed small and lost in the garage and barely filtered back into the car. The men appeared tired and unhurried, their energy apparently sapped by their working day.

Keller glanced at his watch, knowing Prescott would be out shortly, and hoped the two men would leave before he arrived.

After a while, the two executives parted company and walked in opposing directions to two of the three remaining cars--Prescott's was now the only one left.

The sound of the fired engines ricocheted off the walls, but dwindled as the cars left the garage. With their departure, Keller knew there would probably be no one nearby to intervene with his plan. He hoped Elroy had arrived at the security post and realized what it was he needed to do. The thought of Elroy's presence gave Keller a slight margin of confidence, but his anxiety still remained. He stared at the elevator doors and tried to relax his mind without thinking of anything that would compromise his vigilance. He couldn't afford to lose his edge with any form of carelessness.

Before any sound was heard, he saw the red indicator light above the elevator door go on. It flashed like a warning beacon that someone was aboard the elevator. Keller didn't have to guess as to who it was. Every bit of logic and instinct told him it was Prescott. Instantly his heart pounded, struggling to escape his chest cavity. His breathing became rapid and his throat felt hard and dry. Instinctively, his hand felt for the gun that was in his coat.

The doors opened and there he stood, a silent threat, a menacing and formidable opponent on the verge of eruption. The years had only served to amplify his sinister nature. Even from the distance, and in the muted lighting, his face was recognizable. The anger and meanness Keller remembered was still present. An arrogance emitted that knew no boundaries and feared no punishment or reprisal. A self-imposed elevation that caused him to soar above conscience and morality.

Prescott walked to his car and unlocked the door. He threw his briefcase across the front seat and started to get in. Keller reached for the light switch in the dashboard and flicked it on. A direct beam of bright light caught Prescott by surprise. Keller emerged from the car and walked to the front of Prescott's car, positioning himself between the glaring headlights.

Prescott tried to shield his eyes from the direct high beam and discern the figure, but instinct told him who was standing before him.

Each man, in his own perspective, felt a combined rush of antagonism and anger which had fermented over the years and was rekindled by recent incidents. They stood facing each other on a dirty plain that promised a destructive resolution, to nothing more than opposing points of view.

"Here we are again, Emmet," Keller announced, trying to steady his voice.

"Yes," Prescott responded, allowing his aggression to flow freely and become visible. He deliberately started walking toward Keller. His eyes quickly scanned the area and discovered they were totally alone.

Keller responded by placing his hand into his coat pocket and folding his hand around the gun. He knew if he remained still he would forfeit a psychological ground, so he walked toward Prescott. The men stood face-to-face, reacquainted by an old grievance.

"Why couldn't you leave it be? We weren't going to change the course of history," Keller said.

Prescott remained stoic; his glare burned through Keller.

"All that was accomplished was waste...Tennley being the biggest," Keller continued.

"What do you want?" Prescott finally said, his tone threatening.

"Why did you kill Tennley?"

"Tennley's dead?" Prescott responded coyly.

"Don't act like you know nothing about it. I'm sure you know Rayfer's dead too."

"You're still sick. Get help."

"There's no executive privilege to hide behind anymore. I know how you operate Emmet."

"How did you get into this building?"

"Tennley! Tell me about Tennley! I know about Rayfer. Why Tennley? Because you couldn't have your way with Night Shade? I can't believe this is what it's all about."

Prescott didn't want to speak. His training and instincts prevented him from self-incrimination, while his inner urge was to lash out and crush Keller.

"Don't deny you know Rayfer as an assassin. Don't deny you had him kill Tennley. And who can forget Joe Emory, your first victim. After killing him you became immune to it all."

"Emory?"

"Yes."

Elroy sat up in the chair and looked through the glass at the stillness beyond. His attention shifted to the first row of monitors and the idleness they recorded. The bright light from one monitor eventually caught his eye. Elroy leaned forward and studied the two figures, recognizing only Prescott.

"Excuse me," he said to the guard.

"Yes."

"Can you come here and identify these two men?" he asked weakly.

The guard walked over and examined the monitor.

"Mister Prescott is one. I don't know the other."

Elroy didn't need confirmation. It had to be Keller.

"Is this monitor actually recording?"

"Yes...Lieutenant, if there's a problem or a threat to Mister Prescott I need to know now. Protecting employees is my job!"

"I really don't know. Is there a way we can monitor the audio too?"

"Yes."

The guard quickly stepped behind Elroy to a box on the wall and opened the face of it. He flicked a toggle switch and returned to the console. He reached across Elroy and turned a dial which modulated volume. Only a static sound emitted from a tiny speaker beneath the monitor.

"That should be able to pick it up," the guard announced. "I never had to do this before."

"Where are they?" Elroy asked.

"First level. In front of elevator four, second zone."

★★★

Prescott began to become rational. He remembered the monitor behind him and wanted to act fast. He turned abruptly and headed for his car. He sparked the engine to life and drove the car toward the temporary electrical feeder pole. The bumper slammed into the pole and tore it away from the bolts that secured it to the ceiling. Electrical wires sparked and ripped free. Lights in the area blinked off and the camera ceased functioning.

The screen Elroy and the guard were watching went blank, then snowy.

"Something happened to the video signal," the guard said. He reached for a hand communicator and depressed a button. "Bob," he said into it, "there's a problem in zone two of parking level one. Secure my area."

"Roger," came the reply. "Confirm status when evaluated."

"Roger."

The guard followed Elroy out of the office, carrying a large flashlight.

Prescott turned the car and looked for Keller. He saw the red glow of his taillights going to the ascending ramp and followed. He unsnapped the latches of his briefcase causing the lid to pop up slightly. Prescott reached in and withdrew his gun, gripping it firmly. His mind was flashing between killing Keller and devising an excuse and cover-up for the police. He had hoped for a less complicated meeting ground, but his rage made that insignificant.

Keller sped toward the connecting ramp to the visitors parking. He wanted to drive down to the security post and have Elroy intervene. He knew not enough was said to convince Elroy of Prescott's involvement with Tennley, and verify his association with Rayfer. But all that became irrelevant as he was now running for his life.

As soon as he started up the final ramp, he noticed the downed gate which prevented his cross-over and escape. Keller felt instantly trapped and disturbed by his impending demise. He slammed on the brakes and came to a halt just before the gate. He looked in the rear view mirror and saw the headlights of Prescott's car coming straight for him. Keller quickly threw the gear shift into reverse and jumped from the car. The car started descending the ramp on a course for Prescott.

Keller ran with the car, staying on the passenger side. He heard Prescott's tires screech as he tried to avoid the crash. His car stopped then started to go in reverse. Keller's car had gained momentum and hit into Prescott's. It wasn't a forceful crash, but it did jostle Prescott. He hit the brakes, forcibly suspending both cars mid-ramp. Prescott jumped from the car and fired a shot just as Keller ran by. Keller withdrew his own gun and fired aimlessly behind him in a half-hearted attempt at defense. Prescott ducked instinctively but then came up and fired at where he thought Keller might be. The sound of bullets hitting steel and concrete rang out in the parking lot.

Keller reached the bottom of the ramp and ran into the parking area. Prescott followed in angry pursuit.

Elroy and the guard reached zone two. The guard ran the light up and down the felled pole.

"Here's the problem," the guard observed.

"Yeah. They must have gone to an upper level."

"What the hell is going on Lieutenant?"

"Just stay here."

"I can't do that, Lieutenant."

"This is no time to argue. You'll do everybody more good by calling nine one one. Just say officer needs assistance. Now do it!"

Elroy didn't wait for a response. He ran toward the ramp and tried to ignore his sickly condition.

The guard brought the hand communicator close to his mouth and spoke, "Bob!"

"Yes?" came the reply, with static.

"Dial nine one one, pronto."

"Roger."

The guard closed the light in hopes of blending into the darkness.

Keller ran behind a main support beam which was wide enough to protect him. Prescott was heading toward him, trying to use a row of narrower steel support struts for his own protection. The struts were in a straight line running away from Keller. Based upon the angle relative to Keller's position, they almost formed a large sheet Prescott could safely hide behind.

Keller peered around the beam and realized the angle favored Prescott. He suddenly became dejected, sensing Prescott had always bettered him. Now it appeared to be the final battle and Prescott once again had the edge. His ruthlessness was severe and unbeatable, defying recourse and defeat. Keller lamented and became resigned to his fate. The strange acceptance at the instant of one's own mortality seeped its way into his psyche. His defense mechanisms became flawed as his hopes diminished.

Prescott saw Keller, took aim and fired. A pinging sound rang out which was followed by a human cry, as the bullet nicked the edge of the beam then crashed into Keller's shoulder. The force of the bullet knocked Keller to the ground; the gun flew from his hand and out of sight. He tried crawling to safety, but there was nowhere to hide. His fingertips grasped the cold, hard pavement in an attempt to become one with it and use it for protection. Prescott aimed once more and fired. The bullet imbedded itself into the asphalt, inches from Keller's face. Fragments of stone exploded outward, ripping into his face and forehead. Blood poured out, down to his neck. He felt the warmth of the blood and it suddenly enraged him. The realization that there was nothing left to lose made his reactions acute, free from tentativeness. His adrenaline choked off personal fear and replaced it with absolute resolve.

As Prescott neared, Keller struggled to his feet, repositioning himself behind the beam, pressing his back against it. Prescott charged like a rogue elephant. Nothing would deny him.

Keller heard the footsteps approaching, waited until he sensed Prescott was close, then sprang from behind the beam and leaned his entire body into a punch. His fist caught Prescott flush in the face. Prescott staggered back, hurt and surprised. Keller moved in quickly and swung again just as Prescott fired another shot. The bullet grazed Keller's cheek, but caught his ear, ripping it in half. He felt a stinging sensation, but his psychological pitch was such that he felt no pain.

Keller grabbed Prescott's gun hand and forced it into the air, aiming it harmlessly away. Prescott's free hand reached around Keller and wrestled him to the ground.

Keller and Prescott were locked in mortal combat, struggling to impose their wills. Prescott forced Keller backward, then straddled him. Keller grabbed Prescott's hand and twisted the gun away from himself.

Prescott freed his left hand and quickly brought it crashing into Keller's face and Keller's head banged into the hard ground.

Bones cracked in Keller's ears. Prescott struck once more and Keller became lethargic and weak, animated only by injury and acceptance. His grip on the gun became loose and his head was reposed on the ground as though he welcomed sleep.

Prescott tore the gun away from Keller's meek grasp and positioned the barrel just inches from his left eye. A strange reaction suddenly overtook Prescott as the ultimate power was never so imminent and personal. The joy that he assumed Rayfer enjoyed over Tennley was now his alone to experience. It was beyond scope and definition, rivaling all the past pleasures that were ever his to embrace.

He cocked the hammer of the gun as a surge of deranged bliss welled inside him. For a brief instant in his life, he understood the true essence of his existence. He felt a euphoria surpassing the killing of Michael Baylor or the unseen armies he manipulated into abstract combat. This glimpse into the remote mystery of man through the experience of another had no equal.

Prescott was totally consumed with his own intentions, oblivious to Elroy's cries of warning. "You fucking maggot," he growled. "How dare you defy me. Die! Die! Die!" Prescott scowled.

Prescott started to depress the trigger as an explosion rang in his ears. He felt the hot pain tear through his neck and he sensed himself toppling off Keller onto the ground. He felt disoriented and misplaced. His throat was inflamed as he reached for it. Blood filled his hand and he had the sensation he was swallowing his tongue. His eyes studied his surroundings, trying to comprehend his immediate imbalance. Everything around him was surreal. Keller, and his intentions, no longer occupied his mind. A sense of disbelief dragged him further from his destination. He floundered to his knees and recognized

Elroy running toward him. He managed to take aim and fire, missing his approaching target. He fired once more only to discover the gun's chamber was empty. Impulse and fury propelled Prescott to stand. He responded from instinct rather than clarity of thought. The invasion into his unearthly baptism was intolerable, denying him essential gratification. He stepped backward; shock and desperation now consumed him. Prescott ran off into the garage, abandoning his mission and purpose.

Elroy reached Keller and paused before him. Keller appeared serene and relieved, temporarily out of danger.

Elroy turned his head in time to see Prescott stumble behind another pillar in the distance. Elroy's vision was blurred and his walking was strenuous as he struggled against his own sick feeling. He left Keller and followed Prescott. As he neared the pillar, he heard a heavy scraping noise. It was pronounced and amplified in his head.

"Prescott?" Elroy whispered.

As Elroy stepped closer to the pillar, Prescott bounded from behind it, splattered with blood and charging at him. Held over his head was a small but heavy metal sign which read "Handicapped Parking" and displayed the wheelchair graphic.

The wound to Prescott's neck caused him to lose his ability to speak or scream. He attacked in deadly silence, swinging the blue sign at Elroy's head. Elroy struggled to step away and fell over his own feet. The weight of the momentum of the sign pulled Prescott down. He quickly regained his footing and aligned himself for a second attack. Elroy had moved to a sitting position, the gun braced between both hands and aimed directly at Prescott.

There was no hesitancy in Prescott as he raised the sign overhead once more. He visualized the path of it and the destruction of Elroy.

Prescott stepped forward. A malignant determination occupied his eyes. He defied his wound and fostered contempt for the prone policeman before him. He was bound in mind and spirit to kill him then continue with Keller.

For an instant, Elroy paused, noticing the blood flowing from Prescott's throat, realizing the shot only wounded him. He raised his sight. The barrel of the gun aligned with the bridge of Prescott's nose. Elroy squeezed the trigger gently, not jerking. The gun fired and the bullet crashed between Prescott's eyes and tore out a portion of his scalp.

Prescott recoiled violently. The sign went crashing to the floor and his body followed it, rolling over its round base. Prescott quivered, a final attempt to reject his demise. Gradually he became still. His hands that once gripped tightly in anger, now became limp and serene. Everything around him became vague and quiet. He felt a swirling sensation gathering around him. He relived the revelation he experienced as he was about to kill Keller. Perhaps that unfolding mystery was designed as a premonition of his own fate. Killing and dying joined together in his mind, a juxtaposition that was deceptive in nature, and ironic in results.

Elroy struggled to his feet and approached Prescott. He studied the lifeless form and became acutely aware of the waste and folly of humanity. He pondered how Prescott's revenge offered no exoneration, yet satisfied some personal form of justice.

He turned away and started back toward Keller. As he neared the spot where Keller had fallen, Elroy realized he had gone. An obscure fugitive, remarkably adept at vanishing, had once again avoided his grasp. It represented no cause for concern, however. Elroy's confrontation with Prescott provided him with the answers he needed.

In the distance, Elroy heard police sirens growing louder as the cars approached. Flashing lights flew over the ramp as two squad cars raced toward him. Elroy closed his eyes and covered his ears, trying to protect his senses from the invasion. He fell against a steel strut, consumed by his sickness. He would reserve his feelings for what had happened when he felt better.

Now he needed rest--the kind of rest that would deliver him from all the ills that had ever haunted him.

TWENTY-SEVEN

Elroy sat reclined on the sofa with his head on Mary's arm. She gently massaged his forehead and temples, trying to diminish the last stages of his headache which was subsiding reluctantly. She leaned forward and kissed his lips. Elroy opened his eyes slightly and tried to smile.

"Feeling better?" Mary asked.

"A little."

"Good...Will there be a departmental investigation into Prescott's death?"

"Yes. It's procedure."

"What, if anything, will come out about Prescott?"

"Probably nothing."

"Why?"

"Because people really don't want to know. If everyone learned about Night Shade, the only thing it would serve is good parlor conversation. Think of the implications. People don't want to see themselves as prisoners to the system and the power brokers."

"That sounds fatalistic."

"No, just realistic."

"Larry, why did Prescott overreact to Keller, especially when he seemed to stay so cool in front of the cameras?"

"Who knows? His rage got the best of him I suppose. Also understand Prescott was a man who was used to having things his own way. If he had killed Keller, he would have alibied his way right out of it, using his connections and clout. He just didn't figure Keller had set him up with the police there."

"Do you think Keller was banking on his reaction?"

"I know he was hoping for something; it was a good lure. I think when Prescott wasn't admitting to anything and when he crashed into the electrical pole, Keller lost his protection. He had to get back out in front of a camera."

"Why do you think he ran away?"

"I don't know, he got what he wanted."

"Do you think he'll be back?"

"Yes. He needs time to think, sort it all out...He's not a criminal and he doesn't want to be hunted...He's probably weighing his options. Maybe he wants to see my next move."

"What will you do?"

"About Keller?"

"Yes."

"His sister...I still want to know about Thomas Bass. That's where it all started for me. Through her, Keller will have to face the music."

"How about you, Larry?"

"What about me?"

"How do you feel?"

"About what happened?"

"Yes."

Elroy closed his eyes as though to see inside himself. What greeted him was a compendium of logic and emotion. "Through it, or because of it, I met you," he replied with a smile.

"And?"

"And Prescott, Keller, Night Shade are all abstract notions, because there will always be others like them. I know I can't change the way things are. I just try my best and when it's all done, I can feel satisfied and proud."

Mary smiled and hugged his head. Elroy could feel her warmth and her love. He felt protected by her and nothing could hurt him. His mind recalled the burning car that consumed his parents and he was able to keep his eyes closed and face the reality of it. With Mary he had clarity and comfort, and the promise of his own peace and happiness.

 ★★★ The End ★★★